STACY M. JONES

What He Saw

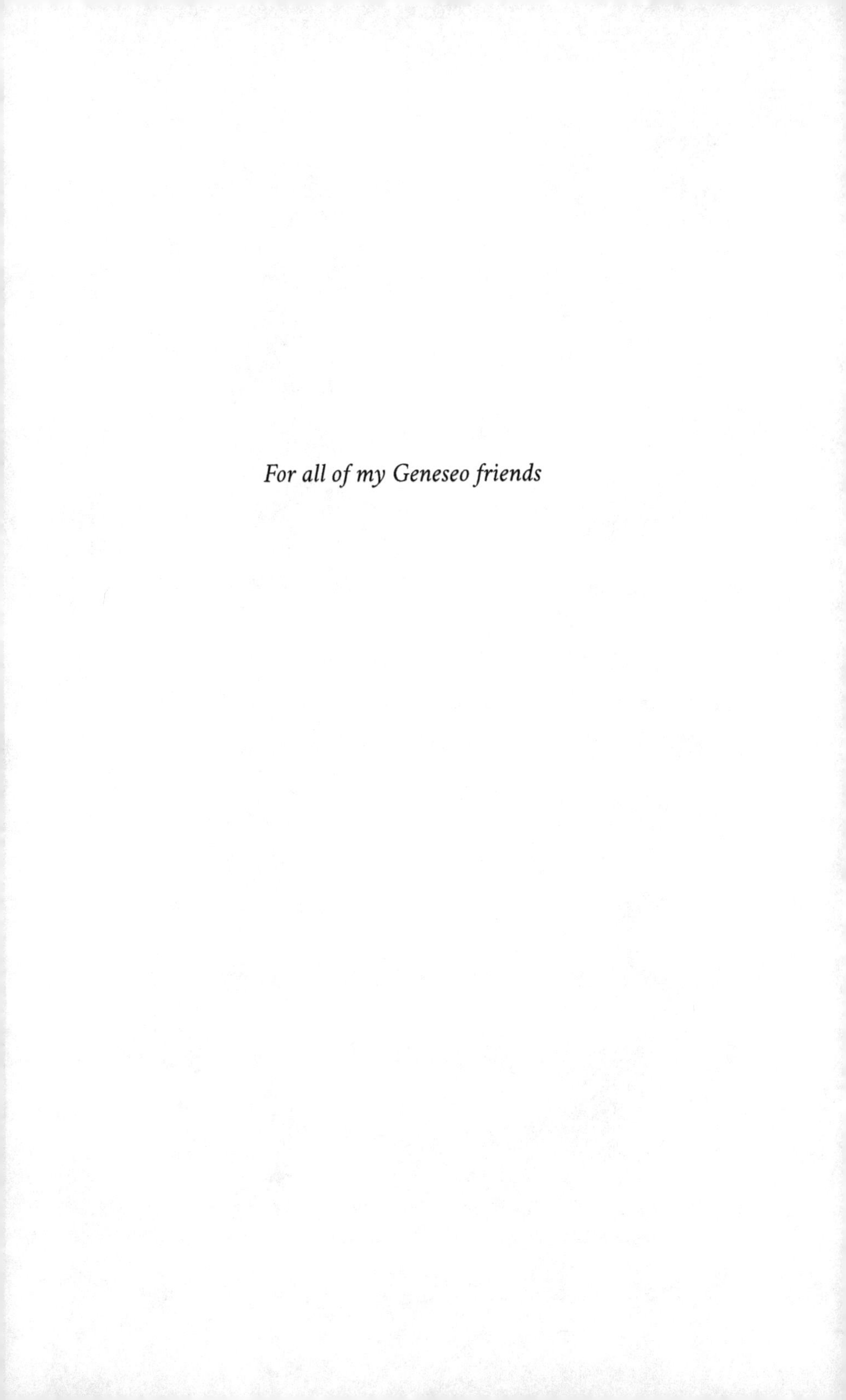

For all of my Geneseo friends

Acknowledgement

Thank you to the detectives and forensics teams I've had the pleasure of working with through the years and the knowledge and expertise shared with me. Special thanks to 17 Studio Book Design for bringing my stories to life with amazing covers. Thank you to Dj Hendrickson for your insightful editing and Liza Wood for proofreading and revisions. Thanks to my family and friends who are always a source of support and encouragement and to my early readers whose feedback was invaluable. Special thanks to my Geneseo friends who made my early college years so enjoyable. It really was the best place to go to college and memories will be cherished forever.

CHAPTER 1

In the haze between sleeping and opening my eyes to the new day, my yellow Labrador, Dusty, licked the side of my cheek and pressed his cold nose against my face. It was all an effort to wake me. He wasn't normally this affectionate, only when he wanted something. I reached out and rubbed his head without opening my eyes. I figured I'd settle him down and then catch a few more minutes of sleep but that wasn't the case.

"Riley," my mother, Karen, called from the floor below. "I've called you three times to get up if you're going to have any pancakes. They are getting cold!" She grumbled something to herself I couldn't hear. "I sent the dog up there to wake you."

She waited to see if I'd rouse myself out of bed. Frustrated, she yelled again, "Dusty, you had one job to do!"

I patted Dusty's head as I rolled to my side. "Did you hear her? You had one job, buddy. What did she give you in exchange for waking me up?" He backed up from my bed and left my room without looking back. I had gotten him in trouble with my mother and that was a sin that wasn't forgivable. It would take treats and belly rubs. Dusty was technically my dog but he'd grown so attached to my mother that when I relocated, he stayed with her. I no longer had his loyalty.

Stretching my arms overhead, I let out a half yawn, half growl. It was only seven in the morning and I had nothing to do until noon.

Being back in my childhood bedroom brought back many memories of trying to sleep in on weekends when my mother simply wouldn't allow it. She made big breakfasts and expected my younger sister, Liv, and I to be at the table when it was ready. I always assumed she did that on the weekends to make up for not being there for dinner during the week because she worked the evening shift at the hospital as a nurse.

I shouldn't complain. In my late thirties and married, I was lucky to still have my mother making me eggs and pancakes when I visited. I put my bare feet on the cool hardwood, tugged the covers back up on the bed, and pulled my bathrobe from the chair.

The smell of brewing coffee hit me as soon as I got to the door of the kitchen. "What is that you're brewing?" I went right to the counter to grab a cup.

"It's salted caramel mocha," my mother said, handing me the creamer and a small teaspoon. She went back to flipping pancakes. "I bought it at that new coffee shop downtown. I thought I'd try something a little fancy." She pointed to the round table in the middle of the kitchen. "Go eat before it gets cold. Liv already left for work."

"On a Saturday?" I asked surprised.

My mother leaned against the counter and lifted her coffee cup to her lips. "Her real estate business is taking off. I'm happy she finally found her niche."

Liv was only a few years younger than me but had struggled to find her career path. She bounced around a lot and even worked for me at my private investigation business for a while before I packed up and moved to Little Rock, Arkansas where I live now with my husband, Det. Luke Morgan.

"I'm glad it's going so well for her. She was excited when she told me about it."

Liv had moved back into my mother's five-bedroom house on the eastside of Troy, New York. The house was too big for her and Jack, her new husband, but there was no way she was ever going to part with it. They both enjoyed having my sister there and some noise in the house.

"Where's Jack?" I asked, sitting down at the table.

With her back turned to me and focused on the stove again, she said, "He had an early morning surveillance case and will be back later this afternoon." She finished cooking and scooped the last of the eggs onto a plate. She turned to face me. "I wish you'd let Jack go with you to Geneseo. It's so rural out there and who knows what kinds of things you'll stumble across while investigating the case."

The case my mother was referencing was an eighteen-year-old homicide that took place in my apartment when I was a senior in college. I had gone to SUNY Geneseo, which was out in western New York, about forty minutes south of Rochester. There wasn't much in the village of Geneseo besides farms, a simple Main Street with a few shops, restaurants and bars, and the college. The village had a population of less than ten thousand people and was surrounded by even smaller villages.

The most iconic thing on Main Street was Emmeline, a statue of a bronze bear hugging a light pole atop a sandstone pedestal in the center of a circular granite fountain. Legend said that Emmeline would only leave her post when a virgin graduated college. So far, Emmeline remains. This was the pinnacle of action in the sleepy little Geneseo village. To say that I had an idyllic college experience right up to the murder would be an understatement. I wished sometimes that I could go back to those early years in school.

The campus sat just south of Main and was small and contained roughly four thousand students. Everyone knew everyone, which made the rare homicide all the more horrifying. The fact that the victim, Alex McCormick, was a good friend and my roommate, was my first lesson that even in an idyllic setting, we weren't safe.

I didn't realize it then but that case set the trajectory of my life. I had been studying psychology and was not quite sure what I was going to do with it. But a knack for writing and a tendency to put my nose where it didn't belong set me on a path to be an investigative reporter and then later a private investigator.

I was so lost in thought remembering Alex and my time at Geneseo, I didn't hear my mother speaking to me. I raised my eyes to meet hers. "I'm sorry. What did you say?"

She came over with her plate and sat down at the table with me. "I said that I'm glad you're taking the case. I remember even back in college you didn't believe the official story of Alex's murder. Of all the cases you've taken over the years, this one might put to rest some doubts you've had. I know it's weighed on you over the years even if you don't want to admit it."

My mother was right. It was something I rarely talked about. It was grief wrapped in a blanket of guilt that was too painful to touch. Tim Rattan, Alex's boyfriend, who was arrested and convicted of her murder, was released from prison after doing sixteen years. His conviction was overturned on an appeal and the prosecutor's office was still debating the merits of retrying a mostly circumstantial homicide case.

After getting out of prison, Tim called my mother's house looking for me. It was the last known number for me given my mother never got rid of the old landline. I had teased her more than a handful of times for still having a house phone and the same phone number for the last forty years. It paid off though because Tim was able to reach my mother who reached me. He wanted me to help him find the real killer.

"When Tim called the house, he was rather adamant that he didn't kill Alex and that he could prove it." My mother took a sip of her coffee and shook her head as she set the cup down. "I don't think I've ever heard someone with so much conviction in their voice. There was fear, too, Riley. The case has been in the news and there's a real fuss that the system let out a guilty man. Alex's family wants the prosecutor's office to retry him. Tim is still facing a life sentence if sent back in."

I took another bite of eggs and silently praised my mother's cooking. She was right about Tim. I had only spoken to him briefly to let him know that I was willing to take the case. He said over and over again that he was innocent and that he hadn't even spoken to Alex on the night she was murdered. He was trying to convince me to take the case, but my mind had already been made up.

I had stopped him mid-sentence and told him I'd help and to gather up whatever evidence he had and meet me in Geneseo. I came to Troy first to meet with a New York State Police investigator who had handled the case. That's the only thing I had planned for today. He was assigned to a local barrack now and was willing to meet with me. I planned to drive out to Geneseo tomorrow to meet with Tim. Then I'd get down to work.

"What do you remember about the case?" my mother asked, finishing the last of her pancakes.

I sat back and remained silent for a moment, letting the images come to me slowly. "It was over Thanksgiving break. Alex and I went out Tuesday night for drinks at a local bar. We were finally old enough to get into them and had laughed about not having to stand in the muddy yard of a frat house drinking from a plastic cup. The bar was barely a step up but we didn't care. We had a few drinks, stopped for pizza on the way home, and then went to bed. I had an early class on Wednesday then left right after for home. The last time I saw Alex was that Tuesday night before bed."

"Why wasn't she going home for Thanksgiving?"

It took me a moment to recall. "Her parents were going out to Los

Angeles to visit her sister and Alex didn't want to go. At least, that's what she told me. Tim said something about staying back with her so she didn't have to spend the holiday alone, but she didn't want him to miss time with his family."

My mother sipped from her coffee cup then asked a rather astute question. "I remember you telling me that Tim and Alex had been dating for close to two years. Wouldn't he have asked her to go home with him for the holiday break?"

"You're thinking like an investigator, Mom." She beamed a smile over at me. "Alex wasn't sure about her relationship with Tim. He was a little controlling but not anything that I'd consider crossing the line to domestic violence. He wanted to take care of her more than she needed taking care of and they bickered frequently about mostly little things. Alex told me she was thinking about ending things with Tim after graduation. She didn't see their lives going in the same direction. She had wanted to be a teacher but possibly teach abroad and he wanted to settle down back in Buffalo where he was from and start working. He was talking about marriage while Alex was talking about travel and adventures. It was a clash for sure."

She peered over at me with a slight frown of disapproval. "Did Tim know how she felt?"

I could tell by the look on her face that wasn't what she had wanted to ask. "Tim didn't know that's how she felt. That wasn't your question though. Ask me what you really wanted to know."

My mother sighed. "I don't want to speak ill of the dearly departed, but it sounds like Alex was being a bit selfish. She knew she wanted to end things. Instead, she was going to string him along for a few more months. Was she seeing anyone else?"

"I suspected but it was never confirmed." Alex and I had argued about the relationship all those years ago. "Tim was a good guy and he cared a lot about Alex. I didn't like how she was behaving. After our initial conversation, there wasn't much I could do. It wasn't my place to tell him. The times Tim tried to ask me questions about Alex when we were alone in class, I told him that he'd need to speak to her. It was a weird situation to be in."

My mother let that line of questioning drop. I knew by her look she wondered if that factored into the murder. "Remind me. When did you learn of her death?"

"Not until I got back on Sunday after the break. I pulled onto my street and could see the cops surrounding the house. The neighbors who lived on the first floor were outside on the sidewalk. I asked what happened and they were the ones who told me Alex had been found murdered. I think I blocked out most of that day but I remember speaking to the cops. I wasn't allowed back into our apartment for several days. I stayed at a friend's house in the meantime and the school offered me accommodation in the dorm."

"I always hated that you went back and stayed in that house until you graduated."

"What was I going to do? I needed a place to live and the landlord wasn't going to let me out of our lease. Besides, Tim was caught right away and I figured it was safe. It was creepy but I did what I had to do."

"I thought you said you weren't sure they had caught the right guy?"

I nodded and took a sip of coffee. "I didn't want to think Tim could be capable of something like that and he was supposed to be in Buffalo for Thanksgiving break. The cops said he came back on Saturday night, earlier than planned, and they argued. They reasoned he killed her in a fit of rage. I was young and I believed the cops."

It sounded simpler than it felt. I still had confusing and conflicted feelings over the whole thing. I didn't think Tim was capable of murder. He was always incredibly nice to me. I was young though and figured the cops knew what they were doing. I was taking the case now in the hopes of losing the guilt and finding the real killer, even if in the end it was Tim.

My mother stood from the table. "I hope you solve it not just for Tim but for Alex's parents. The murder and Tim's release have left a lot of people with many lingering questions. If he isn't guilty, then they deserve to have the truth finally come to light."

I still had lingering questions, including what if any role I played in all of it.

CHAPTER 2

Det. Luke Morgan stood over the body of a man splayed on the grass with his arms and legs outstretched as if he were making snow angels. He wore a white tee-shirt, blue plaid boxers, and a sock on his left foot. His right foot was bare and his pants and shoes were nowhere in sight. A single gunshot wound to the head was the obvious cause of death.

The victim was a white man, with a medium build and dark hair, probably mid-thirties to forties. Without measuring – the medical examiner would do that later – Luke put him right around five-foot-ten and probably one-hundred-eighty pounds. Luke guessed the guy spent a few hours in the gym but probably also enjoyed a burger and a few beers. He had no identification on him and no other signs of trauma.

"Who'd leave this guy here, *like this?*" Det. Bill Tyler, Luke's partner, asked with frustration as he surveyed the area. They were standing right behind the President William J. Clinton Library on the grassy hill that led to the Arkansas River. "How did he even get here?"

"I have no idea," Luke said, standing with his hands on his hips, taking in the scene. They had been called to the scene at eight that morning when the first employees arrived at work. One of them looked out a back window and happened to glance down and saw the man lying below. She thought he might have been sleeping off a drunken night.

Their proximity to the River Market District – right down the road – made the situation plausible in her mind as she marched out the front door and around the back to confront him. It was only when she got close that she realized how wrong she had been. Her scream alerted other employees who came to her aid. Standing outside huddled together, they placed the call to 911.

Now, the area was sectioned off with crime scene tape. The only thing Luke was glad about was that it wasn't right in front of the building where visiting guests could see the body. As it was, people had started to gather. A few minutes ago, the first media trucks pulled up. Luke wasn't giving any statements until he had a better understanding of the situation.

Luke and Tyler had been the first on the scene even before the crime scene techs, who had only just arrived. Ed Purvis, Pulaski County's Medical Examiner, was also on the way, delayed by another homicide in the southeast part of the city that was believed to be gang related.

Luke bent down and assessed the victim. He tugged up the man's shirt to reveal a flat torso with a brush of hair. There were no bruises or other marks on the body. "No wallet or anything to identify him. Let's take his prints and run it in the system," he said to a nearby crime scene tech. To Tyler, he said, "Let's take a walk and see if we can find anything that tells us how this guy got here."

Since they had walked in from the front of the building and Luke didn't see anything that caught his eye at the time, he gestured toward the back and Tyler followed. The two had been partners for almost the entire time Luke had been not only a detective in the homicide unit but the head of the unit as well. Captain Kurt Meadows had paired them early on and it had been a partnership that stood the test of time.

"Did Riley leave for New York?" Tyler asked as they walked with their eyes focused on the ground.

"She left over the weekend," Luke said, his voice soft. He still wasn't sure how he felt about her being gone. He understood why Riley wanted to take the case. But the house was empty without her. He had grown accustomed to their routine and, without her, everything felt off-kilter.

It must have been Luke's tone of voice or Tyler was just really good at reading him because his partner was quiet for a moment and then asked, "Is it bothering you that she's gone again?"

"I'm not sure if it's that I miss her or the house is too quiet. I just feel a bit off this time with her gone," Luke admitted but then quickly wanted to take it back. It felt like weakness he shouldn't admit.

Tyler had been married longer than anyone Luke knew. It wasn't just that he had longevity with his marriage, it was a solid healthy one at that. "You're used to her being around. It's normal. You'll feel better in a few days or she'll be back by then. Temporary feeling."

Luke hoped Tyler was right. "This murder was the last thing I expected to wake up to this morning. Maybe I'm just feeling out of sorts about that."

Tyler chuckled. "A half-dressed dead guy outside of the Clinton library is bound to mess up anyone's morning." They quieted down as they continued their search, but they didn't find much of anything. After they made it down to the river, Tyler said, "I didn't see a lot of blood up there in the grass near the body or anywhere else. I think it's safe to say the guy was dumped there."

"Kind of an odd place to dump a body," Luke said as he ran a hand down his stubbled face. He hadn't shaved in the last few days and was contemplating growing a beard for winter. "Something feels off to me and I can't quite put my finger on it. Why is he half-dressed and where are his clothes?"

Tyler threw out a possibility. "It's possible that he was sleeping with someone's wife. Maybe the guy comes home, catches him right before the act, and shoots him. Then he and the wife panic and they dump his body out here."

The start of the scenario seemed likely for Luke. There was just one catch. "I don't think a husband and wife who have never killed anyone would dump a body here. Look at how he was splayed out. That seems intentional to me. That guy is about one-hundred and eighty pounds and there are no tire tracks on the grass. Someone strong carried him there from the parking lot. That's a lot of dead weight and ground to cover. I'm not sure I could do that alone."

"Maybe the wife is strong," Tyler said with a shrug.

Luke chuckled and shook his head. "I assume you're kidding."

Tyler threw his hands up. "I don't know any more than you do. I admit the scenario seems unlikely that the wife helped her husband carry her lover's dead body across the field and left him behind the library. There are easier dump spots around Little Rock." He looked at Luke with his eyebrows raised. "A lot of people don't like the Clintons. Do you think someone is leaving a political message?"

That had been Luke's first thought when he heard there was a dead body on the lawn. There didn't seem to be any political message with the body or any way to connect it back to the library or the Clintons. While Luke couldn't rule it out, he had no evidence to rule it in either. He told Tyler as much. "We don't have anything that points to anything. I don't want to speculate too much until we have some facts. We won't know more until we get some identification."

They walked back toward the library and made it just as Ed Purvis arrived. "Well, this certainly is new," he said and gave Luke an elbow bump instead of a handshake. They were both gloved up and didn't want the cross-contamination. "I've been to a lot of scenes over the years with you two and this isn't one we've seen before."

"We like to keep you on your toes," Tyler teased.

"It keeps it interesting when the criminals get inventive." Purvis leaned over the body much the way Luke had when he arrived on the scene. "Cause of death is apparent. I don't see much blood." He angled his head to look at Luke. "Are you assuming he was shot elsewhere?"

"That's the theory." Luke made a sweeping motion with his hand around the scene. "Not much to suggest otherwise." He provided Purvis an overview of how the body was found earlier that morning and highlighted some of what he and Tyler had discussed. "We also have some questions about the way he's splayed out like that. He looks like he's about to make snow angels with his arms and legs at those angles."

Purvis stood up and took a few steps back and looked down at the body. "That is an odd way to position him. Let me get him back and I'll do the autopsy today and get the ball rolling. I assume we don't have identification?"

Luke explained that the crime scene techs took prints and that they'd know more when they got back to the office. They stood out of the way as Purvis and his team worked to get the body into a body bag. As they were rolling him to the side, his white tee-shirt came up in the back, giving Luke a glimpse of his lower back. "Hold on!"

"What's wrong?" Purvis asked as he stopped moving.

Luke bent down and with his gloved hand slowly raised the man's shirt and then pulled back in shock. "There's writing on his back," he said then corrected himself. "It doesn't look like writing, more like it's been carved into his back. *Retributio mea.* What does that mean?"

Purvis couldn't move from his position to see it but Tyler stepped around and stood next to Luke. He said, "It's Latin for 'my retribution.'"

"How do you know that?" Luke asked surprised.

Tyler shrugged. "Catholic school, you pick up a thing or two."

"That's a game changer," Purvis said with his eyes focused on Luke.

Luke had no idea what he was looking at but it wasn't like any homicide he'd seen in a long time. "We need identification on him."

He wasn't sure what else they could do right now faced with the limited information they had. He pointed to the library. "We are going to check their surveillance footage. Purvis, as soon as you get anything, call me. I don't care if it's in the middle of the night. I want to know what you know as soon as you know it."

Purvis gave a curt nod of agreement and then went about getting the man into a body bag. Luke and Tyler made their way up to the front of the building where people had gathered along with the media waiting for an announcement. Reporters shouted questions at Luke, who wanted to avoid them for as long as possible. He turned from the grass to walk toward the front of the building when a woman's shouts caught his attention.

"Did you hear that?" Luke asked Tyler. He nodded that he had.

They waited a moment longer and again the woman shouted, "I think that's my boyfriend!"

Luke turned back to the sea of people and scanned the crowd. A petite woman waved frantically at Luke. She shouted for a third time and Luke went straight toward the lion's den of media. He'd have no choice now but to make a short statement.

Luke stood back and gestured for the crowd to quiet down. Then he started. "I don't have much information to release, so I won't be taking any questions. We have a lot of investigative work to do. What I can say is that earlier this morning one of the staff at the William J. Clinton Library found the body of a Caucasian male on the grass adjacent to the library in the direction heading towards the river. The medical examiner is in the process of removing the body and the crime scene techs are on the scene. I'll have more of a statement later when we know more."

With that, Luke lifted the crime scene tape and pulled the woman through the crowd of people shouting questions at him. Luke tuned it all out to focus on the woman. "You said he might be your boyfriend?"

"Yes," she said as she pulled out her phone and handed it to Luke. She showed him a photo of the two of them. "That's from last night. We were at a party and then Nick went out with friends. They all left the bar together but he hasn't been seen since. He's never disappeared like this before."

Luke took in the woman's words and felt the weight of them on his shoulders. He took the phone from her hands and looked at the photo. He tried to keep his expression steady as he handed the photo to Tyler. He glanced at it then gave it back to the woman.

Luke put his arm around the woman's shoulders. "Why don't you come with me so we can talk inside."

"Is it Nick?" she asked and started to cry.

"It seems that way from the photo. He had no identification on him so we'll need to make a formal identification later." Luke did not doubt that the dead man was her boyfriend. All he wanted to do was get her inside and interview her. Hopefully, something would start to make sense.

The body didn't just appear overnight on its own.

CHAPTER 3

"Did you see that they found a body near the Clinton library?" Adele Baker asked her husband, Cooper Deagnan, as she put her lunch bag and a pair of heels into her large brown shoulder bag before she left for work.

"No," Cooper grunted from the couch. He had an edge of annoyance in his voice. Everyone was busy going about their lives while Cooper remained in his downtown loft still healing from stab wounds to the gut he acquired on the last case. The healing process was taking considerably longer than he had planned. Part of it was his fault. He had gone against doctor's orders and went back to work sooner than recommended and tore some stitches. The doctor had to perform some outpatient surgery to repair the mess he'd made of himself.

Cooper was forced to rest. To get a break from the bed and the couch, Cooper was allowed slow walks outside, if he didn't overdo it. Even that was barely possible because pain ripped through his insides if he moved too swiftly. It rendered him immobile in a way he had never been before.

Cooper had knee surgery once and he had been encouraged to get some exercise. He had physical therapy appointments three times a week and he was still able to do surveillance in his truck. It was his left knee and he didn't need that leg for driving. With his current injury, getting in and out of his truck was an event.

It brought out a side of himself he didn't like. Adele didn't like it much either. She had grown tired of his grouching and whining. Two nights ago Adele officially stated that the honeymoon phase of their relationship was over. It was meant as a wake-up call for him. Cooper was self-aware enough to know that. That didn't mean making the mental change would be easy or even possible.

"I'm leaving," Adele said as she bent over and kissed him on the lips. When she pulled back, she twirled for him. Her black hair had been braided and twisted in a knot on the top of her head and she was wearing a new gray suit she had bought for court. "What do you think?"

"Incredible, as always." Cooper gestured for her to bend down so he could kiss her again. He longed for the day when he could wrap his arms around her and lift her off the ground in a hug.

Adele was the one person who could make Cooper smile no matter his mood. It wasn't just that she was beautiful, which she was, it was that she was intelligent and kind and willing to call him out every chance she got. She didn't let Cooper get away with anything, but she did it in such a confident, sweet endearing way, he couldn't fault her for it. She was the push he sometimes needed.

Adele had upended her life in Atlanta, Georgia to move to Little Rock to be with him. They had mutually decided that her criminal law practice was much easier to relocate than the private investigation firm he ran with Riley. Cooper assumed Adele wanted a change.

"Do a puzzle or read a book. I left a few paperbacks on the nightstand." Adele swept his blond hair off his forehead. "Maybe this is the universe's way of telling you that you deserve a break." She kissed him one more time on the forehead and then on the lips. She gathered up her things and then blew him another kiss at the door.

Cooper wasn't much of a reader and he didn't have the desire to start a puzzle. He flipped on the television and caught a breaking news segment with Luke's brief statement about what was happening. Cooper wondered who the woman was that Luke had let under the police tape and guided into the library. He wouldn't call Luke and check in but he wanted to.

Cooper shut off the television and considered checking in on Riley. He reached for his cellphone and stared at it for a few moments and then decided against it. He didn't have anything going on or anything to say.

Cooper inched himself to the end of the couch and got up gingerly the way the doctor showed him so he didn't rip his latest round of stitches. He went across the room to the row of windows lining the living room. Cooper undid the latch, pushed out one of the windows, and breathed in some fresh air. He put his hands on the sill and leaned forward, allowing himself to look directly into the windows across the street. Cooper had done this so frequently he'd begun to make up stories about the people he saw frequently.

There was one woman with her young son. He never saw a husband or any man there. Cooper assumed she was a single mother. He had watched as she rushed around each morning to get him ready for school and out the door in time to catch the bus. Three days in a row, they missed the bus and she had to drive him to school. Cooper wished he could help the woman or at least bring her some coffee and a pastry from the bakery nearby. Really any kind gesture to let her know she wasn't alone in the world.

Maybe she wasn't alone though. Cooper didn't know. All he knew was what he saw each morning when he was spying on his neighbors. Before his injury, Cooper hadn't paid any attention to his neighbors at all. He had lived in the building for more than eight years and the only person he had spoken to regularly was the young woman across the hall who was a nurse at the local hospital. About a year ago, she got engaged and moved in with her fiancé. Since then, Cooper didn't even know the name of the man who had replaced her.

It surprised him what boredom could do to a person. It made them do things they wouldn't normally do. Cooper needed some stimulation, and if all he was doing was watching the world go by outside the window, he didn't see the harm.

It's not like he was a peeping tom. When the brunette woman undressed in front of the window, he turned away. She had a few boyfriends or men she saw regularly. He didn't judge, it wasn't his place. If someone had been watching his place years ago before he met Adele, he'd be embarrassed by what they had witnessed.

Cooper was about to turn away from the window when he caught sight of the brunette and wondered why she hadn't left for work yet. She usually left at seven-thirty right on the dot. Cooper admonished himself for knowing that. But there she was with her phone pressed to her ear gesturing wildly with the other hand. Cooper guessed she was probably in her mid-thirties. He had no idea what she did for work, but she left each morning in sharp skirts or pantsuits and heels. It was a professional job whatever it was.

Today, she had on a pair of leggings and a tee-shirt that looked so wrinkled Cooper imagined she had pulled it from a heap on the floor. Still on the phone, she walked to the window and looked out at the street below. Cooper went up on tiptoes and peered down to see what she might be looking at. He didn't see anything other than a man in jeans and a blue sweater waiting at the buzzer to be let into the building. A moment later, he pulled open the door and disappeared inside. When Cooper looked back at the window, the woman was gone.

Cooper didn't think he'd seen that man in her apartment before, not while he'd been watching. He shrugged and stepped back from the window, not thinking much of it. Cooper turned and faced inside to view his loft. There wasn't much for him to do while Riley had her case in New York. He had hired a few other investigators to help with their business in Little Rock, which ended up being a good thing with Cooper's injury. He fielded calls and sent off contracts but that was about all he could do.

Cooper took a few steps into the living room, leaving his post at the window but a raised voice drew his attention back. He turned and stared across the street. He got up on tiptoes and looked down at the street below but no one was there. His head snapped up at the sound of glass breaking.

Cooper scanned the windows across the street until he realized where the sound originated. He zeroed in on the brunette's window in time to see the man throwing a vase against the wall. It shattered into several pieces. His heart rate quickened as he scanned the four living room windows for the woman. He didn't see her anywhere as the man continued his tirade, grabbing things off the shelves and end tables and smashing them to the ground. When he was done making a spectacular mess, he moved on to the bookcase. He scattered the books to the floor. All the while he yelled words that Cooper couldn't quite make out. The woman was still nowhere in sight.

Cooper scanned his eyes to the left and then to the right finally spotting her cowering behind a closed bedroom door. Cooper's range of sight was limited to two bedroom windows. It was enough to make out the end of the bed and a long narrow dresser against the wall with the door. It was strange because she normally had these drapes closed. Today, they were wide open.

Cooper breathed out in short rapid breaths as he patted down his pockets for his cellphone. He cursed loudly, remembering that it was in the bedroom. Cooper caught sight of the woman one last time still hovering behind the closed bedroom door and the man still in the living room smashing everything he could get his hands on.

Cooper left his post and hurried as quickly as he could across the loft to his bedroom. He made it around to the far side of the bed, sharp pain catching with every step, and grabbed his cellphone.

Cooper made a quick call as he headed back to the window. He scanned the windows again to check on the woman and this time real panic set in. The man was no longer in the living room and the bedroom door had been thrown open wide.

"911. What is your emergency?" the operator asked in a clipped no-nonsense tone.

Cooper could barely get out the words as he tried to make sense of what he was seeing across the street.

"911. What is your emergency?" the operator said again.

"I'm here but not sure what I'm witnessing." Cooper focused on the end of the bed. The man was bent over at the waist straddling the limp legs of the young woman under him. "I think he's strangling her. I need help immediately." Cooper gave her the address of the building across the street. Then he realized he didn't know one important thing. "I'm unsure of the unit number. It's the third floor and she has south-facing windows."

The operator assured Cooper the police would do their best to figure it out. In the meantime, she wanted to gather as much information as possible and asked Cooper a series of questions he couldn't answer. "It's okay," she assured him, "just tell me what you know."

Cooper remained at the window watching the man as he explained to the operator his background, admitted his terrible habit of watching the neighbors and detailed the few things he knew about the woman. The police seemed to be taking far too long to arrive while the woman remained limp on the bed.

The man slowly rose from his bent-over position and stood to his full height. As if he could sense Cooper's presence, he turned sharply to the window and stared out of it. Cooper stepped back from the window, out of sight. The wail of sirens could be heard off in the distance.

Cooper would meet the cops on the sidewalk out front.

CHAPTER 4

Senior Investigator Dave Grogan sat behind his desk at the police barracks and studied me carefully. He had agreed to the meeting, but it was clear he hadn't decided whether or not to trust my motives for taking the case. Finally, he leaned forward and rested his hands on the desk.

"I never once questioned my decision to arrest Tim." If there was a *but* hovering in his statement, he didn't express it.

"Do you still stand by that decision?" I moved to get more comfortable in the small chair across from his desk. I crossed my legs and then uncrossed them. The chair had shorter legs, which I assumed was on purpose to leave me in a position of looking up at him instead of directly across his desk.

"The evidence was there," Inv. Grogan said evenly. "I'll tell you this much. When we got him back to the station and started to interrogate him, he was utterly distraught. I'd never seen a man so upset and it wasn't because he was being questioned by the police. He was dealing with grief or maybe shock over what he'd done."

"Is it possible that it was *only* grief from losing someone he cared about a great deal? I saw Tim with Alex at school and they always seemed rather happy. He doted on her and was in love with her. I had a hard time believing he had killed her. I believe him now that he is innocent. That's why I'm willing to take the case."

Inv. Grogan narrowed his eyes at me. "Did I interview you all those years ago?"

"I was Alex's roommate but wasn't home at the time of the murder. It was Thanksgiving break. You interviewed me a few days later after you had made the decision that Tim was guilty. I questioned it then and you dismissed me. You didn't even take a statement from me since I wasn't home and had, as you put it, *nothing to offer*."

I had meant it as a slight to his investigative skill but he didn't take it as such. He shrugged and asked, "Do you think you have something to offer now?"

"I don't know what I have to offer. Tim asked for my help and I said I'd help him." We remained locked in a staring contest across the desk. I wasn't going to look away first. "I can't say for certain if Tim did this or not. Even though Tim was good to her, they argued often. I know Alex wasn't as into Tim as he was into her. She was going to string him along until graduation and then break up with him. I suspected at the time that she might be cheating on him. I never had evidence to back that up."

Inv. Grogan raised his eyebrows slightly. "No one said anything about another man. I never found evidence of that."

"I tried to tell you then. You said if I didn't have solid proof you didn't want to hear it." I felt angrier and was more combative than I meant to be. I hadn't realized until I sat down with him how dismissed I had felt when he interviewed me. That wouldn't get me very far now. I tried my best to set those feelings aside. "I don't want to argue with you. I'm not trying to call you out on work you should have done then. I want to offer Tim my help. My husband is a homicide detective, so I understand what a retrial means for you. If Tim is guilty, I'll happily turn over whatever I find. But if he's not, and this has been a huge mistake all these years, then the wrong needs to be righted."

Inv. Grogan seemed to appreciate that sentiment. "What can I do for you now?"

"Help me understand the evidence. As I said, I wasn't there that weekend. By the time I got back on Sunday, Alex's body had been found. I know my downstairs neighbor found her, but I don't know how that came to be."

"I shouldn't be sharing this information with you, Riley, especially if the case goes back to court."

"The first trial is a matter of public record. Tim has the transcript. I'll find out sooner or later. I'd rather hear it from you and understand." When he didn't seem to be convinced, I pushed harder. "I'm only asking you to have a conversation with me. If you truly believe that Tim is guilty then convince me."

"A jury already decided that," he said and appraised my response. When Inv. Grogan saw the look of doubt on my face, he gave in. "Your downstairs neighbor, Michelle Hurst, found Alex's body that Sunday afternoon. She had heard some concerning noises the night before but brushed it off and didn't think anything of it. She figured Alex and Tim were arguing again, which she said was constant. Michelle and Alex were supposed to meet for a late lunch on Sunday. When Alex didn't come down in time, Michelle went up and found the door slightly open. She pushed it open farther and called Alex's name but there was no response. She became more concerned and entered the apartment and found Alex dead on her bed. Michelle ran out and immediately called 911."

All of that sounded reasonable enough except for one thing – Alex hated Michelle and would have never scheduled lunch with her.

The story didn't add up and I told Inv. Grogan that. "Those two did not get along in any way. They were like oil and water. I never fully understood why they disliked each other so much but they did. I didn't have a problem with Michelle and sidestepped the drama."

Inv. Grogan didn't appear convinced. "It was Thanksgiving

weekend, Riley. Isn't it possible they put their differences aside? It was your senior year after all and everyone would be going their separate ways before long. Maybe the two of them decided to call a truce."

I shook my head. "Alex would have mentioned it to me. I saw her the night before break. They didn't make up in two days. If they were meeting for lunch, there was another reason or Michelle lied about why she went up there. Did she see Tim at the apartment or just hear him?"

"She heard all the fighting upstairs and saw him leave. Tim denied being inside the apartment that night but we have evidence to suggest otherwise."

"Just Michelle's statement?"

He nodded. "She's credible."

Eyewitness testimony was inherently unreliable. "Tim never admitted to killing Alex," I said and he confirmed. "Isn't it possible that there was another person there that night?"

Inv. Grogan gestured dismissively. "There is no evidence of that."

"My understanding is there is no evidence of much of anything. There was no murder weapon because it was determined to be suffocation. The assumption was that someone had put something over her face to stop her from breathing. There is no DNA evidence or eyewitness evidence either other than Michelle who said she saw Tim leave. Is that correct?"

Inv. Grogan confirmed that to be true. "As you know, there were too many fingerprints around your apartment for the evidence to be considered. You had many people in and out of there, including a party the previous weekend. Fingerprint evidence wasn't going to rule anyone in or out. We did find Tim's in her bedroom."

I scoffed and shook my head. "They naturally would be. Alex and Tim were in a relationship and he was in our apartment day and night for two years. It would have been odd had his fingerprints not been found. That would have meant someone wiped it down removing all of their fingerprints."

There was something about the way Inv. Grogan squinted that made me suspicious.

I leaned into the desk. "Was there an area of the apartment that had been wiped down?"

"Riley…" he started to say and then trailed off as he seemed to consider if he was going to disclose what was on his mind.

I didn't let that stop me. "What area in the apartment was without prints?"

"There were prints everywhere. That wasn't the concern." Inv. Grogan had a question in response to mine. "How did you normally leave the kitchen? Was it tidy or a bit messy?"

"It was never left a mess. I'm a bit of a neat freak and so was Alex," I admitted, thinking back on my time with Alex as my roommate. Our same level of cleanliness was one of the reasons we decided to get an apartment together. I had closer friends at college but none that I could have lived with. Inv. Grogan was watching me carefully. I added, "Tim was even more of a neat freak than the two of us. There was never even so much as an unwashed dish left in the sink or crumbs on the counter."

Inv. Grogan sat back in his chair. "It would be unusual then to find the kitchen a mess?"

"Define mess."

He spun the chair to the side, got up, and went to the cabinet in the corner of the room. He pulled out the top drawer and grabbed a file folder. When Inv. Grogan turned to me, he said, "I won't show you all the crime scene photos but one may be of interest to you." He opened the file folder, flipped through photos, and then handed me two prints.

I took the photos and stared down at them unsure of what I was seeing. It was my old apartment kitchen but left in a state that I'd never seen. "This can't be my kitchen."

There were two dinner plates on the table with half-eaten food, a sink full of dishes, drawers, and cabinets left half-open, and items on the counter left at odd angles to where they should have been. "Alex would have never left the apartment this way."

Inv. Grogan didn't seem interested in my assessment. "Isn't it possible that Alex and Tim started fighting over dinner and it escalated? He's certainly not going to clean the kitchen after he killed her."

"That isn't how they argued," I countered and put the photos back on the desk. "They were verbal people. They could get into hot debates about things, but when it came to the relationship, Alex pulled away more than she argued." I could see it in my mind and it still didn't add up. Even if Tim had tried to start a discussion about their relationship over dinner, Alex would have sat there calmly listening to him and avoiding the confrontation. She would have appeased him, cleaned up the kitchen after their meal, and then she would have asked him to go, feigning being tired. I explained all of that to Inv. Grogan, then stressed, "They weren't violent with each other."

"They could have…"

"No," I said more forcefully, interrupting him. I pulled the photos back off the desk and held them up. "You don't understand. Alex and Tim would have never sat down to dinner with the kitchen in this state. They would have cleaned up the counters, put the pots and pans in the sink to soak, closed the cabinet doors, and sat down to dinner. I don't know anyone that would leave a kitchen like this while they were eating. It's chaos."

"What's *your* assessment?" Inv. Grogan asked the question but there was a hint of sarcasm in his voice I didn't appreciate.

The kitchen hadn't been in this state when I was finally allowed to return to the apartment. The whole place had been professionally cleaned and everything was back in its place by the time I returned to living there. I stared down at the photos and tried to make sense of what I was seeing.

After a few moments, the reality of what I was seeing set in. I raised my eyes at him. "This looks staged or searched after the fact. If I had to venture a guess, I'd say that Alex was having dinner with someone and maybe a fight broke out. It's possible she was killed in the middle of dinner. Then whoever killed her staged the kitchen to look like this or was searching for something. See this pot here," I said, pointing to a small round pot on its side near the stove. "It's clean and not even a pot that would be used to cook this meal. We kept that one in a cabinet near the stove. Why would it be out? This is a staged scene or someone was tearing the place apart looking for something."

Inv. Grogan leaned over his desk and stared at the pot in question. "That does look clean as if it hadn't been used."

"Why did this mess strike you as odd?"

He took a breath and kind of cocked his head to the side to watch me. After a few beats, he nodded his head. "It seemed staged to me too. Tim shuddered when he looked at the photo. He said they would have never sat down to dinner like that, even if they were arguing. He seemed credible and his physical reaction to the photo wasn't faked. The kitchen mess was the one oddity about the case."

It was a lot more than odd to me. It was a real indication that Tim wasn't guilty.

CHAPTER 5

Luke met with Leslie and determined that the deceased man was her boyfriend. He got the full name of the deceased and his address. Leslie told Luke that Nick Day had left the party at her friend's house the night before at close to eight to meet with some friends. They were going to a local bar in the River Market and she had expected him to be back around midnight. When he didn't come home, Leslie assumed Nick went back to his apartment instead. When she couldn't reach him earlier that morning and then saw on the news about the body on the grounds of the Clinton Library, she had a sinking feeling it was Nick.

Leslie insisted that he would have called her by morning if he'd been alive. He hadn't shown up at the small tech firm where he worked. Those two things alone brought her to the crime scene. She didn't know anything more about his night or what happened. But identifying the victim was a huge step forward in the case.

Enroute to Nick's apartment, Luke received a text from Cooper to come to his loft right away. Cooper insisted that he had seen a woman murdered across the street from his loft but that the police weren't doing anything about it.

Luke handed the phone to Det. Tyler. "Does that say what I think it says?"

Tyler read the text and then squinted up at Luke. "Is he that bored he's creating fake cases to solve?"

Luke had known Cooper was struggling with his limited mobility, but he was never one to be overly dramatic. "Text him back and tell him we will stop to see him when we can."

Tyler did as Luke asked and within seconds, the phone rang. Luke engaged the call via Bluetooth so both of them were listening in. "Cooper, I'll be there as soon as I can. We are in the middle of a case. I don't know if you saw the news, but there was a body found at the Clinton Library this morning."

"If you can't get here, you can't get here," Cooper responded with an exasperated sigh. "I'm telling you, Luke, a woman was strangled across the street. The cops said they didn't find anything, but I didn't know the unit number and they wouldn't let me in the building to search with them. They weren't even in there for thirty minutes. They came out and said I must be seeing things. I don't understand how they can say they found nothing. I saw the man's tirade and the result. A woman is dead."

Luke wondered if Cooper was seeing things. He didn't know how to ask the question and not sound insensitive. He figured their twenty-something years of friendship could handle it. "Did you take any of the pain medication the doctor prescribed?"

"I'm not hallucinating," Cooper said dryly.

Luke could tell by his tone that his feelings were hurt. "As soon as I'm done here, I'll come and meet you and we can go into the building together."

"It's fine," Cooper said with an edge to his tone. "I'll take care of it."

The phone clicked and he was gone.

Luke thumped the steering wheel with the palm of his hand. He didn't mean to dismiss Cooper or make light of the situation. Luke knew the medication the doctor had prescribed him was strong enough to cause hallucinations. They had joked about it. Cooper wasn't one for any medication, so Luke assumed he probably wasn't taking much or any of it at all.

Det. Tyler glanced over at him. "Cooper sounded like he meant it. Do you want to head there first before he does something stupid? The victim's apartment is going to be there waiting for us. If it wasn't for the girlfriend, we wouldn't even have had his name yet."

Luke side-eyed his partner and then pulled over to the side of the road to pull a U-turn. "Cooper is probably heading over to the building to search for the woman's apartment. It's not that I doubt what he thinks he saw. I just question if what he saw was accurate. He's watched one too many movies."

Tyler chuckled to himself. "Isn't it usually reclusive women with a drinking problem?"

"If we get there and Cooper is wearing a fluffy pink bathrobe and slippers with a coffee mug filled with vodka, I'm going to leave him where we find him," Luke said, laughing for the first time all morning. "I'm sure he thinks he saw a murder and maybe he did. I've never known him to lie or be dramatic. He's just been bored and grumpy lately and who knows what he's been up to recently."

Luke drove through the streets of downtown Little Rock grateful to hit mostly green lights. They pulled to a stop on the side of the road in front of the building in question. He parked as Cooper entered the lobby and the door closed behind him. He didn't even notice Luke's SUV.

Tyler whistled. "I don't think I've ever seen Cooper moving so slowly."

Luke cut the engine and reached for his door. "Two deep stab wounds and then not following doctor's orders for rest and recuperation. He had to have another surgery to repair what didn't heal right the first time. I can see he hasn't learned his lesson."

Luke and Tyler entered the foyer of the building together. Similar to

Cooper's building, this one had a concierge desk off to the left of the foyer with staff who kept everything in the building running smoothly for its occupants. The desk was unmanned as they entered. Luke made his way through the foyer to a set of unlocked double doors. He found Cooper standing in the narrow hallway in front of the elevator.

"Where are you going?" Luke asked, startling him.

Cooper gestured toward the elevator. "To the third floor to look for the apartment. I thought you couldn't meet me. You said you were too busy and then insinuated that I was hallucinating." He looked away from Luke and stared at the elevator. It was a sure sign his feelings were hurt.

Luke didn't have time for him to be angry. He had shown up. "Cooper, you can't wander around the building looking for a murdered woman."

Cooper glanced over. "That's why I called 911. The cops didn't do their job, so now I have to. Come with me to the third floor, find the apartment, and then you'll see what I'm talking about." The elevator doors slid open and they all stepped inside. "It's the third-floor front of the building. That's all I know. I, unfortunately, don't have an apartment number."

"It should be easy enough to find," Luke said and then hit the button. He ate his words when the doors opened on the third floor. To say it wasn't quite what they had been expecting would be an understatement.

What should have been a simple hallway branched out in four directions. After taking one hallway and then another in the direction of the front of the building, Cooper finally had to stop. He caught his breath and held his side. "This place is a maze. I know it's the third floor and there are big windows into the living room and then another smaller two windows into the bedroom."

Luke watched him carefully as he spoke. He was left with one question. "Do you know this woman?"

Cooper glanced over at him and then quickly looked away. "I wouldn't say I know her. I've seen her around."

"Around where?" Tyler asked, his tone as suspicious as Luke's. When it was clear Cooper wasn't going to respond, he pressed. "Cooper, you have to help us understand what's going on. You seem to know the whole layout of her apartment. If you're involved with this woman, we need to know. I'm not going to tell Adele, but you need to come clean with us."

Cooper shook his head as red filled his cheeks. He quietly admitted, "It's nothing like that. I've been bored at home and it hurts to sit for too long. I've found myself staring out the window often. I guess you can say I've been spying on my neighbors. I see the woman often rushing around to get ready in the morning." More quietly, almost in a whisper, Cooper added, "She's had men in and out of her apartment. It's not a judgment, just a fact. I've never seen the guy who was with her this morning."

Luke didn't want to pile on Cooper's embarrassment, so he didn't comment on his new pastime. He did need to know the facts of this morning if he was going to help. "What did you see this morning?"

Cooper focused his attention on Luke. "She normally is out the door by seven-thirty each morning. Today, she was still at home dressed in black leggings and a tee-shirt. I thought maybe she wasn't going to work. She was on the phone and it looked like a heated exchange. It could have been with the guy who showed up. I'm not sure about that. But he walked in through the front door and then once he got inside, they started arguing and he lost it. He smashed things to the floor and was tearing up the place. She ran to her bedroom but he followed her. I didn't see what happened right when he entered the bedroom because I had left the window to get my phone to call 911."

"What did you see when you got back?"

Cooper closed his eyes and explained in detail what he had witnessed. When he opened his eyes, his expression was pained. "I could only see her legs but she looked lifeless on that bed. The way he was bent over her, I'm sure he was strangling her."

Tyler asked, "Did you see him get up from her?"

Cooper nodded. "He looked out the window as if knowing I was watching him. I don't think he was able to see me. I stepped back regardless and then when I looked out again, the drapes were closed and I couldn't see anything anymore. I headed down to meet the cops."

It was Tyler who said what Luke was thinking. "You don't know for sure then that he killed her. He could have strangled her and then stopped or he could have been bent over her screaming at her or maybe what you saw was them making up."

"She wasn't moving at all," Cooper argued, but a look of doubt came over his face. "It's possible, I guess. He had been in a rage though, breaking and smashing things. She ran and hid from him. I just…"

Luke put his hand on Cooper's shoulder. "You saw a woman who was in danger and you reacted. Let's knock on some doors and try to figure out where she lives. If he was that violent, we can offer her some support if she wants to take it."

That seemed to satisfy Cooper. They still didn't know what direction to go. "She's short and petite with dark hair cut in a bob. I don't even know her name."

It was a good enough description for Luke. They decided to split up and each took one of the hallways. Luke started at the first door closest to the elevator and worked his way down. It took knocking on five doors before he reached a woman who answered. She drew up short when she saw Luke's badge. "I thought you were the maintenance guy. How can I help you?"

Luke introduced himself and apologized for bothering her. "I'm looking for one of your neighbors. I'm a bit turned around in the hallways here. Her apartment faces the road and she has short dark hair. I'm not sure of her name."

The woman squinted and then stepped out into the hallway with Luke. She pointed farther down the hallway to the apartments he hadn't yet reached. "Head down this hall. At the end, take a left and then another quick left. There are four apartments and those are the ones in the front. I don't know who designed this building but I've assumed they were on drugs when they made the design. None of it makes any sense. There are only four apartments with front-facing windows. I'm not sure which apartment she's in. I've seen her in the hall and at the mailbox. Her name is Mandy McKee. I don't know much more about her. She isn't one to socialize with her neighbors that often and I work nights. I barely see anyone."

"You've been a great help." Luke asked one more question. "Do you know if she has a boyfriend? Have you seen her with anyone?"

"I've seen a few men with her. I don't get involved though, so I don't know her relationship with them. They could be family for all I know." She stepped back into her apartment.

Luke thanked her again and she closed the door. He headed down the hallway armed with more information. He'd need eyes on her himself to know that she was safe. That was the only way Cooper was going to let this go.

CHAPTER 6

After I gathered as much information from Inv. Grogan as he would allow, I sat in my SUV outside the police department and searched social media for Michelle Hurst. I had stayed friends with Michelle for a couple of years after college. Enough time to know she had moved to Syracuse and then last I heard she met a lawyer and was moving to the Albany area.

We had planned a few times to meet up for lunch or dinner but that never happened. She got busy with married life and then had a baby. That was the last I had heard from her. In all that time, there had been little discussion about Alex and Tim and the murder.

I found Michelle faster than I assumed I would. She wasn't using her married name on social media so that made finding her even easier. It looked from what I could see on her profile that she was still living in the area and working in development at a local college. A quick search of the college's website gave me both her email address and phone number. It didn't look from her photo that she had changed all that much. Her hair was a little darker and shorter than the last time we saw each other. Tiny creases around her eyes mirrored my own.

I called the number provided and was pleasantly surprised when she answered with a cheery hello. She probably assumed I was a donor and had to be nice. She squealed when she realized it was me. I took the chance and asked if she was free for lunch. I explained that I was only in town for a few days and would love to see her. I left out why I wanted to meet up. I figured any mention of Alex would be better left for later. We made a quick plan to meet in thirty minutes at a pizza place near the college.

Michelle was sitting in the last booth on the left near the window that overlooked the side street. A long bar filled the space to the right. In between the booths and bar was a narrow walkway. It wasn't a big place by any stretch but the pizza was always good.

She slid out of the booth and put her arms around me. "It's so good to see you."

I returned the compliment and sat down. "Did you order yet?"

"Half pepperoni and black olives and half sausage and peppers just like in college," she said with a laugh. Michelle beamed a smile at me then filled me in on her daughter who was heading into fifth grade and her amicable divorce. "It's been kind of a whirlwind lately. I'm happy to be settled into a new house and new job. It's all going well." She asked questions about my life and I updated her.

"You were teaching, weren't you?"

"Eighth grade math," Michelle said and rolled her eyes. "Hard being in a school these days. I desperately needed a change."

After catching up and a little reminiscing while we ate our lunch, I finally told her why I had called. "I'm not sure if you know, but Tim was let out of prison on an appeal."

"I heard," Michelle said with a heavy sigh. "I feel horrible for Alex's family. I can't imagine what they are going through, having to live this all over again. In a news statement, Tim said he had evidence that he was innocent. I wonder what he plans."

I took a sip of my drink, swallowing my trepidation with it, and then put the cup down on the table. "That's why I'm here in New York. I'm going to meet with Tim. He's asked me—"

Michelle screwed up her face in horror. "Why would you do that,

Riley? He's a killer! Alex was one of your best friends. How could you betray her like that."

A few patrons looked down at our table. I shifted my focus back to Michelle and leaned into the table. "Tim asked for my help to reinvestigate his case. If he's guilty, then that's what the evidence will show me. If he's not, then I can make sure the real killer goes to prison." I let the words hang there for a moment and watched her reaction.

Michelle shook her head in disgust. "The cops have the right person. I'm sure of it, Riley. Don't let him manipulate you the way he did Alex for all those years."

For someone who didn't like Alex and didn't know her well, Michelle sure had an opinion on her relationship. "Maybe I'm not remembering correctly, but I don't recall that you and Alex were very friendly back in college. Did you know a lot about her relationship with Tim?"

Michelle pursed her lips and glanced to the side. "I heard things, Riley. We all did, especially after the murder."

"All rumors. I heard them too and they didn't match up to what I knew firsthand about the relationship, Michelle." I waited until her focus was on me and then said what I should have said back in college. "Alex wasn't that easy to date. She was going to end things with Tim after she strung him along until graduation. I had suspected she was up to something Thanksgiving weekend when she didn't want to see her family or go to Tim's. I had even invited her to come home with me, but she turned me down. She said she'd be fine home alone for the weekend. That was not the Alex I knew."

Michelle closed her eyes. "We shouldn't speak ill of her now that she's gone."

"You had no problem speaking ill of her when she was alive," I snapped, not letting her off the hook for the suddenly pious attitude. "Open your eyes and look at me, Michelle."

Her eyes fluttered open. "Riley, I don't want to talk about this."

"We have to talk about it because what if the wrong man went to prison?" The guilt washed over me as I considered what I might have done differently then, including telling Inv. Grogan that I had long suspected Alex of being involved with someone else. I had forgotten that over the years, but when he showed me a photo of that kitchen, those memories came rushing back. I wasn't going to remain silent now.

Michelle folded her hands primly on the table. "What is it you want to know?"

"A few things," I said, glad that she was going to talk to me and hadn't gotten up and stormed off. "First, I want to know everything you remember about that weekend. Second, I want to know why you told Inv. Grogan you were going to meet Alex for lunch on Sunday when you and I know you didn't get along with her. Third, why didn't you ever tell me the circumstances of finding her body?" I didn't care if all my questions at once overwhelmed her. Michelle was stronger than she was acting.

She absorbed the information, took another bite of pizza, and then shrugged. "You never asked me about finding Alex and it wasn't something I liked talking about." She locked her gaze on me. "I was worried you might suspect I had something to do with her death. You, more than anyone, knew Alex and I didn't like each other. You're perceptive, Riley. You always have been. If I told you about finding her, you would have had many questions I didn't want to answer."

"I would have had many questions," I said, agreeing with her with anger in my voice. "You're right about that, but I would never have suspected you. We were better friends than I was with Alex. I knew you well enough to know that you wouldn't have hurt her no matter how much you didn't like her."

Michelle looked down at the table and gave a slow nod to her head.

"I appreciate that. You're right about lunch. We didn't have lunch planned. I couldn't think of a reasonable reason to give the cops why I had gone up there. The reason I had sounded dumb and made up."

I inched closer to the table. "What was the reason?"

"It sounds dumb to me now," she said with a small breathy laugh. Michelle raised her eyes to mine. "Do you remember how loud Alex used to be? It drove me crazy – the stomping around in those shoes she used to wear and she'd play music so loud it drowned out everything else in the building."

"I remember," I said evenly. Everything Michelle mentioned had caused more than one argument between Alex and me.

"I heard her arguing with who I assume was Tim the night before. They were screaming at each other in a way I'd never heard before. It was hard to make out what exactly was being said, but it was a fight to end all fights. At close to eleven, I heard Tim pound down the stairs and leave the house. It's—"

"Wait," I said, interrupting her. "You said you *heard* Tim leave. Did you see him leave?"

"Well, no…" Michelle stopped to consider. "Who else would have been fighting like that with Alex?"

That was certainly the question of the hour. "What time did you hear them start fighting?"

"It started around eight. Then it got quiet and I assumed they were making up. Later, around eleven, Tim came down the stairs and I heard the front door slam shut. I didn't bother looking out the window. I had hoped he wasn't coming back that night because I didn't want to listen to them go at it again."

"What made you then go up and check on Alex on Sunday?"

Michelle gestured with her hand. "As I said, she was always loud. It occurred to me on Sunday that I didn't hear her after the argument. Not after Tim left. It was only one person walking down those stairs, so it's not like she left with him. You remember how those stairs echoed. I'm sure when you were up there you used to be able to hear people walking up and down."

Michelle was right. The stairs were wood and not carpeted, so the pounding up and down the stairs even if someone was light-footed echoed throughout the whole building. It was easy to tell if one person was coming up or more than one. "That's it then? You heard arguing, got worried when you didn't hear her again and went upstairs to check?"

Michelle nodded. "I didn't like her, Riley, but I'm not a monster. It was a bad fight, so bad that Tim didn't spend the night like he usually did. When I heard nothing all Sunday morning, I got worried. At worst, I thought she was sulking. I didn't know what I was going to say to her given we didn't like each other. Still, I felt bad for her. I went upstairs and found your apartment door open. I called her name and then went in when she didn't respond. She would have never left the door unlocked. I saw the mess in the kitchen and I started to panic. I found her in her bedroom…" Michelle trailed off, her eyes getting watery.

I didn't need her to share the details of what she saw then. There was something more important I needed her to understand. "You said you heard Alex and Tim arguing. Had you ever heard them before that night?"

"They argued all the time, Riley," Michelle snapped back at me.

"Right. I remember telling you that. It was fairly common knowledge that they had a volatile relationship because they often weren't speaking. But what I'm asking you is, had you ever heard them screaming at one another like you heard that night?"

After a few beats, Michelle shook her head. "Never. I hadn't thought they had that kind of relationship until that night. I never realized they had that kind of passion between them. As you said, when they argued, I'd heard they went silent with Tim eventually coming back and trying to make everything okay. If anything, I heard he was the one who always gave in first."

"You don't find it odd then that suddenly they were screaming and shouting at one another?"

Michelle looked like she wasn't sure what to say. "I assumed maybe Tim finally snapped." She remained quiet for a few moments and I allowed her to ruminate without asking anything else. When she spoke again, her voice broke. "If Tim didn't kill Alex, then who did?"

"You understand now why I'm willing to help him." There was something she was leaving out. "I spoke to Inv. Grogan and he said that you testified you saw Tim leave the apartment. You're telling me now that you only heard him. Which is it?"

"Riley, they make you say things," Michelle said, her tone implying that I wasn't in the know about how cops worked. "I told them I only heard him and they convinced me I must have seen him. That's what they wrote down and that's what the prosecutor said I should say."

I sat there dumbfounded. "Are you saying you lied on the stand?"

She cast her eyes up toward me and didn't respond to my question.

"Michelle, this is important. I don't care what you said then. Did you see Tim or only hear who you thought was him?"

"It was him, Riley." She sat back and folded her arms over her chest. She stared me down. I didn't look away. "Fine," she huffed. "I heard him but I'm sure it was him. As I said who else would have been up there?"

"Why didn't you tell me this before?"

"Riley, she died and you acted like you didn't care. You went back to living in the apartment and didn't want to talk about Alex again. We tried and you shut us down. You didn't even attend the trial."

She was right. It had been too raw for me. I distanced myself from everyone after it happened. That wasn't the case now. There was more

I needed to know. "Tell me again everything you heard that weekend, every detail you can think of no matter how small or insignificant it might seem."

We spent the rest of our lunch with her going over every detail she could remember from the time I left for break until I arrived back on Sunday. It was clear to me Michelle had thought about that weekend a lot over the years. Her memory was far sharper than mine.

I left lunch with a strong lead and made Michelle promise to call me if she remembered anything else.

CHAPTER 7

Luke made it back to the police station in the later part of the afternoon. After he discovered Mandy McKee's name and apartment number, he had gone to check on her and found no one home. He promised Cooper he'd check later in the day on his way home from work and he'd do some follow-up to try to get a phone number for the young woman.

Cooper wasn't happy with that but didn't push further. He knew there wasn't much Luke could do. It's not like he could break down the door and search Mandy's apartment. They didn't even know for sure that a crime had been committed. All Cooper saw was a man getting angry and smashing things to the ground. He hadn't seen the man actually put his hands on Mandy. If she wasn't calling in the disturbance about her trashed apartment, there wasn't much Luke could do without more information.

Cooper headed back to his apartment and promised Luke he'd wait until later. Luke and Det. Tyler went to search Nick Day's apartment and found nothing that would help them figure out why the man had been murdered.

Nick had kept his place fairly tidy. The bed was made and mail was stacked in a holder in the kitchen. He had a full load of laundry still in the dryer and a filing cabinet of important documents arranged neatly in folders. There was an array of healthy food in the fridge and neatly labeled meat in the freezer. His clothes were folded in the drawers and hung in the closet. He had a few pairs of sneakers and some shoes, nothing extravagant. One gray suit hung in the back of the closet, probably for weddings, funerals, and the occasional fancy night out. He wasn't a business executive who dressed in suits for work each day. Neither was he someone who wore a uniform. His girlfriend had said he worked for a local tech company and his wardrobe checked out.

All in all, Nick didn't appear to Luke as a man who led anything other than an ordinary safe lifestyle.

There was nothing Leslie told them that indicated anything different. She had no idea why her boyfriend would be dead by the Clinton Library with a message about retribution on his back. They had been together for more than a year and were recently talking about moving in together. Nick had been married and divorced in his twenties but had spoken kindly about his ex-wife who lived in Dallas and was married to someone else.

Leslie had been married and divorced years ago. Her ex was in another state and she hadn't spoken to him in close to ten years. There was nothing in either of their pasts that would have led to Nick's death – at least that Luke could find during the initial stage of the investigation.

By the time Luke made it back to the police station, he was filled with far more questions than he had answers. Captain Meadows stood at his office door and shouted for Luke across the detective's bullpen. He went back into his office before Luke responded and sat down.

"What did you find out about the victim?" he asked as Luke entered his office and took a seat.

Luke laid out the details of the case as he knew them but had little in the way of solid leads to offer. "He was dumped in the field near the library. There was no blood evidence to indicate that he had been shot there. We need to find the location of the murder to know more."

"Any ideas?"

Luke shook his head. "His girlfriend said that he was meeting friends in the River Market that night. I have calls out to the list of friends she provided and I'm waiting for calls back. The surveillance video at the library does catch the image of a man in the distance walking to the side of the building but its grainy and doesn't look like Nick Day. I put a call in for street surveillance but, even if we had that right now, it's going to take a while to go through to find him. I'd be better off taking his photo and going to each of the bars and restaurants."

"Do that then," Captain Meadows said and then glanced up at the clock. " If you interview the girlfriend again, formally here at the station, do you think you'll get more?"

Luke shook his head. "Leslie was forthcoming with information. She saw the news report and came to the scene. If she hadn't identified him for us, we'd still be waiting. His prints aren't in the system and he had no wallet on him. I believe she told us everything she knew."

Captain Meadows gave a curt nod. "Let's table that then until you learn more. Has there been notification to his parents or surviving relative?"

"Not yet. Leslie gave me his parents' information and I've left a message." When Luke saw Captain Meadows squint, he quickly added, "They are traveling right now and not at home. It wasn't like I could just go by the house and tell them."

"Understood. Still, I'd like you to go by the home and double-check. There might be someone there, a sibling or someone. I've been getting calls all morning from the media wanting identification on the victim and it's only a matter of time before it's leaked. We need to get to the family first."

Luke agreed with him. They talked for a few minutes more before Luke stood and headed for the door before his boss called him back.

With one raised brow, Captain Meadows said, "I heard Cooper

witnessed something across the street from him. Beat cops weren't able to confirm. They chalked it up to his boredom. Have you heard from him today?"

Luke rubbed his hand over his bald head and stared at Captain Meadows. "News travels fast. I stopped over there and found the apartment, which was more than the cops who showed up did. That said, I can't confirm that what Cooper saw was real. I have the woman's name and planned to do a wellness check this evening. I figured if I could prove to Cooper that she was okay, then he'd feel better. As you know, he's having a rough go of it since he got back from New Orleans."

"Has Cooper ever shown signs of being delusional or overreacting?"

"No," Luke said slowly, not sure what Captain Meadows was getting at with the question. Cooper had worked for the police department years ago and his boss knew him well. "He's under the care of his doctor and on some heavy painkillers. That can mess with anyone's mind."

"I understand that. From the statement Cooper tried to give the cops, it sounds like he had details and a solid timeline of events. If he was mentally compromised on pain medicine, he'd not be able to do that."

Luke realized Captain Meadows wasn't angry with him for checking out the building or entertaining Cooper. "Are you saying that you think we should explore this further?"

Captain Meadows chuckled. "I'm saying Cooper is rarely wrong, so humor him at the very least until you can confirm this woman is safe. If you're unable to reach her and Cooper still has concerns, let's figure something out. We both know that if you don't help him, Cooper will run with it on his own. Then who knows what kind of trouble he could find himself in."

Luke leaned against the door frame. "I appreciate your perspective on it. I wasn't sure what you'd want me to do. I know we all have too many cases as it is."

Captain Meadows leaned back in his chair. "If Cooper wasn't credible, it might be a different story. As it stands, Cooper has given me no reason to doubt him, even if he is on pain medication. Let me know what you find out."

Luke thanked his boss and left. He made a beeline back to his desk, long enough to check in with Det. Tyler. "I'm going to head to Nick Day's parents' residence. Captain Meadows wants me to stop there even if we believe they are on vacation. You can come with me or head down to the bars and restaurants and show Nick's photo around. It might take some time before we get the surveillance footage and the sooner we can nail down where he went last night the better."

Tyler agreed to go canvass the River Market. He pointed to his laptop screen. "I'm running the Latin phrase we found on the victim's body through the federal database. I'm looking to see if any other crimes have the same signature."

"That's a good idea," Luke said, at the same time hoping it wasn't connected to anything else. The last thing Little Rock needed was another serial killer. The city had a long-standing reputation as a violent gang-infested city and the current rash of murders wasn't helping it any.

Luke double-checked Nick's parents' address and then stopped at the coffee shop two doors down from the station before departing. He ordered his usual vanilla latte, spoke with the woman behind the counter briefly as he ordered, and then waited for his coffee.

As he stood there watching the efficient line of customers coming and going, he sent a quick text to Cooper letting him know that he'd be by his place after work and asked if he wanted anything when he came by. His coffee was ready a moment later, so he put his phone back in his pocket and headed for his car.

Luke still hadn't had a response from Cooper by the time he reached Nick Day's parents' house. Even though they were supposed to be on vacation, there were two cars in the driveway.

Luke rapped his knuckles against the door and waited and then waited a few moments more. Nick's parents lived in a quiet suburb in West Little Rock. There was no one on the street that time of day. Most homes had mature trees in the yard and well-manicured lawns that met with brick houses with shutters on the windows. It was an upper-middle class neighborhood, which is exactly how Leslie had described Nick's family.

Before giving up, Luke knocked one more time and introduced himself loud enough that anyone in the home could hear him. He leaned his head toward the door listening for any movement. When he heard none, he turned on his heel to leave. He reached his SUV when he heard someone call to him. Luke turned back toward the house and realized quickly that it was coming from the neighbor.

"They are on vacation but their son should be home," a man quickly approaching Luke shouted. He had a head of sparse white hair and age spots on his hands. Luke closed the distance between them and then the man asked, "Got a badge?"

Luke pulled his badge from the chain around his neck. "I need to speak with Tom and Janet Day as soon as I can. Do you know how to reach them?"

The man shook his head. "They are on a cruise. There's no reaching them until they are back on land."

That was news to Luke. "Do you know when they will be back?"

"Probably a week from now. They only left two days ago." The man squinted up at Luke. "Did something happen? They didn't get robbed, did they? We don't normally have that kind of thing in this neighborhood."

"No," Luke said with his voice constrained. The story would be in the news soon enough with the victim's name. There was no point holding back the information. "Unfortunately, the Days' son was killed last night. I need to notify them."

The man did not look surprised. "I knew something was going to happen to him. That kind of life always leads to trouble. Poor Tom and Janet tried everything to get Jimmy on the straight and narrow. It just never took. You might need to call the cruise lines to get a message to the ship."

Luke barely heard the last part. He was stuck on the name of the son. "I wasn't speaking about Jimmy," Luke clarified. "It was Nick who was killed."

The man's mouth fell open and he shook his head in disbelief. "Nick was always such a good kid. That can't be."

Luke confirmed that it was true. "Are there other siblings?"

"Just the two boys. Jimmy is the older of the two if you can believe it. The oldest is supposed to set an example. They are barely a year apart."

"Do you know where I can find Jimmy now?"

The man pointed back toward the house. "He was supposed to be housesitting. I'm sure I saw him drag himself in early this morning. He's probably passed out and hungover. I've got the spare key to the house. Let me go get it and wake him up for you."

Luke was about to say no but if he had the key and permission to enter, there was no reason to stop him. He waited there on the porch while the man went back inside his house. He returned with a key and then marched across his lawn toward the house, grumbling about how Jimmy was good for nothing. He pounded his fist on the door, calling Jimmy's name. When no one answered, he unlocked the door and pushed it open. He called for Jimmy again and this time was met with a groan and shout to go away.

"I'll take it from here," Luke said as he opened the door wider and stepped inside. The man closed the door behind Luke, promising to return if needed. With the man gone, Luke called out. "Jimmy, I'm Det. Luke Morgan. I need to speak with you about your brother. Please come out to the living room."

Luke moved to a short hallway and heard the squeak of older bed springs and the cursing of a man who hadn't expected to be roused from his sleep. A few moments later, Jimmy appeared wearing a tee-shirt and blue plaid boxer shorts. He had the same height and build as his brother and the same dark hair. Jimmy rubbed his eyes as he stumbled down the hall.

When they moved into the living room, Jimmy moved his hands from his face and looked up at Luke through bloodshot eyes. "Whatever you think I did, I didn't do it."

Luke knew he should take a softer approach. He didn't like Jimmy on sight. "I'm sorry to inform you that your brother, Nick Day, was found shot to death on the grounds of the Clinton Library early this morning."

Jimmy stood motionless staring at Luke. The news had sobered him up. "I need to see him."

"Get dressed and I'll take you to the morgue."

CHAPTER 8

Cooper had tried to keep his word to Luke. As the hours of the morning turned to afternoon and then early evening, his patience gave way to restlessness. There was no point sitting in the living room doing nothing when he could do some searches in his database for background information and go back to Mandy's building to talk to neighbors. That wouldn't be too strenuous for him. Cooper reasoned that when Luke came back, he'd have helpful information to speed things along. Luke couldn't be too angry with him for that.

Cooper knew he was justifying doing exactly what Luke had asked him not to do. He couldn't help but consider that Luke knew him well enough to know he wouldn't just sit idly by and wait. He crossed the living room and looked out the window at Mandy's apartment. He cursed his initial bad luck at not being able to direct the cops there when they arrived that morning. He'd had no idea the building would be such a maze inside.

Cooper went to the small desk he kept in his loft for work. Since Adele moved in with him, he'd taken a formal office in hers. Previously, if he needed to meet a client in person, which wasn't all that common, he'd choose an out-of-the-way coffee shop. Now with Adele's office, he had a formal place to operate. It came in handy now for meetings with the investigators he had hired to work with him, but Adele had barred him from the office for the time being.

Cooper lowered himself to his desk chair, wincing as he sat. Clicking the keys brought his laptop to life and he signed into his database and typed in Mandy's name. Nothing came up under the name Mandy so he tried Amanda McKee instead. The information was there. As Cooper hovered the mouse over her name, he hesitated to click it. It felt like an invasion of privacy, which considering he didn't have an actual case, it was.

Cooper stared at the screen while having an argument with himself about the rights and wrongs of what he was doing. It had been embarrassing to admit to Luke that he'd been spying on his neighbors and would be bordering on ethically wrong to go digging into the woman's background. Still, Cooper talked himself into it. If she had been murdered and he did nothing about it after what he witnessed, Cooper didn't know if he could live with himself.

He leaned forward over the laptop and clicked the tab that brought Mandy's full profile into view. As he scanned the information, he realized that she was a bit older than he had first thought. She was thirty-six, single never married, no children listed, and from Los Angeles, California.

It appeared she had been in Little Rock for close to eight months and had a finance degree from a college unfamiliar to him. Mandy had no significant debts, no bankruptcy, didn't own any property, and had a decent credit score. His database wasn't always able to pull all criminal history, but it didn't appear that Mandy had ever been in trouble with the law.

There was nothing that hinted there was much wrong in her life. Then again, the details were sparse and only gave Cooper an overview. He scanned through the details one more time and then closed the website. He did a quick search of her college and then clicked out of that too.

Cooper turned to look toward the window and sighed at his indecision. Looking in the database was one thing, going to interview people was something else entirely. Despite his better judgment, he got up and headed for the door.

Ten minutes later, he found himself standing inside the lobby of Mandy's building. He followed the same path he and Luke had taken earlier to Mandy's floor. This time, Cooper knew exactly where he was going. He hesitated for only a moment before knocking on her door. When there was no answer, as he assumed there wouldn't be, he left and made his way down the hall. Cooper stopped and knocked at each door but had no luck finding anyone home. He skipped the woman Luke had spoken to earlier, given she seemed to have told him all she knew.

Cooper wasn't deterred. If there was no one on this floor, it didn't mean all hope was lost. He took the elevator to the floor below Mandy's and, starting with the door closest to the elevator, began his process again. This time he got lucky. A woman answered the door at the apartment directly below Mandy's. She had long dark hair, a pleasant smile, and big round brown eyes.

Cooper knew from the considerable time he spent staring across the street that this woman never had the blinds open. This was his first time seeing her. He introduced himself and quickly asked, "Do you know Mandy McKee who lives above you?"

"Not well," she said her eyes growing even wider. "I've only met her a handful of times."

Cooper couldn't very well explain what he'd witnessed, so he did the next best thing. He dropped his voice low. "I'm a private investigator and I was checking in on her wellbeing. I'm hoping you can keep that between us. If I can be assured she's fine without having to bother her, my client would be appreciative." He shrugged for good measure. "You know sometimes family things can be a bit sensitive. I've been having trouble reaching her. I figured talking to some of her neighbors might be helpful. Have you been home all day?"

The woman stepped out into the hallway and looked to the left and then to the right. When she realized he was the only one out there, she stepped back inside and extended her hand to Cooper. "I'm Nora. I assume by the question that you heard about the fight this morning. I don't like getting involved in my neighbors' business, but if Mandy has family who want to know if she's okay, then they must have concerns. Come on in and I'll tell you what I know."

Nora closed the door behind Cooper and locked it. She went across her living room to her laptop, clicked a few buttons, and then gestured toward the couch for Cooper to sit. "I work from home and needed to save a file. I've lost more than my fair share of work by not saving it frequently enough." She came around to the couch and as she sat down on the other end of the couch, stared at Cooper as he sat. "Are you injured?"

Cooper placed a hand over the outside of his shirt above his wound. "I was stabbed on my last case. I'm fine though. Just takes me a minute to get comfortable."

"Is your job always so dangerous?"

Cooper shook his head. He didn't want the focus on him. He shifted on the couch to face her. "You said that you know something about Mandy."

Nora took a moment, seeming to collect her thoughts. She looked up and locked her gaze on him. "I'm not a nosy neighbor. I don't care what anyone does but my apartment is right below hers. Sometimes I can't help but hear what goes on."

Cooper cracked a smile. "No judgment. I live in a similar building and hear all kinds of things I wish I hadn't."

That seemed to put her at ease. Nora relaxed back on the couch. "There seems to be heavy foot traffic upstairs. I often hear different men's voices. Not that I can hear what they are saying. There was one guy named Rob who she was dating for a few months, but I think he broke up with her or maybe she dumped him. Either way, he stopped coming around. He was quiet and nice enough. I saw him in the elevator and he was always polite. I never heard him yell or anything. There's a new guy and I…" She trailed off and didn't finish her thought.

"He yells," Cooper suggested, hoping by saying it for her she'd continue. "Does he do anything else?"

Nora slowly nodded. "I've heard yelling. I never heard things smashing and breaking until the last two weeks. I think this guy she has now is someone from her past because she asked him why he followed her to Arkansas."

"Do you know his name?" Cooper asked, wondering already if the reason Mandy was in Arkansas was to get away from a past abusive relationship.

"Sonny is his first name. Not sure if that's just what she calls him. I don't know his last name or anything about him. I've only seen him once in the lobby downstairs. He gave me a dirty look when I said hello." Nora shrugged and shook her head. "It's not how most people act here. Almost all our neighbors are friendly if you pass them in the hall, elevator, or lobby."

"What does Sonny look like?"

Nora paused for a moment. "He's shorter than you are with dark hair. He might be on the shorter side but he's muscular and strong. He's not a bad-looking guy but nothing too distinctive about his face. I'd say average facial features."

That was close to the man Cooper had seen. "You said he's been coming around for the last two weeks?"

"About that. It was a Tuesday night the first time I heard them fight and I know that because of what I was watching on television. But it wasn't this immediate last Tuesday. It was the one before," Nora explained her sound reasoning. "It's not like I watch her closely, so I couldn't tell you how many times he's been here. I don't think they are in a relationship. There have been other men here over the last two weeks. She seemed to be casually dating a few men. Sonny isn't someone I'd want to spend time with if you know what I mean."

"Understood." Cooper asked her a few more questions about the other men. Nora didn't have many details to add. Now that he knew a little information, he decided to come clean. "I'll be honest with you, Nora. I didn't tell you the truth about me when I first arrived."

He caught the look of fear in her eyes and quickly added, "I am a private investigator as I said. I live across the street and I saw the fight between Nora and Sonny. He tore up her place and then he followed her into the bedroom. I still can't make sense of what I saw. Mandy was on the bed and all I could see were her legs. He got on top of her in a rage and then she was very still. After he got off her, he realized the window was right there and closed the blinds. I don't know what happened after that."

Nora's hand flew to her mouth. "Did you call the police?"

"I did but it's such a maze in here I wasn't able to give them the right apartment number. I guessed and it wasn't correct. The cops assumed I dreamed it up or was hallucinating or something."

"Her family..." Nora said slowly and then realized. "There is no family concern is there?"

Cooper shook his head. "I'm afraid not. I didn't want to scare you if you didn't know anything. I'm sorry for lying to you."

Nora held her hand up to stop him as she stood from the couch. For a moment, Cooper thought she might kick him out. He couldn't read the emotion on her face. She didn't kick him out though. She went across the living room to her desk and grabbed her phone. She scrolled through something Cooper couldn't see and carried the phone over to him. "Read those text messages. When the fight was going on, I texted a friend of mine."

Cooper read the text chain of messages back and forth. It went on for close to twenty minutes and started by Cooper's best estimation right around the time Sonny arrived. Nora had grown concerned about the noise and fighting. Nora heard Mandy tell him to leave and that she was afraid of him. That he was scaring her. She then begged him to stop and promised they could continue their relationship. After a few minutes, Nora indicated the deafening silence as compared to the several minutes before. Then a moment later, she texted her friend about a loud thud and she had expressed concern to her friend that Sonny might have hurt her.

When Cooper was done reading, Nora said, "I didn't know what to do. I hadn't witnessed anything. I left my apartment right after that to go do some laundry downstairs. I took the back service elevator and there was Sonny with a large suitcase. He was talking on the phone. I pretended I forgot something and didn't get in the elevator with him. I didn't know what to make of the whole exchange."

Cooper did. He was sure now that Mandy was dead – her body was brought out in that suitcase. "Are you willing to talk to a detective friend of mine?"

Nora nodded her head. "I'm so sorry, I should have done something sooner."

"I tried and failed," Cooper admitted. "There was nothing more you could have done."

CHAPTER 9

It felt serendipitous that I had remained in Troy for as long as I had. If Inv. Grogan hadn't been located here now, I might have only stayed a day and then gone straight to Geneseo. It seemed far more of my classmates were in the area than I had realized. Other than Michelle, I hadn't stayed in contact with anyone. Once she and I lost touch, I was out of the loop completely.

That's why when she told me that Gail Jensen had started working as a math teacher at Austen Academy for Girls, I was glad to still be in the area. The all-girls boarding school, which was founded in the 1890s, was a stones-throw from my mother's house. I had a previous case there and wasn't sure if I would be welcomed on campus. I figured it was better to ask for forgiveness than permission. Michelle told me where Gail's classroom was. I figured now was as good a time as any.

I parked at the curb in front of my mother's house and walked over. I assumed I'd catch her at the end of the school day. The campus had Collegiate Gothic-style stone buildings perched on a hill behind a wrought iron fence that bordered the entire one-hundred-and-thirty-acre campus. There were more than thirty buildings including dormitories and faculty residences. Girls came from across the globe to attend high school there. But as fancy as it was, there was little security and easy access.

No one stopped me as I walked across the empty main courtyard. I assumed classes were in session. It would still be a few weeks before they'd be on break. I found the building and entered. I climbed the stairs to the second floor and hit the landing just as a bell rang. Doors flew open and a horde of girls in uniforms came spilling into the hallway chattering away with each other. I asked one of them where I could find Gail Jensen and she pointed to the third door down on the right.

I stood in the hallway until the last girl left the classroom then knocked on the open door. Gail was standing over her desk leafing through a book and didn't hear the knock.

"Gail Jensen," I sing-songed from the doorway. She had her blonde hair twisted up on top of her head in a neat bun and dark round glasses perched on her nose. She was wearing jeans and a cute jacket over a light purple shirt. She didn't look all that much different from college. She and I weren't the best of friends but our social circles sometimes overlapped.

Gail raised her head to me and squinted. "Can I help you?" she said and then leaned over her desk when she realized. "Riley, is that you?"

"In the flesh," I said, holding my arms open wide. "Michelle said you were teaching here and I thought I'd stop by and say hello."

"Michelle texted me and said you had questions about Alex."

Bad news traveled fast. I made my way over to her desk and stood in front of it. "I do have questions. It's nice to see you though. I would have come over to see you even if I didn't have the questions. I had no idea you were living here. I thought you had taken a teaching job downstate."

"It's too expensive to live on my own there. After my relationship ended, I needed a change."

I understood that. "It's good you're here then. Troy is an easy place to settle into. It might not be the easiest to make friends right off but over time you should be fine. Plus, you're teaching at an amazing school."

Gail laughed and flashed the same winning smile she had in college. "Sit and we can talk. You know people still mention your name here. I was surprised when I first got the job and I heard your name mentioned."

My cheeks reddened. "Solve a case involving a senator's daughter and people hear about it, I guess."

"It was a lot more than that." Gail sensed I didn't want to rehash an old case. She gestured for me to sit and then came around her desk and sat at one of the student tables with me. "What is it you want to know about Alex?"

I nodded. "Michelle mentioned that you might know something about Alex's murder. You didn't testify at the trial."

"The prosecutors didn't want my testimony because it wouldn't have helped their case."

"Why didn't the defense call you?"

Gail shook her head and frowned. "They should have, but Tim's lawyer didn't think what I had to say would help his case. I should have been called."

Gail had never mentioned to me before that she had anything to do with the case. I was surprised by her admission. "What do you know?"

"I know that Tim didn't kill Alex. There was no way he could because he was with me that night." When she saw the look on my face, she closed her eyes. "Not like that but not for my lack of trying."

This was all news to me. "I don't understand. You had a crush on Tim?"

Gail paused for a moment to collect herself. "Riley, it's more complicated than that. Tim and I had struck up a friendship before he ever met Alex, so we spent a good deal of time with each other. I liked him way before Alex ever did. Tim and I got close to hooking up one night but it never happened. There was attraction and good chemistry.

I thought it would go somewhere, but soon after that night, he started dating Alex. It was no one's fault, just a lot of miscommunication."

That sounded like every one of my *almost* relationships in college. I had never been good at making my interest known. "You and Tim stayed friends then," I said as a statement more than a question.

"We did and he'd often confided in me about his struggle with Alex. You know better than anyone how hot and cold she could be. It messed with his head. Then the summer before her murder, I saw her with another guy. I don't know if you remember that I was in Geneseo that summer too."

"I remember. A lot of us stayed that summer. I was taking two classes before heading into senior year and so was Alex. Tim traveled with his parents and asked Alex to travel with him. She went on one or two shorter trips that I remember." I tried to recall as many details of that summer as I could. I mostly remembered it as a laid-back time with summer parties. "I don't remember Alex seeing anyone else."

"She was trying to keep it hidden," Gail said with an air of agitation. "I shouldn't have even been on that side of campus that day. They were in the Letchworth dining hall. I'm sure Alex assumed none of us would have seen her there. They were cozied up together at a back table. I didn't think anything at first. Maybe she was meeting someone from class and they were just sitting close together to talk. Then he kissed her and I knew it was more than that."

I couldn't remember ever having gone to Letchworth the entire four years I was at Geneseo. We had a closer dining hall to us when we lived in the dorms, and I never ate on campus once I had moved into our apartment. I certainly wouldn't have found Alex there.

I couldn't even fake surprise at the news. I admitted, "I had long suspected Alex to have cheated on Tim. Did you know him?"

"Griffin Lyons," Gail said and I did my best to not react because I was familiar with him. My poker face must have been good enough because she continued. "He was on the rugby team and lived at the rugby house. I had taken a history class with him during our sophomore year. I didn't know him well but I knew him."

Gail's voice was tinged with anger and it was clear she was still upset by what she had witnessed. I imagined if she had testified with the same tone a jury might have wondered if she was blaming Alex for her murder. "How does all of this relate to the murder?"

Gail sat until her back was straight in her chair and she stared ahead. "Throughout that summer, I saw Alex with Griffin a few times and I debated whether or not I should tell Tim when he got back. On one hand, if I did, I might look like I was trying to break them up for my gain. If I didn't tell him, what kind of friend would I be?"

I understood what Gail was saying. I hadn't had romantic feelings like that for Tim, but I had felt bad for the guy. Alex was my friend though and I had remained loyal to her, although it had been a struggle. "Did you eventually tell him?"

Gail nodded once. "I thought maybe once Tim was back from summer break, he'd figure out Alex was cheating or maybe the cheating would stop. Maybe it was just a summer fling. I didn't want to ruin Tim's vacation. But Alex didn't stop with Griffin. I saw them at a restaurant in Rochester that fall. My parents had come to visit and took me out to dinner. Alex and Griffin were there. I don't think they ever saw me but they were clearly a couple. After that weekend, I tried to tell Tim but he wouldn't believe me. It strained our friendship." Gail wiped a tear from her eye and took a breath. She exhaled slowly and looked over at me.

"The night of the murder," I prompted.

"Tim called me and said he was coming back early from break. He said he believed me about Alex cheating and wondered how he should confront her. I told him that he had to do it head-on or break up with her and let it go. He said he wasn't going to stay with her and that he couldn't forgive cheating. He went over to your apartment to confront her. She wasn't alone and he didn't go in."

"What time was he there?"

"Around seven," she said quietly. "He never went in. Tim saw them in the window and never went in. He didn't want a confrontation like that. Certainly not with a guy like Griffin. I think Tim was afraid of him because he came straight over to my place and was there by seven-twenty. He was a mess. He got drunk and ended up passing out in my bed all night. By morning, Alex was dead. There was no way Tim could have done it. He was with me all night. I know he didn't leave."

"You can alibi him for the whole night. Why wouldn't Tim's defense attorney use your testimony?"

"He thought because of my feelings for Tim I might not be credible. It was suggested that the jury would see it as me covering for Tim, or worse, conspiring with him to commit the murder."

I turned to look at her. "How could anyone ever think that?"

Gail lowered her head and looked at her hands on the desk. "I'm not proud of this. A week before she was murdered, I confronted Alex on campus and got into a huge fight with her. I told her I knew about Griffin and that if she didn't tell Tim, I was going to. She told me to mind my own business and said I was sad and pathetic for the way I trailed after him and I needed to get over it because Tim was never going to like me like that. She accused me of trying to break them up. There were witnesses to that argument." Gail finally turned her head to look at me. "No one saw Tim come to my dorm that night because no one else was around. It was during break and there were only a handful of people left in the dorm. No one saw him walking campus that night either."

I couldn't remember what kind of security cameras there were on campus. I couldn't recall any. "Still, the attorney should have put you on the stand."

Gail nodded. "That's partially why his case won the appeal. There were other issues with his attorney but I should have testified. I wanted to, begged him. Tim begged him. He couldn't afford another attorney and his attorney promised that there was no evidence of him being in the apartment that night. There was no proof that he did it, so they'd be fine without my testimony."

None of it made any sense to me. I hadn't watched the trial at the time. All I wanted to do was put it behind me. "Did Tim's attorney put on any defense at all?"

"He had one forensic witness who tried to dispute the forensics found in the apartment but that was it. He advised Tim not to testify." Gail closed her eyes again and sniffed back tears. "I've known all these years that he was innocent and there was nothing I could do. I tried to tell the cops but they didn't want to hear it. I tried telling the prosecutor's office but they didn't want to hear it. I had been seen publicly threatening the victim and everyone knew I was in love with the defendant. No one saw me as credible."

I remembered then she said she had a recent breakup. "Have you stayed in contact with Tim all these years?"

She nodded slowly. "It's part of what ended my last relationship. He couldn't stand that I was keeping in touch with a convicted murderer. No one could understand. Everyone thought I was crazy, but I knew, Riley. I knew he didn't do it because he was with me the whole night."

"Are you willing to testify to that now?"

Gail locked her gaze on me. "I'll do whatever I have to do to make sure Tim doesn't go back to prison."

The sheer desperation in her voice made me question her credibility as any good investigator would. On the other hand, at the time had I known Alex was involved with Griffin, I would have gone to the police with that information. I thanked her and said I'd be in touch.

A twinge of uncertainty about what she told me rumbled in my gut but I couldn't quite pinpoint why.

CHAPTER 10

By the time Luke finished at the morgue with Jimmy, it was close to six. He texted Cooper that he would be there as soon as he could. He still needed to interview Jimmy and didn't trust that the guy wouldn't take off on him. Not that Luke had any reason to hold him. There was something about him, besides his rough drunken demeanor, that Luke didn't like about the guy.

Jimmy had kept it together at the morgue and identified his brother's body. It was only after they were leaving and in the parking lot that he puked on the pavement. After, he slumped down on the ground and held his head in his hands. He rocked back and forth as the tears spilled. It was genuine shock and raw emotion and Luke fully understood how it felt to lose a sibling to a violent act. His only sister had been murdered during her freshman year of college.

Luke did the best he could to console him, knowing full well the interrogation to come. When they made it back to the police station, Luke directed him to one of the interrogation rooms and then left to get him something to drink and a few snacks from the vending machine.

Jimmy had his head down resting on his arms on the table. He didn't look up when Luke said his name. "Why can't I just go home? My brother is dead. I'll come back tomorrow and we can talk."

Luke slid the can of soda and snacks across the table. "Drink something and you'll feel better, at least physically. We need to talk now because every second that goes by without me finding out who did this to your brother, the chances of bringing anyone to justice decrease. You do want justice for Nick, right?"

Jimmy rested his chin on the table and looked up at Luke through bloodshot eyes. "He's dead. He's not going to care if he gets justice or not. It's not going to do me any good either. Just let it go."

Luke pulled out the chair and sat down at the table across from him. "When was the last time you spoke to Nick?"

Jimmy lifted his head but slumped down in his seat. It was like he was having trouble holding his body upright – whether from grief or a terrible hangover, Luke wasn't sure. "About a week ago. He wanted me to meet his new girlfriend. I forget her name."

New wasn't exactly how he'd describe Leslie. She had told Luke they had been seeing each other for quite some time and even thinking about moving in together. "How often do you see and speak to Nick?"

Jimmy clicked his tongue and turned his head. "Why do you care, man? It's my relationship with my brother. It didn't matter how long in between we talked or saw each other. We are still family." Luke didn't respond to that. He watched Jimmy carefully, using the silence between them to force the young man to continue. Jimmy finally shrugged. "We'd talked recently but it didn't go well. We didn't get along that well. Is that what you want to hear?"

"I don't *want* to hear anything. It's the truth that I *need* to hear," Luke stressed, trying to keep the annoyance out of his tone. "I'm not asking you these questions to be nosy. I'm trying to find out what you know about your brother's life."

"I don't know much," Jimmy admitted. "When we did talk, he was focused on me getting my life together."

"The girlfriend, whose name you don't know. What did he tell you about her?"

Jimmy rubbed his brow. "He was serious about her and said that he was thinking about moving in with her. Our parents liked her and Nick said she could be the one. He thought his first wife was 'the one' if that tells you anything. My brother was a romantic...like that crap is real or something. I don't know."

"What do you know about his friends?"

"Same group of guys he's known since college. A few from high school too." Jimmy sighed loudly and stared off beyond Luke. "I don't know who could have done this to Nick. He was the kid my parents wanted. He was a good student, played sports, never got in trouble, had a respectable job, a stable life, and never did drugs or drink too much. Basically, he was the opposite of me in every way. If anyone of us should have ended up murdered, it should have been me."

Jimmy led Luke exactly where he wanted to go. "I can't help but notice that you and your brother look similar enough to be twins. Is there any chance someone was after you and came across your brother first?"

He winced. "Are you trying to make me feel guilty?"

"Not at all," Luke said calmly. "I'm just trying to figure out how your brother ended up dead. By what you're telling me and what his girlfriend said, he lived a low-risk lifestyle. There'd be no reason for someone to want to kill him. You said you lived the opposite kind of life and, from what I can see right now, you're a hard-partying kind of guy. Maybe you owed someone money. Maybe you stole someone's girlfriend. Isn't it possible someone mistook Nick for you or they found out you had a brother and wanted to exact a little revenge?"

Jimmy looked at Luke then. "Why revenge?"

"What do you mean?" Luke asked even though his ears perked up at the way Jimmy asked the question like the word *revenge* had some serious meaning for him.

He stared at Luke with a blank expression on his face. "You said revenge and I asked what that meant. Why would someone need revenge on Nick? He never did anything to anyone. I already told you he was everyone's friend. I can't even name one person who didn't like him."

Luke noted how quickly Jimmy turned that around. To some he might have come across as not that intelligent. Under all the drunken stupor, Jimmy was far cagier than Luke had initially given him credit. "I said they could have killed Nick to take revenge on you."

Even though Jimmy had viewed his brother's body at the morgue, he hadn't seen the carving on his brother's back. Neither Luke nor Purvis had mentioned it at the time.

Luke leaned forward. "Jimmy, did someone want revenge on you?"

He averted his eyes from Luke and stared off at the mirror next to the table. Normally, Det. Tyler would have been watching the interview, but he was out running down leads.

Jimmy shrugged. "I told you my life is complicated."

"Was there any specific threat against you or Nick?"

Jimmy shoved the chair back and slumped down, putting his hands on the edge of the table. "There are always threats. It doesn't mean that anything is going to happen. Nick's death didn't have anything to do with me. Are we done here? I have somewhere I need to be."

Luke had no reason to detain him. "Where were you last night?"

Jimmy cracked a smile to reveal a chipped upper incisor and stained teeth. "I was with friends. I didn't see Nick and I didn't hear from him. Five guys can alibi me all night if that's what you're asking. I didn't kill my brother. That's messed up you'd even think that."

Luke wasn't going to take his word for it. He asked for all five names and a detailed timeline of his whereabouts, which included about an hour's worth of time in a known drug house. Luke didn't lecture or threaten because he might need a cooperative Jimmy later.

When he was done, Luke asked, "How can I reach your parents?"

"I texted my father already that he needed to call me. They'd kill me if I didn't tell them even while on vacation." When pressed, Jimmy provided his father's cellphone number to Luke and then stood from the table. "I know you want to find out who killed my brother. I know you're trying to be the good guy here. Some things are better handled differently."

Luke glared up at him. "That sounds like you know who did this and are planning to get revenge on them."

"I never said that."

Luke stood and stepped around the table, blocking Jimmy's exit. "It's not worth going to prison. Let me do my job, help me if you can, and we'll bring his killer to justice the right way."

Jimmy smirked. "A cushy prison sentence with a cot and three squares? No." He must have thought better of what he said when Luke refused to move from his position at the door. "I'm just talking," he said, backtracking. "I don't know who killed Nick and even if I did, I'm not going to do anything. I'd probably get myself killed if I even tried to go after him."

Although Jimmy had given himself away, Luke knew it wasn't the time to push. "I hope not. No good will come of it for you or your family if you did. I'm going to need you to sign a few things before you leave. I'll be right back and then you can go."

Jimmy nodded and stood by the door as Luke stepped into the hallway. He moved away from the door and placed a quick call to a desk sergeant. He wanted a tail on Jimmy as he left the police station. When it was set, Luke went back into the room. "Sorry, you'll have to sign them later or maybe your parents can do it when they are back. The printer's down."

"Whatever," Jimmy said and looked at the floor. "Call me when you need me to come back."

"Don't worry. I'll be in touch."

Jimmy raised his eyes to Luke and no words needed to be said between them. Luke conveyed the warning with his eyes. As Jimmy exited the room and walked down the hall, Luke texted the surveillance unit to let them know he was leaving.

During the interview, Luke received a text from Cooper explaining he had already found a witness who was willing to speak to him. Luke hadn't thought Cooper would listen to his pleas to lay low, but even so, a wave of disappointment swept over him. He fought the urge to chastise Cooper for not following directions and instead relayed that he'd be there within the hour.

Luke walked back into the detective's bullpen and found Tyler back at his desk. "Did you make any progress on the security cameras?"

Tyler raised his head from his laptop. "I got the city surveillance tapes and confirmed that they weren't in the River Market but rather at Dugan's a few blocks back. I asked for surveillance tapes from there and was assured they'd be dropped off by morning. The staff there didn't recall any issues from last night. Nick Day is known to the staff there. He and his friends are regulars, so I'm sure if something happened out of the ordinary, they'd know about it."

Luke sat on the edge of his desk. "Nick Day has a brother, Jimmy. My guess is when I run his name in the database, he's going to have priors."

Tyler raised his eyebrows in a question. "You're not suggesting that Nick's brother killed him, are you?"

Luke shook his head. "Not given the theatrics of how the body was found. I can see Jimmy losing his cool and fighting with his brother. He didn't strike me as the murdering kind and, with the hangover that he was nursing, I don't think he could have carried a body last night. He seemed too interested when I mentioned the word revenge. Maybe the best way to get revenge on Jimmy was to kill his brother."

"Did he see what was on Nick's back?"

"No. I didn't tell him either. I held that back for now." Luke crossed his arms and considered the information Jimmy had told him and the current of unspoken words between them. "He threatened to go after the person who did this. I warned him against it, of course. But the fact that Jimmy might have a suspect in mind means he knows someone out there might have had a beef with him. He confirmed that Nick was a stand-up guy and couldn't think of any reason anyone would have a problem with him. Either way, I put a tail on Jimmy. Maybe he'll lead us to the killer."

Tyler chuckled. "If only it was that easy."

Luke updated him on the parents' cruise and that he'd call the father's cellphone before heading out for the day. "I need to stop by Cooper's again before going home."

Tyler turned around in his chair to face Luke. "You're going to continue to entertain him?"

"He texted me that he found a witness who lived right below Mandy who has some information to share – information that corroborates what Cooper saw." He noted the look of disappointment on Tyler's face. "Captain Meadows asked me to run it to ground and figure out one way or the other what happened to Mandy. If nothing happened, then case closed. But if something did…" Luke didn't finish his thought because he didn't want to think of the implications of one more missing and possibly dead woman in the city.

Luke's answer seemed to satisfy Tyler at least for now. He could only hope Cooper's witness had more solid information than Cooper was able to provide earlier.

CHAPTER 11

Luke met Cooper in the hallway outside Nora's apartment. Cooper's face was drained of color and he was holding his side. "You look like you're about to keel over at any moment. You should be back at home resting. What did Adele say about your adventures today?"

Cooper ignored the question. Instead, he told Luke all about Sonny and his relationship with Mandy. "Nora can confirm that she overheard the fight at the same time I was seeing it. Soon after, she saw Sonny going down the back service elevator with a large suitcase. I suspect Mandy's body was in that suitcase. She can give a good description of Sonny that you can use."

Luke held his hand up to stop his friend. "Slow down, Cooper. Let me talk to her and figure out what's going on. When I said you look like you need to go home and rest, that wasn't a suggestion. You can introduce me to Nora and then you can leave. I'll meet you back at your place when I'm done."

"But..." Cooper started to argue but Luke shut him down.

"No," he said forcefully, taking a step towards Cooper. "You're not going to argue this with me. If something happened to Mandy, then you and Nora are both witnesses. It's bad enough that you might have contaminated each other's statements and recollections. I'm not going to have you do further damage by sitting in on an interview with a witness. You're going home and sitting down and waiting for me to come over. Where is Adele?"

"She's in the middle of prepping witnesses for an upcoming trial. She said she wouldn't be home until around ten," Cooper said, not putting up a fight to counter what Luke had told him about witness contamination.

Luke pulled his wallet from his back pocket, opened it, and tugged out three twenties. "Stop at the grille and pick us up dinner. I'm starving and we can talk while we eat."

Cooper refused the money. "I can get dinner. I'm glad you believe me now."

"Captain Meadows believes you too," Luke said to Cooper's surprise. "We both know you don't make up things. Let me talk to Nora and then we can figure out a plan. Did you do any digging into Mandy's background that you want to admit before I go in there?"

Cooper admitted the limited database search. "It didn't yield much. She has a clean record, no significant debts, and is from California. I wasn't able to get much on her family life. But that tracks with what Nora told me."

Luke wasn't going to scold him for the search. Cooper knocked on the door and introduced Nora to Luke and then left them to get on with the interview. He stopped only once in the hall and turned back. Luke waved him off and then focused his attention on Nora.

"I appreciate you speaking with me," he said as he entered her apartment. "Cooper said he spoke to you already about your neighbor."

Nora wrung her hands as she sat. She had a painful expression that Luke couldn't read. "I'm glad Cooper came by first. If it had been a police detective, I might have been afraid and not gotten involved."

Luke hated that people were so resistant to speak to detectives. "Why is that? What could you have done?"

She took a deep breath and held it. When Nora released it, she cast her eyes up toward him. "I probably should have called the police other times I heard arguing. I should have called the police earlier today after that fight and then what I saw later," she admitted as her expression softened. "I hope you're not here because of that. I felt tremendous guilt and even more when Cooper told me what he witnessed. I don't like getting involved in my neighbor's lives."

Luke understood why she had looked so pained now. It was a mix of guilt and fear that he was there to pass judgment on her behavior in some way. He quickly corrected her assumption and tried to put her at ease. "My only job is to find out what happened to Mandy. Cooper said you witnessed something." Luke wanted to keep it vague and not coach her.

"I didn't see what Cooper saw if that's what you're asking. I heard the fight and not just the one this morning." Nora explained the history of what she'd overheard from Mandy's apartment, including that she believed Sonny was an ex who had followed her from California. "That's speculation on my part," she corrected. "I don't know where Sonny is from, but he doesn't sound like he's from Arkansas. Given she's from California, I assumed that's where he had come from too. He's only been around for the past two weeks that I know of anyway."

What Nora told him about the fight that morning corroborated what Cooper had seen. He had to prompt her for the other information. "You also mentioned seeing Sonny later in the day."

Nora nodded and sat back. "I did and that's when I should have called you. After hearing that fight, I was a bit rattled and decided to get out of my apartment. I went downstairs to the laundry room. I saw him in the back service elevator with a large roller suitcase. He shouldn't have been able to access that elevator. There's a special code for only employees and residents of the building. Of course, Mandy could have given him the code at some point. It still didn't make a lot of sense why he was using the back elevator. It's farthest away from Mandy's apartment and the front door. I could only assume he wanted to leave via the alley out back."

"How did you feel seeing him there?"

"I didn't get in the elevator with him," Nora said, suddenly standing. "I couldn't. There was this look on his face, pure evil. I've never seen anything like it. I noticed the suitcase and he noticed me noticing it and I turned and ran back to my apartment. It took me another two hours to even consider going down to the laundry room. I had the feeling then that he did something to hurt her. It's not like I could call the police on a feeling though." She turned to focus on Luke. "Should I have called you?"

Luke knew dispatch wouldn't have taken her any more seriously than the cops took Cooper's concerns. "You're talking to me now and that's all that matters. With what Cooper saw and what you heard during the fight and after, we have grounds to investigate. At least to get the ball rolling. When they were fighting, did you hear Sonny make any specific threats?"

Nora stared off into space as she tried to recall the specifics. "It was a lot of yelling. While the noise in this building carries and I could hear the raised voices, it was not always easy to distinguish what they were saying. She didn't want him in her apartment that was for sure. She asked him to leave several times. He told her that he was never going to let her go. There was also some argument about money, but that was unintelligible to me. It sounded like Mandy might have owed him money or taken money from him. I can't be sure. Then I heard her scream and the fight raged on."

Luke asked a few more questions about the fight that didn't yield a whole lot of information. "You said that you left to do laundry. At what point during the fight did you do that?"

"It wasn't until after it got quiet."

"Can you take me to this back elevator? I'd like to see what you're talking about and the alley out back. Are there any security cameras?"

"No," Nora said with annoyance in her voice. "It's in my lease that there are supposed to be working security cameras and even a security guard in the building. I've only seen him a handful of times over the years and we've never had working security cameras."

"What about the cameras I saw downstairs and in the elevator?"

Nora shook her head. "I've come to believe it's all for show. None of them work. We had a building meeting about this a month ago because one of the tenants had a break-in and wanted the footage. The building wasn't able to supply it even though they had promised they were working again. I recently inquired and still no working cameras."

That was the way it went a lot in these buildings. "I'll need you to work with a sketch artist then so we can get a good composite of Sonny."

Nora agreed as she opened her front door and led Luke down a maze of hallways to the back elevators. Each hallway had the same drab tan coat of paint and the same blue doors. A few of the doors had colorful welcome mats and some even had nice wreaths which brightened an otherwise sterile hallway. They reached the back service elevator and Luke noticed the keypad on the outside.

"There's a community code to get the elevator door to open," Nora explained.

That was interesting to Luke. "Who oversees the elevator?"

"You'd have to check with management downstairs." Nora punched in her four-digit code and the elevator slowly made its way to their floor and the doors creaked open. "I don't know how old this elevator is and I almost don't want to ask. It always sounds like it's going to break, but it's so much easier than the front elevator to access the laundry room."

They stepped in and the whole elevator seemed to sag under their weight. Luke laughed nervously. "I see what you mean." He wasn't claustrophobic or had any issues with heights, but still, the elevator didn't evoke any confidence in him. They reached the basement floor quickly enough and then stepped out into a hallway that was in desperate need of a coat of paint and to be swept.

He followed Nora down a short hall and they stepped into a large laundry room with several washers and dryers and an area to fold clothes. There was also a small four-person table in the back. He turned to Nora. "Is the door to the alley down at this level or up one?"

"It's down here," she said, stepping back into the short hallway. She continued on and made a right. She followed that hall for a few feet and took another right, which brought them to the back of the building. There were seven stairs up to a heavy metal door. "It's not locked from the inside, but if you go out and it closes behind you, it locks automatically."

Luke nodded in understanding and then climbed the stairs. He opened the door and stuck his head out. It was a common alleyway for downtown Little Rock. There were trash dumpsters, uneven pavement that looked like it hadn't been paved in fifty years, and enough space for one large truck to go down. Luke turned back. "Hold this door open for me while I check out the alley."

He waited until Nora came up to the landing and held the door and then stepped out into the alley. Luke didn't know what he was searching for, if anything. If Sonny had come this way, Luke hoped there might be evidence of that. He tipped his head back and craned his neck from side to side searching for any security cameras and found none. He walked the length of the alley to the garbage dumpsters. He flipped open the lid and recoiled at the smell.

Luke didn't need to lean over the dumpster and look in to know what he was going to find. He did anyway to confirm. Amid the trash bags was the delicate hand and wrist of a woman. It led to a bare arm and a shoeless foot peeking through the bags. That was all Luke could see or would see until a team of crime scene techs showed up. He had no idea if this was Mandy, but what mattered most was getting a team to the scene.

Luke noticed Nora watching him from the doorway. He waved her back in as he made his way down the alley toward the building. Before stepping inside, he called his team and then called Cooper to let him know he wouldn't make it for dinner.

He had a long night ahead of him and it was just getting started.

CHAPTER 12

"Y"ou got in late last night," my mother said as I made my way from the kitchen door to the coffee pot. She looked up from the newspaper. "Did you find out anything?"

After my interview with Gail, I went to catch up with old friends. The hours slipped by quickly as I tried to put the case out of my mind. My mother had saved me dinner but had gone to bed before we had a chance to talk. I poured myself coffee and popped wheat bread into the toaster.

I spoke to my mother over my shoulder and told her about my meetings with Michelle and Gail. "Gail gave me a tip about Griffin Lyons. I called him but he wasn't at home. His wife said he was out of town for a rugby reunion. I assume he's at Geneseo."

"Does this mean you're leaving today?"

I turned to look at her. "I think I should. I told Tim I'd be up there to meet with him and I'd like a chance to speak to Griffin. I can't sit around here hoping he comes back. Did you need me to do something before I leave?"

"No," she said with a smile. "I like having you here. You didn't even get a chance to see Liv."

I slathered butter on my perfectly barely toasted bread and carried the plate and coffee cup over to the table and sat down. "I'll be back before I head home to Little Rock. I can stay for as long as I like then.

That's the benefit of driving up. No flight schedule to keep to."

"Don't you want to get back home to see Luke?" she asked with eyebrows raised.

She was digging for something that wasn't there. "All is fine at home, Mom. I know Luke is busy on a case and Cooper has a few other investigators. There is no rush. I can spend a few days with you and Liv before I head back."

Assured that all was well, my mother took a sip of her coffee and eyed me over the rim. "Will I be getting grandbabies any time soon?"

I swallowed the piece of toast in my mouth so hard it scraped my throat. I reached for my coffee and took a sip before responding. "If it was up to Luke, you'd have them already. I'm not sure I'm ready yet."

"You're heading into your late thirties. You better get ready." My mother saw the look on my face and thankfully let the subject drop. I was inching closer to being ready but didn't want to say that and have to walk it back later if I changed my mind.

She thankfully changed the subject. "What do you know about Griffin?"

"Not too much. He was a rugby player and lived at the rugby house where I spent a lot of time. He could be a hothead at times, especially on the field. I can recall a fight or two that he started at parties. I didn't know that much about him."

I had spent the previous night trying to remember my encounters with him or if anything should have given me an idea he was involved with Alex. I had suspected there was someone else, but Griffin was a surprise. He wasn't Alex's type by any stretch, so it was an odd pairing to me. Tim and Gail would have been an odd pairing too. I hadn't known until she told me that she had a crush on him. It made me question how well I had known my friends.

"You look like you're lost in thought," my mother said softly. "It's okay if this case isn't for you. I'm sure it's difficult wading through old memories."

I admitted she was right. "It's a lot to process from what feels like a lifetime ago. It's also making me question how well I knew people. There seemed to be a lot going on that I never knew."

Her gaze locked on me. "Does that bother you?"

I didn't want to admit that it did because I wasn't sure why exactly. My mother asked me the question again. "I'm left wondering if I was truly friends with these people. Hearing all these things I never knew made me feel left out. I'm worried I wasn't that great if no one confided in me."

My mother offered me a sad smile. "I can understand why you feel that way. Could it be that you were too much in the middle of all of it and were living with Alex and friends with Tim? You've always had a strong sense of right and wrong – not that you don't ever blur the lines. But it's possible Alex was worried that you'd tell Tim. I can see why Gail wouldn't admit her crush on Tim to you given you were Alex's roommate. Michelle had her reasons for keeping secrets. We don't always know what's going on in the lives of those closest to us."

"Shouldn't we though?" I asked, thinking immediately of Luke, Cooper, and Adele. It was possible I hadn't been listening enough or asking the right questions. We all went through our days mostly focused on work. Did we ever stop to consider how the other was feeling? I'm not sure we did that enough.

My mother was staring at me as if watching the wheels turning in my head. "The fact that you're questioning this will only improve your relationships, Riley. You've been a good friend. Don't doubt yourself on that." She got up from the table and dropped a kiss on the top of my head before dropping her dishes in the sink. She turned to look at me before leaving the room. "Make sure you call me when you get to Geneseo."

The way my mother said that and the look on her face brought me right back to those years I'd drive myself back and forth to school. It wasn't a long drive –straight out the New York State Thruway to Rochester and then south. She always worried about me taking the drive alone. I loved it. It was the first time I had a sense of total freedom and it spurred a lifelong love of long road trips. I promised I'd call and then finished my breakfast before gathering my things to leave.

Pulling into the village of Geneseo, even before getting to the campus, always felt a bit like stepping back in time. There was a lot in the village now but back then there was a Wegmans, a McDonalds that looked straight out of the seventies, one hotel, and an old K-Mart where the manager of the store couldn't pronounce Geneseo correctly and stared at my chest when he interviewed me for a job that I never ended up accepting.

As I drove closer to campus, I passed the old cemetery next to the field that had a bloom of the most beautiful sunflowers in late summer. Alex and I had walked from campus up to the McDonald's a few times freshman year when neither of us had a car or much money but had tired of dining hall food. The sunflower field was always my favorite.

I took a right at Main Street, which was listed on the National Register of Historic Places in 1977. It was filled with shops and Mama Mia's pizza, which I was happy to see still standing. The campus was off to my left.

I headed farther down Main Street and took the left on Court Street, where I spent considerable time at the rugby house, hockey house, and several of the fraternities. I drove down the hill noting how little the buildings had changed and then took another left on Genesee Street. This road was at the bottom of campus and not a road I took often. But it led me directly to the other side of the U-shaped campus.

At Mary Jamison Drive I took a left and second guessed if this is what the road was called when I went to school there. I didn't think back then I knew the name of the road even though I crossed it multiple times a day to get to the main part of campus. I had lived on what was considered the south side of campus in a small section of dorms with our dining hall. I glanced to my right and spotted my dorm, Niagara Hall, as I drove back up toward Main Street.

The dorms looked smaller to me now, but the biggest difference was across the street to my left on the main part of campus. Back then, once we crossed the main road, there was a path that led directly to the educational buildings. We called the path the tundra because it was built into a hill and wind whipped something fierce and the snow often piled higher than we were on both sides. Now, there were townhouses on a paved well-lit walkway. I'm sure the changes made the walk from the south side to the main campus a lot more enjoyable.

At the top of the hill, back at the start of Main Street, I pulled into a parking space and checked my phone for Tim's text. He said he'd let me know when he arrived. There was no text. It didn't matter though because there he was looking out at the campus.

I grabbed my things and got out of my SUV, stopping for a moment to take in the campus myself. It was always such a lovely place and it still was. I watched Tim for a moment, taking him in. He looked similar to how he did then – still tall but with considerably more muscle on his frame. His face had grown more angular and his dark hair thinner but not receding. His skin was pale as if prison permanently drained all the color from his face.

The starkest difference was the way he held himself. His head bent low, shoulders rounded and one hand shoved in his pocket. The other held a thick binder I assumed was a trial transcript. Gone was the natural confidence with which he used to carry himself. I couldn't help but feel the blow of realization that I might have caused part of this.

"Tim," I called out to him softly at first and then louder as I approached. "Tim," I said his name again when I was almost to him.

"Riley," he said with a blink of recognition and then he extended his hand awkwardly and I took it. His hand was strong but cold, much colder than the air outside.

I was suddenly struck with an awkward feeling and like nothing was the right thing to say. "Tim, it's good to see you. I'm glad you called me."

"You are?" he said with a hint of skepticism. Even though he called me and I showed up on time, he didn't seem convinced that I wanted to be there.

"I am," I said forcefully and realized I truly meant it. I wanted to set the record straight and prove that he hadn't murdered Alex because, for the first time, I believed he didn't do it. "Tim, I know it might not seem like anyone is on your side or wants to help you, but I do. That's why I'm here. It's why I came from Little Rock to help you."

He raised his eyebrows at me. "I still can't believe you live down there."

"Story for another time." The last thing I wanted to do was go over the last several years of my life while Tim had been sitting in a prison cell for a crime he didn't commit. "Where do you want to talk about this? You said you know who might have killed Alex. Let's start there."

Tim slowly nodded his head. He handed me the binder. "I don't know that anything in here will help you."

"Better to have it and not need it than not have it." I walked it back to my car and tossed it in the backseat. I would read it later. It was too heavy to lug around with me all day.

As he stood next to me, he looked up Main Street. "For old time's sake, let's get some pizza at Mama Mia's and I'll tell you what I know."

I knew why he wanted to do that. Tim and I had many, many lunches eating pizza and talking about his relationship with Alex. It was a good way to bridge the past and the present. I put my hand on his arm and smiled up at him. "It's the perfect place to start."

CHAPTER 13

Luke's morning was a swirl of activity that didn't necessarily produce results. It was a lot of checking off boxes of things that needed to be done. The evening before, after he found Mandy's body, he had ushered Nora back inside her condo and told her to remain there. He explained what he had found and remained with her for a few minutes until she calmed down.

After that, he called Cooper and explained why he was going to miss dinner. Luke asked him to come to the scene and identify the body for him. While Luke had seen photos of Mandy, he wanted a positive identification, particularly with what she had been wearing. He didn't want to ask that of Nora. The bruising on Mandy's face had changed some of her features and while Luke was sure she was the woman in the dumpster, he didn't think another identification could hurt.

Cooper had arrived within minutes of the call and was visibly shaken when he confirmed that it was Mandy. The guilt washed over Luke for not initially believing him. They stood there and waited while Purvis came and removed the body and the crime scene techs did their job. Luke had called Det. Tyler and Captain Meadows to report what was happening. Thankfully, only one news station had heard and showed up at the scene. Luke had made a brief statement without disclosing many details.

The suitcase Nora had suspected Mandy had been stored in was nowhere to be found in the dumpster or the alley. Sonny might have taken it with him to remove traces of his DNA and because Nora could identify him with it.

Without it, there left room for some doubt that Sonny was the person responsible for the murder. Luke felt it unlikely that he was innocent of the crime, but there was no smoking gun. He had trouble imagining him lifting the body out of the suitcase and tossing her in the dumpster. Why not just leave the body in the suitcase in the alley? There were questions still plaguing Luke.

Cooper hadn't seen enough to say with certainty he had witnessed a murder, and Nora hadn't heard anything specific to murder either. Until they received the medical examiner's report and the crime scene techs processed the scene, they were still dealing with circumstantial evidence. At least they had found her body fairly quickly.

Luke could thank Cooper's persistence and Captain Meadows for urging him to explore the case more. He didn't take any credit for himself. All he did was show up and happen to explore the alley based on Nora's tip.

While Luke had spent the morning trying to find out more about Sonny, which was proving impossible so far, Det. Tyler had been busy exploring leads in the death of Nick Day. Neither of them had made much progress by the time they returned to the office.

Luke sat down at his desk. "Mandy McKee was from California and moved here several months ago. She worked for a local bank and seems to have dated a lot. There was a range of prints found in her apartment. Sonny must have cleaned up after the fight because Cooper said he saw him smashing things and Nora confirmed she heard things smashing to the floor. However, once we got inside, the place was spotless. Almost a little too spotless, if you ask me."

Tyler didn't have a chance to respond because Luke's desk phone rang. He picked it up and couldn't believe what he was hearing from

Purvis. He gave a series of curt yes and no answers while Tyler looked on. "We'll be down there in fifteen minutes. Don't release any information to the media." Luke said the last part even though he knew it wasn't warranted. There were never any leaks from the medical examiner's office. He wished he could say the same about the police station.

"What is it?" Tyler asked as he stood.

"Once Purvis started the autopsy this morning and saw Mandy's back, he couldn't believe what he was seeing. That same Latin phrase about revenge was carved into her back." Luke shook his head as if he couldn't believe it either. "Purvis apologized and said that whoever in his office undressed her last night and sent her clothes off for evidence wrote down what was on her back but no one alerted him to it, which is why we are only hearing about it now."

"I don't understand," Tyler said with Luke's same confused expression. "You mean to tell me that Mandy McKee and Nick Day are connected?"

"I don't know how we can take it to mean anything else."

"The motives are completely different. Mandy was killed by an abusive boyfriend," Tyler countered as they headed down the stairs to the front door of the police station. They walked the few blocks to the medical examiner's office as they talked about the likelihood the cases were connected. There was one point Tyler couldn't get past. "I thought we agreed that Nick Day was most likely killed by a stranger or someone connected to his brother."

Luke knew what he had said and the whole thing didn't make a lot of sense. He admitted as much as he pulled open the glass door to the medical examiner's office. As he stepped inside, he turned back to his partner. "I'm sure once we see the body, we'll have a sense of whether it's connected or not. I find it as strange as you do."

"It has to be connected," Tyler said with his voice constrained.

"There is no way Mandy's boyfriend could have known that detail. It hasn't been on the news."

Luke let the subject drop as he approached the administrative assistant and flashed his badge to her. "Dr. Purvis is expecting us."

She pushed the silver button on the side of her desk and the door to the back of the morgue opened. Luke moved down the hall to the room where Purvis did the autopsies. Outside of the room, there were gloves and gowns. The gowns weren't always needed but Purvis was in the middle of an autopsy and he demanded as sterile an environment as possible, which Luke and Tyler had no problem obliging.

Once suited up, they entered the room. Purvis raised his head and pointed to the far end of the room. "Body is back in the freezer," he said matter-of-factly as he snapped off a pair of dirty gloves and chucked them in the bio-bin. He pulled a clean pair from the box and then went to the freezer. He tugged the metal handle and pulled out the drawer. "She's on her back so you're going to need to help me turn her. I took photos, obviously, but I want to show you the body so you get a better sense of it."

Luke had been around the deceased for so long in his career that it didn't bother him anymore. Respectful always, but the turn of his stomach that he had in his first year of being a detective had long ago subsided. He helped Purvis position the body so that he and Tyler could look at her back. There, in between her shoulder blades, just like Nick Day, were the words *Retributio mea*.

Luke would need to compare the two photographs to compare the style of the carving but they looked the same to him. Besides, it's doubtful there'd be two people running around the city murdering people and carving that into the backs.

He raised his eyes to Purvis. "Was that carved post-mortem?"

"Same as your other case," Purvis said and lowered the body back to the table. He covered her with the sheet then slid the drawer back in and relatched the door. "I don't know what to make of it. We will need to wait for the toxicology but I didn't see any signs of long-term drug use or violence for that matter. No broken bones that have healed or injuries that indicate long-term domestic violence. I see that sometimes with victims."

Luke stepped back from the freezer doors. "I spoke to one of Mandy's neighbors who said that the suspect was someone from the victim's past. She believes he started coming around about two weeks ago. What was the cause of death?"

"Manual strangulation from the back." Purvis demonstrated on Luke by standing behind him and mimicking the way the killer gripped her neck. "He had to have been taller than her, strong, and have big enough hands."

Luke and Tyler shared a look and unspoken words passed between them. It wasn't exactly what Cooper believed he witnessed. "What was the time of death?"

"I'd say close to nine that morning," Purvis said leaving Luke flustered.

"That doesn't make any sense." Luke did the mental math. "Cooper saw a man strangle her at a little before eight yesterday morning. Nora said that she saw Sonny in the elevator leaving shortly after. The cops were in the building probably around nine. They didn't see a thing." Luke couldn't make sense of it.

Tyler turned his attention to Purvis. "Her body was found in the dumpster right behind her building with easy access from the alley and the basement door to the dumpster. We were working on the assumption that she had been killed in her apartment and her body dumped there. Do you have any evidence to suggest that wasn't the case?"

"There's nothing on the body to suggest where she was killed," Purvis explained as he gestured to their gloves and gowns and the bin where they could dispose of them. "Let's head back to my office and I can go over the preliminary report and we can look at some of the photos."

As they disposed of their protective gear, Tyler asked Luke if he was okay. It was met with a solemn nod. Luke was ruminating over the fact that the cops might have been able to save Mandy. Tyler knew it without Luke ever uttering a word. "They couldn't have known, Luke. They couldn't have saved her. Right now, we don't even know what we've got here."

"You're right," Luke said and snapped off his gloves. He knew Tyler was right, but he also couldn't make sense of the timing. Purvis had always been correct on cases. The man was like a machine in his accuracy. Not that he was infallible. Luke had just never known him to be wrong.

Luke and Tyler stood at the edge of the desk and watched as Purvis flipped open a file and read from it. Mandy's hyoid bone had been broken and she had other medical signs of strangulation. The bruising imprint of fingers was found on her neck indicating that the killer had been behind her as she was strangled. Luke reasoned she couldn't have been killed lying on the bed as Cooper had thought. It didn't mean Sonny hadn't killed her, but it wasn't what Cooper had witnessed.

Purvis pulled out the photos of Mandy's back and slid them across the desk. While Luke and Tyler examined the photos, he turned and grabbed another file from the cabinet. Purvis pulled out two photos and lay them side by side.

Luke was no handwriting expert, but the carvings were the same. He'd bet money they were made by the same hand. "These are nearly an identical match," he said, lifting two photos and giving them a closer inspection. The placement of the carvings was nearly identical as well.

"An inch and a half from each shoulder blade," Purvis said and then admitted, "I didn't catch this at first. You know we take measurements of everything. When I compared the measurements of the carving on Mandy's back to Nick's file, I realized that it's dead center of the upper back an inch and a half from each shoulder blade. These words weren't haphazardly carved. There is precision here that took time and considerable effort. It also means they had time with the body after the murder."

Luke placed the photos back on the desk. "Do you know what the killer used to carve this into their backs?"

"A small, serrated knife would be my best assumption based on the wound pattern. It's something that could be found in any kitchen."

"That doesn't help us much," Tyler said with a deep sigh.

It was clear to Luke that he wasn't the only one frustrated with the case. He didn't want to ask the next question but he knew he wouldn't sleep that night if he didn't. "Purvis, I've never known you to be wrong, so I apologize ahead for the question."

Purvis held his hand up and cut him off. "You're worried about the timeline. I assure you, Luke, the body was already in full rigor and based on her body temperature when she was found, considering all the factors, she was dead at nine or a few minutes after. I know it doesn't make sense given your timeline. I can only give you the facts."

Luke nodded and apologized for second-guessing him. He turned to Tyler. "Looks like we are back to square one."

CHAPTER 14

I had eaten more pizza in two days than I had over the last year. I gave myself a break since finding good New York-style pizza in Little Rock was harder than finding a diamond in Arkansas' Crater of Diamonds State Park. I finished the last bite and washed it down with some soda. I had waited the whole lunch for Tim to say something about the case or his time in prison or even the evidence that he had. He never said anything. He seemed to savor each bite in quiet refuge.

When Tim was done, he grabbed my paper plate and his and tossed them in the garbage. He offered to refill my drink and came back with two filled cups. Tim slid into the booth. "Let's get down to business. I believe I know who killed Alex."

As much as I wanted him to start there, I didn't. I wanted to know why he was innocent first before I started focusing on another suspect. "Before we get to that, I want to understand your case. I know why you were convicted and it all sounds circumstantial. I want to know why you're innocent. Start with that night or the lead-up to it and convince me why you didn't do this. Then you can tell me your suspect."

Tim seemed a little caught off guard by the approach. It took him a few beats before he agreed. "You know my relationship with Alex. I was always the one who loved her more and felt like she was going to leave me at any moment. She did that on purpose to keep me guessing.

Did you know she told me that once? That she could leave me without caring I was gone?"

I hated hearing she played games like that. "I didn't, but it doesn't surprise me."

Tim sat back and appraised me. I wondered if he was feeling the same nostalgia of years ago sitting in the same booth having yet another conversation about Alex. She had consumed far too much of his life. He didn't seem to regret it. That's not what his expression or body language told me.

When he spoke again, his voice was soft. "I loved her, Riley. I would have spent the rest of my life loving her. It was a messy and toxic love. I know that now, but then I would have given her anything she wanted." Tim frowned and closed his eyes. "Alex wanted to break up with me. I could feel it and knew it was coming. I thought if I tried to show her how much I loved her by having her spend more time with my family, she'd know how serious I was about her." His eyelids fluttered open and he looked at me. "It sounds so juvenile now."

"We were kids, Tim. It was your first love. We all did silly things back then." I didn't want him to shut down from embarrassment. He used to say that when we were in college. That he was embarrassed by how much Alex impacted him and how much he loved her.

"As you know, Alex didn't go home with me that Thanksgiving break. What you might not know is that after I left, she called me a few times and sounded upset. She thought someone was watching her and that she didn't feel great staying by herself that weekend." He paused as if to weigh his words. "Alex said something felt off and she didn't know what it was. I asked if she wanted me to come back early, but she said she'd make it through and that she'd see me Sunday night."

"Alex never called me that weekend. She had stayed alone in our apartment before, so I wonder what was wrong. Did she give you any indication?"

"None. Just that something felt *off* and she didn't elaborate further. At first, I thought she meant she felt upset about our relationship. She assured me it wasn't about me. I told her to go talk to Michelle because I remembered that she wasn't going home for Thanksgiving either. She told me she didn't want to do that either."

"Alex and Michelle never got along."

"I don't think I knew that then." He touched his forehead with his fingertips. "Maybe I did. Being in prison for so long and one day rolled into the next with not much difference, memory starts to play tricks on you. Either way, Alex chose to remain alone and deal with whatever was bothering her. At the time, I thought maybe she was testing me or looking for attention. That's why I came back that weekend. Even though Alex told me it wasn't necessary, I didn't want to leave her there alone. I knew you had gone home and if she wasn't going to talk to Michelle, then she needed someone."

Tim stopped then and took a drink. A flash of anger came over his face. When he placed the cup back on the table, the tips of his ears were red and his cheeks flushed. "Alex wasn't alone when I arrived. I saw from the window that she was with another guy. I bailed on my family and drove all that way to make sure she was okay and there she was with another guy. I can't even tell you how angry I was, Riley."

I could imagine the anger and humiliation he felt. "What did you do?"

Tim shook his head and looked down at the table. "Nothing. I was a wimp, Riley, especially when it came to Alex. I wasn't going to go up and confront them. I wasn't going to fight the guy. I stood on the street watching them for a few minutes, feeling resigned, and I left. I drove around for a while and thought about going back home. I should have done that and no one would have known I was back in Geneseo that weekend. Only I couldn't go back home. What was I going to tell my family? That I left them and drove all that way only to find my girlfriend cheating on me? No. My humiliation was enough. I didn't need everyone to know."

Tim's story didn't exactly match up with Gail's. "Where did you go when you drove around?"

"I went back up towards Rochester and then looped back down and drove through some of the smaller towns. I had the radio on and I was trying to clear my head. I didn't want to be around anyone and my roommates didn't leave for Thanksgiving. I wasn't ready to answer any questions or talk about Alex." Tim took another sip of his drink. "Everyone was going to find out soon enough. I didn't need to rush my embarrassment."

"Why would they have known?"

Tim shrugged. "How would they not have known? I was pathetically in love with her, Riley. But I wasn't going to keep seeing her if she was involved with someone else. Even I had my limits."

"Did you see who the guy was with her?"

Tim shook his head. "I still don't know who it was. I had heard it was Griffin Lyons, but I didn't know him. I couldn't identify him if I had to. I didn't get a good enough look at the guy through the window that night to identify him anyway. I told the cops I couldn't identify the man. They didn't believe that anyone else was there. Once I heard it might have been Griffin, I still didn't have proof and I didn't want to tell the cops without any. What was happening to me was so terrible that I didn't want it to happen to anyone else."

That was Tim in a nutshell. Even when he was facing a murder charge, he wasn't going to randomly throw someone under the bus unless he was sure. "Who told you it was Griffin?"

"Gail Jensen," he said slowly not sure he wanted to disclose the information. I encouraged him to go on without telling him that I had already spoken to her. Tim explained, "I confided in her what I saw that night and she admitted that they had been involved for a while since the summer before that semester. I was angry of course and even angry at her that she hadn't told me."

"Was that before or after you went to Alex's house that night?"

"It was after, hours after in fact. The only reason I saw Gail that night was because she called me as I was driving around. She wanted to see how I was doing and when I'd be back." Tim took a breath and let it out slowly. With his eyes mere slits, he rubbed his brow. "The only reason I went to Gail's that night was because I knew how much she liked me and didn't like Alex. I figured I could vent my frustration to her and not seem pathetic."

"What time did you get there?"

"I went to Alex's place around seven and didn't see Gail until close to eleven. I stayed there until mid-morning when I had my head clear and then went to speak to Alex around noon. I was going to end things with her. There were cops everywhere. That's how I found out what had happened and that I was a suspect. I don't know that the cop even looked at anyone else."

What Tim was telling me was in stark contrast to what Gail and Michelle had said about the events of that night. Michelle said the fight started at eight, long after Tim would have left. I didn't want to push too hard. "What was your relationship like with Gail?"

Tim gave me a half-hearted shrug. "We were friends, but I knew she liked me more than that. I took advantage of that."

"How so?"

"I confided in her about Alex, even though I knew she had feelings for me. I didn't like her that way, so I probably should have kept up better boundaries. I had made my feelings known and she said she could handle being just friends. In hindsight, I don't think she could."

"Gail never testified for you in the first case. I don't remember seeing her name. If you spent the whole night at her place couldn't that have helped you?"

Tim shook his head and reached for his cup again. He traced the condensation down the side. "I wanted her to testify and pleaded with my defense attorney to put her on the stand. The problem was that she lied to him initially. She said I was with her longer than I was that night. I had already told him the truth that I didn't get there until around eleven. She said I arrived close to seven-thirty. There were other discrepancies as well."

"I spoke to Gail yesterday," I said and registered the surprise on his face. "It was a tip I received that she might have information to help you. I admit that I didn't find her credible. There was something in her statement and what she was telling me that didn't ring true. There is one thing I need to clear up right now. Did you know about Griffin before the night Alex was murdered?"

"No," Tim said firmly. "I did not know that Alex was cheating on me and I certainly didn't have a name. I didn't even know the guy's name that night when I was standing on the sidewalk in front of your apartment, watching Alex cheat on me. Gail provided that later when I went to her place. But even at that, I never saw the guy's face that night. I didn't see enough to identify him other than he looked like a muscular guy. He had a bigger build than me. I couldn't identify him from a line-up though. Even when Gail showed me a photo of Griffin, it didn't help me. When my attorney interviewed Griffin, he denied it and provided an alibi for that night. I had no other reason to pursue that. As I said, I knew what I was going through, I wasn't going to throw him under the bus when I had no solid proof that he did anything. All I had was Gail's observation."

The information was more than troubling for me. We locked our gaze on each other and it held firm while I told him what she had said. "Gail confided in me that she told you about Griffin before that night and the reason you came back was to confront Alex. She told me that when you got to the apartment, you saw Alex with Griffin and didn't want to confront them. She also said she knew you were coming back that night and that you went over to her place soon after leaving Alex's."

Tim tipped his head back and focused his eyes on the ceiling while a noise almost like a groan escaped his lips. He lowered his head and looked at me. "If I could have alibied myself for that night, don't you think I would have, even if Gail wasn't the most credible?"

Tim had a point there. "Is any of what she told me true?"

He looked like he wasn't sure what to say. "A partial truth, I guess. But it's all flipped around. She told me about Griffin *after* I went to her place that night not before. She had no idea I was coming back into town and only knew because she called me that night. I know what time I got to her place because I remember looking at the clock and wondering if my roommate would be asleep yet. I remember thinking that I should just go home. But I didn't. I went to Gail's for the reason I said. Maybe that's pathetic. I knew she liked me and I knew she'd be sympathetic."

I asked a few more questions about that night. Tim's story remained consistent. He had context to his statement and he didn't waver. I believed what he was telling me. I looked around but no one was paying any attention to us. I leaned into the table. "You said you had a suspect in mind."

"I've thought about this for all these years behind bars, Riley. I'd never want to accuse an innocent person, so you have to know I don't say this lightly." He held steady eye contact with me and I reassured him. Then as if letting all the air out of his body, he said, "I believe that Gail killed Alex in a jealous rage and then panicked and tried to pin it on me and then offered me half-hearted support. I think she thought she could pull it off and win me over at the same time."

I sat with that information for several moments. I didn't know what to think of it, but it was certainly possible – maybe even likely.

CHAPTER 15

"Are you going to say anything?" Tim asked, watching me closely. His back was ramrod straight and his fingers clenched around the plastic soda cup, pushing in the sides of the cup and forcing the liquid to rise.

I needed a moment to process what he told me and explained that. "You can't spring something like that on me and not give me time to digest it. Gail told me that she's been in contact with you all these years while you were in prison. Is that true?"

Tim released the cup and fixed it so the sides popped back into place. I couldn't tell if he was stalling or if the cup's dents bothered him. He met my eyes and laid out the evidence. "It's true and why I'm even more convinced. Gail, by her admission, was madly in love with me for a long time, possibly even still. She had wanted to date me long before I was with Alex even though I had made it clear to her that I wasn't interested in anything more than friendship. She also told me she knew about Alex and Griffin but hadn't wanted to tell me because she assumed I wouldn't believe her and it would lead to a fight between us. She didn't want to lose me as a friend, but that never stopped her from speaking badly about Alex. Once out of the situation and with all that time in prison, I thought long and hard about my interactions with Gail. She was in many small ways always trying to undermine my relationship with Alex."

"None of that means Gail killed her," I countered half-heartedly. The more he talked, the more convinced I became that it could have been Gail. "There must be more than that. In what ways did she try to undermine you with Alex?"

"Besides not liking Alex, she actively said that I needed to end the relationship. Every time I confided anything in her, her answer was to end it. Then she'd list all of Alex's flaws and how the relationship was bad. That's why I went there that night. I knew she'd tell me what I already knew – that it needed to end."

I had never been that direct with him. "The relationship was bad. I wish I had told you to end it with Alex. If I had, you might not have been in the situation."

"She might not have been murdered," Tim said solemnly. "There's a difference, Riley. We were true friends. When I came to you for your opinion, you gave it to me without bias and an agenda. Back then, you did tell me to end it more than once."

"I did?" I said, interrupting him.

Tim nodded. "More than once you tried to warn me that the relationship wasn't healthy. You were doing it from a place of concern for me. You saw how much I loved and cared about Alex and, without trashing her in the process, you also saw how she treated me. That's the difference from Gail. You weren't attacking Alex to try to knock her down a peg and paint yourself in a better light. You suggested that I should consider breaking up with Alex but it wasn't a demand. You offered other suggestions and said you'd support me no matter what I did."

Everything he said was true, even though I had no recollection of suggesting a breakup. It wasn't out of character for me. "Even if Gail was madly in love with you and actively trying to break you up, that doesn't mean she went so far as to kill Alex. You saw a man with her that night. Wouldn't he be the most likely suspect?"

"He would be but we don't seem to know who that is. It couldn't have been Griffin because he had a solid alibi."

"Unless that alibi was a lie. Gail was willing to lie for you. Who knows what his friends were willing to do for him." There was more that Tim wasn't telling me. The accusation was weak at best. "There must be more."

Tim had left the best evidence to last. "There was no reason for Gail to call me that night, especially not that late. We were friends at school. She'd never called me at home before then. When I saw her, she was flustered and amped up and she had fresh bruises on her hands and one on her face. I asked if she was okay and she said she had a mishap at the gym. Gail was much stronger than she looked and she had been taking some martial arts classes. She could have easily overpowered Alex. Once I arrived at Gail's, she kept asking me if I had gone back to Alex's apartment. She wouldn't let it go. I assured her I had been there around seven and hadn't gone back. I had been driving around. She asked if I was alone and I said yes. She was happy about that. I asked her what she had been doing all night. Gail told me she went for a run alone and then came back to her dorm."

Tim took another sip of his drink and then gestured with his hands as he spoke. "In the end, Gail didn't have any more of an alibi than I had. Once I settled into her dorm, she didn't want me to leave. She kept telling me to stay away from Alex and not confront her, to give it a few days. That was the opposite of what she had been telling me for more than a year. *Break up with her* was the constant refrain. Now that I had real ammunition to end things with Alex, I was being encouraged to wait. It was odd at the time and became a real concern the more I thought about it."

What he said was making sense, but it was impossible to prove. "Is there any physical evidence to all of this?"

"There's a necklace," Tim said and let me sit with that for a moment.

When I didn't register any recognition, he explained, "I had given Alex a star necklace with a diamond in the middle for her previous birthday. I saved and saved to buy her that."

"She rarely took it off." Now that Tim had reminded me, I remembered the necklace clearly. It was something Alex had wanted for a long time. We saw it at a shop on Main Street. Whenever we passed by the jewelry shop, she'd stand there for a moment and look at it. I was the one who had mentioned it to Tim in passing. I never thought he'd buy it for her. We were broke college students and it cost a few hundred dollars, more than most of us had. Alex rarely took off the necklace. She was wearing it the last time I saw her. I don't recall ever seeing it again, even after her parents came to clean out the rest of her stuff.

I raised my eyebrows in a question. "What does that necklace have to do with anything?"

"Gail had it on her dresser. It had a broken clasp. When I asked her about it, she got flustered and immediately put it in a jewelry box. She said her father had bought it for her but the clasp had broken."

"You didn't think that was odd?"

"Of course I did, but what Gail said was plausible." Tim rubbed his forehead again as if he couldn't believe it had taken him so long to put the pieces together. "I don't know how I didn't see it then. But I didn't know Alex had been murdered when I saw that necklace. For all I know, her father did buy it for her. By the time I knew Alex was dead and the cops were looking at me as a suspect, seeing that necklace was the last thing on my mind. Had I been the one who found her body or had gone through her belongings after she died, it might have occurred to me to look for the necklace. None of that happened and my thoughts about that necklace couldn't have been further away from the pressing matters at hand."

I could easily see how he hadn't thought about it after getting that explanation from Gail. At that age, I wouldn't have connected the necklace back to Alex's murder. "What do you think? That Gail ripped the necklace off Alex when she murdered her?"

"Alex was killed by suffocation," Tim explained. "I saw the medical examiner's report. They said there was some kind of altercation in the apartment first. There were signs of that in the kitchen. I think Gail surprised Alex and a physical fight ensued. Then Gail got the better of her and suffocated her. It's possible either during the altercation or after her death, Gail ripped the necklace off and kept it."

It was as good a theory as any I'd heard in previous cases. "What about the guy Alex was with that night? Where does he fit in this scenario? It was suggested to me that there was still uneaten food in the kitchen."

"I can't explain any of it," Tim admitted. It was clear he had tried to come up with an explanation for how Alex had been murdered and he thought he had a solid case. "What do you think?"

I didn't want to dash his hopes. "There's a lot to be explored. I wouldn't say you have a solid case, let alone one I'd put in front of a jury, but it's a start. Let's get out of here and walk up to the apartment. I also have information that Griffin is here this weekend."

"He's been alibied and can't be the killer." Tim stood from the table and cleared the rest of the trash including my cup and extra napkins. He reminded me of someone's dad ready to jump in and get things done. "What would be the point of speaking to him?"

I put my hand on Tim's back and gestured toward the door. Once we were on the sidewalk and walking down Main Street, I explained about Griffin. "I want to hear his side of the story. If he was telling the truth and he wasn't with Alex that night, someone else was. It's possible if he was seeing Alex as regularly as Gail told us then he might know more than he said all those years ago. He might know who was there that night. I'd also like to know his alibi because then I can double-check for you. I don't think it's unreasonable to think that someone covered for him. We are talking about college students. It's possible they didn't even realize that Griffin was connected to Alex."

Tim looked down at me. "My lawyer didn't think going after Griffin was a solid strategy."

I raised my eyes to him with skepticism on my face. "Your lawyer is also the reason your case was overturned on an appeal. Had he been doing his job in the first place you might never have been convicted."

"Fair point."

We walked down Main Street, turned on Center Street, and then up two blocks to the short Elm Street which sat bookended by South and Center Streets. It was a short road with one-family homes, some of which had long ago been converted into multi-unit apartments. It was a tree-lined street with a sidewalk and sizeable yards dotted with flowers in the spring and summer. It was the kind of street I had walked down in the wee hours of the morning without a care in the world – before the murder. Sometimes we even forgot to lock our doors.

It's partly why the murder was so devastating not just for Alex's friends and family but the whole community. Horrible violence had touched a location most people thought to be safe. It shook people's worldviews. It was also why the police so desperately needed to catch the offender.

In a way, identifying the threat and arresting him made people go back to feeling safe again. It always amazed me how quickly we could slip in and out of our bubbles. In truth, we were never as safe as we thought and, at the same time, not as unsafe either. It was a complex set of conflicting emotions that had led to the wrongful conviction of a college senior who had his life in front of him and who, too, was grieving.

We got to the curb in front of my former residence and stopped.

They had painted the yellow house blue and added white shutters. I was sure it was a way of distancing from the past. Otherwise, it looked the same.

For some reason when Tim explained that he was looking in the window, I had forgotten the large front tree. I had imagined him standing at the curb watching. I realized now standing in front of the house that couldn't have been the case. I couldn't see through the thick branches that had lost their leaves weeks ago.

"Where were you standing?" I asked.

Tim pointed past the tree toward the front of the house. "Almost right under the front window. Michelle saw me standing there and saw me leave. That's why I was so surprised that she testified against me. She had to have known I didn't go in."

That stopped me cold in my tracks. "Michelle saw you that night?"

Tim nodded. "She passed by the window and saw me standing in the yard. I had seen enough at that point, so I waved and then left. I'd bet money that she watched me walk away."

If that was true, it meant Michelle had lied to me too. The lies were deeper than the fall leaves we were standing in. What I didn't understand was why.

CHAPTER 16

Cooper had been summoned to the police station for a meeting at one that afternoon. He wasn't sure why. Luke had called him close to eleven that morning and asked if he felt well enough to walk the few blocks to the police station and sit in on a meeting. Luke hadn't told him why and didn't respond when Cooper asked.

He had assured Luke he'd be there.

Cooper skipped the pain pill he should have taken early that morning. He was getting tired of the fuzzy-headed blur that followed. He had initially promised that if he was feeling any intense pain he'd take it with lunch. It didn't matter how he was feeling. After the call from Luke, he wasn't taking anything and would wince his way down the street if needed. Luckily, Cooper was starting to feel a bit better, a bit like himself after months of feeling anything but that.

By the time he made it to the police station, he felt stronger than he had in a while. Even though sweat dripped down his back and there was dampness under his arms, the exertion felt good. He was starting to feel useful and alive again.

Cooper waved to Captain Meadows and headed straight for the conference room where he found Luke and Det. Tyler sitting at the table, which was filled with photos and paperwork. Cooper glanced down and grimaced at the sight of what looked like carved corpses.

"What is that?"

Luke raised his head from one photo. "I'm glad you're here." He waved Cooper in without answering the question. As Cooper sat, Luke slid a photo to him. "It's possible you witnessed our only suspect in two murders."

"Two?" Cooper asked with confusion in his voice. He lifted the photo from the table and stared at a dead man's back with a carving of a Latin word.

"As you know, we found Mandy's body."

Cooper knew that but Luke hadn't told him much else. He had been trying not to take it personally that he was suddenly out of the loop on a situation that no one even believed he saw. Adele had reminded him earlier that morning that Luke would update him when he could. She was far more patient than Cooper.

He glanced up from the photo and admitted, "It's been hard not knowing what's happening. I wanted to help."

"We know," Luke reassured him with a smile. "That's why you're here. Given what you saw and if this ever goes to court, you'll be called in to testify. I wanted to clear it with the prosecutor's office that we could bring you into the investigation without compromising your later testimony. Given that this case goes beyond Mandy, and we don't even have a last name for Sonny, let alone know anything about this man, we were cleared to do that."

Cooper let the photo fall to the table. "What do you mean this case goes beyond Mandy? Is that the second murder?"

Luke nodded and then pointed to the dry-erase board at the far end of the table. Cooper turned his attention to it for the first time. He'd been so struck by the photos on the conference table, he hadn't noticed the notes on the board in Luke's handwriting. They had connected Mandy's case to another. Both victims had the same words carved on their backs.

That was news to Cooper. He looked between Det. Tyler and Luke. "Mandy had a carving on her back? I've never seen that with a domestic violence case."

"We aren't sure that Mandy was killed in a domestic violence incident," Tyler said evenly. "From the outset, it certainly looked like she had been involved with Sonny romantically. It's what you thought and even what her neighbor, Nora, thought. That hasn't been confirmed because we can't find out any information about Sonny. For all we know, it's a nickname and not even connected to his real name. We have crime scene techs pulling every print in her apartment right now in the hopes that we will find something. If he's not in the system, it's not going to give us anything. That said, given the other murder, we suspect there might be more at play. As you said, a carving like that in a domestic violence case would be out of the ordinary."

Cooper felt stunned by the information and tried to go over in his mind what he saw through the window. Had he seen them embrace? No. Had he seen any warmth between them as if they were a couple? Not really. Cooper realized then that he had only assumed they were a couple. It was an assumption on his part and one that was wrong.

"You look like you're remembering something," Luke said, bringing Cooper back to the present.

"It's the lack of what I'm remembering that's caused me to reconsider. I assumed that they were a couple but never saw any proof of that. I don't know that she even wanted him in her place that morning. She was not dressed for work like she normally was at that time of day. She didn't look happy to see him there. Although, she did let him in."

"Mandy had taken the day off," Tyler said, interrupting him. "We were able to confirm with her office that she had told them the previous afternoon she had a few personal things to handle and she'd be off the next day. No one who worked with her had any knowledge about her personal life. No one knew who she was dating or involved with and didn't know Sonny. We were told that Mandy kept her work life professional. She didn't even attend happy hour or socialize with co-workers outside of work. She kept her head down at the office."

"Did anyone find that odd?" Cooper asked, thinking about his few work environments. It was mostly the police station as a former detective and his private investigator firm. He wasn't someone who let a lot of personal things slip at the office either, but he wasn't avoidant.

Tyler explained, "It was a quiet office and most everyone focused on work but they did host happy hours and tried to have a more relaxed atmosphere when they could. No one thought it odd that Mandy didn't participate. What did you know about her?"

"I don't know anything," Cooper said as his cheeks warmed. He was still embarrassed that he had been spying on Mandy and his other neighbors.

Tyler saw his discomfort and reassured him, "I'm not trying to make you feel bad. I'd be going stir-crazy if I were you. You knew she wasn't dressed and ready for work that morning, so you do know more than you think about her. That's what I'm asking. Even if it was only the day before that you saw her for the first time, you know more than we do right now. Anything can help to solve her murder."

Cooper relaxed into the chair, letting some of his defensiveness go. "It was more than a day that I watched her. I first noticed Mandy about two weeks ago," he admitted and saw a hint of amusement in Luke's eyes. Cooper glanced away and continued. "I saw her getting home from work one day and she looked tired, but she got in and must have turned up some music because a few minutes later, she had poured herself a glass of wine and danced wildly around her place. It was amusing and mesmerizing to watch. A part of me felt bad for doing so, but I didn't think it'd do any harm. She wasn't undressing or doing anything other than dancing. Most mornings I saw her it was the same. She'd be in the kitchen getting coffee ready in a blue travel mug she had. I've never seen anyone look so calm so early in the morning."

"You're an investigator, Cooper. It's in your blood to watch. Don't feel bad about it," Det. Tyler said, trying to normalize it for him in advance of the next question. "What else did you see her do? You said she had men in her apartment? Was there…"

"Sex?" Cooper asked with his voice strong and steady. He wasn't a child and wasn't going to dance around the topic, even if his cheeks burned red. "I didn't see sex. Her bedroom drapes were always closed and I would have stopped watching at that point. Mandy did have a few men there over the two weeks. I don't want to be judgmental and say a lot of men because that isn't for me to say."

"How many?" Tyler asked no judgment in his tone.

Cooper nodded once. "At least six. I also wasn't watching every evening over the two weeks. Adele was working late a lot of the nights. When she was home, I was focused on her. There could have been more men. I don't know."

Luke pulled his chair into the table, scraping the legs on the floor and drawing Cooper's attention. "How did it go when men were there?"

Cooper paused for a moment and then it dawned on him that it was the same each time. He said that and added, "They always came in the early evening even on the weekend. They had drinks and talked in the kitchen area. Never any food. Then they'd head into her bedroom. As I said, her drapes were always closed so I never saw what happened after that. I didn't stick around watching to see if the men left or not. One time though, Adele was working late and I told her I'd pick up dinner from the grille below our condo. When I went downstairs and outside to go to their door, I saw one of the men leaving. At that point, he'd maybe been there an hour or so."

"Did you ever see them embrace?" Luke asked.

"No. I don't think I ever even saw her touch them. But they went into her bedroom."

Tyler didn't say anything for a few moments. Luke was quiet as well. When Tyler finally did say something, Cooper didn't like it. "Sounds like she was a working girl. Maybe she was a prostitute and these were her clients."

Cooper started to protest, defending her for reasons he didn't understand. "Just because she liked to have a good time and isn't committed to one man you think she's selling herself? What kind of misogynistic crap is that?"

"Slow down, Cooper," Luke said. "Think about this logically. It was the same with every man. The drinks, talking for a few minutes, and then the bedroom. That's not normal for dating."

"I never saw any money exchanged," Cooper countered.

"Happens on websites and apps now," Tyler said. "They list their businesses as a whole range of things. Vice caught one a few weeks ago who was advertising psychic readings and she was charging them for spiritual counseling. Not my kind of church," he added with a laugh.

Cooper didn't know that. He hadn't exactly kept up to date with how prostitutes ran their businesses. "I'll concede the point that it might look that way. Do you think Sonny was a client too? He didn't interact with her the way the other men did."

"Could be her pimp," Luke suggested. "Maybe he tracked her here and wanted her to get back in business with him."

It sounded reasonable to Cooper. "How does Nick Day factor into this?" He asked to see the man's photo so he could see if he'd been one of the men who had visited Mandy.

Luke slid a photo across the table and asked him to take a look. It wasn't an autopsy photo but rather a candid shot with his friends. Cooper studied it carefully and then tried to recall each of the men he'd seen in Mandy's apartment.

Cooper put the photo back on the table and looked over at Luke. "He's not anyone I've seen before. It doesn't mean he was never there. As I said, I didn't see what was going on over there every night. I assume Mandy didn't wake up two weeks ago and become a sex worker."

Luke agreed with that. "We also don't know that she was a sex worker, Cooper. It's a working theory. What else do you know about her?"

"I don't know," he responded with a shrug. "I know she worked a professional job during the day. I know she liked to decompress with wine and dancing at the end of the day. I came to learn that men came over often around seven. I rarely saw her speaking on the phone, except that morning before Sonny came over to her apartment."

Luke stopped him there. "He called her?"

"I don't know who called who. I saw her standing in the middle of her living room on the phone. She didn't look too happy. A moment later, a cab pulls up and drops off a guy who enters her place a few minutes later."

Two points made Luke and Tyler happy – the cab and the phone call. Both had the potential to identify Sonny. They might have continued with their questions, but a knock on the door interrupted them.

It was one of the other detectives. He pushed open the door and stuck his head inside. "There's been another body found. We think it's related to your case."

"Where?" Luke asked, getting to his feet.

The detective hesitated slightly as if the information was difficult to deliver. "The Old State House."

"What?" Cooper, Luke, and Tyler asked in unison. The Old State House was a museum.

The detective confirmed and Luke and Tyler hurried out of the room with Cooper in tow.

CHAPTER 17

Tim wanted to come with me while I went to find Griffin. I wouldn't let him because I didn't think Griffin would be forthcoming with information if Tim was there. While Tim said he'd never met Griffin and didn't know anything about him, I didn't know Griffin's perspective. For all I knew, he hated Tim and was glad he'd gone to prison.

As far as I was concerned, even though it seemed Tim was credible in his statements with me, nothing was a fact until I could prove it. I didn't truly know the relationship between them and an initial interview wasn't the time to find out. I promised Tim we could meet later in the day.

It turned out locating Griffin wasn't difficult. I went to the rugby field first and found no one there. I then walked across campus to Court Street and found the dilapidated white rugby house still standing, just as it had been all those years ago. I was amazed and slightly horrified that it was still in use as the rugby house. I hadn't noticed when I had driven by earlier since it sits a little back from the road. The house was falling apart when I was in college. I couldn't imagine what it would be like inside now.

The front door was open and there were several people on the front lawn standing around talking and drinking. There were groups of five and six of them in clumps. There was also a swell of people in the back part of the driveway, and I assumed that would extend to the backyard as well. It was a bit like stepping back in time and arriving for a weekend keg party. It was mostly men and their ages varied.

I walked up the broken gravel driveway feeling a bit out of place and not sure how I was going to find Griffin in the sea of people. People were friendly enough and several said hello or gave me a friendly nod as I passed. Geneseo had always been one of the most friendly college campuses and it was nice to see that hadn't changed.

I stopped when I reached a group of men who appeared close to my age. "Do you know if Griffin Lyons is here?"

"He was out back a few minutes ago," one of the guys said and then asked me my name because he said I looked familiar. I told him and a broad smile appeared on his face. "We had an English class together." He rattled off a professor's name and I remembered the class but not him. I pretended for a moment that I did and shared some memories of the class. He offered to get me a beer and I declined, thanking him as I walked away.

I entered the house through the side door and ran right into a tall kid with dark hair. His beer sloshed over the top of the plastic cup and landed on my sleeve.

"I'm so sorry," he said and grabbed some napkins off the table.

"It's okay," I responded, not paying attention. I leaned to the side to see around him into the house but he was determined to dry my sleeve. I glanced up at him. "Do you happen to know Griffin Lyons?"

"My dad," he said, still apologizing. "He's in the living room. I can take you to him. Did you go to school with him?"

I barely registered the question. I was looking up at the kid's face wondering how old he was. I pulled my hand back from his and shook out my sleeve. "Do you go to school here?"

He laughed showing off a row of white teeth. "I'm a sophomore in high school. I want to go here when I graduate." He held up the cup of beer. "I was getting this for Dad's friend."

I hadn't even considered the drinking age. I was busy doing the mental math to work out when Griffin became a dad. He would have only been about a year out of Geneseo when he had him. "I sort of knew your dad. I don't know that he'll remember me."

"That's okay," the kid said. He refilled the beer from the keg and then stepped past me and opened the door. "I'll be right back and can take you to my dad."

I didn't wait for him to return. I pushed by a few more groups of men and found Griffin sitting on the arm of the couch, holding court and talking about his days at Geneseo. He had the same broad build. His dark hair was graying now and lines formed around his eyes when he smiled. He looked like a slightly older version of his son. He barely glanced in my direction even after he saw me.

"Griffin," I said loudly, talking over him and interrupting his story. He turned and raised his eyes to me. "Riley Sullivan. We went to school here together."

Recognition took hold and he smiled, flashing the same grin as his son. He stood and wrapped me in a hug, even though we hadn't known each other quite that well. "It's been a long time. How have you been?"

I wriggled back out of his embrace. "Do you think I can speak to you for a few minutes?" I glanced around the room at the others watching us. "Privately?"

"Sure. Let's go out back." He led me back through the house and out the side door. I waved to his son as I exited, glad to see he had given away the cup of beer, and then followed Griffin to the backyard. When we were far away from everyone else, he turned to me. "What's up?"

I explained that I was looking into Alex's murder and that his name had come up in the investigation. "I was told that you were involved with Alex. That she was cheating on Tim with you the summer before she was murdered."

Griffin winced at the word cheating. "I guess that's technically right. My wife, Elise, and I dated all through college. We took a break that summer because she was off in California doing an internship. We decided not to try to make it work long distance. At that age, it seemed impossible. I met Alex on campus one afternoon and we struck up a conversation. We started dating if that's what you want to call it. It was never physical. We never had sex, if that's what you're asking. It was mostly harmless flirting and fun. It was taking my mind off Elise being gone. I hadn't realized until the end of summer that she had been with Tim. She told me right before classes resumed. I'd like to say that we broke off our relationship but we continued to see each other."

"That doesn't sound like anything more than a friendship," I said with confusion in my voice.

"It was more than that," Griffin admitted. "We kissed and fooled around a little and spent a good deal of time together. When Tim got back, we snuck around to see each other. I liked Alex and I knew that she liked me too. It was me who held things back and not because of Tim. I was in love with Elise. I felt like I was cheating on her even though we had agreed we'd go our separate ways. It never quite worked. We didn't want to walk away from each other. While it wasn't *just* friendship with Alex, it wasn't a full-blown relationship either and was never going to be one. She understood that. I don't think she wanted a relationship with me." He ran a hand over his head. "If I'm being honest, I'm not sure Alex wanted a relationship with anyone. She acted like being with one person was too confining."

Alex had said similar things to me back then. My response was that she should be single then. She craved attention and didn't know how to do that. I didn't want to tell Griffin all of that so I told him simply that I understood. "What about the night Alex was murdered? She was with a man that night. Was it you?"

"No," Griffin said firmly. "I had an alibi, Riley. I was with Elise. Instead of the both of us going home Thanksgiving break, Elise came back here to Geneseo. We hadn't seen each other in months and we were holed up here at the rugby house. Alex and I hadn't even seen each other in the few weeks leading up to Thanksgiving break. If I recall, we met for dinner up in Rochester one night and she told me she was thinking about ending things with Tim. She asked me about Elise. I knew at that point I would see her at Thanksgiving and told Alex that."

"How'd she take it?"

"She seemed fine and said that she had met someone else anyway." Griffin must have seen the question on my face. He dashed my hopes before I could raise them. "I have no idea who that was. I don't know for sure that there was someone else. She might have said it because of what I said about Elise."

I shook my head. "Alex was with someone the night she died. If it wasn't you and it wasn't Tim, then there was another man. Did she give any hint during that conversation or before who it might have been?"

"Nothing she ever told me." Griffin grew quiet and reflective for a moment. I wasn't sure what he was thinking about or replaying from the past but the look on his face was one of determination to remember. After a few beats, he said, "I did see her with Jason Thatcher a few times. I don't want to shift the blame to him. I have no idea about the nature of their relationship. Jason was an education major too. For all I know, Alex was tutoring him or they were working on a group project together. He was on the hockey team. Do you remember him?"

I had a vague recollection of a tall guy with a muscular frame and a head of dark hair that always looked like it had been under a helmet or freshly washed. There was no in-between. I explained my recollection to Griffin who confirmed that to be true. "Do you have any idea where I can find him?"

"Here in Geneseo," Griffin said much to my surprise. "He was a hockey coach here for a few years and then left to coach at the high school. I know it seems like a step down but he was only an assistant here and got a head coach position at the high school. More money he said."

I hadn't realized they were friends or that they had kept in touch. "When was the last time you saw him?"

"The last time I was here in Geneseo, about a year ago. I was surprised to see him but he told me what he was doing. His sons go to the local high school and his wife is a nurse at a local hospital. He should still be around." Griffin looked across the top of my head and told someone he'd be right there. When he focused his attention on me, he said, "I wish I could help more. I told the cops back then that I'd do anything I could to help. I felt bad about what happened to Alex, but I didn't have anything to do with it. I swear to you, Riley, we were over at that point. I'd never hurt her like that."

I knew I only had a few minutes left with him. "Did Tim ever confront you about Alex?"

"No. I don't even know Tim. Alex never talked about him other than saying she wasn't ready for the serious commitment that he wanted."

"When you heard that Tim killed Alex, did you think it was true?"

Griffin shrugged. "As I said, I didn't know Tim and Alex didn't talk about him much. It was shocking that it could have been one of our classmates. I assumed the cops knew what they were doing."

I glanced over my shoulder at the group of guys waiting for Griffin. They'd have to wait a few minutes longer. I turned my attention back to him. "What about everyone else? What were the rumors swirling around at the time?"

"You're asking about rumors from a long time ago, Riley. I'm not sure I remember."

"Try," I urged. Sometimes rumors were just rumors. I knew with other cases, sometimes they held a bit of truth. "Anything you can remember might be helpful."

Griffin stood there rocking on the balls of his feet. He took a few sips of beer and peered over my head as if he couldn't wait to be on the other side of this. Finally, he looked down at me. "There was one rumor that she had been involved with one of her professors. Lance Donovan. I don't know if that's true or not. I don't know anything about him. I never saw her with anyone else or heard other rumors. I know she was your friend, Riley…" His voice trailed off.

I knew there was more. "Say it, Griffin. Good or bad, say what you want to say. Alex is dead, so we can't do much to her now."

"She was hard to like." Griffin furrowed his brow as he said it. "She didn't have many female friends because she was always snipping at people. She could be your best friend and then toss down a biting remark out of nowhere. People didn't know how to take her. She flirted with guys one day and then treated them like dirt the next. It was always hot and cold with her. Even if Elise and I didn't get back together, I wouldn't have been able to stay with Alex. It was too much of a rollercoaster. Her mood never seemed stable to me." He reached out and put a hand on my shoulder. "It was good seeing you. If I think of anything else, is there a way I can reach you?"

I gave him my phone number and let him walk away. I stood there considering for the first time Alex's mental health back in college. Griffin had been right, she never seemed stable. There were big shifts from one day to the next. Sometimes even hour by hour. I didn't know if or how it related to her murder.

CHAPTER 18

By the time Luke made it to the Old State House, media had swarmed the front, blocking his entrance. He pushed past reporters and cameramen jockeying for position. He led the way with Tyler right behind him and Cooper a few steps after that. He wasn't moving too quickly and Luke had to wait a moment for him to catch up.

In that time, a reporter stuck a microphone in his face and barked a question about dead bodies all over the city and what exactly was he going to do about it. Luke explained that he hadn't even had time to assess the scene and didn't know much more than she did at that moment. He promised to brief them all when he knew more.

As Luke pushed through them, another reporter asked a question that stopped him cold. "Do you think Captain Meadows is past his prime and it's time for him to retire and let someone else take over? Is he the cause for the spike in crime in the city?"

Luke tried not to laugh at the sheer audacity of the question. He turned on the reporter. "Asking that question tells me you have little understanding of how crime works. That said, Captain Meadows has dedicated his entire career to working in law enforcement in this city. He's been a dedicated public servant and not only my boss but my mentor. When he retires, it will be on his terms and a great loss to the city."

With that, Luke turned on his heels and marched toward the yellow crime scene tape. He grabbed the uniformed cops by the shoulder and leaned in. "Push the media back even farther. Clear the whole street for us. We need room for the medical examiner's van and the crime scene techs."

The young, uniformed cop made no movement other than to shift his eyes slightly toward Luke. "They are both parked around back."

Luke cracked a slight smile. "I know. Move the media back anyway."

The young cop understood the request and began his work which was met with groans by the news stations. Luke kept his smug satisfaction to himself as he ducked under the crime scene tape and was met by the first cop on the scene. Together they walked up the red brick sidewalk, moved toward the right on the path around the fountain, and continued toward the front door of the Old State House, stopping only briefly to look up at the two-story building with four wide columns in front. The cop briefed Luke and Tyler on the scene inside.

Luke hadn't been inside the building in years. He couldn't even remember the last time. The Old State House, which was the original state capitol building of Arkansas, was now a museum. Construction on the building started in 1833 and it was the oldest standing state capitol building west of the Mississippi River. The building had seen its share of history.

In 1837, Speaker of the House John Wilson fatally stabbed Representative Joseph J. Anthony after a debate over taxes. In May 1861, all but one delegate voted for the state to secede from the Union. The building was home to the Confederate government until Union forces captured Little Rock in September 1863. It was also the site of many segregationist bills that passed after the war. It was a building that taught its history well – the good and the bad.

Luke remembered touring the museum on a school field trip and never liked the vibe of the place. Riley had joked more than once that the place was haunted. Luke had no idea if that was true or not, but he never spent time there to find out.

"Where was the body found?" Luke asked the cop.

"On the second floor in a back room that's rarely used. That's why it took so long to find the body. Hardly anyone goes up there. He was sitting in a chair and slumped over the desk. At first, the woman thought he was asleep. She thought maybe some drunk guy had stumbled in the night before and was sleeping."

"Has that happened before?" Tyler asked.

"She said a group of teens broke in a few years ago and they found two of them passed out the next morning. They got better security after that, so she had no idea how this guy could have gotten in." He provided Luke with her name and office number.

Luke thanked the cop for being first on the scene and for calling in Purvis and the crime scene techs. The cop assured Luke that even though they were all in the building, no one disturbed the scene until he arrived. That was good. Luke liked to take it all in fresh, rather than see it in photographs later.

Luke, Tyler, and Cooper made their way into the building and then climbed the stairs to the second floor. Luke got to the landing, said hello to the crime scene techs, then made his way down to the back office. Purvis was waiting outside for him.

"The carving is on the victim's back. The same as the others," Purvis said as Luke approached.

Luke and Tyler got gloves and booties on before heading down the rest of the hall and entered the office while Cooper waited outside. As Purvis and others told him, the man was slumped forward on the desk resting his head on his arms. It was easy to see why the woman might have thought he was asleep at first. He was facing the front of the room nearest the door so Luke had to walk around the desk to see the man's back. He lifted the man's shirt and revealed the same Latin carving. It looked as precise in placement as the others.

Luke bent down and looked at the back of the chair and the floor under the man. There were no signs of blood anywhere. With Tyler's help, they moved the man's body gently enough so Luke could look at the desktop. There was no blood there either. He searched the man's front pockets and didn't find anything. They moved the body so Luke could see if there was a phone or wallet in his back pockets. They had another unknown victim.

"He wasn't killed here." Tyler said aloud what Luke was thinking. "He was placed here just like Nick Day was placed in that field by the Clinton Library." There were only a few blocks between the Clinton Library and the Old State House Museum. "Mandy's case still doesn't seem to fit for me."

It didn't fit for Luke either, even though she had the carving on her back. The location of her apartment was several blocks farther into downtown, away from the River Market area. Her body was not left in any area of significance. She was thrown out like trash and left not far from where she lived. She was a woman and the other two victims were men. There was a violent assault before her death, which was not witnessed in the other two cases. At least with the information they had to date.

There were major differences in the cases but still, the carving tied all three together.

"I don't know how but they are all connected," Luke said, sure of that. It might be the only thing he was sure of in the case. "There has to be some common denominator among them that we are missing. Let's get out of here and let the team get the forensics done. Purvis can take the body while we go interview the staff."

They stepped back out of the room and met Cooper and Purvis in the hallway. Cooper declined seeing the scene for himself and Luke understood. There was nothing for Cooper to do with them and Luke felt a little foolish for having brought him. He turned to his friend. "You want to come with me while I interview the woman who found the body?" Cooper agreed and Luke asked Tyler to check in with some of the other staff to assess for cameras and general security.

As they made their way to the staff office, Luke turned to Cooper. "You don't have to be here if you don't want to. I know there isn't much for you to do."

"I don't mind sitting in. I might pick up something you miss." Cooper slapped Luke on the back. "It gets me out of the house. Besides, I want this guy caught as much as you do."

Luke wasn't sure anyone wanted this guy caught as much as he did. With the third victim within a couple of days, this was looking more and more like a serial killer and Luke would do anything to avoid that label. They walked down the narrow hall until they found the office. The door was open and Beth Murphy was sitting at her desk staring down into her lap.

Luke didn't want to startle her, so he knocked gently and said her name. She raised her eyes to him and then stood. Luke entered followed by Cooper and introduced them both. "I know this must be a terrible shock for you. I'll try to be brief with my questions."

"It's fine," Beth assured them. "Please sit and we can talk." She moved around to the front of the desk and closed the door behind them. She stood at the door for a moment, seeming to assess them. Then she went behind her desk and sat with her hands folded on the desktop. "Do you want me to start?"

Luke wanted to let her talk as much as she wanted, even for her peace of mind. "Before you get started, do you know the victim?"

"I've never seen him before," Beth said and then sucked in a breath. "I don't think I do, anyway. I wasn't able to get a good look at his face. When I entered the room and saw him slumped over, I assumed he was someone who had broken in and fallen asleep. The room was dark and I hadn't turned on the light. As you saw, the desk is some distance away from the door and you couldn't see his back from that angle. It was only when I got closer I knew it wasn't like the other time the boys had broken in."

Luke was hearing two things – that she didn't know him but that she also might not have gotten a good enough look to determine that. He'd circle back. Luke encouraged her to continue.

Beth touched her hand to her throat and sighed. "I'm a little disturbed that I've been up here alone on this floor for most of the day without having any idea that there was a dead man there." After admitting that, she seemed relieved to have gotten that out of the way. She relaxed her shoulders. "We don't use those offices much. We have extra items stored in there and it's not part of any of the tours. We had staff in there years ago but we've faced budget cuts and have had to do more with less. As a result, we have empty offices."

"Is there any significance to that office?"

"No," she said firmly. "Various staff have had that office over the years. I'd have to check our records but I think the last person was from our fundraising staff. Maybe it was a coincidence that they picked an empty office. I wouldn't have even gone into that office today, but we have some old donor files stored in there. I needed a contact that I hadn't saved on my computer. I was hoping it was in one of our older files. That's when I found him. I feel foolish now for the way I yelled at him to wake up and get out. I even threatened to call the police."

"It happens," Luke said with his tone calm. She had no reason to feel badly about anything she did. "Did you see or hear anything suspicious today?"

"It's an old building so there are always creaks and groans. A few people have said the building is haunted, which wouldn't surprise me.

Nothing out of the ordinary. Honestly, I might not have even gone down there for days or weeks but I needed that file. It was as simple as that."

"Is it fair to say that area of the building isn't used much?"

Beth bobbed her head up and down. "There is only a handful of staff who'd ever have reason to go down to that end of the hall. I feel fortunate I found him when I did." She crinkled up her nose and Luke didn't have to ask what she was thinking.

"What about the cleaning staff from last night?" Cooper asked and then looked to Luke in apology for speaking up.

"We have a cleaner come up here to the offices once a week and that was two nights ago. Every night, they clean the areas downstairs where the tours are held. I can give you their number."

She provided the contact information and Luke wrote it down. "When was the last time someone was in that room?"

"I'd have to ask the other staff. I haven't been down there in a couple of weeks." Beth went on to explain the inner workings of the Old State House Museum. It all seemed routine to Luke.

"Do you have any idea how he might have gotten in? Doors or windows unlocked?"

"Never," Beth said and then paused. "The back door has a pin code and then there is the alarm code inside the door. For safety, each should be different four-digit numbers but it's the same for both. We often have groups in here for catered events, so there are more than a few people who have access. I can check with the company to see if anyone accessed that. The alarm was engaged when I came in this morning. But if they have the code, they could have reset the alarm before they left. The doors are sometimes open when the cleaning staff is here. They could have snuck in. That's how the boys got in that one time."

That opened up an array of possibilities for access. Before Luke could ask another question, Beth added, "Do you think this case is connected to the other recent murders? I knew Mandy McKee. She regularly came to events. It was terrible what happened to her."

"You knew the victim?" Cooper asked before Luke could respond.

"She was a lovely woman. I had met her a handful of times. The bank where she worked sponsors events that are frequently held here."

"Did you know Nick Day?"

"I knew of him," Beth admitted. "His parents were among our donors and he'd been to a few events. His death was shocking as well. His parents must be devastated."

They might be if Luke could reach them. He still hadn't had any luck. "Do you know if the two knew each other?"

"They met briefly," Beth said and Luke asked if she was sure. "They were at the same event over the summer. I introduced them myself." Seeing the expression on their faces, she added, "It wasn't romantic. Nick had his girlfriend with him. They were both interested in the history of the building. I gave them a tour together."

It was the first connection between them. The first thread to be pulled. Luke hoped once he tugged it, more would unravel.

CHAPTER 19

Griffin had given me two more leads but I was running out of daylight. Tim had already texted me twice asking for an update. I didn't have much to tell him. I certainly wasn't going to give him the names Lance Donovan or Jason Thatcher until I explored those angles to see if there was any weight to the rumors. From what Griffin said, it sounded like I'd be able to find both of them locally.

There was something I wanted to do first that I hadn't wanted to do with Tim earlier in the day. After leaving Griffin, I found myself standing at the curb in front of my old apartment. I wanted to go back inside. I knew there would be nothing left over from the time Alex and I lived there. But still, I wanted to stand in the space I stood all those years ago and see if any memories came back. I was learning a lot this trip about Alex that I had long suspected but never knew.

Each time my old suspicions were confirmed, guilt washed over me. It was different learning personality defects in old friends who were still alive. Speaking poorly of the deceased never sat right with me. Alex didn't have a chance to give me her side of the story. What Tim and Griffin told me wasn't wrong though. Alex had never been easy to deal with, but she was one of my best friends.

While I saw the side of Alex men saw, it was easy to overlook. We were young and had our whole lives to settle down. I chalked up her indecision as simply not wanting to be tied down in a relationship and there was nothing wrong with that. But Alex did court attention from men as a way to boost her self-esteem. It was a messy complicated dance she did with them.

People were living in my old apartment. There were lights on in the living room and the kitchen. I crossed the front yard and stood under the tree. Tim was right that you could see into the apartment, but the low-hanging tree branches got in the way if I stood too far back.

I took a few steps forward and the tree was no longer an issue. I had to look straight up and that would make it nearly impossible to see much into the kitchen unless someone was standing right near the window. I wanted to test something out and would need help to do that.

I crossed the front of the house, climbed the few steps to the porch, and rang the upstairs doorbell. Moments later, someone called out to come in, which was followed by the old creak of the staircase. I turned the knob and pushed open the door. I stepped inside the old foyer as a young woman appeared in the middle of the steps.

"Hi," she said casually.

It wasn't the safest approach if I was there to do someone harm. She had already let me in. It's interesting to me the things you think about in your late thirties that never crossed your mind in college. I introduced myself. "I used to live upstairs in your apartment. I was visiting campus and thought I'd see if I could take a look at my old place."

"Come on up," she said with a wave of her hand. "I'm Penny and my roommate is Cassandra."

I glanced to the right at the door to the downstairs apartment. Michelle and I used to argue whose turn it was to clean the foyer, neither one of us wanting to take responsibility for the task, especially in winter when everyone would toss their wet muddy boots on the tile floor.

I climbed the steps and smiled as I hit the fourth stair from the top. It sunk under my weight and let out a low moaning creak. I laughed. "This stair hasn't been fixed in all this time. We used to be afraid that it would collapse on us."

"Same," Penny said with a giggle. "If I can step around it, I do. I kind of like it because no one makes it to our door without making noise." I wanted to remind her that it was the enemy she knew and would probably let in who'd do her the most harm. I didn't want to scare her before I even stepped foot into the apartment though.

I stepped through the open doorway and was awash with memories. The place looked similar to when I lived there. The walls had a fresh coat of paint, but the old wood floors looked like they hadn't had a good shine in fifty years. The girls had a blue and white throw rug on the floor with matching pillows on the couch. Their couch looked newer than the one Alex and I had begged some boys who lived next door to carry in for us. I forget now where we acquired it. In the end it only cost us two large pizzas for the moving help.

A young woman, who I assumed to be Cassandra, called out from the kitchen. "Oh," she said, pulling up short when she saw me. "I didn't realize we had company." She squinted her eyes and then they flew open wide. "Oh my god, you used to live here. You're the roommate of the girl who was murdered!" There was no trace of fear in her voice.

"How did you know?"

"Your photo was in the newspaper!"

I had forgotten about that. The local newspaper had shared a photo of a few of us with Alex and indicated that I was her roommate. It was a risky thing they had done if the killer wanted to come back and finish the job.

I didn't want to scare the girls. I had no idea if they knew about the history of their apartment and the last thing I wanted to do was freak them out. The excitement in Cassandra's voice hinted that they had no fear at all.

I turned to Penny. "I didn't know if you knew what had happened here and didn't want to scare you."

"Everyone knows about this apartment and the legend of Alex McCormick," Penny said with equal excitement. "We heard they were going to do a podcast about her murder seeing as how the killer was let out of prison. You don't think he'll come back here, do you?"

I hesitated, not sure if I should tell them that I was working for Tim. I needed their help though, so there was no point lying. "I'm working for Tim, trying to figure out who killed Alex."

They squealed in unison. "Can we help you with your investigation?" Cassandra asked and then dashed off back into the kitchen while she shouted about shutting off the oven.

I didn't know what to make of the pair of them. They were both more excited than they should be by the prospect of a murder having taken place in their apartment and the suspected killer's private investigator showing up at the crime scene. Given the rise of true crime shows and podcasts, I assumed they were fans of the genre. I swallowed hard, not sure where to start. Probably sorting fact from fiction would be a good start.

"What do you know about the case?"

Penny pointed at me. "You were gone for Thanksgiving break and Alex was here all alone. They think her boyfriend was here with her and they got into a huge fight. The place was a mess and then she was smothered probably with a pillow on her bed. Cassandra has Alex's old room. Do you want to see it?"

"Not yet," I said, stalling. After Alex had been murdered, I rarely went in there and only if I had to. I never had another roommate move in. Back then, murder wasn't something exciting. No one wanted to share my stigmatized apartment with me. I certainly tried not to dwell on it either. "Has there been any talk around campus now that Tim is out of prison?"

Cassandra plopped down on the couch and crossed her legs under her. "There's some mixed reaction. We still have professors who taught here then and they seemed more stressed by it than anyone else. Everyone knows about this house and the landlord knocked off considerable rent for someone to take it. It sat empty for a long, long time. Most people think the place is haunted by Alex."

"Is it?" I found myself asking without meaning to. I wasn't sure I was much of a believer. Like many who had lost friends too young, the grief was still there, a dull ache somewhere inside of me. I wanted to tell the girls I didn't mean to ask about it being haunted and that I didn't want to know. They seemed too excited by my interest to walk back what I said.

"It's definitely haunted," Penny said, sitting next to Cassandra on the couch. She gestured toward the chair across from them. "We heard it was haunted before we moved in. I love that kind of stuff, so it didn't bother me. Convincing my parents was much harder. We love this apartment and can deal with the occasional bump in the night."

"Alex is here," Cassandra said as I sat. "I talk to her all the time. One time I caught her voice in a recording on my phone. I couldn't understand what she was saying. We also held a séance after we found out Tim was being released from prison. I wanted to know what Alex thought about it. We wanted to see if she could tell us who killed her. She's not the easiest spirit. She's moody."

I had to hold back a laugh and couldn't help but smile. My friend wasn't easy in life, so it made sense that her spirit would be giving these girls a hard time. If Alex was hanging around this apartment, which didn't make sense to me, she probably enjoyed toying with them. I didn't want to encourage them, but if they had information from the great beyond, I'd listen. "Can I hear the recording?"

"Definitely. You knew her better than anyone. You might be able to tell me what she's saying." Cassandra leaned forward on the couch and grabbed her cellphone from the coffee table. She scrolled and when she found what she had been seeking, placed the phone back down so we could all hear it. She glanced up at me and asked if I was ready before she hit the button.

A crackly static hum masked the voice I heard underneath. There was a distinct voice there. It was metallic and I had trouble hearing it. "Is there a way to quiet some of the static?"

"I've done all I can with it. Do you want me to send you the audio file?"

Not that I was putting any stock into this. What could it hurt? "Yes, send it to me. You said you held a séance. Did Alex come through then?"

"It was terrifying," Penny said and looked sheepishly at Cassandra. "We didn't want to use a spirit board so we used the audio again. It was better this time because we had more people here. I think Alex was better able to feed off our collective energy. We used a recorder like you see in those ghost shows."

They were dragging this out and making it dramatic while I wavered in belief. A part of me desperately wanted to connect with my old friend. Another part of me knew that wasn't possible. I'd entertain them to a point. "Can I hear it?"

Penny got up from the couch and went down the hall towards the bedrooms. That was an area of the apartment I didn't want to see. Even after all these years, I didn't want to see where Alex had drawn her last breath. There was no reason to do that to myself. While she was gone, I asked Cassandra, "Is there anything else Alex does to let you know that she's here?"

"She slams the kitchen cabinet doors and sometimes creaks the step on the stairs. I can't tell you the number of times we've heard the creak and looked out and no one is there. You know it takes some weight on that step for it to make the noise."

That was true. The house was old and made some distinct sounds for its age. That step needed a bit of force. "What do you think she wants?"

"For someone to find her killer. Tim didn't do it and she feels bad that he went to prison for something he didn't do. She said she's felt bad all these years for how she treated him in their relationship."

That knocked me back a bit. "How do you know that?"

"In addition to the audio files, we used a flashlight and asked her yes or no questions. She was able to turn the light off and on depending on her response. We asked her if she knew her killer and she indicated yes. We asked if it was Tim and she indicated no. We asked a range of questions trying to figure out why. The audio helps to explain that better. We asked if the killer was male or female and she indicated yes to both. I'm not sure what that means." Cassandra called out to Penny and then turned back to me. "It's better to hear the recording."

Penny came into the room holding a small audio recorder, not unlike one I'd carried during interviews or even when trying to record without the other party knowing. She handed it to me and told me to push play.

A distinct woman's voice pierced through the recorder without the static or the metallic sound. I didn't raise my eyes to look at either of the girls. I swallowed hard as the recording continued. It was Alex. I was sure of it.

On the recording, Cassandra asked a question and the response back would be a word or phrase, almost as if Alex didn't have the strength to speak in whole sentences. I'd seen the ghost shows too and always assumed they were fake. I had no idea how Cassandra and Penny could fake this.

Alex, plain as day, responded *no* to the question if Tim killed her.

When asked who did, the response wasn't clear. It sounded to me like the word *complicated*. The following words were *cheating uncovered*. The girls asked a few more questions that all elicited a response from Alex and then the recording ended.

"What do you think?" Cassandra asked, sitting on the edge of her seat. "You can listen again if it helps."

I didn't need to listen again. The voice was Alex, no matter how much I couldn't understand how. What I heard couldn't have been faked. "It was Alex," I said softly, my throat suddenly dry. I raised my eyes to each of the girls. "Are you willing to help me?"

They both nodded. "Anything you need," Cassandra added.

I put the recorder down on the coffee table and explained what I wanted to do.

CHAPTER 20

I made it back to my hotel at close to nine exhausted and hungry. I picked up a turkey sub and a bag of chips on the way to the hotel and tossed them down on the table once inside my room. I spent a little time going through the trial transcript and then gave in to my exhaustion and closed the binder.

My stomach growled but what I needed more than the food was the comforting voice of someone who might understand what I had experienced. Luke should have been my first call, but I found myself clicking Cooper's contact in my phone. Luke was not a strong believer in the paranormal and I didn't want to be challenged right off the bat. I needed to talk it through first to decide how I was feeling.

Cooper answered after a few rings. "How's it going out there?" He sounded tired and there was an edge to his voice.

"Are you okay?"

"Fine. We can talk about it later. Update me about what you've been doing."

I shrugged off my cardigan and sat down on the edge of the bed. I inched back to get comfortable. I gave him the overview of my initial meetings with Michelle, Gail, Tim, and Griffin. I saved going back to my old apartment for last. "This is going to sound completely out there, so you're going to have to bear with me." In one breath, I let out what I had been holding in all evening – that I truly believed the girls had captured Alex's spirit on the recording.

Cooper listened quietly not judging or dismissing me.

When I was done, I asked, "That can't be what I heard, right? I must miss her so much and being there in the apartment must have brought back memories. I must have imagined it, right? I wanted to hear her on that recording, so I did. Isn't that what happened?"

I wasn't prepared for Cooper's question. "Why can't it be Alex?" When I didn't have a response, he continued. "Riley, I spent years being a skeptic and that didn't get me anywhere. I was stubbornly a non-believer. Now I'm skeptical but open that there are things in this world that maybe I don't understand. And because I don't understand them, doesn't mean they don't exist. Did you feel better hearing Alex's voice?"

That was a complex question I hadn't sorted through yet. "I didn't like feeling like she might be stuck in that apartment."

"How do you know she's stuck? Maybe she showed up when someone wanted to talk to her. Alex might have figured out those girls cared enough to reach out."

"I don't know," I said and rubbed my brow. "I don't know how any of this works. It was good to hear her voice. It's good to know she's still around, and it was especially good to hear her say Tim didn't kill her." I explained to Cooper about the girls' séance and their trick with the flashlight. "I heard everything Alex said on that audio recording. She blamed her murder on cheating being uncovered. That should point to Tim but Alex was clear that he wasn't the one."

Cooper remained quiet for a moment. "You know there are all kinds of cheating. Maybe Alex wasn't talking about her relationship with Tim. I know you said you discovered that she was cheating on Tim with Griffin and he pointed you to two other men. It could be connected to one of them. Maybe she was involved with one of them and their girlfriend found out. She could have surprised them during the dinner and a fight broke out, leading to Alex's death."

That reminded me of what Cassandra had said. "When asked if it was a man or woman who killed her, Alex said the word complicated. Your scenario fits."

"Have you tried to speak to Alex directly?" Cooper asked.

"I don't know that I could do that. I'd feel awkward."

Cooper laughed. "You talk to yourself all the time. What would be different?"

I wanted to tell him I didn't talk to myself, but I had no defense. He often found me at home muttering to myself as I talked through evidence on a case. "I guess I could try it."

"What else did you uncover?"

"I had the girls stand in the kitchen window the way Tim had described seeing Alex. He was right that if the man was tall enough, Tim would only have been able to see up to his chest and not his face, depending on how they were standing and if the shade was low. I only wanted to prove that was possible and I did."

"Do you believe Tim?"

"He's credible, Cooper. I don't get any sense that he's lying to me. I can't say the same for Gail, who lied about nearly everything she said."

"Could she be considered a suspect?"

I had been considering that. "She loved Tim enough to want to get rid of Alex. Tim wasn't breaking up with her and it was clear that's what Gail wanted. She could have gone to the apartment and in a fit of rage attacked Alex. Then called Tim to see where he was."

Cooper yawned. "It sounds like you have a lot left to uncover."

"You sound tired. I hope you're taking care of yourself."

"It was a long day." Cooper updated me about the cases and his work with Luke. "A body was left at the Old State House, and we found out both of the other victims had been there earlier for an event and had met. There must be a connection. That can't be a coincidence."

It certainly sounded that way. There was something in Cooper's voice I didn't like. "You sound off. Is everything okay?"

"I'm fine physically if that's what you're asking. Getting stronger every day and feeling better. I've also been able to cut down on the pain pills. I…" Cooper started and then his voice trailed off. I remained quiet and allowed him to work through whatever was on his mind. Finally, he admitted, "I don't think Det. Tyler and Luke are right about the direction of Mandy's case. They both believe she was a prostitute and I feel bad I might have led them to believe that."

"How would you have done that?"

"I told them about the men she was involved with. They are right that it sounds like she could have been selling sex. That's not the vibe I got. Also, would a professional woman with a good job in a bank bring clients back to her apartment? Would she have taken that risk?"

"It doesn't sound like it to me. It also doesn't sound like she needed the money."

Cooper agreed. "That's the only thing I was considering. I haven't been able to explore her financial records. Luke is still waiting for them and he probably won't let me see them. Mandy didn't socialize at work. To me, she seemed like a woman with secrets but not prostitution."

"Did you tell Luke and Tyler that?"

"They think I'm being emotional over it and had been watching her for a while. They said I might have become attached. I don't agree with that either."

I didn't want to judge Cooper for doing that. In his situation, I might have spent my time checking out my neighbors too. I didn't know the answer but a past case of ours came to mind. "Do you remember that adultery case we had a few months back? The woman was involved with several different men."

"The one where I did all the surveillance?" Cooper asked with sarcasm in his voice. I hated surveillance and until he'd hired new investigators, all the surveillance went to him.

"That's the one," I confirmed, not feeling the least bit bad. I knew my strengths and surveillance wasn't one of them. I didn't have the patience it required. "Do you recall the result of the case?"

It took Cooper a moment but then he hit on it. "She was a sex addict. Her husband stayed with her when she promised to go get the help she needed. Do you think that's a real thing?"

"Sex addiction?"

"Yes. I wondered at the time if it was something she was saying to excuse her actions or if it was a real addiction. I never did any research on it because the next case needed my attention."

I didn't know much but I knew it was real. "There are twelve-step programs for it like drugs and alcohol. If I'm remembering correctly more women identify with love addiction than sex. That may be what you were witnessing and why it seemed so transactional. It would also be a reason why she didn't mind having them in her apartment. She wasn't doing anything illegal."

"It's a leap," Cooper said but his tone told me that he was mulling it over. "It feels more plausible than this professional banking woman being a prostitute on the side. She also moved from California to Little Rock. We haven't hit on the reason why yet. She doesn't have any family here and no friends that we've been able to track down. She doesn't interact much with her neighbors or her co-workers. She may be trying to manage or hide her addiction."

"It's something to explore," I said, fighting a yawn. We finished up the conversation and then I told him I was going to call Luke.

"Call me if you need anything," Cooper said and then disconnected.

I caught my reflection in the mirror. I looked as tired as Cooper sounded. I pushed myself off the bed and grabbed my sub. I called Luke and chatted with him while I ate dinner. I left out all the details about my recent paranormal exploration and my suggestion to Cooper about sex addiction. I didn't want Luke to think I was encouraging Cooper to get involved with his case.

Luke sounded frustrated and told me that he was working late but promised to get some sleep. We ended the call promising that we'd have more energy for a better call tomorrow. I didn't think that was a promise either of us could keep.

I finished eating while I contemplated the case. I had told Tim that I'd meet him for breakfast and we could go over the events of the day. I still had Lance Donovan and Jason Thatcher to track down tomorrow. Even after sifting through all the interviews, I didn't feel any closer to figuring out Alex's death.

If anything, I ruled out suspects – Tim and Griffin. That would have to be enough for one day.

I went to the bathroom and washed my face and brushed my teeth. There was something niggling in the back of my mind I was trying to ignore. I wondered if I could make contact with Alex outside of the apartment. The girls had wanted me to try there with them. That hadn't felt right, particularly the questions that I needed to ask her. I had a flashlight and a recorder. There was no reason I couldn't replicate what the girls had done.

In the short time brushing my teeth, I talked myself into and out of and then back into trying it. I felt completely foolish even contemplating such a thing.

I flipped off the bathroom light and the main overhead light in the room, leaving on only a small bedside table lamp. The air was cool and still. The room was quiet. If there was ever a time to try it, this would be it.

I dug through my suitcase until I found my flashlight and tossed it on the bed. Then I found my small recorder. Once I had everything assembled, I sat down in the chair at the table.

"Alex," I said slowly and then stopped for a beat. "I don't know if you can hear me. I went to our old apartment tonight and spoke to Cassandra and Penny. They said that you have been interacting with them. I'm still not sure how that's possible or if I believe it. But I'm here to help find out who killed you and thought I'd try to talk to you directly. The girls told me that you said Tim didn't kill you. I'm working with him to find out who did. Can you help us?"

I glanced down at the recorder wondering if there was a response. I pointed toward the flashlight and asked her to turn it on for a yes answer. "Did Tim kill you or have anything to do with your murder?"

The flashlight remained dark. I'd listen to the recorder when I was done.

"I heard you, Alex. You said that your murder was the result of cheating uncovered." The flashlight jumped to life. I inched back from the table, cursing under my breath. "You startled me," I said with a nervous laugh and turned off the flashlight. "Do I know the person who killed you?"

The light went on as my eyes darted around the room. Goosebumps prickled my arms. I persisted.

I ran through a list of names hoping for a response but nothing happened. "Was this about cheating in a relationship?" The light remained dark. "Is it about cheating in another way?" The flashlight turned on and then slowly went dim. I picked it up and tried to click it on and nothing happened. Twice more I clicked the button to make it work. It was like the batteries had been drained in that short amount of time.

A chill ran up my spine and the air grew colder. I shivered. There was something in the room with me changing the energy. I could feel it, even though the rational side of me wanted to believe it was in my imagination. "I'll find whoever this is, Alex. I'll do my best to make sure Tim doesn't serve any more jail time for something he didn't do." In a matter of seconds, the air returned to normal and the heavy energetic feeling passed.

I was alone again.

I tentatively played the recording. All I heard was static. I wasn't sure if I was relieved or not. The flashlight still had my heart thumping.

I climbed into bed and turned off the table light. Alone in the dark, I told myself that I was perfectly safe. I closed my eyes and minutes later opened them again. I got up and went to the bathroom and plugged in the nightlight. I didn't know what a small amount of light was going to do for me, but it was comforting enough for me to drift off to sleep.

CHAPTER 21

Luke drummed his fingers on his desk while he sifted through the evidence that the crime scene techs had taken from the first and second scenes. There was nothing that stood out from Nick Day's murder outside the library. Not that he expected they'd find much evidence on the lawn. Outside scenes like that were notoriously difficult for finding evidence, especially because it was clear he hadn't been killed in that location.

Mandy's scene was nearly the opposite in every way. There were so many prints found in her apartment that it was a mountain of fingerprint files to sort through. Most taken were not in the system. Only one set of prints hit and that was an attorney with the U.S. Attorney's Office for the Eastern District of Arkansas. Luke set that aside for now because it was going to be a tricky call. The dumpster where her body was found was also a nightmare to sift through to determine what was evidence and what was simply trash.

Most difficult of all, they still didn't have a positive identification on the man found at the Old State House. He, like Mandy, had been strangled. That was why at the scene it hadn't been clear to Luke how the man had died. On a call that morning, Purvis confirmed the cause of death and that the carving on the victim's back matched the other two. That was all he was able to determine so far. The victim's prints didn't match any in the system. There were no missing person reports that matched his physical description. He was a John Doe for now.

"Luke," Captain Meadows called from his office. "I need an update about the cases."

Luke turned in the direction of his boss and gave him a thumbs-up. Captain Meadows retreated into the conference room. As he gathered his files, he asked Tyler, "Did you find anything on the surveillance?"

Tyler had spent the morning going through all the surveillance footage from the city and the bar on the night Nick was murdered. "I'm not sure yet. Take a look at this." He moved out of the way so Luke could see his laptop and then he hit play on the video.

Grainy footage showed the outside of Dugan's Pub. Nick walked out in a group of four guys. Two walked down the block to the right and one to the left, leaving Nick standing alone. He looked both ways before he crossed the street and then headed toward the parking lot directly across from the pub. Once he crossed to the other side he disappeared behind a large dark blue truck. The vantage point of the camera cut off the truck at the small door of the double cab, not allowing Luke to see the driver. A few seconds later, the truck pulled into traffic and disappeared along with Nick.

"Do you pick him up on the surveillance camera from the parking lot?"

"No," Tyler said. "Not from the camera down the street either. Unless he vanished into thin air he got into the truck and left. I tried to find the truck on other surveillance cameras but had no luck. He must have made an immediate left and gone down roads that don't have cameras. We don't have a license plate number or any identification on the driver."

"At least we have the truck."

Tyler turned his head to look at Luke. "Do we though? It could be a rental or something borrowed or stolen. We have no idea who this is. Nick could have met up with a friend and was killed sometime later."

That much was true. "We need to run it to ground," Luke said and then waited while Tyler got up and they both walked toward the conference room. He wasn't going into the meeting feeling confident. They hadn't made much progress as the body count notched up – three in two days. That wasn't a good sign of things to come.

"Any new evidence?" Captain Meadows asked as they entered the room. He was sitting at the far end of the table, looking more relaxed than his tone indicated. "We identify the John Doe yet?"

"No identification," Luke said, wishing he could give a different answer. "We don't have much in the way of new evidence either, other than one set of prints found in Mandy's apartment."

Captain Meadows hitched his chin forward. "Who is it?"

"Terry Jordan. He's with the U.S. Attorney's Office. I figured given the sensitivity of the case that I might meet with him outside of the office."

Captain Meadows shook his head. "Three homicide cases all connected. Go straight to his office. He knows something about something. We aren't in the business of cutting anyone slack."

"But what if Mandy…"

"What if Mandy was a prostitute and he was her client?" Captain Meadows asked what Luke had been thinking. "Then he committed a crime and doesn't get a pass. We aren't holding their hands, Luke. Get in there even if it makes the whole office uncomfortable."

"Will do." Luke's instinct had been to play the politics of it because in the past that's what Captain Meadows would have asked him to do. "I'll head over there as soon as we finish this meeting."

Captain Meadows turned to Tyler. "What about the surveillance?"

Tyler explained in detail the video surveillance that Luke had watched. "We don't have anything else. There were no issues with him at Dugan's Pub. I interviewed all his friends and they said Nick parked in the parking lot and was headed home. We have no reason to believe his friends had anything to do with this. They all went directly home and we have statements from their wives about the times they arrived home. All of them remained at home. We've ruled out the friends."

Captain Meadows absorbed the information without comment. "We have a press briefing this afternoon. We've gone long enough without giving a formal statement. We are going to have to say the cases are connected without talking about the carvings on the victims' backs. I don't want that out in the public yet. I'd like to keep that from the public for as long as possible."

Luke agreed he'd run point on the press briefing. He had been getting used to doing that even though it was the part of his job he hated most. There was one point they could make public. "The Old State House itself might be a connection point for all of them. Nick Day and Mandy McKee both went to events there. Nick's parents were donors. The two had met during a tour. Beth, who runs the museum, confirmed that during our interview with her. Given that meeting and the most recent victim was found there, we've been wondering what, if any, connection the facility might have to the murders."

"Anything other than what you found?"

"No. But we have employment files and I'll be exploring current and past employees for any other connections to the victims."

"Could be a coincidence," Captain Meadows said, somewhat dismissively. "Many people have toured the museum or gone to events there. I went to two last month. See if you can find any other connections but don't spend too much time on it." He waved them off to continue work on the cases. He didn't let Luke get too far though. "Luke, have you considered what we talked about a few weeks back? I'm going to need an answer soon."

Luke leaned on the doorjamb. Captain Meadows's retirement was coming fast and he had asked Luke if he'd consider taking his job as captain. "I've considered it. I'm still on the fence. A promotion and pay raise would be nice. I'm just not sure I'm cut out to sit behind a desk all day or deal with the politics of the job."

Luke had broached the subject with Riley and she told him it was entirely up to him. Financially, they were fine. She wanted him to do what he loved and he still wasn't convinced that he'd love the politics and paperwork.

Luke glanced behind him, eased the door closed, and then took a few steps back into the room. He dropped his voice low. "What about Tyler? He's been here longer than I have and he's great at what he does. He would also do a better job dealing with the higher-ups than me. The detectives respect him and he's always fair."

Captain Meadows didn't appear as disappointed as Luke assumed he'd be. "Tyler was my next choice. I agree with all the points you made, Luke. Are you sure you want to give up the promotion? Tyler is only a few years older than you. If you don't take this promotion, you'd have to transfer out of the unit for a promotion later on."

Luke had considered all of that. "I thought about that. Truthfully, I'm not cut out for administration. I love being a detective because I'm out in the field solving cases. That's where I thrive."

"You think you're going to love that another twenty years?"

Luke could retire sooner than that with a nice pension. He didn't see himself doing that though. He nodded. "It's why I became a cop. I'm doing exactly what I always wanted to do."

Captain Meadows tried one more time to convince him and, when he realized he wasn't going to be able to, said, "I'll talk to Tyler. We'll have to get you a new partner."

"We can think about that down the road."

"Let me know if you have anyone in mind."

Luke promised he would and then headed back to his desk to gather his things. Tyler was at his desk running down a few more leads. "Do you want to come to the U.S. Attorney's Office with me?"

Tyler turned his head slightly to look at Luke. "I have an interview set up with some of the Old State House staff. I figure we should clear that as quickly as possible in case it doesn't lead to anything. Divide and conquer, right?"

"Call me if you get anything," Luke said before heading out. He walked the few blocks to the office and texted Cooper on the way. He hadn't heard from him since last night and wanted to see how he was doing. Luke didn't get an answer before going through security and heading up to the office.

"I need to speak to Terry Jordan," Luke said to the young woman sitting at the front desk. She asked what it was regarding. "A case. He might have some information I need."

The woman thankfully didn't question him further. She picked up the phone, punched in some numbers, and announced him. She hung up the phone and looked at Luke. "Down the hall to the last door on the right."

She buzzed him through the secure door and he followed her directions. He got to the last door and knocked twice. A gruff male voice told him to enter.

Luke turned the knob and pushed it open. "Mr. Jordan," he said as he stepped into the man's office. Luke had been expecting someone established and middle-aged or even new and young, possibly fresh out of law school. The man behind the desk was none of those things. He was as short as he was wide and balding. What hair was left was completely white. He had age spots on his hands and a weathered look on his face. Luke would put the man's age somewhere in his sixties.

"Call me Terry. How can I help you?" he asked and waved Luke in and gestured toward the chair. Luke started to introduce himself and Terry stopped him. "I know who you are. You've got quite the reputation for solid police work."

Luke offered him an embarrassed smile. "I aim for solid police work." He sat in the chair and then said, "That's why I hope you know I'm a straight shooter. Your prints were found in the apartment of a murdered woman. I need to understand your relationship with her."

"Relationship?" Terry asked and then a flash of understanding came over his face. "Oh no, there was no relationship like that. I don't deny being in her apartment."

"You know who I'm talking about then," Luke said and Terry nodded. "How did you know her?"

Terry sat straight-faced. "I'm not sure I'm willing to give you an answer."

Luke shifted uncomfortably in his chair and tried to keep the judgment out of his tone. "Terry, we suspect that Mandy might have been working as a prostitute. If you were seeing her, I'll do my best to keep that out of my file. I need to understand your relationship with her. You might have the information I need."

Terry shook his head. "It's nothing like that. Mandy McKee was a witness for a case pending at the U.S. Attorney's Office Central District of California. I've been working in collaboration with that office for some time. That case is connected to Little Rock and several other cities."

Luke had so many questions. "How did Mandy end up here?"

"She refused witness protection until the trial was over. She was willing to move from California and we assumed that might keep her safe. That is until we realized the case had connections to Little Rock."

There was a lot to be explored but one main question was top of mind. "Were Nick Day and another man connected to those cases?"

"Nick Day is not a name I know. There were many people connected to the case. Why?"

"Because Mandy wasn't the only victim. We have clear evidence that connects her murder with two others."

Terry slumped back in his chair. Confusion fell over his face. A second later that was replaced by concern. "Then we've got a real problem on our hands. Bigger than either of us realize."

Luke's stomach dropped. "You need to start talking and don't leave anything out."

CHAPTER 22

The next morning, I dragged myself out of bed only to receive a text from Tim asking if we could meet later in the day. I allowed myself another hour of sleep and then went about my day. The first thing I wanted to do was track down Lance Donovan. After a few internet searches, it seemed he was retired and living not far from campus. I stopped for coffee and a breakfast sandwich and then made my way to his house. He lived a few blocks back from Elm Street.

From the outside, it looked like he owned one of the few remaining old single-family Victorian houses in the neighborhood. Most had been chopped up to make smaller apartments. His house looked like something out of a magazine with a wide rounded porch off to the right side, steeply pitched roof, textured shingles, and stunning oversized windows. The blue house had maroon and white accents. The pathway was clear from the sidewalk to the porch, which was good because I didn't dare step on the perfectly manicured lawn.

I walked up the steps and rang the bell. A moment later, an older man with wrinkled khakis, a ballcap, and a brown cardigan over a blue tee-shirt answered the door. "Can I help you?"

"Lance Donovan?" I asked before introducing myself.

"That's me, young lady. You're too old to be selling candy bars." There was a glint in his eyes when the corners of his mouth turned up in a laugh.

I introduced myself and asked if I could come in and speak with him. "It's about Alex McCormick."

Lance straightened his stance and frowned. "Come on in. I'd be happy to talk about Alex." As I walked into the home, which was as neatly and perfectly maintained as the outside, he got a better look at my face. "Aren't you her old roommate?"

"I am. I never had you for any classes but my understanding is that you taught Alex."

He gave a solemn nod. "It was a bit more than that." He moved past me in the foyer and asked me to follow him down the hall to the back of the house to the kitchen. It was warm and bright in blue and beige tones. It reminded me of my mother's kitchen. "Sit and let me get us some tea or coffee if you prefer."

"Tea is fine," I said as I sat. I didn't want him to go to any extra trouble considering I was there to question him about having a fling with a student and possibly being her killer. I try not to make snap judgments or underestimate people, but nothing about Lance Donovan said anything to me other than a nice old man. "You taught art history, right?"

"I taught several art history classes and was the department chair for the last fifteen years before I retired." He still had his back to me while he was fixing our tea.

"That's why I never met you. I don't think I took one art class while I was at Geneseo. I filled those requirements with theatre classes."

"You should have taken an art class," he scolded with a teasing tone to his voice. Lance finished making the tea and brought it over to the table. He refused my offer to help him. Before he sat, he went to a far cabinet and pulled down a package of cookies from the top shelf and carried them over to the table. "It's never too early for sweets," he said with a grin. "My wife is at her water aerobics class, so I have to get them in while she's gone. Otherwise, she's yelling at me for eating too much sugar. What do you want to know?"

I could have started with an accusation but that didn't feel right. "You said that your relationship with Alex was a bit more than teaching. What did you mean?"

"Oh, just that she was thinking about changing her major from teaching to art history. Alex had talked about working in a gallery or a museum." Lance sipped his tea and, if he noticed the surprise on my face, he didn't comment on it. "I know she was set on becoming a teacher. She was a senior already and had her teaching practicum lined up. She was having a late change of heart. Part of what we discussed was how much longer she'd have to stay in school to get her art history degree. Many credits would count. I think in the end, she'd have to do two more semesters and maybe some summer classes."

"Alex never told me," I said sadly. I hated that she didn't tell me much about her life. I was starting to question our friendship. "Is it fair to say that you were meeting with her a lot during that last semester of college?" I took a sip of the light berry tea and held the warm cup in my cold hands. It felt as good against my fingers as it did to drink it.

"Over the summer too," Lance said, drawing my attention. "That's when Alex first came to me about changing her major. She had taken two art history classes her junior year and then visited me during office hours asking all sorts of questions about the field – what kinds of jobs she could get and so forth. She had a keen eye and a real interest. I was happy to discuss it with her."

I stalled by taking another sip of tea. I looked at him over the rim of the cup and couldn't believe I was even going to ask the question. "Your name came up when I was interviewing someone Alex was dating. He said that Alex might have been involved with a professor. Do you know anything about that?"

Lance chuckled. "It wasn't me if that's why you're here. I was nearing fifty when I was helping Alex. I was married with kids her age. I know some of the younger professors have a hard time sorting out those kinds of interactions with their students. I've never had trouble with that. There was always a firm teacher-student line for me. I wanted to mentor but I was careful about the amount of time I spent with students and the relationship we had. I assure you there was nothing but professional mentorship involved in my interactions and conversations with Alex. I wasn't aware of any relationships she had either with students or professors. We didn't discuss personal things."

There was a straight-forward honesty to his tone. "As you might have read, Tim, Alex's boyfriend at the time, was convicted of the murder but was recently released on an appeal. I'm investigating the case. I don't believe that Tim is guilty of anything."

Lance agreed. "A lot of the Geneseo community found that hard to believe. I never taught Tim, but I had colleagues who did. They couldn't believe he was the one responsible. Did you get my name from him?"

"No," I said with a sigh. "It was someone else. I'm learning that Alex had many secrets I didn't know. She was cheating on Tim with someone else and that's who mentioned your name. There was no confirmation that he witnessed anything but chalked it up to a rumor."

"Those happen sometimes," he said with a wry chuckle. "It's true I was spending a good deal of time with Alex. I was helping her sort out what she wanted to do with the rest of her life, which if you remember back then for yourself was daunting. Those decisions aren't easy to make." Lance grew quiet for a moment. "You said you are learning about secrets Alex had. Did you know that she was concerned about someone cheating on tests in her education classes?"

I lurched forward at the word *cheating*. "She never told me anything like that."

Lance took another sip of tea and then grabbed a cookie, making me wait far too long for him to fill in the details. After he finished, he looked over at me. "As you know, Geneseo was originally a teaching college. It started as Wadsworth Normal and Training School, which issued state-certified teaching credentials. As a result, the education department was highly competitive not just to students in New York State looking to become teachers. We had students coming from out of state as well. Any accusation of cheating is taken seriously. If she went forward, Alex would have been leveling a serious accusation."

This was all news to me. "Do you know who Alex suspected of cheating?"

"She wouldn't tell me. She said that she was still trying to get evidence." Lance locked his gaze on me. "Riley, she brought it up in conversation to ask me what she should do. The most frustrating part was that Alex refused to tell me if it was a student who was getting an education degree or someone just taking classes. Every time I asked a question to try to gather more information, she shut me down. I went to the head of the education department to ask what I should do. I didn't want to tell them it was Alex because I didn't want to put her on the spot like that but the allegations were serious."

It was something that would have ended the student's academic career. There was a lot at stake. *Was it worth murder?* "Do you know if it was ever resolved?"

"The secret died with Alex," Lance said and studied my face. "Are you sure she never told you anything about this?"

"Nothing. I swear to you," I said with emphasis. "I never took any education classes, so I couldn't even venture a guess who it might have been." Even though that's what I said, two people came to mind. Gail and Michelle had been education majors with Alex. Both had lied to me recently.

Lance sat back in the chair. "I always wondered if that had something to do with her death. You're right that Alex had a lot of secrets. Was

Tim an education major?"

I shook my head. "He was a history major. He and I had a few classes together. I know for a fact that none of Tim's classes overlapped with Alex's. Did you ever go to the cops after Alex was murdered?"

"I tried but they didn't want to hear from me." Lance took a deep breath in and then sighed it out. He sipped his tea. "I've always felt like there was a huge miscarriage of justice on this case. Not only with Tim going to prison for something he didn't do. Alex never got justice. Her case was never solved and her murderer is out there running free."

I wasn't sure what to ask him at that point. I had no reason to suspect him. We sat there chatting like old friends eating cookies and drinking our tea. Before I got ready to leave, I asked one more question that came to mind. "Did Alex ever mention Griffin Lyons or Jason Thatcher to you?"

Lance paused and gave it some thought. "Do you mean Jason Thatcher the hockey player and one-time coach here?"

I confirmed that's who I meant. "His name came up during my investigation, but I'm unsure of his connection to Alex."

Lance put a hand to his forehead. "My memory isn't what it used to be. I haven't thought about this in years."

"That's okay. Take your time," I assured him that we were in no rush.

Lance spoke slowly as if he was putting the memory together piece by piece. "There was one day when Alex was in my office and we were looking at grad school requirements. I remember we had master's program brochures laid out on my desk and a guy came to the door looking for Alex. He was quite angry. I can't remember why – something about being late to meet him or she didn't call him back. He was so angry that he shoved brochures off the desk and became so belligerent that I kicked him out of the office and told him not to return. When I asked Alex what that was about, she said that she was late getting her half of a project done for a group project. She joked that he was type-A and that he was difficult to work with in the group. She even joked that's how education students were and one of the reasons why she didn't want to continue in the program. She couldn't work in a school full of teachers like him. I assured her from an education standpoint that wasn't the case. I don't think she was being serious. It was clear his anger caught her off guard and she was trying to make light of it."

"Do you remember his name?"

"I didn't know it at the time. I never followed hockey and he hadn't taken any classes with me. I forgot the incident soon after it happened. I do believe though Alex called him Jay. She said, 'Come on, Jay. This isn't that big of a deal.' That's when he went off and yelled at her and knocked the brochures off my desk." Lance shook his head in uncertainty. "I can't be sure that was Jason Thatcher. I didn't know the young man then. I can tell you that Jason Thatcher, the hockey coach, had a violent temper and that's one of the reasons he was fired. There was an incident with a player in the locker room. We don't tolerate that kind of thing here."

"He was fired? Didn't he take a job at a high school as the head coach?"

"That I don't know."

"I appreciate everything you've told me," I said, standing and bringing the tea cups to the sink and tucking the cookies back in the cabinet. I ran some water over the cups and turned back to Lance. "I wish I had taken some art history classes. Are you still teaching?"

Lance turned in the chair and thanked me for clearing the table. "I give a guest lecture now and then. I'm mostly retired. I think you ended up right where you were supposed to be, Riley. I hope you'll be able to solve the case. I'd hate to see Tim go back to prison."

The way he spoke about him made me question how well he knew him. "You asked me if Tim was an education major. Did you know him? You seem to have a real attachment to the outcome of his case."

"I suppose I do," Lance admitted, standing. He shoved his hands in his pockets. "It's not so much about Tim as it is Alex for me. She was an exceptional young woman and I never quite got over her murder. None of us in the community did. Those of us still around are still shocked by it all these years later. Nothing like that happens in this quiet little village. As I said, those who knew Tim couldn't believe he'd do something like that. I guess they have convinced me."

"Is there anyone else you think I should speak to while I'm here?"

"Have you spoken to Mary Maguire? She taught American history while you were here. She lives across the street and two down from where you and Alex lived on Elm Street. I know she tried to speak to the police about that night but they didn't take a statement. She was very frustrated that they wouldn't listen to what she had to say."

I knew her well. "What did she see?"

"It's better to let her tell you," he said and then thanked me for taking the case.

It was off to Mary Maguire's next.

CHAPTER 23

Cooper had been hunched over his laptop all morning going over the case files that his investigators had submitted. Not that Cooper liked doing paperwork, but he was happy that his business was growing and that he finally had some work he could do.

The only noise all day was the heater that occasionally kicked on and off. It was the sound of the heater that masked the initial jiggle of the front door. Cooper almost missed it. He glanced at the clock on his computer and assumed that Adele was home from work early. He started to call her name when the door thumped loudly once and then twice as if someone thrashed against it.

Long ago, Cooper had installed a security camera outside the front door. The building security didn't always have their cameras on and, in his line of work, he wasn't going to take any chances. Before grabbing for the phone and checking his security app, Cooper got up from the chair and moved as quickly as he could to his bedroom where he kept his Glock. He checked to make sure that it was fully loaded, unlatched the safety, and headed back to the front door.

The person on the other side had stopped thrashing against it but was now trying the doorknob again. Even if they were able to pick that lock, he had a second deadbolt only accessible from the inside. No one was getting inside his home unless they were invited.

Cooper kept the gun in one hand while he thumbed open the app. He clicked two buttons and engaged the video of the security camera. Cooper sucked in a sharp breath when he saw who was on the other side. It was the same man he had seen with Mandy days earlier. Sonny was the name he was given by Nora, the downstairs neighbor. Luke still hadn't had any luck identifying him beyond the first name.

Sonny had on a dark jacket, a wool hat pulled low on his head, and black driving gloves. He also had lockpick tools in his hand. Cooper stepped away from the door and quietly called the police. If he could engage the man long enough, the cops might make it there in time. The only caveat was that Cooper couldn't open the door and confront him. In his physical condition, he was no match in a fight. Unless he planned to kill the man, there wasn't much Cooper was able to do and that enraged him.

The 911 operator explained that the cops would be there soon. Cooper begged her to tell them not to put on their sirens. She assured him they wouldn't. She asked to remain on the line with him, but Cooper declined.

Sonny tried one more time to use his weight to force the door open. Again, he got nowhere. By the look on his face, he was close to giving up.

Cooper had no choice but to keep him engaged. "What do you want?" he yelled through the door as he watched the man's reaction on the app.

Sonny looked up at the ceiling and around the hallway to try to look for the camera. Cooper had it well hidden because he wasn't allowed to have it in the building. He had done a good enough job that Sonny didn't find it. Finally, he stared right at the door. "I want to talk."

Cooper knew nothing the man wanted included talking. "Talking doesn't include knocking my door down or using a lockpick to break in. I can see everything you're doing."

Sonny narrowed his eyes, cursed, and kicked the door twice. He slammed his fist into it. "Open the door! I know you were watching Mandy. I saw you!"

As much as Cooper wanted to admit it and ask what he did to her, he didn't. He'd pull him in more first. "I don't know what you're talking about."

"Yes, you do! I saw you through her window. You don't know what you saw. You got it all wrong."

"What did I get wrong?" Cooper asked, not admitting anything one way or the other.

"Let me in and we can talk about it."

"That's not going to happen. If you have anything to say, say it through the door." Cooper's heart raced and he checked the phone for the time. He didn't know why the cops were taking so long or how much longer he could keep Sonny at the door. "What is it you think I saw?"

Sonny paced a small circle around the hallway, muttering and cursing to himself.

"This is important to you. Important enough that you'd try to break into a stranger's home. What do you think I saw?" he asked again.

That question was met with silence.

Cooper wasn't sure if Sonny even knew his name or had only figured out what condo he was in because he had seen him looking through the window. "This is getting us nowhere. What's your name?"

Still, no response. Frustrated, Sonny pounded his fist against the door again. "If you don't let me in, I'll be back. I need to make you understand and I might not be so forgiving next time."

"If there is something you need to clear up, do it now. If you come back, next time you won't be so lucky," Cooper cautioned him. "I'm armed and have no problem using it."

Sonny stopped pacing and stared at the door. He took a step back, seeming to recalculate his choices. "I didn't kill her!" he shouted and punched the door. "I swear to you I didn't kill her. When I left her apartment, she was alive."

Cooper didn't believe him. "Why would I think you killed her?"

"We fought, okay? I tore up her place and then I went after her to her bedroom. I even got right in her face and yelled at her. That's when I saw you. We both know I closed the blinds and hours later her body was found in the dumpster behind her building." He smacked at the door. "I didn't kill her. We got over the fight and then I left. Mandy was alive when I left. I swear to you she was alive." He punctuated each word.

"Then what are you doing here?"

"I thought you recorded what you saw. I wanted to get it so you couldn't give it to the cops because I didn't kill her."

"Don't you think if I had recorded it, I would have already given it to the cops when Mandy's body was found?" Cooper asked, wondering about the intelligence level of the guy.

"I don't know what to do. The cops are looking for me."

"Sounds easy enough to me. Turn yourself in. If you didn't do anything wrong, explain what happened. Call Det. Luke Morgan. He'll be able to help you out. He's handling the case. I know him and he's more than fair."

"I can't go to the cops!" Sonny kicked the door again, this time harder.

"Knock it off!" Cooper yelled back as frustrated with Sonny's rage as he was that the cops still hadn't arrived. "Calm down and talk to me. If you didn't kill Mandy, then someone else did. Do you have any idea who might have done that?"

"No," Sonny said with resignation in his voice.

Cooper was starting to wonder if this guy wasn't as tough as he tried to appear. He still wasn't going to open the door and test his theory.

"It's possible you know something without realizing it. If you speak to Det. Morgan, he might be able to jog your memory. Running from the cops isn't going to help you."

Sonny backed away from the door and leaned against the wall. "I can't turn myself in."

"You're not turning yourself in. You're going to the police department to discuss what you know." There was no way Cooper was going to let on that the cops didn't even know the guy's name. "If you care about Mandy as much as it sounds like you do, then you owe it to her to try to help the police figure out who killed her. If you do that, the cops will stop wasting their time going after you." Cooper could tell by Sonny's expression that he was wearing him down.

Sirens wailed off in the distance. Sonny pushed himself from the wall. "You called the cops on me?" Oddly, there was betrayal in his voice.

"I didn't call anyone," Cooper lied as his heart started to race harder than before. He heard the thumping through his ears. If Sonny got away now who knows if they'd ever find him again. Cooper tried stalling. "There are always sirens in the city. It's probably some robbery..." He didn't get to finish his thought.

Sonny disappeared down the hall. Cooper could only assume that he'd be gone by the time the cops arrived. He had a clear shot of him on video surveillance, but that wasn't enough. With his gun by his side, Cooper unlocked the bolt locks and pulled the door open. He shouted down the hallway for Sonny. No response.

Cooper closed his door behind him and went down the hallway slowly, waiting for him or the cops to appear. He got to the elevators and looked left and right. There was no one there. Cooper hit the elevator button and waited. It seemed to be taking longer than normal. Cooper wished he could race down the stairs but that wasn't going to be possible with his injury. He had no choice but to wait.

Finally, the doors glided open and revealed two uniformed cops inside.

"What took you so long?" Cooper barked. He didn't recognize the officers. They clocked his gun and put their hands on theirs. Cooper quickly identified himself. "I'm the one who called you. I have the guy on surveillance video. I was going after him since you hadn't arrived."

The cops seemed unsure. "We need your identification," one of the cops said with uncertainty in his voice.

"Don't you want to go search for him? He couldn't have gotten far." Cooper explained what Sonny looked like and asked if they had seen him in the lobby. They hadn't. "Could one of you go search while I show the other my identification and the surveillance video?"

"Put the gun on the ground and step away from it." The bigger of the two cops gestured for Cooper to step back. They were holding up the elevator. Cooper did as they asked and they stepped off into the hallway.

Cooper pulled his wallet from his back pocket and showed him his private investigator credentials. "I'm friends with Det. Morgan," Cooper added. The cops allowed him to pick his gun up from the floor.

The bigger cop said, "We'll all go back to your place. That guy is long gone now. We can take an incident report. Did he break in? Steal anything?"

Cooper let out a frustrated sigh. He hated being at the mercy of anyone. He had no choice but to give in to what they wanted. "Fine," he said, his voice full of unspoken frustration.

Once inside his condo, Cooper placed his gun on the kitchen counter and grabbed his phone. Cooper showed them the video of the entire exchange with Sonny.

Once the cops took the report and Cooper promised to email a copy of the video, they left. Cooper stood in the middle of the living room wondering what he should do. He couldn't sit back down at his desk and go back to work like nothing had happened. He was too amped up and wanted badly to get out on the street and look for Sonny, even though rationally Cooper knew he'd probably never find him.

Cooper grabbed his gun, wallet, phone, and keys and headed for the door. He stopped long enough to text Luke what had happened. He explained that he was going for a walk but could be reached whenever Luke was available. The doctor said he should get some exercise. At least, that's what Cooper justified to himself as he headed for the elevator.

An hour later, with his side knotting in pain, Cooper arrived at Adele's law practice. He hadn't found any sign of Sonny and Luke hadn't called him back yet. All he wanted to do was hug his wife and see her for a few minutes. More than anything, he wanted to debrief what had happened with Sonny.

Cooper would have to wait to see Adele. Her receptionist said she was in with a client but should be done soon. Cooper made his way to the small kitchen in the back and waited. He sent Luke another text and then called Captain Meadows. He left him a message and updated him about Sonny's arrival at his door.

As he was finishing the message, Adele's voice drifted down the hallway as she promised her client that everything would be okay. The client responded with relief. Cooper heard the familiar voice before he saw him and it launched him from his seat. He made it to the hall in enough time to stop them dead in their tracks.

"What are you doing here?" Cooper snarled, reaching for Adele and pulling her away from Sonny.

Startled, Adele wriggled lose from Cooper's grasp. She put her hands on his chest and pushed him back, glaring at him. "What do you think *you're* doing? Go in my office and wait for me."

Adele turned back to Sonny. "I'm so sorry about this. My husband can be a bit overprotective."

Sonny looked between the two of them and swallowed hard. "You're married to him?"

"I hope that's not going to be a problem," she said calmly.

"It's a huge problem," Cooper and Sonny said in unison.

Sonny tried to move past Adele but only made it a few feet. Cooper blocked his path. He looked around Sonny and spoke directly to Adele. "This is the man I saw kill Mandy McKee."

Adele's eyes got wide. "I had…" She couldn't finish her thought.

Cooper grabbed Sonny by the front of the shirt. "You're not going anywhere."

CHAPTER 24

Luke sat in the conference room at the police station with Det. Tyler and Captain Meadows. The door was closed and they sat at the far end of the room out of earshot from any of the other detectives. What Luke had learned at the U.S. Attorney's Office was not for public consumption. The only thing he could do was bring the information back to his team and strategize.

Tyler didn't look happy. "You called me in from the field, so this better be important. What did you find out, Luke?"

"We had everything wrong," he admitted, sitting back in the chair. He glanced over at the board they had created with information about each victim. He had missed so much. Luke turned back to his partner and boss. "I still don't know how Nick Day or John Doe fit into this. Mandy McKee was a witness for federal prosecution against the Andino family. She worked at a bank in Los Angeles and noticed some discrepancies with an account. They were depositing large amounts of money and then moving it from account to account, some off-shore accounts at other banks. The family only dealt with the president of the bank and there was never any reporting to the Internal Revenue Service as there should have been with those large deposits.

"Mandy started exploring internally what was going on and stumbled across the truth. It turned out the bank president was on their payroll and was money laundering for this family. She took the information to the FBI and an investigation was opened. They kept her name confidential for now, but the amount of information she was able to uncover about their financial crimes was staggering. She refused witness protection but did allow them to move her here to Little Rock to keep her safe. She quietly resigned from her job in Los Angeles and said she was moving with her boyfriend. She didn't think anyone even suspected she had uncovered anything."

"What about the men in and out of her place?"

"I'm getting to that," Luke said. "Terry Jordan had been working in collaboration with the office in Los Angeles. They had identified criminal ties here in Little Rock. The Andinos run guns and drugs across the country. There were networks of people connected to this family in cities across the United States, some of them here in Little Rock. Mandy had done such a good job of uncovering past crimes, she begged to help more. She was working with Terry. Mandy said she was willing to try to get more information. She had a strong foundation in the case already because of what she initially uncovered. She knew how this family worked. It was dangerous but she was determined."

"She brought them to her home?" Tyler asked.

Luke held his hand up. "I know. It wasn't smart of her to do. Terry hadn't realized that until recently. The FBI was using her as an informant. I can't believe they didn't caution her better."

"Not a prostitute then?" Captain Meadows said with confusion in his tone.

"Nothing of the sort." Luke recalled Terry telling him where the confusion had been and he could hardly believe what he heard. "About two weeks ago, Mandy noticed Cooper watching her. She didn't know who he was and, once they learned he was a private investigator, they got spooked thinking he might work for the Andinos. She started bringing the people she met back to her bedroom to discuss things.

She figured she always kept her drapes closed and Cooper wouldn't suspect. Terry didn't want her to change her routine until she threw Cooper off her trail. If she started closing her living room drapes, it might set off suspicion. She figured Cooper might just assume they were her lovers. After that, Terry wanted her to change how she met with them."

Tyler whistled loudly. "That's a lot to take in. How does Sonny factor into this?"

"Terry believes Sonny is the boyfriend she left behind in Los Angeles. To keep him safe, she couldn't tell him what she was doing. The guy had a temper which is what Cooper saw. Terry believed that Sonny had killed her. Mandy had told him that Sonny had shown up and was demanding answers for why she left her high-paying Los Angeles job to come to Little Rock. She had no real answer to give him because she couldn't tell him the truth."

Captain Meadows drummed his fingers on the table. "Is it possible Mandy confided in Sonny once he arrived here?"

Luke thought it was possible. Terry didn't share the same opinion. "Mandy assured Terry she hadn't. He said she was smarter than that. But whoever killed Mandy took some of the recorded evidence she hadn't handed in. He suspected Sonny found the recorder and got curious. Terry wants that information. He *needs* that evidence."

Tyler gestured with his hand. "It's not like we have any idea who Sonny is or where he can be found. Did Terry have a last name or know anything about this guy?"

"No," Luke said with a shake of his head. "Mandy only referred to him as Sonny. She said she ended the relationship in Los Angeles and she wasn't even sure how he found her."

Tyler didn't understand the same thing Luke had asked during the meeting. "If Sonny found her, isn't it reasonable to think that the Andino family could find her too?"

"Terry didn't think so because no arrests have been made yet. There'd be no reason for the Andino family to connect Mandy to an investigation because they don't know an investigation is happening. None of the low-level guys here in Little Rock had ever heard of the Andinos. It was a wide and deep network. Mandy was helping to gather the information that would hopefully connect back to the Andinos. They were hoping to flip a few along the way."

"No arrests have been made yet?" Captain Meadows asked and Luke confirmed. "The U.S. Attorney's Office is working with the FBI before any arrests are made?"

"That's what Terry said. He wouldn't share the full scope of the investigation with me."

Captain Meadows said, "I didn't think he would. The feds like to keep things close to the vest, especially an ongoing investigation. When you told Terry you believed Mandy's death was connected to two others, did he have any response?"

"He didn't believe me at first. He said it had to be a mistake. Terry truly believed that Sonny had killed her. They were scrambling to replace her and figure out how to keep the investigation going here. Mandy had gotten in deep and was getting them some good information." Luke recalled the horror on the man's face when he told him about the carvings. He relayed that to Tyler and Captain Meadows. "With that information, Terry became convinced that the Andino family must have figured it out. He said a carving like that sounds like their particular brand of brutality."

"What a mess," Tyler said, stretching his arms over his head. "Did Terry have any suspects in mind?"

"Basil Andino. He's the oldest son of the main boss. He also has a violent temper but is known to be a bit obsessive-compulsive, which would account for the precise measured carving. Terry is going to contact the FBI to find out if they have eyes on Basil. We have a name now so we don't need to wait. We can run our investigation."

Captain Meadows and Tyler agreed with that. They were also relieved that the case finally made some sense. Captain Meadows only had one question for now. "Do we know if or how the Old State House factors into the murders?"

Tyler explained, "No connection so far. Seems like it might just be a coincidence like you said initially. We need an identification on the John Doe and figure out how Nick Day fits into all of this."

"I think I might know," Luke said and then recalled Jimmy Day's criminal history. "I guess that Jimmy is in deep with someone connected to the Andinos and maybe they think he was going to flip. We've not been able to reach him to see if he knew Mandy. I need to focus on that today."

The conference room door opened and Cooper stood on the other side. His red face beat like a pulse. Beads of sweat dropped from his forehead. Luke stood from the table worried he might keel over. "Cooper, are you okay?" Luke asked, knowing full well that his friend wasn't okay.

"I found him. I found Sonny," Cooper said, moving quickly into the conference room. He held his side and winced in pain as he walked to the table. He leaned on the back of the chair as he caught his breath and explained how Sonny had shown up at his condo to confront him and, upon fleeing Cooper's, went to the nearest criminal defense lawyer he could find, which happened to be Adele. "Sonny decided to come to the police station to speak to you but he didn't want to do that without an attorney present. I can't say for certain that he killed her, Luke. Maybe I didn't see what I thought."

Luke knew that was true in several instances. "Where is he now?"

"With Adele in one of the interrogation rooms."

"Sit down, Cooper, before you fall. You look like you ran here," Captain Meadows said and Cooper gratefully pulled out a chair and sat. "He didn't hurt you, did he?"

"I'm fine. It took the cops too long to get to my condo and I specifically asked them not to turn on their sirens. Sonny heard them coming and took off. It was a good thing he wanted to come in and talk." Cooper looked to Captain Meadows and then to Tyler and Luke.

Luke didn't want to chastise the cops. He had no idea what they were faced with earlier today. Instead, he focused on praising his friend. "We are grateful that whatever you said got him here. I'll go interview him now and see what we can find out."

Luke left Cooper there and made his way down the hall checking each interrogation room until he found the right one. He pushed open the door wider, said hello to Adele, and then introduced himself to Sonny.

As Luke sat, Adele explained, "My client, Sonny Ramono, came in today voluntarily to discuss the murder of Mandy McKee. Sonny had nothing to do with it. We are willing to let you interview him with me present."

Luke nodded his head. "I'm fine with that." He turned his attention to Sonny. "How did you know Mandy?"

Sonny didn't look ready to talk. He turned to Adele and she urged him on. He leaned his arms on the table and focused back on Luke. "Mandy was my girlfriend until she left. She gave me no explanation for why she was ending the relationship or even where she went. There are people worried about her back in Los Angeles. It took me a while to track her down. I was hoping she'd explain what happened or come back with me."

It was exactly like Terry had told him. "What happened when you found her?"

"She was angry. Angrier than I'd ever seen her. Mandy used to be so even-tempered. When I showed up, she was ready to rip off my head," Sonny said with an expression of shock to drive home the point. "It was like nothing I'd ever seen. We'd been together for two years. I couldn't walk away like that. I hung around for two weeks trying to convince her."

"There was arguing?"

"Lots of arguing. Fighting and yelling. I wasn't going back to Los Angeles without her." Sonny put his hands in the air as if to surrender. "I swear to you I never laid a hand on her. You can say my behavior was over the top or even stalkerish. I felt foolish coming all the way here and trying to convince her to come home. Something had changed and I was worried about her."

"Were you only worried because she ended the relationship abruptly? Women can do that. It's possible she wanted to leave for a long time and hadn't told you."

Sonny slammed his fist down on the table, making Luke and Adele jerk forward in their chairs. "It wasn't like that. We were talking about getting married one day and the next she says she's leaving and moving and won't tell me where she's going. She was getting strange late-night phone calls and not the kind that made me think she was cheating. The kind that made me think she was in some kind of trouble."

Luke sat up a little straighter at that. "What exactly did you hear?"

"There was talk about money." Sonny shook his head in confusion. "None of it made any sense to me. At first, I thought she had done something wrong at work because she worked at a bank. Then I came to realize that she had caught someone doing something wrong. After she left, it occurred to me that maybe she was running away because someone was after her. That's why it was so important for me to find her. I thought I could keep her safe."

"What happened the last day in her apartment?"

Sonny looked at Adele. She told him to continue and he focused back on Luke. "We had another fight. She didn't want me to come over and I called her that morning and told her to stay home from work.

That if she talked to me, I'd leave. When I got there, she wouldn't listen. She said she had to be there for work. She said it was over and I lost it. I smashed things and scared her. I felt horrible about it and went to her room. She got on her bed and I climbed on top of her and yelled right in her face. I'm not proud of it, but when she started to cry I stopped and got off her. That's when I saw Cooper watching me."

"What happened after that?"

"We made up and I told her that I was leaving and wouldn't bother her anymore. She had an old suitcase by the door and she asked me to take it to the trash for her. I had her code to the back elevator and I took it down and left." Emotion filled his voice and he turned his head from Luke. "I couldn't keep her safe. I don't know what she was involved in but whatever it was got her killed. The same with those other guys who visited her last week."

"What other guys?" Luke asked, inching to the edge of his seat.

"The dead guys," Sonny said evenly, looking at Luke like he couldn't believe he didn't catch what he was saying. "I saw the morning news with the composite sketch of John Doe. That guy and Nick Day, the other victim, were at Mandy's last week."

Luke couldn't believe what he was hearing. "You know that for a fact?"

"Yeah. I don't know who John Doe is but I saw him there with my own eyes. Both times I showed up when they were leaving. Mandy wouldn't explain who they were."

Luke wanted to get up and rush out of the room. There were just too many questions he had left for Sonny. Patience would have to win out.

CHAPTER 25

Mary Maguire wasn't home when I went to see her. I waited a few minutes outside her house and then left and went to Mama Mia's for a slice of pizza. It was as good a place as any to wait. I texted Cooper and Luke earlier that morning to see how the cases were going. There had been no response from either yet. My mother and I texted back and forth while I ate.

After lunch, I met Tim and gave him another brief update. I could tell by his tone and the way he fidgeted that he was worried about how all of it was going. I assured him the case would come together. I was sure he didn't like hearing investigations couldn't be rushed. He should have known that, since it was a rushed investigation that landed him in prison.

After spending time with Tim, I made my way back to Elm Street. This time, there was a car in Mary's driveway and a dog running circles out front. I didn't know what kind of dog but she was small, white, and fluffy. As soon as she spotted me on the sidewalk, she let out three loud yips. I tried to sweet talk her but she wasn't having any of it.

Her bark grew louder as I stepped onto the driveway and made my way to the front porch. After a few sniffs and a head scratch, she sat back and determined I was no threat. She went back to running circles.

"She's not very scary is she," Mary said from the doorway. She had the same bob haircut as she did when I had taken two of her classes. Her blond hair was now more of a silvery gray and she had wrinkles around her eyes she didn't have then. She still had a rosy glow about her cheeks and an easy relaxed smile as if she didn't have a care in the world.

"I'm not sure if you remember me," I started to say as I walked toward the porch.

"Riley, I remember," she said, opening the screen door and stepping outside. "I always thought you should have majored in American history. You were good at it. What did you end up doing?"

I was surprised she remembered me after so many years and the countless students she taught since I was in her class. I loved American history and sat in the front row of her classes and could have listened to her lectures for hours. I always stayed after class to ask questions, so my pestering might have made me memorable. "Journalist turned private investigator. It's funny, I always thought if I wasn't doing that, I wouldn't have minded teaching history."

"You would have been good at it. What brings you by?"

I had assumed Lance would have called her. She didn't seem to know though. "I met with Lance Donovan earlier today. I'm investigating Alex's murder. Lance said you witnessed something but that the cops didn't want to take your statement. I thought you might be able to tell me."

Mary frowned and nodded. "You were her roommate. I remember you both living right over there. It must have been so difficult for you."

"It was then and it is now," I admitted. "I'm finding that Alex kept a lot of secrets from everyone including me."

Mary opened the door and gestured for me to follow. "I didn't know Alex well. I didn't teach her. She'd wave if she saw me in the yard. What I know might not help you find the killer but it should exonerate

Tim. I tried telling the cops and they didn't listen. Neither did the prosecutor's office or Tim's defense attorney. All of them said what I saw wasn't enough."

I thanked her for being willing to speak to me as I followed her into the house. She offered me snacks and coffee but I declined. I was full from lunch. We sat at the kitchen table and just as I remembered her, Mary got straight to the point.

"I saw Tim that night," Mary said with her eyes wide remembering. "He never went into the apartment."

"You saw him the whole time?" I asked, hardly able to believe what I was hearing.

"It might be helpful if I start from the beginning," Mary said, gesturing as she spoke. "I had family in town that weekend for the holiday. We got home that Saturday night and I saw a young man going into the house where you lived. It gave me pause because it was Thanksgiving break and I knew you had gone home for break. I wasn't sure who else had remained that weekend. The street was quiet and I had never seen him at your house before, so it registered with me. I don't know why with all the kids coming and going. That night though, maybe because it was so quiet, it made me stop and watch."

I stopped her. "Did you know him?"

"Sure," she said with an enthusiastic nod of her head. "It was Jason Thatcher. I had watched enough Geneseo hockey games to know him and he'd been in one of my classes the previous year."

Finally, a confirmation about who Alex was with that night. "Until your statement, I had not been able to identify who was with Alex that night, so your statement is incredibly helpful. Did you happen to notice the time?"

"No. I was with family and wasn't paying that much attention."

"Did the police even speak to Jason Thatcher?"

"I don't know. I told them he was there and they said they'd look into it. His father is well-connected. He was involved in county politics at some point. If they spoke to him, they cleared him quickly. His name has never been connected to the investigation."

I would need to speak with Jason Thatcher. "Did you see anything else that night?"

"A lot more," she said, focusing on me. "Later that same night, I had to run back out to the car and that's when I saw Tim standing under the tree staring up at the house. I knew him well enough. He'd taken a few classes with me. I called over to say hello, but I don't think he heard me. He didn't turn around and look at me or acknowledge me. It was like he was in a trance staring up at the window. I couldn't see what he was looking at but I knew Jason had gone up there earlier. I wondered if he was seeing Alex with another guy. I didn't know what to do. We try not to get too involved in the lives of our students. I saw them together enough to know that he was probably dating Alex. I didn't know the status of things."

I barely knew the status of things between Alex and Tim. It made sense that a professor wouldn't. "What happened then?"

"There was something about the way Tim was standing there. I couldn't stop watching him watch your apartment. He was there when I walked outside and I probably watched him for ten minutes. But he never went inside. He turned and left, walking up the street and then turned as if he were heading toward Main Street." She paused for a beat and then added, "That wasn't all I saw."

"What else did you see?" I urged, sitting on the edge of my seat.

"There was a car down the street in the opposite direction Tim walked. They waited until he got down the block and then turned their lights on and drove away. I wasn't able to see who was behind the wheel. I saw that same car probably an hour later parked next door to your apartment. By morning, when I looked again, that car was gone."

I wasn't sure of the relevance. "Do you think that car is connected to Alex's murder?"

"I do," she said, nodding her head enthusiastically again. "I can't say for certain why I feel that way. It was like whoever was in the car was watching Tim, and when he left, so did they." Mary paused for a moment and collected her thoughts. "It's possible they weren't watching Tim but watching your apartment. They could have been watching Alex. I don't know what they were doing. It gave me a creepy vibe. I'm sure that sounds silly and not much you can do with that. It's why the cops didn't take it seriously. They said that Tim could have left and come back and I wouldn't have known the difference. I don't think Tim came back."

Neither did I. "Tim's story matches yours, except for the other car. He admitted to being at the apartment and standing at the window. He saw Alex with another guy. Don't discount your creepy vibe. Intuition is a real thing and, if you got the sense they were up to no good, then you are probably right. What can you tell me about the car?"

"I didn't get the license plate. I didn't think to do that. It was a small four-door black car. A Honda Civic, I think. If not that, then something like it. There was a distinctive sticker on the back window. It was a bright yellow and red sun decal. The sun had a face and wild rays off of it."

I knew I had seen that sticker someplace. I might have even owned one. Stickers like that weren't uncommon when I was going to college. They were also sold at our hippy-run local bookstore. It was a lead, even if I couldn't do much with it right now.

"Is there anything else you can think of about that night?"

"That's about it," Mary said with a forlorn look on her face. "I tried, Riley, I did. I went to the cops before they arrested Tim and again after. I tried to get them to listen. They had their minds made up."

I put my hand on top of hers. "At least you tried. I didn't even do that. I moved back into our apartment and finished out my senior year. I tried to act like it hadn't happened because I didn't know what else to do. I knew how tumultuous the relationship was between Alex and Tim. I had a hard time believing he could have killed her. I trusted the cops had done a good investigation and found the right person. I feel terrible now."

"You were young, Riley. There wasn't much you could do," Mary said with sadness in her voice. "It was a terrible thing that happened to Alex and it was a terrible miscarriage of justice for Tim. You're going to right the wrong."

I hoped she was right. "I'm certainly going to do my best."

Mary turned my hand over and saw my engagement and wedding rings. "How does your family feel about you being an investigator? I'm sure that it can get scary and even violent at times."

"I'm safe and my husband, Luke, is a homicide detective. My business partner, Cooper, is Luke's best friend. My mother has come around to the idea. She wasn't supportive at first, but then she saw the cases I solved and recognized that it was important work. Her husband is a homicide detective turned private investigator, so it kind of runs in the family."

Mary sat back and appraised me. "That must mean you are good at what you do. Don't forget that when you're out there trying to solve this case," she said with a wink.

That's why I loved Mary's classes. She had a way of recognizing when I was struggling and, in a few words, could give me the confidence boost I needed. "You seem to have good intuition. Who do you think killed Alex?" When I noticed Mary hesitate, I nudged her. "You're allowed to speculate. I'm not a cop. I can't make an arrest or do anything without evidence. Even if you accuse someone and you're wrong, nothing bad will happen."

"I know in my heart it wasn't Tim," Mary said with a renewed strength in her tone. "I don't even have a question about that. I know it wasn't him. No matter what the cops said, he did not come back that night. If you could have seen the dejected way he walked off. That wasn't a man enraged. That was a man who was broken and sad. Jason has a temper. He did then and he does now as an adult. I would not be surprised if it was him. That said, that car has always bothered me. If you're asking me seriously who did this, I think whoever was in that car might be the key to all of this."

I had a feeling that's what Mary was going to say by how she had initially talked about the car. "I'm going to focus on that right after I interview Jason," I told her as I stood from the table and thanked her.

"If he's not at home, you can find him at the ice rink up the road. I heard after he left Geneseo he started playing for a local men's league. I don't know if he's found another job, but I heard he can be found at the local rink most days."

I walked to the front door with her. Before I left, she gave me a quick hug and said, "I'm sure you'll solve this. You're welcome to come back if you need anything else."

I got outside and Mary closed the door behind me. I walked down her driveway and stopped at the point where her car might have been parked that night. She had a good vantage point to our apartment and to the corner where Tim turned toward Main Street.

I knew in my gut too that what Mary saw was the key to all of this.

CHAPTER 26

Luke made it to the final moments of the press conference when a reporter in the back called out one last question. "Can you confirm that the John Doe is Mitch Katz?"

Luke stepped back from the podium and looked at Det. Tyler and then over at Captain Meadows. Both shook their heads. That wasn't a name they knew. He stepped back to the microphone. "As we said earlier in the press conference, we are still listing him as John Doe as we've had no credible information to identify this man yet. If you are aware of who he might be, please let's meet after this press conference. The name you mentioned is not one we have heard."

All the other reporters turned to the guy in the back who had asked the question. Other reporters began shouting questions at him. He thankfully remained tightlipped and Luke pointed to the door to the station.

He held the door for the reporter who pushed his way through the crowd. At the door, he shook Luke's hand and introduced himself. "Lee Best from the Gazette. I'm new to the crime beat and sorry if I threw you for a loop. I received a tip after your press conference started that the victim was named Mitch Katz. You can listen to the voicemail when we are inside."

Luke pushed the rest of the reporters back as Lee went inside followed by Tyler and Captain Meadows. He locked the door behind him and then led the group upstairs to the detective's bureau and found an available conference room.

"I didn't mean to end your press conference like that. I thought it was a fake tip and you'd be dismissive of it," Lee said as he sat at the table. He put his phone down, turned up the volume, and hit play.

The man's voice was loud and clear: *"Lee, I was too worried to call the cops. I believe the victim is Mitch Katz. He used to work as a mechanic at Katz Auto on Markham. His father owned the shop until a few years ago. I don't know if he's still at the shop or not. Maybe you can confirm this for me. I didn't want to waste the cop's time."*

Lee hit stop on the voicemail and looked up at Luke. "I guess I should have confirmed it before asking the question. It came in while I was listening to you talk and I assumed better now than later."

Luke couldn't fault the young man. He might have gone directly to the cops too. Maybe just not in the same way. "Is there a number attached to that voicemail?"

"No," Lee said, turning his phone and showing Luke that it came up as a private number. "I assume he's someone who has been to the shop and saw Mitch. The man sounds older than your John Doe. He referenced Mitch's father. That may be how he knew him."

"Is that all the information you have?" Captain Meadows asked.

"That's it. I didn't hear my phone ring but when the voicemail came through it buzzed against my hip and I checked it. That's when I heard the name. I asked Det. Morgan the question less than five minutes after hearing the message."

Tyler laughed. "You've got a lot to learn about being a reporter. You were supposed to hold onto that name and run your exclusive if you found out that it was true."

Defeat came over Lee's face. "As I said, I haven't been doing this for very long. My editor is probably going to be angry with me."

Luke sat down next to him. "Det. Tyler is teasing you. Some

reporters would have kept the information from us and that's why they don't have access when we want to put out information. Coming to us in a press conference probably wasn't the best course of action. We can work with it though. If we confirm that it's Mitch Katz, tell your editor we will give you the exclusive interview. No one else. You can run it first before we release the information."

A huge smile came over Lee's face. He reached out and shook Luke's hand. "I appreciate that. Do you need to keep my phone?"

"No. We'll get a copy of the message before you go. It's probably as you said, just a concerned citizen." Luke walked Lee to one of the tech guys for them to copy the message and promised he'd call the young reporter if he confirmed his tip. Lee was so excited that he tripped and then righted himself. Embarrassed, he looked back at Luke and thanked him for taking the time to speak to him.

Once back in the conference room, Luke said, "Sonny confirmed that he saw Nick Day and our John Doe at Mandy's a few days before they were both killed. They went there separately for reasons unknown. I reached out to Nick's fiancé and she did not know that he knew Mandy. When I mentioned the tour of the Old State House, she remembered touring it with another woman but hadn't remembered her name. She had no idea why Nick would have gone to her place."

"Was she concerned he was cheating?" Tyler asked.

Luke shook his head. "She didn't seem to be. It sounds like they had a good relationship. Other than the tour, I haven't been able to find another link. I still need to track down his brother. If I had to guess that's the connection. We haven't ruled out that Jimmy wasn't involved in criminal activity. He's got a drug habit and it's possible he was a low-level guy for the Andino family. The same with our John Doe."

Tyler asked, "How would Nick have become mixed up in that?"

"That's the question," Luke said and checked his watch. There were about two hours of daylight left. "I'm going to try to find Jimmy and get to the bottom of this. The surveillance team didn't catch much other than him going out and getting drunk and then back home. I need to confront him again and add a little pressure."

There was another pressing matter to handle before he left.

Before the press conference, Luke officially turned down the job as captain. He told Captain Meadows that he was happy to remain as head of the detective bureau. He asked if he could be there when he told Tyler.

Tyler waited and looked between Captain Meadows and Luke. When the tension reached a peak, he joked, "You firing me?"

"Not quite," Luke said with a laugh.

Captain Meadows leaned his arms on the table. "As you know, I'm getting up there in years and planning to retire. I've decided who I'd like to take over my position."

Tyler looked at Luke and started to congratulate him.

"Just listen," Luke stopped him. Tyler turned his attention back to their boss.

"As you may know, I offered the job to Luke but he turned me down. In retrospect, I should have known he wasn't the fit I needed. When Luke turned down the job, he recommended you. It occurred to me that Luke was right. You're the best fit among the detectives for this position. Is this something you'd consider?"

Tyler turned sharply to Luke. "You turned it down?"

"I should never have been offered it in the first place," Luke said honestly. "I'm a great detective but I'm not cut out to be an administrator. I don't have the skills needed to deal with all the other work. You are naturally skilled in all the ways I'm not. That's why we are such good partners. I hope you'll consider it."

Tyler's cheeks reddened at Luke's flattery. "I need to speak to my wife first."

That was the response Luke expected. With that, Captain Meadows dismissed them.

As they left the conference room, Tyler pulled Luke aside. "Are you sure you don't want this promotion? They don't come along often."

Luke put his hand on his friend's shoulder. "I'm not right for the job. I had a long time to consider it. I never could get my mind around sitting in an office all day and not taking cases. I'm not good at playing the politics of it all. You're a natural at that."

"I'd be your boss."

"And a good one at that," Luke said with a smile. "I'm serious. Talk it over with your wife and seriously consider it. I think you'd be perfect."

Tyler thanked him and then went to his desk. Luke could tell he was flattered by the offer but still somewhat hesitant. It was a huge responsibility.

Luke gathered a few things at his desk and then headed out to find Jimmy. He had tried to call him a few times. He couldn't leave a message because the voicemail was full. Luke still hadn't received a call back from Nick's parents either.

Luke drove to the parents' house and pulled into the empty driveway. It took a few minutes of banging on the front door for Jimmy to stagger out to answer it. He had no shirt on, a pair of ripped basketball shorts, and his feet were bare. His hair flopped all over the place and he appeared to be sleeping off another hangover.

"We need to talk, Jimmy." Luke shoved past him into the house.

"You can't come in here like that," Jimmy said, closing the door behind them. "What do you want? I told you everything I know."

Luke put his hands on his hips and stared him down. "I don't think you did, Jimmy. I need to know how you know Mandy McKee and how that involved your brother. We can talk about it here or we can go down to the station. It's up to you."

"I don't know what you're talking about. I don't know any Mandy

McKee."

"I think you do. I think you got in something over your head and you asked your brother to help bail you out," Luke said, taking a wild guess. That was the only thing that had made sense to him so far. "What was it that you did? Rip off your dealer? Take money that wasn't yours?"

Jimmy slumped down on the sofa and put his head in his hands. "You have got to stop talking. My head is pounding."

Luke didn't have time for this. "Look at me!" He waited until Jimmy raised his head and stared up at him. "Your brother is dead. You need to start talking or I'll take you right down to the station and throw you in a cell until you sober up. Got it?"

"You can't do that."

Luke reached for his handcuffs. "You don't know what I'm willing to do. I have three murder victims and you're impeding my investigation. Last time we talked, you acted like you knew who did this to your brother. You'll either start talking here or you can sit in a cell until you're ready to talk. Do your parents even know your brother is dead?"

Jimmy swallowed hard and shook his head. "My father hasn't called me back yet and I didn't want to leave it on voicemail." He slowly pushed himself off the couch. "If I tell you what I know, I'm as good as dead."

"We can protect you."

"I don't think anyone can protect me."

Luke leveled a stare at him. "You don't have a choice. Either you trust me or you get arrested and they assume you're flipping to save yourself. This way is much easier for you."

Jimmy's mouth drew in a tight line. "I don't want them to think that."

"If I arrest you and the judge lets you out on bail, you're on your own." Luke knew he was playing hardball and skirting an ethical line.

He was done playing games. "It's your choice. What's it going to be?"

Jimmy wrapped his arms around his naked torso and avoided Luke's eyes. "I knew Mandy McKee. She contacted me a few months back and said that if I wanted to get out of selling drugs she'd be able to help me. She wouldn't tell me anything until I met with her. We met and she told me all I had to do was tell her who I was selling for and she'd help me out. I didn't know if I could trust her. She said there was a federal prosecution and she could be in touch with the person who could cut a deal for me."

"How'd she find you?"

"Got my name from someone else. She said that's how the whole thing worked." Jimmy shook his head. "I couldn't do it. I was too afraid. Later, when I changed my mind, Mandy wouldn't talk to me. She said she didn't trust me at that point."

That made sense to Luke. "How does your brother fit into this?"

A resigned sigh escaped Jimmy's lips. "I told Nick what had been offered and he told me I was crazy for turning it down. He knew that I'd been trying to get out from under this for a long time. I sent Nick to plead my case. They must have found out and killed him to keep me quiet."

Luke pointed down the hall. "Go pack a bag and get dressed."

"Where am I going?"

"Just get your stuff. I'll get you someplace safe and then you can tell me everything you know." While Jimmy got himself ready, Luke sent a quick text to Tyler to find an available safehouse. It was going to be a long night.

CHAPTER 27

There was something about the car that Mary described that was bothering me. I knew I had seen it somewhere before. I couldn't quite place it. Who else would have wanted Alex dead?

Jason fit that bill in every way.

From Mary's house, I walked back to Main Street where I had parked my car and then drove the short distance to the ice rink. There was a lone red pickup truck that had seen better days in the parking lot. One dim light lit up the front of the building, leaving the back in total darkness. I checked my phone and it was nearing six o'clock. I worried that I might have missed Jason and that would be the end of investigating for me today.

I got out of the car and walked toward the building, stopping briefly outside to gather my courage. The red metal door's rusted handle chilled my hand under its touch. The door creaked open and I walked inside. A pungent mix of sweat and ice hit my nose. Geneseo hockey games flooded my memories. I had watched Jason and his teammates play. We had a good hockey team then.

I scanned my eyes around the dimly lit main lobby. There was a concession stand off to my left and two double doors directly in front of me that I assumed would take me to the ice. As I approached, I heard the grinding sound of blades and the crack of the stick to the ice. I didn't have to see him to know that whoever was on the other side of the door was probably running drills.

I nudged open the door and looked inside. The rows of five-high metal bleachers surrounding three sides of the rink were empty. The Plexiglas around the rink appeared as if it hadn't been cleaned in the last fifty years. It blocked my view of who was on the rink.

I stepped onto the rubber floor mat and made my way to the rink, looking for the small door in the boards. I didn't see one from my vantage point so I started down the right side when someone shouted for me to stop.

"You can't be in here," a man said from behind me. "This is private property and you need to leave." His tone was stern but not angry.

I turned and came face to face with Jason. His appearance hadn't changed that much over the years. His hair had thinned and there was gray at his temples. He had gained a few pounds and some lines had formed on his face that hadn't been there when we were twenty-two. Otherwise, he was still the same. I couldn't recall if we had ever met back then. I had seen him play and had gone to plenty of hockey parties. I had no memory of ever having a conversation with him.

"Jason, I'm Riley Sullivan. I was here at Geneseo at the same time you were a student."

There was a flash of recognition on his face. "I remember you. You still can't be in here. There's no open skating."

That wouldn't be a problem. I hadn't been on ice skates since I was a child and I'd probably break several bones if I attempted. "I'm not here to skate. I came here hoping to speak to you."

He put his hands on his hips and watched me. "How'd you know where to find me?"

"I heard that you skate here sometimes and you're playing in a men's league." I turned back to the ice. Only one person was skating out there.

"I used to coach at the high school. I stopped doing that a few months back. I do one-on-one coaching with players now," he said, answering the question I hadn't asked. "Why did you want to speak to me?"

I turned my attention back to him. "I know you were involved with Alex McCormick. I'm not sure if you know this but I was her roommate on Elm Street."

If Jason knew that or remembered it, he didn't let on. "Did Alex tell you that?"

"Yes," I lied, keeping steady eye contact with him. "She didn't tell me much about your relationship. I knew she was cheating on Tim with you. She had told me before Thanksgiving break that she was going to see you that weekend. I never heard your name connected to the investigation, so I assumed you didn't stick around town over break."

Jason furrowed his brow. "Is there a question in there?"

I shook my head. "There might have been a question yesterday. I have confirmation that you were there that night. Someone saw you. What happened, Jason? The place was trashed and Alex would have never left it like that."

Jason turned away from me and, for a brief second, I thought he was going to kick me out. He balled his fists and I stepped back. Whatever demons he was fighting, he won. He turned back to me and calmly said, "Go sit on the bleachers and we'll talk. I have to take care of something first."

I stood there while Jason walked off toward the rink. I waited until he disappeared and then went to the other side and climbed the bleacher steps. It was then I could see onto the rink. Jason called the young man over, said a few words to him, then they both glanced in my direction. The kid, who couldn't have been more than fourteen or fifteen, slapped his stick down on the ice and started more drills on his own. I sat there watching him skate and practice shooting the puck at the net until Jason joined me.

"I didn't want to shortchange the kid on his lesson today," Jason said as he sat. He stuffed his hands into his coat. "What do you want to know?"

"All of it," I said and looked over at him. "How long were you and Alex together? When did it start? What happened that night?"

"Why are you bringing all this up now? Alex has been dead for so long. Does any of it matter?" He didn't seem angry. There was sadness on his face and he seemed more than a little resigned. Before I could answer his question, he looked over at me. "I know it probably didn't seem like it, but I loved Alex. I asked her to marry me."

"You proposed?" I couldn't help the shock on my face or in my tone. I had been thinking this was some fling they had. I had no idea that the relationship had gotten that deep. Tim hadn't even been thinking of marriage, especially given the rockiness of the relationship. That led me to question something else. "Did you know Alex was still involved with Tim?"

"I did and I hated it," Jason admitted, pulling his hands out of his pockets. He linked his fingers together on his lap. He leaned back against the wall behind us. "I wanted Alex to break it off with him. She told me a few times that she wanted to. She never did it and when I asked her why she'd only tell me that Tim wasn't like me. He was sweet and sensitive and she didn't want to hurt him like that. She said that when we graduated, they'd go their separate ways naturally and then she and I could be together."

I knew what he was saying was true because that's how Alex was with men. She dangled the carrot of a future time when things would be good. She strung them along. I watched her do it with Tim and now Jason was telling me she did it with him too. "I suspect that you didn't believe her."

"It got to a point where I didn't know what to believe. I proposed because I thought Alex didn't understand how serious I was about her.

I thought if I proposed, she'd know."

"What did she say?" I asked, knowing she didn't say yes. I wasn't prepared for how badly Alex had responded.

"She laughed at me and told me I was crazy. Alex said that she never wanted to get married and that she'd never marry a townie like me. That she had bigger dreams for herself than marrying a hockey player and living in some tiny town. She was headed for New York City after her graduation."

His words tugged on my heart. I had to remind myself that he was my prime suspect and he was handing me motive. "Alex could be cruel like that. I've come to learn that I didn't know as much about her as I had assumed. I had no idea that you proposed. When was this?"

"It was about a month before she was murdered." Jason looked up at the ceiling and cursed. "You'd think I wouldn't have been such a sap. Something like that should have ended the relationship. I still had hope that I could convince her to marry me. After graduation, maybe, or later. I wasn't sure that she was being serious about going to New York City." He looked over at me again. "We started seeing each other in May right as the semester ended. Then we saw each other over the summer and kept seeing each other that fall semester. I didn't want the relationship to end. I knew it wasn't a good relationship. I mean she was still seeing Tim. I didn't have my head screwed on right. But when she started talking about becoming an artist or whatever she was going to do, I lost it. I knew I couldn't compete in that world."

He was opening the door, so I was going to walk through while I had the chance. "Were you an education major like Alex?"

Jason nodded. "We had a few classes together, which is how we met. I noticed that she seemed to lose interest in teaching. She said as much in one of our classes. Then she started talking about art and visiting a professor. That previous summer we had talked about finding a school where we could teach together. I felt like she was throwing our dream away when she started talking about art. It didn't make any sense to me and I blamed the other guy."

I pulled back with confusion on my face. "What other guy?" *Griffin? Tim? That didn't make sense to me.*

"That artist guy in Rochester. She met him at an art show. I didn't think they were involved." Jason shook his head and his voice grew louder with anger. "Alex said they weren't but that she was learning about art from him. That's what the argument was about the night she died."

"You trashed the place like that?"

He paused and looked out over the ice. "I did."

I recalled how staged the kitchen looked. I didn't want to push on that, so I set it aside. "Help me to understand what you're saying. I didn't know anything about this other guy. I only recently learned that Alex was considering a career in art history. Who was he?"

"Tate Butler. He's a famous sculptor. Alex met him at one of his shows and they talked on the phone. She said she was going to New York City with him. That he was going to be featured at a gallery there and he was opening up a studio." Jason eyed me. "You didn't know any of this?"

I shook my head. "What happened the night she died?"

"Initially, she said she wanted to be alone that weekend. Alex said she had a lot to think about. I lived in the next town over but I lived in the hockey house here in Geneseo, so I was going to be around. She called me Saturday afternoon and asked me to dinner. She said she wanted to talk. I thought for sure she was going to tell me she broke up with Tim and was going to stop all this art talk nonsense and commit to our relationship."

"That isn't what happened?"

"Not even close," he said with disdain. "It was another chance for her to humiliate me and I lost it. I trashed your whole apartment. I'm sorry about that. I've spent my life trying and failing to control my temper. I didn't kill her. I left them there and stormed out."

"Them?" I asked, not sure I heard him correctly. The fact there was yet one more man in Alex's life floored me. There was so much she had kept hidden.

Jason blinked rapidly like he wasn't sure what I meant. "Yeah, Tate was there that night. I left them alone together. I couldn't stand the sight of her anymore. I swear to you Alex was alive when I left."

I was in such a confused state, I didn't even know what to say. I sat there silently collecting my thoughts while Jason kept his eyes on me waiting for my reaction. My backside felt glued to the cold bleacher as I tried to process a life I had known nothing about even though she lived feet from me.

CHAPTER 28

"Say something," Jason demanded, red fanning up his neck and cheeks even in the cold of the ice rink. "This is the first time I'm telling anyone this. I didn't even tell the cops. My friends covered for me. I felt bad all these years that Tim went to prison for something he didn't do. I knew if I told the truth no one would believe me. Do you believe me, Riley?"

I didn't know what to believe. I started this case thinking Alex had been dating Tim and now I had a roster of men in front of me. I wasn't judging her. We were in college and it was a wild time. I wish she had ended it with Tim first.

I wasn't as convinced as Jason would have liked me to be. I'd give him one chance to change my mind about him. As far as I was concerned, he had the temper and motive to kill Alex in a fit of rage. "Tell me everything that happened that night."

Jason started to ask if I believed him again, but then he saw my face and thought better of it. "When I went over there for dinner, Tate showed up as we sat down to eat. Alex said she wanted me to meet him like we'd all be friends or something."

"Did she say why she wanted you to meet him?"

"I don't know," Jason said, brushing off the question.

I had never known Alex to be stupid, and introducing one man she was involved with to the other who she knew had a temper wasn't something I could imagine any sane woman doing. There was an element of this I was missing. "I'm sure you asked her why she wanted you to meet him. What did Alex say?"

Jason was quiet for a moment and then said, "Alex wanted Tate to explain how good she was in the art world. That she had a natural talent for recognizing quality art. She wanted me to be happy about her change of career." Jason cursed and shook his head. "Why would bringing some guy that was only going to take her away from me help me to understand? It was the worst thing she could have done."

His anger bubbled up in his tone. I didn't feel like dealing with an outburst, so kept my voice steady and calm. "You must have had a response to that. What did you tell her?"

"I tried reasoning with her. He kept interjecting that it wasn't my place to tell Alex what to do with her life. I knew he was right…" Jason grumbled something I didn't understand. When I asked him what he said, he shook his head. "It was an impossible situation, Riley. I hope you see that. She kept promising me a relationship and then kept moving the goalpost. She'd break up with Tim once we graduated. We were going to teach together. She mapped out an entire life she saw for us and then snatched it away overnight. What was I supposed to do?"

I wanted to tell him he should have walked away and let Alex live the life she wanted. Driving home that notion was pointless now. "I don't want to know what you were supposed to do. I want to know what you did."

"I completely lost it," Jason said without any hint of remorse in his voice. "I trashed the entire kitchen. I screamed and flipped out. Alex screamed back and she threw things at me and I threw things back at her. Alex and I fought like we never had before. I had lost my temper with her before but never like that. She never screamed back at me. She'd wait until I calmed down. Maybe she felt like she had to put on a show or felt safe doing that because Tate was there. I don't know. The more she came at me, the more my temper raged. Do you know what that idiot Tate did?"

I didn't respond because I was too caught up in the scene playing out in my mind that had left a wave of destruction in the kitchen.

Jason didn't wait for me. He went on. "Tate sat at the table like nothing was happening. He didn't yell. He didn't tell us to calm down or try to stop us. He let us go at each other. I'm sure he even got hit with food. All the while, he had a smug smile on his face like he was winning. He was a weird guy. I'd go as far as to say creepy. I should have never left Alex alone there but she kicked me out in the middle of the fight. I was more than happy to leave."

"Where did you go after you left? You said your friends covered for you with the cops. If that wasn't true, where were you?"

"I went home after I drove around and calmed down. I didn't tell my parents what had happened. They were asleep by the time I got there. I went in and ate some leftovers from the fridge and then about one in the morning, I went back to my room at the hockey house."

"Did your parents know you went there that night?"

Jason shook his head. "After I found out the next day that Alex had been murdered, I didn't want them mixed up in that. They never saw me and it was easier to get my friends to lie."

It didn't surprise me that his alibi had been faked. "Did you ever tell the cops about Tate?"

Jason lowered his head and looked at his hands which were balled into fists on his lap. "If I admitted to Tate being there, I would have had to admit I was there. That wasn't something I could do. I know how bad it looked for me. I knew given my reputation as a hothead that if I said I was there they'd pin her murder on me. I had to protect myself."

It was my turn to be angry. My voice rose several octaves. "You let

Tim go to prison knowing he wasn't there that night. You knew who you left Alex alone with right before she was murdered. How could you sit with that kind of secret your whole life?"

"I did what I had to do," Jason said softly. "I've felt bad all this time about it. There was no way to direct the cops to Tate without explaining how I knew it."

"You could have left an anonymous tip. You could have done anything to help Alex and to make sure Tim didn't pay for someone else's crime."

Jason turned his head and side-eyed me. "I didn't know, Riley. After I left, I didn't know what happened. I didn't know if Tim came back and saw the mess and saw Alex with Tate and killed her. I figured it was best to stay out of it."

I turned my body to face the ice. I couldn't stomach looking at him for a second longer. He was as pathetic now as he was then. "Why are you telling me this now? You could have lied to me and said you were never there. That my information was wrong."

"You'd have found out the truth eventually." Jason breathed heavily and didn't respond for several moments. "I think the guilt is getting to me. I don't believe Tim did it. He spent enough time paying for someone else's crime. If I can help keep him out of prison now, it's the least I can do."

"You'll have to speak to the cops. Do you understand that?"

He gave me a curt nod. "I'm older now and my father isn't pressuring me. My life is a mess so what's the difference if I mess it up more? Besides, it's about time I do the right thing. Are you going to call them now?"

I wasn't going to call them. I didn't think the investigator would speak to me if I tried to bring him a witness without any evidence. "I'll let you know when. Is there anything else I should know?"

"Are you going to try to find Tate?"

"I have to. If he was the last person to see Alex alive, then I have to see what he knows."

"He could be dangerous, Riley," Jason said, suddenly seeming concerned for my safety. "I don't think you should go alone. You are alone, right?"

There was something in the way he said *alone* that sent shivers down my spine. His gaze remained fixed on me. I shivered again. It wasn't the cold from the ice rink. It was the icy way he watched me. "I'm never alone, Jason. I thought you killed Alex. Do you actually think I'd come in here alone to interview you?"

He looked out over the ice rink. "It doesn't look like anyone is here."

"Appearances can be deceiving." I stood from the bench. His student, who was still practicing drills, glanced up at us. "Are you trying to be intentionally creepy?"

"What?" Jason said, tipping his head back to look at me. "I'm sorry. I was worried about you going to speak to Tate. I'd never hurt you. I was worried about you."

"Then don't act so weird." I climbed down the metal bleachers and didn't look back. It didn't matter what he had told me about leaving Alex with Tate, I didn't believe his story. I didn't believe he'd get that angry and just leave Alex alone with another man. I also couldn't get past that the kitchen mess looked staged.

I made it to the bottom of the bleachers when Jason followed with his heavy footfalls clanging the metal. I looked over my shoulder. "Is there anything else you need me to know?"

"Tate is in New York City. I have his address if you want it."

I turned around fully to face him. "How do you know that?"

Jason didn't respond until he reached the floor. He shoved his hands in his pockets and shrugged. "I've kept track of him over the years. If he was the one responsible for Alex's murder, I wanted to keep track of him. I also wanted to make sure he didn't hurt anyone else."

"How were you going to make sure of that?" I asked, a sinking feeling growing in my gut.

"I might have talked with him at some point."

I cocked my head to the side. "Did you hurt him?"

Jason turned and looked out at the ice rink. "I made sure he knew he was being watched. I made sure he knew that I knew what he did. The justice system isn't the only way to solve things."

I didn't know how to respond to that. I didn't even know if it was true or just posturing from a man who still couldn't get over losing a woman like Alex to an artist – if that was even what had happened. "What's the address?"

"He has a gallery on Bleecker Street in Greenwich Village. The last time I was down there, he was still living above it." He gave me the address and directions to the closest subway stop. I knew my way around the city but I listened to him anyway. It was clear he had made the trip more than once.

"When was the last time you were down there?"

"About three months ago." When he saw the disgusted look on my face, Jason added, "I told you, I've been keeping an eye on him. I didn't want him getting too far away."

None of that made any sense to me. I thanked him for the information and headed toward the door. Jason followed right behind me asking again if I believed him. Once I reached the door and pulled it open, I had a taste of freedom and turned and faced him. "What does it matter if I believe you or not? You gave me a lead and I'll follow up with it. This is all for a court to decide."

Concern fell over his face. "What if Tate lies to you about that night? What if he doesn't admit to being there? I don't have any proof that he was there. This could fall back on me."

"I thought you were willing to take that risk?"

"I want the man responsible for Alex's downfall to be held responsible."

"Alex's downfall? What does that mean? She was murdered, Jason." I stared him right in the eyes now and wouldn't look away. His story might have pointed to another man but his words told me that I might very well be staring into the last face Alex saw. "The truth will come out one way or the other."

He had no response to that.

I left and rushed back to my SUV. I had my Glock under my coat, but I didn't want to have to use it.

Once in my car, I turned the ignition and put my car in drive. I didn't realize until I reached for the steering wheel that my hands were shaking. I didn't think it was just from the cold. My stomach flipped and I swallowed down the acid that rose in the back of my throat.

Jason stood in the doorway watching me. I couldn't read his expression as his face was cast in the shadow of the light inside the building. I didn't stick around to find out. I put the car in drive and sped out of the lot. If Jason wasn't guilty of the murder, he had never figured out how not to make himself look like a creepy predator. I wasn't sure why Alex wanted to be with him in the first place, but I could certainly understand why she'd want to leave him.

I made it back to my hotel and looked around before getting out of the car and going inside. It wasn't until I was safely locked inside my room that I pulled my phone from my pocket and hit stop on the recording. I was glad New York was a one-party state and I could record him without his knowing. Jason could change his mind all he wanted about going to the cops with a new statement. He wasn't going to get far given everything he had already told me.

CHAPTER 29

Cooper stood in the kitchen putting the finishing touches on the pancakes and eggs he made for breakfast. Adele was in the bedroom getting dressed for work and he wanted to make sure she started the day with something substantial in her stomach. She had a long day of court ahead of her, and she was prone to skipping meals when she was stressed. If Cooper wasn't able to be in the field investigating cases, the least he could do was cook his wife a decent breakfast.

Cooper transferred the eggs from the pan to the plate as Adele wrapped her arms gently around his middle. She laid her cheek on his back. "What did I do to deserve such a great husband?"

Cooper set the pan down on the stove and turned to wrap his arms around her. "You put up with me." He dropped a kiss on her lips and then gestured toward the table. "You should eat something before court."

"I'm not going to argue with that. Yesterday wiped me out." Adele pulled out a chair at the kitchen island and sat down. She admired the plate with scrambled eggs, pancakes, and even orange slices neatly arranged. She took a bite of the scrambled eggs mixed with cheddar and peppers and smiled. "Where did you learn to cook like this? Has there been another woman here? Only two months ago, you could barely use the stovetop. If it couldn't be cooked on the grill, it wasn't worth cooking was your motto."

Cooper didn't want to let on how happy he was that Adele was impressed. He gave a non-committal shrug. "I watched some YouTube videos." That was only partially true. He had been reading food blogs, watching cooking videos, and learning from step-by-step tutorials. Spying on his neighbors wasn't the only thing he'd been doing. "I figured you shouldn't have to do all the cooking all the time."

"I'm not going to argue with that."

Cooper sat across the island from her and dug into his food. Between bites, he asked, "Have you heard from Sonny since his interview with Luke yesterday?"

Adele put her fork down and took a sip of coffee, fixed how she liked it with a little milk and one sugar. "He's been staying at a local hotel since he arrived two weeks ago. Luke was clear that Sonny couldn't leave town. I don't think he's in the clear yet. Do you still believe he murdered Mandy?"

"I don't know. It's hard to reconcile what I saw with the turn in the case." Cooper had been struggling to make sense of it all. It was possible what he saw was only part of the story. There were so many questions left to be answered about what Sonny had been doing during the time of the murder. As far as Cooper was concerned, Sonny still didn't have an alibi.

"I can see on your face the mental gymnastics in your mind," Adele said and reached over and patted Cooper's hand. "I trust Luke to do his job. If he doesn't believe that Sonny is a suspect in Mandy's murder, then I believe him. When I interviewed Sonny, he was more credible than most of the people I'm defending."

"The anger," Cooper said and let that sit with them. "He was out of control when he was here. I find it hard to believe that he didn't strangle her. Then again, there was the carving on her back." Cooper hadn't been allowed to tell Adele about her connection with the U.S.

Attorney's Office. Sonny didn't seem to have any ties to that or the other victims.

Adele agreed with his reasoning. "Let Luke run down the other leads and sort it out. If he had suspected Sonny of killing her, he would have made an arrest."

Cooper knew that was only partially true. "Even if Luke thought he was guilty, if he didn't have the evidence to bring a case against him, he'd wait to arrest."

Adele agreed. "Let Luke do his job and, if the time comes, I'll do my job and pass him off to another attorney to defend him. You know I can't represent him with what you witnessed. What do you have planned for the day?"

Cooper knew that the discussion was closed. Once Adele was done with a subject, she rarely pivoted back. "I have a few reports to go over from my investigators and Riley wants to go over her case. She said she needed some advice. We are going to video chat." Cooper checked his phone and the time was rapidly approaching. "She should be calling me in a few minutes."

"Sounds like a full day." Adele finished the rest of her breakfast and carried her dish over to the sink. She turned around to face him. "I know it's hard not being able to do everything you're used to doing. It's temporary and you'll be back to full capacity soon. I know that's easy to say. I didn't mean to dismiss you about Sonny. I don't want you to stress about something that Luke has handled."

Cooper appreciated what she said. He looked over at her. "You're right, I need to let it go. I'm having trouble getting the image of him over her on the bed and everything else I saw out of my head. I'll feel better when Luke solves the case."

Adele hugged him before she went into the bathroom to finish getting ready while Cooper cleaned up from breakfast. He rinsed the dishes and put them in the dishwasher before pouring himself another cup of coffee. He checked the time again and headed over to his desk in time to answer Riley's video chat request.

He saw Riley's video image before his own connected. When they were finally face-to-face on the screen, he said, "How's it going out there?"

"It's going," Riley said with frustration in her voice. "I'm glad you had time to talk to me this morning. I'm trying to figure out the best course of action. Can I give you a case overview?"

"Hit me with it." Cooper sat back and sipped his coffee as he listened to the details.

Before she dug into the meat of the case, Riley admitted, "I walked into this case thinking it was one thing and realized quickly I had no idea what happened the night of Alex's murder. I need solid evidence to bring to the state police if I have any chance of stopping Tim's second prosecution."

"Do you have evidence now?"

Riley nodded. "I'm a step closer. Tim told me someone else was there with Alex the night she died. I have a witness who saw Jason Thatcher going into her apartment that night. When I interviewed him, he confirmed he was there for dinner. He said he'd been involved with Alex for quite some time and had even discussed a future together. I have another professor who saw Jason show up at his office and yell at Alex. Their relationship was volatile. Jason admitted to trashing the kitchen that night. It still looks staged to me. None of that adds up."

Cooper shook his head. "What is with these rageful men destroying everything? That's what happened here. Can't anyone control their temper anymore?"

"It happens far more than you realize, Cooper." Riley looked down at the desk and held up a few pages, which Cooper assumed were her notes. "Putting Alex's muddled dating life aside, she was also in the middle of trying to make some long-term career decisions when she died. I spoke to a professor who said Alex was going to change from being an education major to an art history major. She never mentioned anything like that to me. I still thought she wanted to be a teacher. This decision caused fighting between her and Jason. It also opened the door to an artist named Tate Butler. Jason claimed Tate was there that night and that's who he left Alex with alone in the apartment the last time he saw her alive. I don't know that I fully believe him."

"Was he not credible?" Cooper asked, trying to piece together all the details of the investigation. There were many people Alex had in her life, similar to Mandy. There were parallels in their two cases that Cooper hadn't realized before now.

Riley explained her interaction with Jason and the way the interview ended. "It wasn't so much the questions he asked but how he asked them. He admitted to lying about his alibi. He'd also been fired due to his temper, so even as an adult, he's not gotten it under control. The oddest part is that Jason told me he's been keeping his eye on Tate who lives in New York City and has a gallery for his art and other artists. I looked it up online and it's where Jason said it is and it's quite successful. I can see Alex's attraction for him, if that's what it was. He's a good-looking successful guy. I'm sure he was even more attractive back then. I called and left him a message last night and he called me back and said if I wanted to speak to him, I needed to do it in person."

"Do you think Alex was involved with this guy?"

"I don't know what to think anymore. She seemed to bounce from one guy to the other all while stringing along Tim. The truth is I don't know if Tim went back to that apartment or if Tate was there or if it was Jason trying to blame someone else."

"You mentioned the other night something about cheating. Have you figured out what that means?"

Riley exhaled loudly. "If it's cheating in a relationship, that's clear. The professor I spoke to said Alex suspected other students in the education department of cheating. I don't have any information like that. Jason took education classes, but I didn't ask him about this. I was so thrown with the information about Tate. Gail and Michelle were also education majors, so I can go back and ask one of them if they knew anything."

It sounded like Riley had the case under control. Cooper wasn't sure of her question. "What's your plan now?"

"That's what I wanted to figure out. It seems like I've done all I can here. I was thinking about going back to my mom's house and taking the train into the city. I assume interviewing Tate is a good next step. I have so many lingering questions about Jason." Riley slumped down at the desk and rested her head in her hand. "It's been weird coming back."

Cooper noted how tired she looked. Dark circles had formed under her eyes and her hair was pulled back in a ponytail, which Riley never did unless she was tired. It was hard being on cases all alone. It was one of the reasons why he liked partnering with Riley.

"If it were me, I'd go back and ask Jason about the cheating. I'd make it broad and ask if he knew about any cheating rumors from back then," Cooper said and then watched her reaction. It was clear Riley didn't like the idea of going back to speak to him. He thought it would be a wasted opportunity if she didn't. Riley didn't say no, so Cooper continued. "After that, I'd head to New York City. If you have a statement that Tate was the last person seen with her, you have to rule him in or out. If he'll only talk in person, you're going to have to go to him. How far away is it?"

"It's about three and a half hours home and then another two and a half hours on the train," Riley said. "I should be able to make it to the gallery by the time he's closing up for the night."

"Has Tim heard of this guy?"

Riley shook her head. "I ran it by him last night on the phone without explaining much. He said it wasn't a name he'd heard before from Alex or anyone else. I called Professor Lance Donovan and he told me Tate had been on campus a few times – once at an art show and then he gave a lecture to an art class. Lance had no idea if Tate knew Alex."

"They could have interacted," Cooper said and Riley agreed. "It's worth a trip to sort it out. I find it odd that Jason would be keeping track of him. Do you know if they had any interaction beyond that night?"

"Jason alluded to it." Riley seemed hesitant as if she wasn't sure she wanted to continue. After a moment, she added, "He didn't outright give me the details. It sounded to me like Jason might have threatened Tate or physically assaulted him. I suspect that's why he also wanted to speak to me in person."

"That's something definitely to explore." Cooper leaned toward the screen. "I wish I was there with you. I wouldn't mind some field work. Have you heard from Luke?"

"I haven't had a chance to catch up with him. He brought someone in for questioning last night and texted that it wasn't going well."

"I'll check in on him today."

They spent a few more minutes catching up about life before ending the chat. Cooper finished with a sense of satisfaction. He didn't feel like he did much other than suggest Riley do what she already knew to do. Even so, it was good to be back at the grind.

CHAPTER 30

After ending the video chat with Cooper, I knew I had to go interview Jason again. I had considered it briefly last night and then pushed the thought aside. I realized when I listened to the recording, he had distracted me with the new information about Tate, I never asked about the cheating. There was a lot left to be explored. I also felt safer going back to him during the day right before I headed out of town.

I texted Tim and let him know that I had one interview to wrap up before meeting with him that morning. He suggested meeting on campus so we could walk and talk. I agreed that would be fine and let him know I'd text him when I was headed that way.

I finished getting myself ready and checked out of the hotel. I had no plans for coming back. It was clear that whatever I needed to know to solve the case probably wasn't going to be in Geneseo unless Jason was planning to confess.

I drove back to the ice rink and saw the same beat-up old pickup truck in the parking lot. The whole building seemed a lot less menacing in daylight. I parked, set the recording on my phone, gave myself a quick pep talk, and headed into the building.

I entered through the same door as I had the night before and was met with the smell of eggs and bacon cooking. A woman looked over from the concession stand and waved. "We aren't open," she said pleasantly with a smile on her face. "Can I help you?"

I walked over to the woman who was about my height and had short dark hair. "I'm looking for Jason. Is he here?"

"He's in his office. Are you here to register your child for lessons?"

I shook my head. "I went to college with him and wanted to say goodbye before I headed out of town." It wasn't technically a lie.

She pointed to the double doors. "Follow the rink to the back and his office is through the next set of double doors. He should be in there."

I thanked her and then hightailed it to the rink, grateful she hadn't asked me any further questions. There was no one on the ice today. I walked down the right side of the rink and passed through the double doors. I passed locker rooms on my right and an equipment room on my left. Past that there was one more door left slightly ajar.

I rapped against it. "Jason, it's Riley."

"Come on in," he said with a gruff annoyed tone.

He was sitting at his desk hunched over a laptop when I entered. "I won't take up too much of your time. I had a few follow-up questions."

Jason raised his eyebrows. "You had a chance to talk to Tate that quickly?"

"This isn't about Tate," I said, taking a seat without being invited. "I have questions about some of your education classes."

Jason pursed his lips. "I barely remember my classes. I'm not sure I'm going to be much help."

I paused as I considered how I wanted to frame the question. Jason looked at me expectantly. I took it head-on. "I've heard that there was a cheating scandal in the education department. Do you remember anything about it?"

Jason cocked his head to the side. "Are you accusing me of cheating?"

"No," I said, trying to keep my tone even. "I'm only trying to understand if the rumors I heard were true. It's believed that Alex might have been aware of the cheating. I know from a witness that she was considering whether or not to go to the department head."

"If Alex knew about cheating, she didn't mention it to me. I never knew of anyone cheating on tests or anything. Those are not rumors I heard. Do you know who was being accused of cheating?"

"I don't know anything," I said honestly. I tried to hide the disappointment. I had been hoping he would know something. "It was something I heard recently. I never took any education classes and Alex never mentioned it to me."

A slow smirk spread across Jason's face. "Alex didn't tell you a lot, did she?"

If he had slapped me, it would have hurt less. "It's true I'm finding out things now I didn't know then."

"Have you asked yourself why she kept you in the dark?"

A part of me wanted to get up and leave. Not that I'd believe anything he said, but curiosity got the better of me. "I don't have any idea."

"Alex didn't like you, Riley. She said that you played both sides of everything when you should have been on her side for everything. You were friends with Michelle when the two of them didn't get along. You were friends with Tim even when they were fighting. Alex thought you were disloyal."

Much to my dismay, Jason wasn't lying. Alex and I had a few arguments about that. I felt the need to defend myself now as I did then. "I'm not sure if you know this. I was friends with Michelle and Tim long before Alex met them. She met them through me. Alex and Michelle never got along and both tried to put me in the middle of it. The only thing I could do was step back and remain neutral. Because Alex was my roommate, I listened to her about the arguments more than I listened to Michelle. Alex asked my opinion all the time and then was angry when I gave her an opinion she didn't like. As far as Tim goes, I never liked the way Alex treated him and strung him along.

When asked, I let her know that. Otherwise, I listened to Tim and remained a friend to him."

"Like you are now." Jason snickered. "I see a ring on your finger. I wonder how your husband feels about you rushing here to come to Tim's defense."

I wasn't going to defend my marriage to a man I still thought could be a killer. I got up and headed for the door. Before leaving, I turned and asked one last question. "Do you remember anyone with a small four-door black car like a Honda Civic? It had a decal of a sun on the back. I can't quite remember the owner."

There was a flash of recognition on his face. He sat with it for a moment, then shrugged. "Sounds familiar to me, but I don't know who it belongs to."

"Thanks," I said and purposefully pulled the door closed behind me, leaving it slightly open. I moved down the hall a few feet from the door and waited.

Almost immediately, I heard Jason on the phone.

He only said a few words. "Riley is getting closer to the truth. I gave her Tate, so hopefully, she gets off our back. Don't mess this up now."

I waited a second longer and then moved swiftly down the hall and out of the ice rink as fast as I could, hoping I'd never have to see Jason again. If he wasn't responsible for Alex's death, then he knew who was and was responsible for covering it up.

After arriving on campus, I found Tim sitting on a bench near Sturges Hall. I had taken a few classes in this building. I always liked the brick exterior, double wooden doors, and clock tower. It was one of the prettiest buildings on campus. Tim had his head bent and was focused on his phone. He raised his head when I called his name.

I wanted to manage his expectations more than anything else. "I've made some progress. I'm optimistic but there's still work to be done."

Tim nodded in understanding. "You said last night that Alex might have been involved with someone named Tate Butler. I spent some time looking at his website. He doesn't seem familiar to me at all."

There was a lot of ground to cover. "Did Alex ever tell you anything about changing her major from education to art history?"

"Alex talked about changing all the time. She was flighty, Riley. One day it was art history and the next day it was American history. She was studying to become an English teacher. She bounced from one idea to the next. If you're asking me if she was serious about the change, I don't know. Alex was hard to pin down in that regard. I know her parents were frustrated with her. At least, that's what she told me. Her father encouraged her to get her degree and start working. If she didn't like it, then she could figure it out. I always suspected Alex didn't want to graduate. She was scared of the next step in life."

Her lack of commitment to future employment mirrored her lack of commitment to a relationship. None of it was unusual for someone in their early twenties about to graduate from college. "Do you have any idea who you saw that night with Alex?"

"As I said, I never saw his face. He was a bigger guy and wasn't someone I wanted to go inside and take on. I would have lost that fight and the humiliation wouldn't have been worth it."

"Jason Thatcher admitted he was with Alex that night. He was the person you saw because after seeing photos of Tate, I don't believe it was him."

Tim rested his phone in his lap. "Jason admitted being there?"

I pulled my phone from my pocket, scrolled to my audio recording app, and hit play. I had previously queued up the portion of the audio where Jason admitted to being there for dinner. I knew even this many years later, it would be hard for Tim to hear.

When I was done with that section of the recording, I hit stop. I turned to Tim and put my hand on his arm. "While Alex was involved with Griffin casually, he was in love with someone else and it wasn't serious. It sounds like she had an ongoing relationship with Jason. They had talked about teaching at a school together. I don't know that Alex was ever as serious about him as he was with her. He had proposed and she said no. She kept pushing him off until graduation."

A loud sigh escaped Tim and he sat back deflated. "If Alex was so unhappy being in a relationship with me, I wish she had just ended it. I could have taken that. There would have been a finality to it. Instead, we remained in an ambiguous state with her telling me she wanted me but acting like she didn't. I can't tell you how confusing that was for me. I was such an idiot."

I wanted to find some way to comfort him. I didn't think that anything but time would help. "This might be painful to relive all these things you didn't know then and I'm sorry for that. This is good for your case. We know Jason was there that night. That it was him who had the fight and trashed the apartment. I have the audio of him admitting to doing that. I can give this to the police and to the prosecutor. This creates enough reasonable doubt that they might not retry you."

"Yeah," Tim said and shook his head. "How does Tate fit into all of this?"

I gave him the overview of what Jason had told me about Tate being there that night and leaving Alex alone with him. "I don't know if I trust Jason. He was clearly jealous of Tate and his relationship with Alex. I don't know if they were involved or if he was a mentor to her. Tate is willing to speak to me. I'm going to leave today and head to New York City."

"Is there anything else I need to know before you leave?" Tim turned on the bench to face me. He frowned and bit at his lower lip.

I wasn't going to disclose going back to my old apartment and the séance. I didn't think I'd ever admit that to anyone other than Cooper. "Did you ever hear Alex talk about anyone cheating in her education classes?"

Tim thought about it for a moment. "I remember something like that. She was concerned that someone was getting better grades than she was because of cheating. I thought she was jealous and being petty. Alex was determined to figure out if there was cheating happening. She never mentioned who she suspected. That's one of the reasons I didn't take it seriously. She didn't have anything to substantiate the claim." Tim looked up at me. "Is that relevant?"

"I'm honestly not sure. It came up during an interview and I wanted to see if you knew."

Tim shook his head. "Not anything more than Alex's overactive imagination."

I explained to him that Mary Maguire had seen him that night. He hadn't seen her but he wasn't surprised that someone had noticed him. "Mary also saw a car she thought was suspicious."

I explained the details of the car and how it drove off after he left and then circled back around later. "It was parked in front of the house for a period of time and then gone in the morning. I'm certain I've seen the car but can't place it."

"You're right that it's familiar." Tim thought about it but couldn't place it either. "Do we know if this car has anything to do with the murder?"

"I have no idea. It's another possible angle. It was something Mary saw and made her suspicious. If you remember anything, please let me know."

Tim agreed. "Will you call my lawyer and tell him what you have?"

"Let me talk to Tate first and try to put a few more pieces together."

We took a walk around campus before I went back to Main Street. Before getting in my car, I stood there surveying the area. I smiled at the rush of memories because even though it ended with Alex's murder, there were many good memories to hold onto. After I was ready, I said goodbye to Tim and headed back to Troy.

CHAPTER 31

Luke had spent considerable time the night before at the hotel with Jimmy trying to make sense of his statement. He had been too hungover and tired. Luke left him at the hotel with a cop standing guard outside of his room and went home to get some sleep.

The morning brought a whirlwind of activity. Det. Tyler had received positive confirmation that their John Doe was Mitch Katz. Although his father had retired and the shop sold, Mitch remained employed. The reporter's tip had been correct.

After having the man's name, Luke was able to run it in the system, but like the man's fingerprints, he came back with nothing. Mitch had no criminal record or any involvement with law enforcement.

Luke was now headed to speak to a few of the other employees to get a better sense of who Mitch was and how he could possibly be involved with Mandy McKee or the Andino family. Tyler was busy with Captain Meadows and a meeting with the big bosses. He had accepted the promotion earlier that morning.

Luke pulled his SUV into the autobody shop parking lot and parked in a row of cars. He went straight to the front desk instead of walking into the bay and disturbing the mechanics.

"How can I help you?" the young man behind the counter said as soon as Luke stepped inside. There were three people sitting in a dank waiting room either focused on the small television affixed to the wall at an odd angle or had their faces buried in magazines. The old tile floor looked like it hadn't been mopped since it was installed and the window looking out to the road had a thin film, making everything look gray and cloudy.

Luke got to the counter and flashed his badge. "My partner, Det. Tyler, was here this morning and spoke to someone about Mitch Katz. I'm here to ask some follow up questions."

The young man nodded. "Terrible thing that happened to him. Everyone around here liked Mitch. We liked his father too before he retired. Did you know he was only retired a week before he had a heart attack and died?" The young man shook his head in disbelief.

Luke had learned those details this morning. Both of Mitch's parents were deceased and he had no siblings. The autobody crew had been the closest people to him. One of the mechanics had gone to the morgue with Tyler to identify the body. Luke noticed the few people in the shop were now staring directly at them. He turned back to the young man. "Is there a place where I can speak to people away from everyone else?"

"There's a desk in back the manager uses, but he's at lunch. I'm sure he wouldn't mind you using it." He left his post at the desk and took Luke down a narrow hallway to the office.

Before leaving, Luke asked him how well he knew Mitch. "Anything you can tell me would be helpful."

"I've only been working here about a month. I don't know anyone that well. Mitch was a good guy. People who worked here and the customers liked him. They trusted him, which is important in our business." He stepped back to the doorway and leaned against it. "I never heard anyone say a bad word about him. I'll get you Mitch's friend Curtis. If anyone knew Mitch, it was him."

He turned and left before Luke could ask anything else.

Tyler had spoken to Curtis that morning but held off on a formal interview. Luke glanced around the office for somewhere to sit. He didn't want to sit behind the desk littered with papers and three old Styrofoam cups stained with coffee. There was only one chair in the room. He chose to stand awkwardly in the middle of the office.

A few minutes later, Curtis came into the room wiping his hands on an old red rag that had seen better days. "I'd shake your hand, Det. Morgan, but I'd get grease all over you. You wanted to ask me a few questions about Mitch."

"I don't know how much Det. Tyler explained to you about the nature of Mitch's murder. We believed that it's connected to two others."

"He told me that. I saw the carving on Mitch's back. Det. Tyler explained that was done after Mitch was dead, which I was grateful to hear he didn't have to suffer. I don't know who could have done that to him if that's what you're here to ask me." Curtis stuffed the rag into a back pocket and kept his focus on Luke.

"I have a few questions you might not want to answer. I wouldn't be asking them if they weren't important." Luke waited until Curtis said he understood. "To your knowledge, was Mitch involved in any criminal activity? Selling drugs or guns or anything like that?"

Curtis stared down with an expression on his face Luke couldn't read. "Do you think that's what got him killed?"

"It may have played a part. That's why it's so important." Luke paused to see if that would be enough. When Curtis didn't look convinced, he added, "We don't want to say this publicly, but I don't have many leads on this case. We think it's all connected to something bigger. I have to put the little pieces together to have it start to make sense. Mitch is a part of that puzzle. If I can figure out how he fits into all of this, the case could be solved. If you have information that could help me, I urge you to tell me. You can't hurt your friend now."

Curtis raised his eyes. "What if it hurts me?"

Luke was in no position to offer any kind of immunity. "I can promise that if you witnessed something or knew something and didn't call the cops, I don't care about that. If you're involved in criminal activity, then tell me what you know and we can make a deal."

Curtis wavered for only a moment. "Mitch stole cars and brought them back here to the shop. Sometimes someone came and picked them up and sometimes they were taken apart and the parts sold, depending on the car. I didn't know he was doing this until about two months ago. I had forgotten my phone at the shop and came back around ten. I have a key and I found him here."

"Okay," Luke said evenly, showing no judgment in his expression or tone. "Did you get involved in the operation after that?"

Curtis shook his head. "I have a wife and kids and I was raised better than that. I work an honest day for an honest day's wage. It might not be as much as other people, but I'm no thief. I told Mitch he had to stop. He told me he'd been doing it for years. It started long ago when his father owned the shop and he didn't have a way out. Mitch said that the people he was working for wouldn't let him stop. I told him he had to figure it out or I was going to tell the new owner. I figured I was doing it for his own good. Maybe if he stopped, he could turn his life around and stay out of trouble. I had no idea it might get him killed."

Luke saw the guilt on the man's face. "It's not your fault, Curtis. Mitch made the choices he made and you did a good thing encouraging him to stop. Do you know if he tried?"

"I'm not sure." Curtis leaned against the desk and blew out a frustrated breath. "About a month ago, I went back to him and asked if he had stopped. Mitch said that he thought he found a way. It would require working with the FBI and he wasn't sure he wanted to do that. There was a woman he said who could help him make a deal. I don't know how she found him or if he found her but she had come to the shop a few times with her car. They got talking and I assume that's how the connection was made."

"Do you know her?" Luke asked even though he was sure of the answer.

"It was the woman who was murdered like Mitch. When the news broke she had been killed, Mitch freaked out. He left the shop and said he had to take care of something. That was the last time we saw or heard from him. I tried calling but he never answered." Curtis stared down at the floor. "I didn't know how to help him."

"There wasn't anything you could have done, Curtis," Luke said, feeling badly for the guy. It was clear Curtis had been a good friend and if he could have done something to help Mitch, he would have done it. "It's good that you didn't get involved. It's possible that you could have been a target. This is bigger and more complex than the average murder. Do you know anything about the people Mitch was involved with? Did he ever tell you anything?"

Curtis raised his head. "He didn't tell me much. I didn't want to know anything because I didn't want to get in trouble. I know you probably think I should have called you guys when I first found out. I just wanted to give Mitch the chance to do the right thing on his own. His father had a great reputation and I didn't want to destroy that because of something stupid Mitch did."

"That's understandable. I don't know if I would have done anything differently than you did." Luke wasn't sure that was true, but if it had been Cooper or someone equally close, he didn't know that he'd be able to turn him in to the cops. "Can you think of anything Mitch might have said about them?"

"There's only one thing." Curtis pushed himself off the desk until he was standing to his full height. "Mitch told me he had to go to a house out in West Little Rock to pick up his pay for two of the cars.

Mitch said it was just past the Walmart out there on Highway 10. It sits back up on the hill and has a long driveway. It's gated and looks like a normal farm. There are even horses out front. He said that once inside, it didn't seem like a normal house. He guessed they were running whatever else they were doing out of there."

That was probably the first solid lead Luke had found. "That's great information, Curtis. I appreciate it. What about any person he dealt with regularly?"

"Mitch never told me any names. He called one guy the Greek and left it at that. I don't know anything about him other than that. I couldn't pick him out of a lineup if you had one. As I said, I only found out all this about two months ago. I hadn't even resigned myself to tell the boss yet." Curtis looked toward the door. "I need to get back to work. If I think of anything else, I'll let you know."

Luke thanked him as Curtis headed for the door and then disappeared into the hallway. A few minutes later, another mechanic was sent in to speak to Luke and then two more followed. He didn't learn any information more useful than what Curtis had provided.

All in all, Mitch was well-liked and did his job and didn't cause trouble for anyone. That's all anyone seemed to care about at the shop. No one else, that they were admitting, was privy to Mitch's afterhours activity.

Luke left the shop and headed straight back to the hotel where Jimmy was holed up. He double checked with the guard outside and then relieved him of his duty, telling him to take a break and come back in thirty minutes. Luke rapped on the door once and then slipped the keycard into the slot and pushed the door open.

The room was bathed in darkness even though it was nearing ten in the morning. Jimmy was sprawled out on his back with the sheets twisted around one bare leg. There were four empty bottles of water on the floor and a half-empty one on the nightstand. Luke headed to the window and yanked back the dark curtains to reveal the first hint of sunlight in the room.

"Jimmy," Luke said, turning to look at his witness. "Jimmy," he called again, growing frustration in his voice. He could see the man's chest rise and fall, so Luke knew he wasn't dead. That had been one of his concerns the night before when he had placed him in the hotel. Luke second-guessed himself and wondered if Jimmy should have been in a rehab facility instead. He didn't know the detox process. All Luke knew was he needed Jimmy clean and sober enough to tell him what he knew.

"Jimmy!" Luke shouted this time. "Get up. We need to talk."

A groan escaped Jimmy's lips as he rolled over to face away from Luke.

Luke went to the bed and stood over him. "You need to get up and tell me about the man called the Greek and the house in West Little Rock."

Jimmy mumbled a curse and flopped himself back over on his back. He stared up at Luke. "How'd you find out about that?"

"Not your concern." Luke checked his watch. "I'm giving you thirty minutes to get showered and get yourself together. I'll be back with coffee. You better be ready to talk when I get back or I can bring you to a jail cell."

With that, Luke left and didn't look back. His patience had run out.

CHAPTER 32

At close to ten-thirty when Cooper couldn't stand being at his desk any longer, he decided to take a walk. He decided he'd go to a coffee shop he liked in the River Market and grab coffee and pastry. He'd people-watch while he ate and then walk back.

Cooper had texted Luke right after talking to Riley. When Luke responded an hour later, he said he was deep in interviews and would catch up with Cooper later. That was about all he could do on that front. Two of his investigators were in the field and, unless they needed something, Cooper was free to roam. He wished he was with Riley heading to New York City.

Cooper walked the few blocks to the River Market, enjoying the crisp air and sunshine on his face. The walk shook him out of the boredom that had settled in his bones. Cooper entered the coffee shop, ordered a caramel macchiato that Adele told him had too much sugar and stared into the pastry case.

"There's too much to choose from," a woman said, stepping closer to him. "You're Cooper Deagnan, right?"

Cooper righted himself and glanced to his side. The woman stood about Riley's five-foot-seven height and had her hair in a short messy dark bob with strands of purple through it. She had a row of earrings up both ears and dark lipstick.

"Do I know you?" Cooper asked tentatively, hoping she wasn't someone he'd slept with in his single years and had long since forgotten.

The woman stuck out her hand to shake his. "I'm Cat O'Conner. I have a podcast called Rock City Killers. I've been wanting to speak to you for some time. Have you listened?"

During Cooper's recuperation, he listened to a few episodes that were focused on their past cases. Cooper's name along with Luke and Riley were frequently mentioned, even though none of them had ever been interviewed. He had considered more than once reaching out to Cat but never followed through. Cooper wasn't even sure why he hadn't. He shook her hand. "I've heard of it and caught an episode or two. They were quite good."

"I'm flattered," she said, blushing. "I've been an admirer of yours for quite a while. Care to sit and talk with me for a few minutes?"

"Sure," Cooper said, not having anything else to do. The company might be nice. Cooper ordered a blueberry muffin along with his coffee and then waited while Cat ordered. He paid for both even though she argued with him about it. They found a back table away from other patrons.

Cooper sipped his coffee. "I found out about you while I was in St. Thomas. There was someone who knew us from your podcast."

"It's grown over the last year," Cat said with a big smile. "I assume you might want to know how I got started and why."

"I'm always interested in why people gravitate to what they do," Cooper said, honestly. He was interested in her background as well as why she had zeroed in on him and his friends. Cooper assessed right away that Cat was the kind of woman who seemed to ooze confidence. Whether she knew she was doing that Cooper couldn't be sure.

"I went to college for journalism and I've been freelancing for years. I'm from Chicago and ended up following my boyfriend to Little Rock. He wanted to be back living near his family. We broke up about a year ago and now I'm just kind of here. I guess the podcast started as a way to help me through the breakup. I needed to focus on something else. To my surprise, I quickly had followers who were interacting with me. They felt like friends and family I didn't have here." Cat held her coffee cup as she talked, taking little sips during pauses.

Cooper found her to be surprisingly open and honest for someone he'd just met. "I know what it's like to only have a handful of people in your life."

"I have family and friends back home in Chicago." Cat smiled and laughed at herself. "It's probably me being stubborn. I didn't want to go back home even though my relationship ended. It felt a little like admitting defeat and crawling back."

"Would anyone think that?"

Cat tapped the side of her temple. "Just me and I'm my own worst critic. I made this big move and I wanted it to mean something. I wanted to leave my mark here even if I don't stay forever."

Cooper understood that. "Have you always had an interest in crime?"

"Always!" Cat said with an enthusiasm that Cooper felt in his soul. "I have a bookshelf full of true crime novels. Once my ex and I broke up, I was living alone in a strange city. I started paying attention to the crime stats because as a single woman safety is important. It's something we are naturally aware of, keeping tabs on it in a way. I stumbled across all these cases no one else was talking about locally or nationally. You've had some fascinating cases. Not only did I want to highlight your work but also the nature of these crimes. They made for compelling episodes."

Cooper didn't disagree with her. She made them sound more interesting than they were while the investigation was happening. "I can't speak for Luke because he would have to clear it with the police department. I would have given you an interview and I'm sure

Riley would have as well. Is there a reason you didn't reach out? More than anything, we all felt a little shocked that this was happening and we didn't know it."

Cat apologized for that. "It wasn't my intention to do that. I didn't think anyone would take me seriously at first. There are some huge true crime podcasts and I was an unknown in a smaller city in the middle of the United States. I sourced all my information using the Freedom of Information Act. But I didn't reach out to any of you as I should have because I wanted to establish myself first. I didn't want you to think that this was a side project or hobby. I'm making a full-time living now as a podcaster. I even have a full-time assistant and technical person who helps me. Before coming to any of you, I wanted you to take me seriously. I only covered the cases that I could without interviews. There are others I haven't tackled."

The way she looked at him, Cooper had a feeling which one she meant. "The one where I was drugged?"

Cat nodded. "That case, the one you were just injured on, and what's happening now. I know that you weren't mentioned in the news. I have a source who says you witnessed the murder of Mandy McKee."

Cooper turned his head to look away from her. He hoped this meeting was by chance and that she hadn't followed him here for this reason. He leaned into the table as he glanced to his left and right. He needed to set the record straight. "I didn't witness Mandy's murder," he started and when she didn't look convinced, he pushed harder. "I thought I witnessed it. That isn't what I saw. She was killed sometime later. Where did you hear that?"

"I can't say," Cat said and stared intensely at him. "If I reveal my sources, they won't tell me anything anymore."

Cooper assumed it was someone at the police department like a crime scene tech or one of the beat cops. They'd be the only ones who knew. "Your source wasn't correct this time because I wasn't," Cooper said and sat back. "This case is ongoing and the police have it under control."

"Do they?" Cat asked and her tone indicated that she knew something more.

"What do you think you know?"

Cat shifted her eyes to the side and then looked back at Cooper. "I don't think we should talk about this here. Will you come with me to my studio?"

"I'm not being recorded talking about this," Cooper said firmly. "This is an open and active investigation. If you have information to help the police, we need to go directly to Luke and tell him."

"This isn't about an interview for the podcast," she clarified. "I don't want to record you. I want to go someplace more private and speak about this. I don't want to talk about it openly."

Cooper wasn't sure if he should trust her. He wavered for a beat too long.

Cat pushed her chair back from the table, making a scraping noise on the floor. Others in the café turned to look at them. Cat eyed them and then lowered her voice. "I have what could potentially be sensitive information that I don't like having. I was hoping given your background you'd be willing to help me. I don't have all the pieces together enough to give the information to the cops. I thought you might help me with that."

Cooper would go with her. There was something he wanted to know first. "Did you follow me here?"

"I did," Cat admitted. "I hadn't planned on that. You walked by my studio and I saw you out the window. I decided if I was ever going to speak to you, I should have it look like we ran into each other. I didn't know if you'd return my calls."

"You could have tried," Cooper responded, standing from his chair. "I don't like being followed." What Cooper wanted to say was that he didn't like *not knowing* he was being followed. He was normally more on his game than this. He pulled out his phone and texted Luke that he might have a lead on his case and he'd be in touch as soon as he could. For good measure, he mentioned that he was heading to the Rock City Killers podcast studio with Cat O'Conner.

Once back at the studio, which was only a block away from Cooper's loft, he settled into a chair in a small conference room with sidewalk-facing windows. Cat had surprisingly good office space for what Cooper had considered a start-up project. An assistant manned the front door and the phones. Cat had introduced the young woman as Lorna as they entered.

"You got me back here. What do you think you know?"

Before Cat joined Cooper at the table, she closed the conference room door and closed the blinds. "Do you know the name Brody Barrett?"

"Should I?"

"He works at the U.S. Attorney's Office here in Little Rock. He's been involved in the investigation of the Andino family. Do you know who that is?"

Cooper knew the name from what Luke had told him. He knew very little about the investigation or background about the family. Cooper's search hadn't turned up much. "I know the name."

"Let me tell you what I know and we can go from there." Cat sat back in the chair and continued. "The Andino family is to California what the five Italian families were to New York City. They run the state and the west coast. Over the last ten years, they moved east and have a reach into other cities. I'm talking about all kinds of crimes from running drugs and guns to art theft, money laundering, and car theft. You name a crime and they have their fingers in it."

"I know all of that," Cooper said, surprised but also impressed Cat knew as much.

"Do you have any idea how they have been able to grow this quickly and not get caught? Do you know how they have avoided the kinds of prosecution that have taken down other crime families?"

"I assume you're going to tell me it's not because they are better at getting away with it," Cooper said with a hint of a smile. He was warming up to Cat. He liked how animated she got when she talked and how her excitement level matched her tone.

"It's not. They have someone on their payroll who tips them off on investigations and has even stolen and destroyed evidence. Worse still, they have given up the names of people who are willing to testify against them." Cat looked over at Cooper with a look that said she wanted him to add it all up for himself.

"Brody Barrett," Cooper said after a moment. Then he leaned into the table not sure that he was hearing it correctly. "Are you telling me that a U.S. Attorney, responsible for federal prosecutions, is on the Andino payroll?"

"That's exactly what my source told me. She said that she has the evidence to prove it. But she's terrified that he will find out and have her killed before she can go to the cops. She said she is being watched all the time."

She had Cooper's attention now. "How did you find this out?"

"This woman told her daughter who stalked me until she staged an impromptu meeting with me in public, not unlike what I did to you today. When she did that, she slipped me a note. From there, it was all rather clandestine between this woman's daughter and me. We met a few times as she relayed information about what Brody has been doing. They are both hoping I can go to the cops with the information."

Cooper wasn't sure he understood. "Why haven't you?"

Cat scrunched up her nose in a way that made her seem much younger than she was. "How do I know it's true? A woman told me her mother said it. I never saw documents to prove it. I never spoke to the mother, who works for Brody in his home as an assistant. She has seen several people connected to the Andino family in and out of his house. I've never seen proof of that either. I assumed if I went to the cops with no evidence, they would assume I was pulling some stunt for the podcast."

"How long have you known about this?"

"A few months," Cat said and leveled Cooper a look. "I'm coming forward now because this woman believes Brody is connected to the recent murders. She said he ordered them killed."

"Why did they come to you and not the cops?"

"The daughter listens to my podcast and assumed I'd have a connection to the cops. Neither one wanted to be seen going to the police directly."

"They will have to. Your information is hearsay and so is the daughter's."

"I know that, but what do we do?"

The truth was if he hadn't already heard the name Andino from Luke, he might not have believed Cat's story. "Let me call Luke and I'll be in touch. For the time being, lay low. We don't want you to end up another victim."

Cooper left Cat sitting at the table with an expression of concern on her face. He was glad because she needed to be worried. As soon as he got to the street, he turned right instead of left and walked the distance to Adele's office. He'd talk to her and then take it straight to Luke.

CHAPTER 33

Luke had stood outside the hotel room door until the uniformed cop returned. When he got back, Luke went to make some calls and get coffee. He returned to Jimmy's room twenty minutes later and found Jimmy sitting at the table nursing a cup of coffee he had made in his room.

"This doesn't taste as good when you make it yourself," Jimmy said, looking over at Luke. "I'm awake and showered. What do you want to know?"

Happy to see Jimmy had done what he'd asked, Luke handed him the coffee he bought at the shop across the street and got down to business. He sat across from Jimmy at the table. "Tell me how you started working for the Andino family."

"I didn't know that's who I was working for initially. I needed a job, mostly to pay for the drugs I was taking. My parents and brother had cut me off financially. They tried more than once to get me into rehab. I went that route a few times and it never stuck. Anyway..." Jimmy took a sip of coffee. "My dealer hooked me up with his guy and I started selling. It was as simple as that to start. Once they realized that I was good at selling, they pulled me in more. Dealing weed turned to dealing pills and cocaine. I never went harder than that with the drugs. I didn't have those kinds of connections, and I wasn't looking to make them."

"What's the timeframe on this?" Luke asked, jotting down notes in his phone as Jimmy gave him the details.

"It was about three months between the time I was dealing weed before dealing pills and cocaine. I was bringing in a lot of money. A lot of money," he stressed. "Not that I was seeing much of it. But I was getting by. It was enough."

"How long have you been dealing for them?"

"In total?" Jimmy asked and Luke confirmed that's what he meant. "About four years. I was approached and asked if I wanted to get involved in other things, running guns and stealing cars. I never had an interest. I was doing so well dealing drugs that they left me alone for a while. About five months ago, there was more pressure. They told me one of the guys I knew might be talking to the cops and they wanted me to take care of it."

"What does that mean?" Luke asked even though he knew.

Jimmy locked his gaze on Luke and sent a message just with a look. "I've never killed anyone, and I wasn't going to start. I gave him bus money and told him to get out of town. I told my contact that I threw the body in the river."

Luke had heard similar stories of people that had gotten caught up in mob activity. He was glad Jimmy had the fortitude to not go through with murder and instead sent the person away. He'd be in serious jeopardy if the person ever returned. "I assume since you're still alive that they bought your story."

"They did," Jimmy confirmed. He glanced out the hotel room window. "That was enough for me, man. I wasn't going to stick around after that. I didn't know what to do. When I met Mandy and she said she could help me, I thought I had a way out. Fear got the better of me. I didn't know if I could trust her. I wish I had just said no and didn't involve Nick. Then he'd still be alive."

The guilt was starting to set in for Jimmy. Luke knew that the more it did, the more he'd want to turn back to drinking to dull the pain. He needed to keep Jimmy on track. He asked a series of questions about people he'd met while selling drugs and then jotted down names and how they connected to Jimmy and one another. "I assume at some point you figured out this was all connected back to California and the Andino family. Tell me about that."

"There isn't much to tell," he said with a shrug. "It was right before they wanted me to kill someone. I had to meet a man they called the Greek. He's a big hulking specimen of a man. He said he was the son of the head of the Andino family and that's who was running the operation. He came to me directly and gave me the gun. He said I had to shoot this other person. When I said I couldn't, he said he'd kill me. They don't shy away from getting their hands dirty. I believed him."

Before Luke asked about the house in West Little Rock, he wanted to know one important fact. "Both your brother and Mitch Katz were left in public places. Do either of these locations mean anything to you?"

"No," Jimmy said loudly, stressing the word. "That's the one thing I know about them more than anything else. They like to make things public. It was all for show." Jimmy stared at Luke from across the table. He pointed at him. "I want to know how they knew about me. I was good at playing loyal right up until Nick's body was found. I never told anyone but Nick that I was willing to rat them out. He wasn't going to tell them. He was trying to help me, so how'd they know?"

Luke wished he had more answers for him. "We are still working on that." Luke was still hung up on the locations where the bodies were found. "You're telling me the location didn't mean anything? Why take the risk?"

"That's how they roll. Those locations mean something to the people in Little Rock and that's the only point they are making. They can kill people and cause destruction anywhere. These murders were meant to send a message." Jimmy raised his eyes to Luke. "I know there's no way I'm getting out of this alive unless they are caught. Even then, I'm not sure I'll make it."

"You'll make it, Jimmy," Luke reassured even though he wasn't sure that drugs and alcohol wouldn't do the job better than the Andinos. "I need you to tell me about the house in West Little Rock. What's the purpose and who is out there?"

"When the Greek is in the city, that's where he stays. He has someone else out there too – another big guy. I only met him briefly and don't remember his name. It's something weird. That's where the Greek gave me the gun. I know they have guns out there and drugs. There is a basement in the home that has all the drugs. They aren't making anything like meth but the supplies are coming in and it's being sorted and then sent to people like me."

"I assume they have security?"

"Some. Less than you think." Jimmy yawned and took another sip of coffee. As he brought the cup to his lips, Luke noticed the slight tremor in his hand. He wasn't sure if he had missed it before or if it was a sign of detoxing. "The one thing you have to know about the Andinos is they are cocky. They know they are going to get away with everything. I don't know why but they have no fear of anything. That makes them dangerous. They have been operating right under your noses for a long time. They may have more security if they think you know about the house. But my guess is they believe they have eliminated all the threats."

Luke was glad to see Jimmy was finally seeing the situation for what it was. He asked a few more questions about the layout of the house and the people who were there often. When Luke was satisfied with the information, he added, "I'm going to do everything I can to make sure you remain safe. I've spoken to the prosecutor and if you're willing to testify, we can offer you immunity for any crimes you committed. Is that understood?"

Jimmy nodded. "Will I remain in protective custody?"

"Yes. I'm going to have medical staff come here today and evaluate you and see what you need. We need you clean and sober. I want to make sure we provide you the resources you need to do that." Jimmy agreed to the medical visit. Now that most of the information Luke needed had been provided, he had one last pressing question. "Have you reached your parents about Nick? I don't want them to see this on the news. I also don't want them coming home to danger."

"They haven't called me back yet. I'll leave them another message and tell them it's not safe to come home and that they need to go to my uncle's house in Florida. They will be right near there when they get off the ship. I'm sure by the time they dock, my father will call me back." Jimmy looked to Luke to see if it was a good plan.

"That sounds like the best thing we can do." Luke had left a few messages too. "Is there anything else you think I should know before I go?"

There wasn't anything about the Andinos. When Luke stood from the table, Jimmy asked him to wait. He stood and shoved his hands in his pockets. "I wasn't always this messed up. I know I gave you a hard time but I do want to help. It's going to take me a long time to get back on my feet. I'm going to do it for my brother because I don't think I can ever forgive myself for what happened to him."

"You have to forgive yourself or you're not going to be able to stay sober. Take the lesson learned and grow from it." Luke meant every word. He offered a few more words of encouragement and then left. The medical staff Luke had called earlier would be there soon. He left instructions with the uniformed cop at the door and then headed back to the station.

Luke heard the commotion at the top of the stairs before he saw what was going on. Cooper and a woman he didn't recognize were standing at Captain Meadows's door with Det. Tyler right behind them. There seemed to be a buzz of activity and Captain Meadows's voice carried throughout the bullpen. Luke didn't understand what he was seeing or hearing.

He came up behind Tyler and touched his arm. "What's going on? Has there been a break in the case?"

"Not a break so much as a complication," Tyler said and then got Cooper's attention. "Let's head to the conference room and Cat can tell Luke what you told us. We can take it from there."

As Cooper and the woman Tyler had called Cat went to the conference room, Luke stepped into Captain Meadows's office. He realized what he heard was his boss shouting instructions into the phone. When he saw Luke, he waved him into the office and then slammed the phone down.

"Is your witness safe?" Captain Meadows asked, his face was flushed and beads of sweat had already formed at his sparse hairline. "We need to make sure he's safe, Luke. Does that U.S. Attorney you spoke to know where he is?"

"No," Luke said slowly, still not understanding. "I didn't tell him anything about our case. I haven't spoken to anyone else at their office and have no plan to update them about our case. What's going on?"

"It's better if Cooper and Cat tell you. I'm glad Cooper brought her here directly. So far, her story checks out." Captain Meadows moved around his desk and stopped when he got to Luke. "When was the last time you spoke to your witness?"

"I just left there. I called in a medical team to check him over. It's people I trust."

Captain Meadows hesitated for a moment. "Did you give them any information about who they were coming to see?"

"No. I told them I had a witness in protective custody who'd be detoxing and that was it. I didn't even provide a name." Luke furrowed his brow. "Is Jimmy in danger?"

"He shouldn't be if you didn't tell the U.S. Attorney's Office." Captain Meadows put his hand on Luke's shoulder. "Let's go discuss this and then you can decide what you want to do."

Luke's heart raced with worry and confusion. He followed Captain Meadows down the hall to the conference room and was introduced to Cat O'Conner. Once he heard her full name, Luke realized this was the same woman who ran the podcast. He couldn't imagine that Captain Meadows would be meeting her about an upcoming show on the podcast. It had to be something more.

As Luke sat at the table, he looked at her and Cooper. "Someone needs to fill me in quickly. I have a witness I need to make sure is safe."

Cat didn't waste any time. She locked her gaze on Luke. "I have reason to believe that Brody Barrett with the U.S. Attorney's Office is working with the Andino family. My understanding is that he's on their payroll and passes off any information he hears about potential cases against them as well as witness information. He's protecting them."

The information was certainly concerning. What was more pressing was how Cat had come to the information. "How did you hear about this?"

She hesitated and looked at Cooper who urged her to continue. "There's a woman who works in his home as an assistant who found out the information and passed it to her daughter who told me. Of course, I've not been able to verify it. This is why I brought it to Cooper who brought me here. I don't want to cause any trouble for anyone. I didn't know what to do with the information, but it seemed important I share it with someone. The woman feels like their lives would be in danger if Brody found out she knew and was sharing it."

"They would be," Det. Tyler said and then turned to Luke. "There's no real way to verify this. That said, we need to take it seriously given all we know."

Luke didn't disagree. "Cat, had you heard of the Andinos before you were approached by this woman?"

"It wasn't a name I'd heard before and even when I tried to research them not much came back." Cat picked her phone up off the table and tapped at the screen. She turned it so Luke could see a website. "I was able to verify that Brody Barrett worked for the United States Attorney for the Northern District of California and had transferred here to Little Rock two years ago. I found out where he went to law school and that he had worked at the District Attorney's office in San Francisco before that. That was as far as I got in research because I didn't want to start asking questions and have anyone wonder why."

"That was smart," Luke said, commending her for laying low with the information.

"Det. Morgan," Cat said her tone even but firm. "I don't know if the information I'm receiving is accurate. The one thing I do know is the woman telling me is scared for herself and her mother. They have thought about leaving the area but are worried that any sudden movements, like quitting, might spark concern. Brody seems to trust this woman because he's talked extensively in front of her."

"Either he trusts her or dismisses her," Captain Meadows suggested. "Cat, we appreciate you coming forward with this information. If there isn't anything else, we can take it from here. Please don't share it with anyone as you could be in danger."

Cat thanked them for listening and then got up with Cooper and left.

When the door closed behind them, Captain Meadows looked at them both. "Do you raid the house or bring in Barret first?"

Tyler and Luke shared a long look.

Finally, Luke said, "We raid the house first. Let's go to Barrett with ammunition."

CHAPTER 34

I had such a late start leaving Geneseo that I didn't stop at my mother's house. I headed straight for the train station and called her on the way. I told her I'd be home later that night or I'd stay at a hotel in the city and be back tomorrow. She was glad I called to let her know. She asked if I wanted Jack to come with me. I figured a one-on-one conversation would be better.

I enjoyed the train and the time it afforded me to reflect on the case without interruption. The one thing I knew to be true was Tim wasn't the one who killed Alex, and she had entangled herself with a few men. I wish I had known Alex was thinking about changing her major and what she wanted to do after graduation. I would have been encouraging of that. I had to admit that I could be quick to cast judgment on her back then and that was probably why she hadn't told me anything. It was a tough pill to swallow.

I spent time researching Tate and came back with nothing but glowing reviews of his art. He was also a philanthropist, sitting on boards of nonprofits and giving back to his community. He held an art show once a year to raise money for a local food bank and often donated his artwork for silent auctions at other nonprofit events. He also opened his gallery to showcase upcoming artists who couldn't get shows anywhere else.

The photos of him didn't make him seem very big. I would guess no more than five-foot-eight and he seemed to have a medium build. He was fully dressed in long sleeves and pants so his body wasn't fully on display. I didn't know what he looked like when I was in college. If I had to guess based on the description of the man Tim saw, Tate wasn't the guy.

In all likelihood it was Jason he saw.

I kept coming back to two things – the car sitting outside of the house that night and the cheating scandal. Neither of those two things seemed to fit with the rest.

Jason could have killed Alex and the cheating meant nothing. I wasn't ruling that out, particularly given how I had obtained the information. Taking a statement from the deceased would never hold up in court. I could see myself sitting on the stand having to admit that I contacted Alex's spirit for answers. I'd be kicked out of the courtroom and the case would be over.

The train pulled into Penn Station on time and I quickly walked through the station to the street. No matter how many times I visited the city, the first blast of being in the center of it all smacked me in the face – overwhelming my senses. Car horns blared, the lights of the cars and buildings lit the street like it was still late afternoon, the mix of sour city street smells, the bustle of people rushing past me. I wasn't sure where to focus my eyes.

I stood still for a moment and absorbed it all. I wasn't one to have anxiety, but New York City had a vibe all its own that I never felt anywhere else. It always took me a moment to orient myself, put on a certain energetic armor, and then proceed. I stepped to the curb and quickly hailed a cab that took me to Tate's gallery.

The street was a mix of small shop storefronts with residential units above and old brownstones. It was a narrow side street out of the way of the hustle and bustle. I paid the driver, thanked him for getting me there quickly, and exited the cab.

A bell over the door chimed as I entered. There was no one in the gallery but it was still well-lit. The walls were lined with photographs and there was a row of sculptures that went all the way to the back. The space was narrow but long.

"Tate Butler," I called, not too loudly because the space didn't feel like one where people yelled. I moved through glancing at the photographs, mostly unique cityscapes. I couldn't tell what many of the sculptures were, but I didn't have a refined art palate. Even if I spent time studying them, the pieces wouldn't speak to me the way they did to others. I liked looking at them but rarely found myself finding all the deeper meaning everyone else seemed to take away from the experience.

"Tate," I called again as I made it to the back of the room. I knocked on the single door in the back of the gallery.

"I'm coming," a man responded and then pulled open the door. Tate had a splash of red paint across a gray tee-shirt and ripped jeans. I introduced myself and he stuck out a hand to shake mine. The grip on my hand was strong and masculine. He pulled his hand back when he realized it was covered in paint. He disappeared behind the door and came back with a rag in his hand.

"Sorry, a hazard of the job. I have a table and chairs in the back if you want to sit and talk. Let me lock the front door and we can head back." He left me standing there as I watched him walk away.

I had been thinking on the train ride that one look at him in person and I'd be able to rule him out. I realized how wrong I'd been. I had been working off some misguided notion of artists. I thought he'd be more softly spoken. While he looked the same as in the photos, what they hadn't shown was the muscle definition of his arms and the strength of his hands, which I should have assumed given he was a sculptor. He wasn't tall but I'm pretty sure he'd be no slouch in a fight.

Tate came back to where I was standing, studied my face for a moment, then opened the door. "It's a bit messy back here. We have an upcoming show and I have several art pieces ready for exhibition." He guided me past the stored sculptures, paintings, and photographs, down a short hall and then to another room. "I'm working on a painting," he said gesturing toward the paints and brushes on the floor. "I don't paint often but when I do, it consumes me."

The canvass was turned away from me so I couldn't see the work and he didn't explain further. I took a seat at the small two-seater table. It looked like someone's old kitchen set they had dragged into the space. "I appreciate you taking the time to speak with me. Have you ever been interviewed about Alex?"

"Not formally," Tate said and sat down. He splayed his legs wide and leaned back in the chair, commanding the space.

"What was your relationship with Alex?"

Tate shook his head. "I wouldn't call it a relationship. I barely knew her. I had given a lecture at Geneseo and she visited one of my art shows in Rochester. We struck up a conversation and she said she was interested in working in the art world. She wasn't an artist but she had a good eye. I was encouraging her to explore that more, even if it was something she did while she considered another career. Alex had a ton of questions. Many I couldn't answer. I had resources, books, and things that I provided her to help her."

"Never romantic?" I asked with my eyebrows raised.

"Never romantic. Not even a hint of romance. She was younger than me and we were at different stages of our lives. I know the cliché is a man and younger woman but Alex wasn't mature enough for me. She didn't know what she wanted, and I was full steam ahead at the start of my career. I was seeing enough success that I could give back and help young people like Alex. I wasn't going to have a relationship or even entanglement with her. I wasn't about to let anyone or anything derail the career I was busy building."

There was enough conviction in his voice that I believed him. "How long did you know her?"

"Briefly, barely at all. That's why it's been crazy how I've been caught up in this."

We held steady eye contact as I asked, "You were the last one to see her alive. I'm not sure why you'd believe you shouldn't be caught up in this. You should be more caught up in this. I can't believe the cops didn't take a statement from you or Tim's defense attorney to have you testify in court."

Tate stared at me for a moment as if he couldn't believe what I just said. He closed his legs and sat upright in the chair. He poked his chest as he said, "I wasn't the last person to see Alex alive. I was there the night she died, but I wasn't the last person there. I was only there in her apartment for about ten minutes. About a week prior, Alex borrowed a book from me and I needed it back. She said she'd be home that night and I asked if she'd mind if I picked it up. She said she wouldn't be back up to Rochester for a while and it was worth the drive to get it back. That was the first and only time I had been to her apartment. There was another guy there. I spent a few minutes talking to them and then left."

"You weren't there to meet her boyfriend and convince him that Alex should change her career path?" Saying it aloud felt foolish. The look on his face drove home that feeling.

Tate smiled broadly. "I didn't care if Alex had a boyfriend. I certainly had no reason to meet him and convince him of anything. Who told you I was the last person to see her alive?"

I ignored the question. "Did you sense any tension while you were there with Alex and the other guy?"

"Tension isn't a strong enough word for it. Seething anger was more like it," Tate said and raked a hand through his hair. He expelled a breath. "That's the reason I didn't stay long. I felt like I walked into the middle of a fight."

"What was the apartment like when you were there?"

"What do you mean?" he asked with confusion in his tone.

"I was told while you were there, the other guy went ballistic – throwing things and causing a scene. You sat there calmly and watched it unfold. He stormed out and left you there alone with Alex."

Tate said *no* four times in a row, growing louder each time. "None of that is true." The frustration was written all over his face. He bit at his upper lip and then leveled with me. "Listen, the guy that was there is named Jason Thatcher, which I assume you know. I'm guessing he's the one who said I was left alone with Alex. He's a creep. He's come here to the studio several times over the years and threatened me. He threatened to tell the cops that I killed Alex. It got so bad that I had to take a restraining order against him. I assumed for a time that he was Alex's boyfriend but then I saw on the news that Tim, the guy who went to prison, was her boyfriend. I didn't know what to believe. My name was never dragged into it and I didn't know anything, so I didn't volunteer that I was there that night. For all I know, Tim showed up after me and saw Jason there."

"Jason didn't cause a scene while you were there?" I asked. It didn't surprise me that Jason had lied. I was hearing two vastly different stories and it was a matter of who I believed.

"I could tell that he was angry to have me there," Tate admitted. "There were some raised voices when I was coming up the stairs, but he didn't throw any kind of fit while I was there. If he had, I wouldn't have left Alex alone with him. I didn't know her well, but I wouldn't leave any woman in an unsafe situation."

I tried to piece together the scene in my head. I assumed Alex probably told Jason that Tate was going to stop by and that started the argument. It then bubbled over after he left. "Did Jason say anything to you at the time?"

"Nothing," Tate said, his eyes studying my face again. The intensity with which he looked at me unnerved me. He cast his eyes up to mine. "Sorry for staring at you. You're pretty and your features are symmetrical. Artist's habit." He paused again and took a breath. "As I was saying, Jason said nothing to me which is why it's been so surprising that he's been stalking me and accusing me of killing Alex. I never quite understood it."

I decided then to opt for the truth. "It was Jason who told me that he left you there. The story he presents is much different than your own." I gave him the full rundown of what Jason had told me. "Do you have an alibi for the time after leaving the apartment?"

In response, Tate told me to wait there. He went to a bookcase in the far corner of the room and pulled a slip of paper out of a book and brought it over to me. "Here is the order of protection still in place. The second page is the log of dates and times that Jason showed up at my old studio in Rochester and then here in the city. He went to my first studio and then came here when I moved to this location. The man is obsessed."

I read over the legal document and what Tate had told me was there in black and white. The second page had dates and times going back close to a few months after Alex was murdered. "You did a good job of documenting this."

"My lawyer advised me to do it. I was freaked out after the first visit. You don't get accused of murder and take it lightly." Tate sat back down and held steady eye contact with me. "I don't have an alibi. I left the apartment, drove back to Rochester, and was in my apartment alone all night. What I don't understand is Jason wasn't the only one who saw me leave that night."

"What do you mean?" I asked not hiding the surprise in my voice.

"There was a girl on her way up the stairs as I was leaving. She said she was looking for Alex and I told her that she was home. Someone else saw me leave and I can guarantee you no one saw me return because I never went back there."

Tate watched my reaction closely as I processed what he was saying.

"Did you catch her name?"

"No." Tate could, however, describe what she looked like.

I knew immediately who it was.

CHAPTER 35

Own the road from the Andino estate, Luke assembled his team including Tyler, other detectives, crime scene techs, and SWAT and made last-minute assessments about the best way to breach the residence. Luke had pulled the plans for the house and property so they had an understanding of it before breaching. Night had fallen and they chose the time when they thought the least people might be present on the property.

The SWAT team would position in the trees and watch the back of the property. Luke and Tyler would go the front way to serve the search warrant, which had been kept as quiet as possible. Luke had worked with the judge and explained the situation regarding the U.S. Attorney's Office and why secrecy was so critical.

They were as ready as they could be. Luke hoped that the SWAT team was unnecessary. Given the history and the guns on the property, he wasn't taking any chances. On Luke's signal, they all dispersed to their positions.

He and Tyler pulled up to the front gate and Luke rang the buzzer. A man came over the speaker and asked what they wanted. Luke identified himself and Tyler and asked to be let in. To his surprise, the gate slowly inched open and he pressed on the gas. He didn't worry because he knew SWAT had eyes on them and the house.

Luke pulled right up the circular drive in front of the house. It was a two-story home with an attic and a basement. The total structure had over seven thousand square feet. It was going to be a beast to search unless everything Jimmy told him was true. Then Luke knew exactly where to go first.

Luke put the car in park as a large man about six-foot-four exited the house. His biceps and chest strained the fabric of the gray tee-shirt.

"What can I help you with, Det. Morgan?" he asked walking right up to the driver's side of the SUV door nearly blocking it so Luke couldn't get out.

Luke shoved the door open wider, making him step back. "Who are you?" he asked when he was on solid footing. The man was taller than Luke and he didn't want to have to look up, so he stepped back away from him.

"Atlas," he said not giving Luke a last name even when he ordered him to do so. "I don't have to tell you anything. This is my home."

"Great, then you get this." Luke handed him the search warrant. "How many people are in the house?"

Atlas read the document as the vein at his temple pulsed. He widened his stance and glanced back at the house. "A few," he said curtly.

"Don't get any ideas. We came prepared." Luke didn't want to raise the tensions any more than they were. Not at least until he'd have to. "There is an entire SWAT team surrounding the home right now."

Atlas shoved the document back toward Luke. "This is unnecessary, Det. Morgan. You could have come out here and spoken to me about your concerns. I don't know where you're getting your information, but there is nothing criminal happening here. This is my home with my wife and daughter. I don't understand anything about that search warrant. You must have the wrong house."

Luke looked up at the house. He hadn't heard anything about a wife or daughter. "Where are they now?"

Atlas followed Luke's gaze. "Let me go in and get them. My daughter will be scared that the police are here. Let me reassure her and we can come out together before you go in."

"No," Luke said and took a step toward him. "You're going to wait out here. I don't believe for a second that you have a wife or daughter in there."

Luke signaled for the rest of the cops who had been waiting farther down the driveway to join him. He took another step toward Atlas. "I'm going to ask you again, how many people are inside?"

Before Atlas could answer, three shots rang out at the back of the house. Luke assumed someone was making a run for it. He didn't need to concern himself with it. That's what the SWAT team was for and why they were positioned back there.

At the sound of the gunshots, Atlas jerked to the side and then spun around as if he were going to make a break for it down the driveway. He came face to face with the rest of the cops heading toward them. He cursed loudly and turned to Luke with fire raging in his eyes. "I haven't done anything wrong. You can't treat me like this." He balled his hands into fists and took a menacing step toward Luke.

"Don't be stupid, Atlas," Luke cautioned him. "Turn around and put your hands behind your back." He didn't want to pull his gun if he didn't need to. Tyler already had his at his side ready if Atlas didn't follow directions. When Atlas didn't move, Luke urged him again. "Turn around now or we will force you down on the ground."

"I'd like to see you try," Atlas said and then more shots in the back of the home rang out. He shifted his eyes to Luke and then to Tyler. He was outnumbered and outgunned. He turned around and linked his hands behind him.

Luke put the cuffs on and then patted him down. He pulled a handgun from the man's waistband and then passed him off to two uniformed cops. Luke handed the gun to a crime scene tech. "Bag that for me."

"You have no right to take that," Atlas said as he was dragged off with two officers.

"You want to see what's going on around back?" Tyler asked.

"SWAT has it covered. Let's get inside."

Luke climbed the few steps to the front porch taking an offensive position with his gun in front of him. He glanced in the window to the right and then to the left. The front room was cleared. He pushed open the front door and barked an order for anyone inside to come out with their hands up. They waited and then waited some more. No one came.

Luke, Tyler, and a few officers behind them entered.

The others took the stairs to the right to the second floor while Luke and Tyler took a path from the formal living room to an office and then down a hall to a dining room and kitchen. Each was clear. Whoever cared for the home did a good job of keeping it tidy. There wasn't a cup or dish out of place. Luke assumed this main floor was set up for show rather than functionality.

Luke followed the directions Jimmy had provided to the large walk-in pantry that was stocked with food. Jimmy told him there was a switch on the wall to the right behind the canned goods. Jimmy said flipping that switch would open the back wall to reveal a set of stairs down to the basement.

Luke moved items on the shelf and saw the switch. His hand hovered for a moment before he flipped it in the upright position. The wall in front of them eased opened, forcing Luke to step back out of the way. He peered into the dark doorway to the stairs that descended into the basement. "I wasn't told where to find the lights," Luke said and pulled a flashlight from his pocket. He positioned it above his gun as he walked.

He got to the first step and called out, "This is Det. Morgan with the Little Rock Police Department. Identify yourself!" Silence met his command. Luke moved forward a few inches and felt along the wall for a light switch. He didn't find one but that didn't stop him. He kept going to the top step and he called his command out again. Silence.

Luke descended the flight of stairs to the basement, shining his small flashlight as he went. The basement walls were cinderblock and there were several workstations set up with scales, bags, and other equipment used for cutting, weighing, and packaging drugs. Items were tossed in disarray as if people had dropped what they were doing and made a run for it.

What Luke didn't see were any drugs.

He shined the light across the basement and stopped in surprise at the size of the space. The basement spanned far wider and longer than the imprint of the house above. He realized then that he couldn't see the entirety of the space from where he was standing. They'd need a bigger search team. Most pressing was finding the light because Luke didn't need to hear someone respond to him to know that there was someone else in the basement with him. The electric charge of fear and indecision hung heavily in the air.

Tyler was right behind him covering his back. He had read the energy in the room too. "We aren't alone. There is someone else down here and there's got to be another way out of this basement other than the stairs."

Luke had been thinking the same. SWAT still hadn't radioed about what had happened outside. He assumed that several people ran and fired at SWAT and they returned fire. "Let's keep moving forward and look for a light switch as we go."

They made it several feet when the sound of a box moving across the floor echoed across the room. Luke pivoted sharply to the right and put his light on the spot. There, behind a stack of boxes, were the long slender fingers of a woman gripping the top of the box.

"I can see you," he said calmly. "Put your hands up and get up slowly."

The woman slowly stood from her position. She had her head down so Luke wasn't able to see her face. As her slender shoulders rose and her torso came into view, she raised her chin ever so slightly and cast her eyes on him. It was then Luke realized this wasn't a grown woman. She was a young girl, probably not more than fourteen or fifteen.

"Step out here with your hands up. Are you alone?"

"I think so," she said softly. "They left me down here and told me not to follow them. Please don't shoot me."

Luke had seen ploys like this before. Keep their focus on a child and distract from a shot that comes from behind. He turned his head slightly and noted Tyler had prepared for that. His attention was focused on the rest of the space, covering both of them. "How do you turn on the lights?"

With her hands raised, she pointed to the wall near where she had crouched. "There's a switch here and then two farther back in the room. There's a switch at the top of the stairs too but it's hard to find."

"Turn the light on for me, please," Luke instructed not taking the gun off her. Although she was young, he wasn't giving her a pass. As she slowly made the move to turn on the light, he asked, "Is there anyone else down here with you?"

She shook her head. "They went out the door down here and made a run for it in the field behind the house." She flipped the switch and large fluorescent lights turned on overhead. She blinked and lowered her eyes to the ground.

Luke wanted to do the same but fought the urge to shield himself as he adjusted to the brightness. "How many people were down here with you?"

"Eight or so. I wasn't paying attention." She lowered her hands and stepped to the side of the boxes, showing Luke she didn't have a weapon. "I'll show you everything if you let me call my mom. I want to go home. They said that I'd be able to go home if I worked off the money for the bus ticket. I did that months ago and they still won't let me go."

"How old are you?" Luke realized quickly that this young girl might be as much a victim as Mandy, Nick, and Mitch.

"I turned fifteen last week. My name is Amelia Jenkins and my mom is in Berkley, California. I ran away from home about six months ago. I was trying to get to New York." Her words rushed out as tears stained her cheeks. "I want to call my mom and go back home. I'm sure she's worried about me."

"I'll let you call her but first show me the rest." Luke lowered his weapon and gestured for her to come to him. "Is this all drugs down here?"

"Guns too," she said as people began descending the stairs. She pulled back and looked over. "Are we safe? Are they gone?"

"It's other cops, Amelia. You're safe now." With other reinforcements with them, Luke barked orders for what the other cops and the crime scene techs should do. He holstered his gun and guided Amelia by the arm toward the rest of the room. "Show me where they keep everything."

Over the next thirty minutes, Amelia walked Luke around the space showing him all the hidden switches and levers that opened parts of the cinderblock walls and hid a cache of guns and money.

Amelia saved the best for last.

"Are you ready for this?" she asked as she flipped what looked like nothing more than a light switch. As she did, a large metal door rolled to the side exposing the cherry on the top of their criminal enterprise – a massive underground growing room for marijuana. There was an entire light system that hung overhead and a water system spouting from the ceiling.

There were far too many plants to even count.

Luke pulled his phone from his pocket and handed it to Amelia.

"Call your mother and tell her you're safe."

CHAPTER 36

The next morning at ten, I sat around the kitchen table with my mother and Jack. She had made us all ham and cheese omelets with spinach and a side of toast and coffee. We ate chatting about the weather and traffic and then got down to what they wanted to hear.

After speaking to Tate the night before, I hadn't wanted to waste any time staying in New York City. I caught the last train back to Albany and got in around midnight. They both were asleep by the time I got home. Dusty was the only one who greeted me. He sniffed me twice and went back to my mother's room where she kept his bed. I had torn my clothes off and tossed them in a heap on the floor and slid into cool sheets. I had fallen asleep before my head even hit the pillow.

My mother let me sleep in and then tempted me downstairs with breakfast. They were eager to hear how the trip to Geneseo and New York City had gone. I spent some time filling them in with the details, leaving the most important for last.

I took a sip of coffee and held the cup, enjoying the warmth in my hand. "It all circles back to what Tim had told me at the start. He thought Gail might have killed Alex. It didn't make sense to me at the time. I had no idea how many things about Alex's life I didn't know. In the end, Tate was the one who gave me the evidence that Gail had been there that night. I assume that's who Jason called as I left yesterday morning."

Jack raised the cup to his mouth. "Are you sure about that? Seems like a lot of missing pieces still."

He wasn't wrong. There was still a lot I didn't know. "Jason isn't going to confess, so my only shot is getting Gail to confess or incriminate herself in some way. Tate is willing to testify that he was there that night and he provided me with a signed statement for me to give to the police to get the ball rolling. Even if I can't bring the cops the killer, we have reasonable doubt for the district attorney's office to stop another case going forward against Tim."

They both nodded in understanding. "What are you going to do now?" my mother asked.

I had been considering my next steps. I still didn't know anything about the mystery car or the cheating. Both still nagged at me, but it was possible neither was important. Mary might have imagined the importance of the car and I might have imagined my brief conversation with Alex's spirit. It might have been the power of suggestion by the girls living in our old apartment.

My mother said my name and pulled me out of the spinning narrative in my head. I blinked and looked at her. "Sorry. I'm going over to the school to speak to Gail again. I'm going to tell her I know she killed Alex and see how she responds."

"What about Michelle?" my mother asked with curiosity in her voice.

"What about her?"

With her eyebrows raised and a look I couldn't read on her face, she asked, "She lied to you, didn't she? She said only one person was upstairs that night and that wasn't true by a long shot. Also, you said Tim said she saw him outside not inside."

I had been so focused on the information about Gail I had overlooked all of that. I applauded my mother for keeping track so well.

She might make a good investigator after all. "I'm going to have to speak to her again. I'll do that after I speak to Gail. It's possible Michelle just doesn't remember or maybe she was drunk that night. We all drank a lot in college and it was a holiday weekend. I don't even know if she had company that night."

"Didn't she testify against Tim?" Jack asked, giving me a knowing look.

He didn't want me to let her off the hook because we had been friends. He was right though. I read the testimony from the court case on the way back on the train. Michelle stated that Tim went inside that night and she saw him leave. She didn't testify that anyone else had been there. If she was truly home and saw Tim, then she saw the rest of them. Most of the case against Tim hinged on her testimony. The prosecution didn't have anyone else. The defense only called one witness and that was to refute the physical evidence.

I raised my eyes to Jack and nodded. "I'll go speak to her again."

They were satisfied with that answer. I helped my mother clear the table and loaded the dishwasher before saying goodbye. I promised I'd update them later. I had no idea where I'd find Gail today, but I'd start with her classroom.

I didn't have any luck. The classroom lights were off. I asked one young woman standing in the hall at a bulletin board if she knew where I might find her. She directed me to the bottom floor teacher's lounge. I walked back down the two flights of stairs I had climbed and made my way through a wide hallway.

All was quiet this morning. I found the door to the teacher's lounge and knocked twice before pushing it open. I found Gail sitting at a round table alone. She had her head bent over a stack of papers and a pen in her hand. I assumed she was grading.

"Gail," I spoke her name softly to not startle her. When she didn't even glance in my direction, I said her name again louder this time.

She raised her head and looked over, confused at seeing me. "I hoped that I'd be able to ask you a few more questions."

Gail let go of her pen and it dropped to the table. "Riley, you shouldn't be here. I don't know any more than what I told you the other day." She sighed a deep breath of frustration. "You really need to let the past stay in the past. I don't know why you're dredging all of this up again."

I let the door close behind me as I covered the distance to the table. I didn't sit but leaned down on the back of a chair. "Gail, how can you say that? You said you cared about Tim. You gave me an alibi for him that night. What's changed?"

Tim's words from the first time we met about the case came back to me. Gail had called to check on him later that night and urged him not to go back to the house. She was probably trying to stop him from finding the body and calling the cops. Seeing her now and the way she was trying to stonewall me convinced me even more of her guilt.

Gail threw her hands in the air. "It doesn't matter anymore. Tim is out of prison. They won't retry him and there's not a lot left to say." She stared at me directly. "Besides, it's not like I'm getting anything out of helping you. Tim still doesn't want a relationship with me. He didn't love me then and certainly not now. All he wanted was Alex. I was right in front of him and he never saw me. I was kind and considerate and always there for him. Did he want that kind of stability? No. He wanted her – that ridiculous train wreck."

"You sound like you didn't like her very much."

A cruel mocking laugh escaped her lips. "What was there to like? Alex ran all over everyone. She didn't care about anyone's feelings but her own. She hurt or dismissed everyone she came in contact with. She wasn't even a good friend to you!"

"Is that what you were there to talk to Alex about the night she died?" Gail sat motionless watching me. There was fear in her eyes but she wasn't expressing it. I leaned down farther on the chair, putting my weight on my palms and pressing them into the plastic. "I know, Gail. That's why I'm back. I know you went to our apartment that night. I don't know why and, before I accuse you of something unspeakable, I want to understand why. I *need* to understand what you were doing there that night and what you saw."

Gail pushed the chair back from the table, loudly scraping the legs on the tile floor. "I can't talk about this in here. Let's take a walk."

I didn't care where we had the conversation. All I cared about was that we were having it. I followed her out of the teacher's lounge and then back down the wide hallway to the front door. She pushed the door open and breathed in a deep breath. "This isn't what you think, Riley," she said as she stepped out onto the sidewalk.

I caught up with her. "Help me to understand. What it looks like is that you went there to confront Alex about something and in the process you and Jason killed her."

Gail's head snapped sharply to the side to look at me. "You know about Jason?"

"I know most of it, Gail," I said evenly, making it sound like I knew far more than I did. "I already spoke to Jason. Tate Butler saw you that night as he was leaving the apartment. He's willing to go to the cops with that information."

"I don't know what Jason did or didn't do, Riley. I wasn't there for that," Gail said, walking briskly in front of me. She was on the move and didn't want to slow down to talk. She cut in between two buildings and headed toward the back of campus. She didn't say anything more until we were clear of the buildings and standing on the expanse of green lawn behind the school.

"Why were you there?" I asked when she stopped walking.

Gail turned to me with rage in her eyes. She jabbed a finger at me as she spoke. "Did you know Alex was dropping out of the education department to pursue art?" The way she said it made it sound like it was completely distasteful to her.

I was apparently the only one back then who didn't know. I smacked her finger away from me. "I heard that recently. I didn't know it then. Alex never told me. Why does that matter to you?"

Gail rolled her eyes to the sky and cursed. She marched ahead toward the back black iron gate of the property. "You don't get it, Riley. Alex took the Hamilton Prize for Education. She won a fifty-thousand-dollar award for graduate school in education that she was never going to use. She put herself up for that award knowing full well she was going to drop education and get a degree in art history. She took that prize away from someone who needed it."

There was something about the way Gail said that, a certain desperation in her voice that I finally understood. "She took the prize away from you. Is that what happened?"

Gail turned her head to the side and looked away. "I needed that money for graduate school. Alex only did it to prove she was better than everyone else. She didn't think about someone else who might have really needed the money."

As she said that, I remembered Alex had won the award two weeks before she was murdered. "If the person getting the award doesn't use it, what do they do?"

Gail threw her arms wide. "Nothing. There's no runner-up or second place. It's just not used that year. That's why I was so angry. She wasted scholarship funding she knew she wasn't going to use. If I had lost to someone who was going to use it and deserved it, I could live with that. What Alex did was unconscionable."

She had every reason to be angry. I wasn't going to fault her for that. "Is that why you went to our apartment that night? Did you go to confront her about it?" I remembered what Tim said about the bruises on her hand and face. "Did you get into a physical fight with her, Gail?"

"You really don't know anything," she spat and folded her arms across her chest.

"I'm trying to find out. That's why I'm here asking you about it." When Gail still didn't make a move to tell me, I pushed harder. "I wasn't in the education program. There was a lot going on I didn't know about. Alex and I were friends but clearly, she didn't tell me a lot. I'm trying to sort it all out."

"Eighteen years too late," Gail said with a smirk. "Did you know right before Thanksgiving break, Alex went to the head of our department and told him several students had been cheating? She said she was going to give him names after the break. He demanded to know and Alex refused. She said she had a few things to consider first. She was toying with the head of our department!"

My stomach dropped and my tongue felt like it was too big for my mouth. I couldn't speak. The cheating had been real. It took me a moment to collect myself. "How did you find that out?"

"I heard it from some of the other people in the program. There were rumors Alex had caught someone cheating. I'm fairly certain she started those rumors. She was toying with people and dangling it over our heads for weeks. We didn't know if she was serious or if it was something she was making up." Gail's chest rose and fell with each hard breath. "I wasn't cheating and I don't know who was. I went to her that weekend to talk her out of destroying someone's college career unless she had actual proof. I also confronted her about the scholarship."

"What happened when you got there?"

Gail made steady eye contact with me then. "You think I killed her?"

That was exactly what I thought. We stood in a stalemate while I waited for the truth to be confirmed. Gail rocked back and forth until the tears streamed down her face. All at once, she tipped her head back and she let out a howl that she seemed to have been holding in for a long time. It was a guttural release of anger and frustration.

CHAPTER 37

I was sure with a scream like that the entire school would be racing to see what was going on. I kept turning my head to watch for them while Gail broke down in front of me. I wasn't sure what to say to comfort her. I was afraid anything I said would have her walk back what I thought she was about to tell me.

Several minutes passed while Gail sobbed into her hands. No one at the school came running to see what was happening. Finally, I reached out and touched her shoulder. "Gail, whatever you have to tell me, it's going to be okay."

She shrugged back out of my grasp and raised her head to me. "My life was miserable because of Alex. I hated her but I didn't kill her. I wanted to. God help me. I wanted to. I didn't have the ability to do it." Gail wiped her tears on the back of her hands. "When I confronted her, she laughed at me, Riley. She tried changing the subject about how I was in love with Tim and how he didn't want me. He wanted her. I lashed out and hit her. She hit me back. Jason broke it up before either of us could do much damage to the other. I didn't kill her but I'm glad she's dead."

Her words stung like a slap across my face. I kept my focus on what was important. "Did you see anyone else there?"

Gail sniffled and wiped her hand across her face again, drying it. "Some guy was coming down the stairs as I was going up. I didn't know his name or who he was. He told me Alex was up there when I asked and he left. I'd never seen him before or since."

"Tate Butler," I said filling in the blanks for her. "He's an artist who Alex knew briefly. She had borrowed a book from him and he was there getting it back. He described you. That's how I knew it was you."

"When I got upstairs, Alex was arguing with Jason. I heard them through the door."

"Do you know why they were arguing?"

"Jason was accusing her of cheating on him with the guy who had been there. Alex was yelling back just as loudly that she wasn't involved with him. That he was someone who was teaching her about art. They went back and forth like that. There was a pause in the argument when I knocked on the door." Gail looked up at the sky. "I thought about not going in at all. I had walked all the way over and was angry. I needed an outlet. Alex opened the door and I barged right in, yelling at her. I didn't wait. I had summoned all that courage up on the walk over and it all came pouring out."

"Did Jason say or do anything while you were yelling?"

"He initially went to the kitchen and ignored us. Once I hit her, he came running to her defense. Alex didn't need it. She hit me back harder than I hit her."

"That had to have made you angrier," I said, watching Gail's reaction. She was more in control of her emotions now, but I was waiting for them to bubble back to the surface.

Gail hugged her arms around her body. "I don't know what I expected. It's not like Alex was going to apologize or tell me who was cheating or even be nicer to Tim. She couldn't take back the scholarship decision. I shouldn't have gone there. I felt deflated and defeated after, more so than before. I left right after. I don't think I was there more than fifteen minutes."

It was a story I wasn't sure was true. I took a step toward her. "Come on, Gail. You expect me to believe Alex hit you back and you didn't do anything? You had all that rage inside you. She called you pathetic. She took your scholarship and the man you loved. You just gave up?"

Gail didn't say anything for several moments. Her chest rose and fell with each breath. Finally, she looked up at me. "After she hit me back, Jason came running. I couldn't take them both on. Once Alex hit me, it was like all the anger drained from my body and I realized I was as pathetic as she said. There was no fight left in me."

"No," I said my anger rising. "Isn't it true you and Jason attacked Alex and killed her together? You've been covering it up all these years."

"That's not true," Gail said her voice tight with emotion. "I hit her once and Jason stopped us."

"What about her star necklace. I know that you have it."

Gail cursed and shook her head. "I knew Tim saw it that night. I had pulled it off her during the short fight we had. I left without even realizing it was in my hand until I got outside. I wasn't going to go back. When I got home, I threw it on my dresser. Then she was dead and I didn't know what to do. I wasn't going to tell Tim I had a confrontation with Alex. I wanted him to like me and figured he'd be angry with me."

I wasn't sure I believed her. I pushed harder. "Isn't it true that after you hit her, Jason did as well? He saw you attack her and took the opportunity to finish her off."

"I never saw Jason hit her," Gail said with conviction in her voice. "I had a few classes with Jason. We were in the same program after all. We all knew each other. I didn't like him much, so he wasn't someone I spent much time around. I had no reason to protect him if he had done something to her."

"But you did protect him by not telling the cops he was there that night," I said, my anger growing now. "You could have gone directly to the cops and told them."

"I tried telling them that Tim was with me!" she shouted back.

"It's not the same as telling them you saw Alex that night with Jason." I lowered my voice and zeroed in on her face, watching her carefully. "Were you afraid Jason killed her and, if you said anything, he'd be after you?"

"That was part of it." Gail swallowed hard. "His father was involved in city government, Riley. I had hit her. I put my hands on her and no one was going to believe he was there that night. All he had to do was deny it or say that he was there and left me alone with Alex. If he admitted to being there, then he could say that I hit her and how angry I'd been. It would have been my word against his and everyone knew I was in love with Tim. They would have called me unstable and said I went after her because I was jealous. It was a lose-lose situation for me."

I couldn't argue with any of that. She was right. "Did anyone see you besides Tate and Jason?"

"I don't think so. I knocked at Michelle's door before I left but there was no answer."

"She wasn't home?" I asked my confusion evident. Michelle had told me that she was home the entire night.

"There were lights on and music playing. It's possible she didn't hear me knock. I didn't stay long as I was upset. I stopped to ask her if she knew Jason was upstairs. I thought he'd been dating a friend of hers. I was surprised to see him there."

"Do you know who he was dating?"

"Taylor Lewis," Gail said, her body finally relaxing. "Jason was always a loudmouth in our classes. The one who knew it all, and in one class I told Michelle I didn't like him much. She told me he was dating Taylor and that he was often hard to take. She seemed neutral on him and I let the subject drop."

"You never mentioned being there to Michelle after the murder?"

She looked at me with eyebrows raised as if I was missing something. When I didn't say anything, she admitted, "If Michelle didn't see me leave that night then it was my word against Jason's. I said I wasn't going to take that risk. I didn't tell anyone."

"Including the cops…" I left the most important part unspoken. She could have easily created doubt for a jury with her testimony. I could understand why Tim's attorney didn't want her on the stand. He had probably sensed she was lying about something.

"I couldn't, Riley. I never told anyone, not even Tim."

"Why didn't you want Tim to go back to the apartment that night?" When she hesitated, I explained, "Tim already told me that you didn't want him to go back. He said you begged him not to."

"He avoided a fight with Jason once. I was worried if he went back there'd be an altercation and he'd get hurt." Gail looked up at the school. "I need to get back. I have a class to teach." She turned back to me. "I didn't kill Alex. If I knew who did, I'd tell you."

"When was the last time you were in contact with Jason?"

Gail furrowed her brow. "I haven't spoken to him since graduation, Riley. I told you I didn't like him. I worried if he was the one who killed Alex that at some point, he'd pin it on me. I figured it was safer to move on and never look back." She started to walk off toward the school and I followed behind her.

"Do you remember a black Honda Civic with a yellow and red sun sticker on the back?"

Gail turned to me. Her face registered that she knew what I was talking about. "Is it relevant to that night?"

"I don't know," I said honestly.

"I know I've seen it," she said. "I can't recall where though."

"If you remember, call me and let me know." I watched her walk back to the cluster of buildings, feeling dissatisfied with how our conversation had gone. It's not that she convinced me of her innocence. I couldn't make sense of Jason and her working together.

I walked back toward the side gate of the school and proceeded home. I found my mother and sister, Liv, sitting at the kitchen table laughing and eating cookies. I checked my watch. It was nearing eleven. Liv got up from the table when she saw me and wrapped her arms around me.

"I've been so busy with work I've missed you being home," she said into my shoulder and then pulled back. "I'm so excited about my job. I had the top real estate sales for three months in a row."

"I'm so proud of you," I said, sitting. "Tell me all about it."

Liv went on excitedly gesturing with her hands as she gave me the full update about her listings and her most recent sales. When she ran herself out of breath, she looked at me. "Mom said you figured out who killed your college roommate. Did she confess?"

"No," I responded with frustration in my voice. "She didn't confess. I'm not so sure now that it was her."

"Then who is it?" my mother asked from across the table.

"I don't know." I tried not to sound as defeated as I felt. "Where are my old photo albums from college?" I was old enough that I didn't have digital photos of my whole college experience. I did have a great camera that my mother had bought me for Christmas one year. I had two albums full of college photos. I was hoping by looking back at the photos something might spark a memory.

"Everything you had is in your closet upstairs. I didn't move any-thing," my mother responded, eyeing me. "Looking for something?"

"Anything that might jar something loose." I excused myself from the table, promising Liv we'd have dinner together later that night. I headed up the stairs to my room and closed the door behind me.

I pulled open my closet door, crouched down, and pulled a few bins out. I kept things fairly organized. I pulled off the lid of the first and rummaged through without any luck. The second was the same. When I got to the third in the far back of the closet, I got lucky and found the albums I hoped would be there.

I sat back on the floor and crossed my legs, resting the album on my knees. I flipped through page after page, stopping occasionally to examine a photo or smile at an old memory. I had many photos with Alex and some of the two of us with Tim. Then I had other photos of Michelle and a group of her friends and me. There were even more photos of me with groups of other friends who I had classes with or knew from parties. I knew more people than I realized looking back.

It took me three-quarters of the way through the second photo album to come across one that stopped me cold. There I was with jeans, blue Converse sneakers, and a tee-shirt from some band I stopped listening to long ago.

Three of us were standing at the back of a black Honda Civic with the sun symbol, looking exactly as Mary had described. I stared up into my closet, finally all the pieces fitting together.

Once I knew, it was hard to believe it had escaped me for so long.

CHAPTER 38

While Luke took Amelia back to the police station, Tyler remained with the crime scene team who were combing over every inch of the home and cataloging everything. They had called in the U.S. Drug Enforcement Administration, and SWAT remained on standby in case anyone else showed up.

During the initial breach, three people escaped into the woods behind the house, two had been killed by SWAT after they fired at them, and another five were arrested without incident. Atlas was sitting in a holding cell refusing to speak to anyone. He immediately invoked his right to counsel.

Before Luke left the house, he asked Tyler to keep an eye out for a knife that could have been used in the murders and any ties at all to Brody Barrett. Luke believed that Cat had been provided the information. She had no reason to lie, but he wasn't sure how credible it was and wasn't going off accusing anyone of anything without the evidence to back it up.

This was an all-hands-on-deck situation and a few of the other detectives were hard at work interviewing the suspects that had been arrested. Luke was focused on Amelia and what he hoped she could tell him. She had been the most cooperative so far.

Once back at the police station, he offered her a change of clothes and a shower. She eagerly said yes and headed off with a female officer.

While she was doing that, Luke went to the corner deli and picked her up some lunch. He could only assume given the paleness of her complexion and her scrawny limbs that she was in need of some food. He didn't imagine that the Andinos were feeding her well. Luke also had a doctor on stand-by should Amelia need any medical assistance.

When she called home, her mother was overjoyed that she had been found safely. Luke spoke to Amelia's mother briefly and updated her on the situation. He assured her that he was not arresting Amelia but he needed her cooperation to ensure she remained out of trouble.

While Amelia was freshening up, Luke also called the police department that was handling her missing person's case and reported she had been found. That would be a closed case for that department, and Luke was hoping today would be a significant step in closing his case as well.

He knew he had probably messed up the U.S. Attorney's and the FBI's case but he didn't really care. He had three homicides to investigate, and he found an entire cache of weapons and cash on his own – something the FBI and U.S. Attorney's office had apparently been working on for some time. There might be broader implications down the road for the federal prosecution but that wasn't Luke's job to worry about right now.

A few minutes after settling into the conference room, Amelia was back wearing a tee-shirt and gray sweatpants. She had her wet hair tied up in a clip and her freshly washed face made her look even younger.

Luke gestured to the array of sandwiches, chips and cookies on the table. "I thought you might be hungry."

Amelia nodded once and bit her lip. "I don't have any money to pay you for this."

"No money needed," Luke reassured her. "I spoke to your mother and she said it was okay to speak to you without her if you're willing.

I wanted you to be comfortable while we did that."

Amelia smiled shyly and walked over to the table and sat. She reached for a turkey and cheese sub and unwrapped it. Luke also had a few soft drinks and bottles of water on the table. He thanked the officer who escorted Amelia back and then closed the conference room door.

Luke grabbed a Coke for himself, unscrewed the lid, and took a sip. He watched her as she took a few tentative bites. "How are you feeling?"

Amelia cast her eyes up toward him. "Scared but better."

"You don't need to be afraid of me. I want to understand how you got here and what you've been doing. That was a lot of drugs and guns. I need to understand how you're involved in all of that. You're only fifteen years old and that's too much for anyone your age to deal with."

Amelia took a few more bites of the sub and then took a Coke for herself. She took small sips and then looked back up at Luke. "I was at a grocery store in Los Angeles. I had made it there from Berkley and was going to take a bus to New York. I didn't have enough money and was trying to save the money I had. I was hungry and had stolen a few things from the store. That's when Atlas saw me."

"Was he working in the store?"

Amelia shook her head. "He was shopping there. He saw me and said he could give me a job to earn the money for a bus ticket." Her cheeks blushed and she averted her eyes. "I thought it was like sex stuff. I had heard about that kind of thing happening to girls who ran away. I put the stuff back and left the store. He followed me and promised it was nothing like that. He brought me to a big warehouse and all he said I had to do was count pills out and put them in containers. That was it."

Luke knew asking her straight out if she had been sexually assaulted might shut down the conversation. He needed her to remain open but it had to be asked. "Was he or anyone else abusive toward you?"

"No. Nothing like that ever happened. Atlas kept his promise about that." Amelia took another sip of her soda and traced the condensation down the bottle. "He never hit me either but I saw him hit other people. There were guns all around and he could be mean. Atlas said I couldn't leave until I earned the money for the bus ticket. I figured out quickly he wasn't going to pay me."

"Did you ever try to leave?"

Amelia glanced up at him. "There wasn't a chance to try. In California, I slept at his house and the doors were always locked in a way I couldn't unlock. Here, I slept in that house and he was always watching."

"Was it just you and Atlas in the house?"

"Yes, that slept there. He gave me a room and some clothes and fed me, but I worked twelve hours a day, mostly without any break. He wouldn't let me call my mom or even be near the phone."

Luke had no doubt she was being held captive. "What about other people? Was it like today or are there more people around?"

"More people usually." Amelia grabbed one of the chip bags and tore it open. She popped one in her mouth and then another. "The scary guy has been there more than usual. I thought he was in Los Angeles but he showed up here a few weeks ago."

Luke sat up a little straighter. This was the kind of information he was hoping she'd know. "Do you know the scary guy's name?"

"Basil Andino. Atlas told me to never make him angry. That when he's around I need to keep my head down and focus on work." Amelia took another sip of soda. "They are all scary to me, so I've been trying to keep my head down focused on work. Atlas is sometimes scary but he's never hurt me. Basil is mean. He yells a lot. I heard from a few of the other people that he's killed people who were going to go to the cops. I don't know if that's true. It's what people said."

"Did they say who Basil killed?"

Amelia shrugged and looked up at Luke. "A lady, I think, and maybe a man. Nobody was sure. Basil was arguing with Atlas and said that everything had gotten out of his control. It seemed like Basil was mad at Atlas, but I didn't see them get into a fight or anything."

Luke asked a few more questions but he wasn't able to get more details. Amelia didn't know who supplied the drugs to the house or where they got the guns. She also didn't have any direct knowledge about the murders.

Luke was basically out of luck until he asked one final question. He pulled his phone out and pulled up a photo of Brody Barrett. He turned the screen to Amelia. "Have you ever seen this man at the house?"

Amelia leaned into the table and looked at the photo. She squinted her eyes and pursed her lips in concentration. She slowly nodded. "He was at the house a couple of weeks ago. He was there with Basil and they were arguing with Atlas."

"What were they arguing about?"

"A lady from California. At first, I got scared and thought they were talking about me. Then that guy said she was working for the FBI. He said they had to stop her or otherwise there would be trouble. Basil said he'd take care of it. That guy said that whatever Basil did, he needed to make the problem go away."

Luke was surprised she had overheard all of that. "Where were they when they were saying all of this?"

"I was in the kitchen. They came in and Atlas sent me to my bedroom."

"You were able to hear them from there?"

Amelia bit at her lower lip. "They didn't know but I stayed at the top of the stairs and could hear them. If they were in trouble like the man said, I figured we'd either have to leave or maybe the cops would come and it would be my chance to escape. I wanted to know what was going on."

"That was brave of you but risky," Luke said and she smiled, taking it as a compliment. "It's brave of you to talk to me and tell me all of this. Is there a reason you ran away from home?"

Amelia sat back in the chair and shrugged. Luke asked her again. He wanted to make sure she was safe and didn't run away again.

Finally, she admitted, "We lived in New York and, when my mom got remarried, we moved to Berkley. I don't have any friends and wanted to be back at my old school."

"Do you like living with your mother otherwise?"

Amelia nodded. "Even my stepfather isn't bad. I just wanted to be back in New York. I figured if I got there, I could stay with one of my friends and then I'd tell my mom. I hoped by then she'd let me stay."

"I'm sure if you give it a little time, you'll be able to make friends."

"It's okay," Amelia said. "Even if I don't have friends, I want to be back home with my mom."

Amelia didn't seem like the kind of kid who'd normally run away. It seemed like she had come out of the situation relatively unharmed, for that he was grateful. "I'm going to have you wait with the police officer you were with earlier. Your mom said that she would be landing this afternoon. It was the earliest flight she could get. I have to go take care of a few things."

"Thank you for rescuing me and getting me lunch," Amelia said, smiling up at him.

"I'm glad you're safe now." Luke headed out the door, texting Tyler as he went. His partner responded a few seconds later to tell him there was still no definitive proof at the house of Brody Barrett's involvement. Luke confirmed with him that he had a witness and that was all he needed.

Luke could have pulled in a full team to go to the U.S. Attorney's Office but that's not what he wanted to do. He had a plan he hoped would bring him directly to Basil Andino. He made a few calls as he drove the short distance to the U.S. Attorney's Office.

By the time he went inside, all the pieces were in place.

Arriving at the front desk, Luke asked to speak to Terry Jordan and was ushered promptly to the man's office. The door was slightly ajar and Luke knocked once and announced himself.

"I can't say I'm happy to see you, Det. Morgan," Terry said as Luke entered. He moved the laptop he'd been typing on out of the way and gestured for him to sit. "We've been working on this case for a long time. You caught a smaller fish. I'm not sure if our federal case is blown or not. We wanted them all including the very top of the Andino family. I assume you haven't arrested them."

Luke confirmed that he hadn't. None of the Andinos were at the house. "I have a case of my own. I know Mandy was working with you, but she was murdered in my jurisdiction. I'm here because…" Luke didn't get to say much else because there was a knock at the door.

"Come in, Brody. This is Det. Luke Morgan," Terry explained to the attorney who stood about Luke's height and had a wave of blond hair. "You don't mind if Brody sits in with us, do you? He's been involved in the case."

Luke stood and shook the attorney's hand. "I appreciate any help I can get."

Brody sat down next to Luke but remained quiet. Luke assumed in deference to his boss.

"Anyway," Luke said, taking a big breath and trying to appear as casual as possible "I don't want to take up too much of your time. I want to know if you know how I can find Basil Andino. A few of the guys we arrested flipped, and I know he's directly responsible for the murders. That in addition to all of them working for him and the evidence we found, I have an arrest warrant for him."

Terry stared at Luke across the table. "You have direct evidence tying the murders to Basil Andino?"

"Yes," Luke said with confidence. "As I said, I was able to flip a few of those who worked for him."

"Who flipped?" Brody asked.

"I can't say. That's between me and the prosecutor's office."

"We're the U.S. Attorney's Office," Brody stressed and then looked to Terry.

Luke watched the older attorney across the desk, trying to convey a message with just a look. It must have made an impact because a beat later, Terry shrugged. "I'm sorry, Det. Morgan, we don't know the location of Basil Andino, but if we find him, we'll call you. I guess we need to thank you for making our case for us."

Luke stood from the chair. "I appreciate that. I'll be in touch soon." He left the office and closed the door behind him. Luke stood at the door waiting for the argument that followed. Brody urged his boss to call Luke's captain to find out more details of the investigation. Terry gave a firm no and asked the younger attorney to leave his office.

Luke made his way down the hall with a sly smile on his face. The real work was about to begin.

CHAPTER 39

Luke slipped into the driver's seat of his SUV and drove the short distance to his designated watch point. He had officers in unmarked police cars along every route Brody Barrett might take – whether he went farther into downtown Little Rock or left the downtown area completely. He had even asked Cooper to assist, given how good he was with mobile surveillance.

There was no way after saying people flipped on Basil that Brody wouldn't deliver the news. Even if it was only stepping outside to make a phone call, he'd take action. Luke didn't think there was any way Brody would make a call like that in his office.

Luke checked in with Tyler and Cooper and radioed the other officers. All were ready and waiting. They didn't have to wait too long. One officer spotted Brody's truck pulling out of the U.S. Attorney's secured parking lot. He took a right, traveled down the road for a short stretch, and took another right. He stopped at the light and, when it turned green, made a left to head to Cantrell Road, which would take him out of downtown Little Rock.

Luke waited nearby as he figured that's exactly the direction he would have gone. Cooper was parked in the Heights at the top of the hill, not too far from Luke's house. The goal was to follow for a short bit and pass off surveillance to the next person, so Brody wouldn't get suspicious.

Luke pulled out into traffic three cars behind Brody when he passed by. He followed him to the top of the winding Cantrell hill. They got to the light at Kavanaugh and Cooper pulled into the traffic. Luke was able to make a quick right and would cut through side streets to catch up with them later.

In the meantime, Luke pulled to the side of the road and radioed the other officers and Tyler of their location. As Luke put the car in drive to pull back into traffic, Cooper called him.

"He pulled into a driveway in the Heights. He's on Country Club Boulevard. He turned on the side street near Kroger. I assume maybe he thought he was being followed. It was good we switched off. He went back down Kavanaugh and then cut into the neighborhood." Cooper gave Luke the address so he could run it in the database and see who lived there.

A few clicks on his phone and Luke came back with the details. It was owned by a holding company. "I'm coming back with a business name that isn't familiar. Are there any other cars in the driveway?"

"A black Mercedes. Brody is sitting outside the house in his truck. He hasn't made a move to go in yet. What do you want me to do?"

Luke was only a few blocks away. "Sit on it for now. Let me know if he goes into the house and if you see anyone else." Cooper confirmed and Luke got down to work sending everyone else the location. His goal was to go into the house and make an arrest without incident. SWAT and the rest of his team would take a low-profile position. He needed them in position before he made a move.

The minutes ticked by as Luke waited for his team. Cooper called him again a few minutes later. "He's getting out of his truck and walking toward the house." Cooper gave him the play by play. Brody didn't appear to be concerned now whether he was being followed or if anyone was watching his actions. He strode up to the house with a casual ease and knocked on the door. A moment later, it was answered.

He stood at the threshold long enough for Cooper to snap a photo of the man inside the house. "I sent you a photo of who he's meeting."

Luke's phone chimed as the texted photo arrived. He opened the text and enlarged the photo. "It's Basil Andino," Luke said, confirming what he had already suspected. "You hang back. Let me get everyone in place and I'll be over."

Luke secured his vest and radioed the team to ensure they were in position. Tyler would meet him at the house. It would go the same way as the raid at the other house. SWAT was positioned all around, but hopefully this time, no one was sneaking out the back.

Luke pulled to the curb two houses down and got out of his SUV. Tyler had done the same in the other direction. They met at the driveway, shared a look and fist bump, and walked to the door. Luke banged his fist hard against the wood and did not announce himself. He'd wait to do that once the door was opened.

"Can I help you?" a woman said as she answered the door. She stepped back out of the way when Luke flashed his badge.

"Where are they?" he asked with his voice low.

The woman shook with fear and backed up. She pointed to a hallway off the foyer. "Second door on the right."

Luke pointed to the front door and she ran out. He kept his footfalls light as he made his way down the hall. Tyler covered his back. The door the woman had indicated was closed. He turned back to Tyler and when they were both ready, Luke turned the handle and pushed open the door.

"Who..." was the only word Brody Barrett got out of his mouth before Basil Andino gripped him around the neck and positioned him in front. He put a gun to the attorney's head and threatened to pull the trigger if Luke and Tyler got any closer.

"This is going to end here, Basil," Luke said with his gun focused on the man. He could take a shot right now and hit him dead center of his forehead, but Basil would probably pull the trigger either as reflex or intentionally. "Let's talk this out. Put the gun down."

"I'm getting out of here. Do you understand me?" Basil said and turned his head slightly to look out the glass sliding doors right behind him.

"There's a SWAT team out there and a full police force in your neighborhood. You're not going to get very far." In some hostage situations, Luke might lower his gun as a sign of good faith to negotiate but there were no deals to be made. He didn't trust Basil and had no doubt he'd kill Brody if he thought it would buy him his freedom.

Basil's pupils dilated and beads of sweat formed on his forehead. His grip on Brody grew tighter and the attorney screamed in pain. He tried to elbow the large man but nothing seemed to have an impact.

"I can help you, Basil. Let me go," Brody begged, squirming to be let free. "Don't listen to this guy. He's a local detective. He doesn't have anything on you. Let him take you in and your attorneys can get you off like they have before." It seemed Brody was willing to implicate himself to save his life. When Basil didn't lighten his grip, Brody looked over at Luke. "Help me, please."

"I'm just a local cop, remember. Not much I can do," Luke said with a shrug. He didn't care whether Brody lived or died. The only reason Luke wanted him to live was so he'd face the humiliation of a trial and to see him face justice for helping this criminal family.

Brody flailed his arms against Basil. "Let me go. After all the help I've given you this is how you repay me? If you kill me, you'll really fry," Brody ranted at the man.

All the while Basil remained tightlipped. He stared directly at Luke never breaking eye contact or wavering. Luke wished he could read his mind.

Finally, after a few beats too long, Basil let out a low guttural laugh. "How'd you like my handiwork, detective?"

Luke's mouth went dry. A confession meant only one thing. "Are you talking about the precise carvings on the victims' backs?"

Basil gave such a slight nod of his head Luke nearly missed it. "They deserved what they got."

"Nick Day didn't do anything to you," Tyler countered, drawing everyone's attention to him. "All he was doing was trying to help his brother."

Basil shook it off. "It silenced Jimmy."

Luke wanted to tell him Jimmy had broken away from him and confessed but that would only put him in danger before any trial. "What about Mandy? How did you kill her? Her boyfriend was there with her." Luke still hadn't understood the timing.

"After Sonny slipped out the door, I knocked. She thought it was him coming back. I strangled her within thirty seconds. It was lucky they had such a volatile relationship. He provided cover for me. I watched her for a long time that morning and heard the fight between them. The whole building heard. That's when I decided it was the perfect time to strike."

"There were two cops and a private investigator searching the building after the fight between them. How did you slip past?"

Basil laughed. "It's easy to slip past people who aren't looking for you. I saw those cops – said hello and answered their questions in the lobby while I pretended to check my mail. I went upstairs while they went to the second floor. She was dead before they got to the third floor. I was inside while they searched. No one ever knocked on that door. I had plenty of time to work."

"Blood?" Luke asked, knowing none had been found in her loft.

"I clean up after myself, Detective. I carried her out over my shoulder, down the back elevator, and threw her in the trash where she belonged," Basil said with an air of pride. "She had no right to cross us and revenge was ours for the taking. Nick was eager to make a deal for his brother's life. I went to him directly and he came with me willingly. Then I killed him in some dirty alleyway. Mitch was a little harder," Basil said, chuckling at some memory Luke didn't want to know. "He was cagey that guy. Didn't trust easily. Brody left him a message that the U.S. Attorney's Office wanted to make a deal with him and to meet that night at the Old State House. I figured I'd make a splash on that one – let the whole city know that you can't cross us and not pay for it. I killed him behind the place, carved him up nice and good and snuck past the cleaning crew. I couldn't believe my luck to find the back door open. I was just going to leave him outside like I did Nick."

Luke focused his eyes on Brody. "You're the one who lured Mitch to his death?"

For a few moments, Brody said nothing. Then he whimpered. "If I didn't, he was going to kill me. He didn't leave me any choice."

"No more talking. You have what you need," Basil barked, meeting Luke's eyes. All at once he shoved Brody to the ground. He fired two rounds at Luke in quick succession. Almost instantaneously, Basil's body absorbed the full impact of the bullets fired by Luke and Tyler. His body jerked with each hit and he crashed backward into the glass sliding door, shattering it and falling to the ground.

Brody remained in a fetal position on the floor.

Luke caught his breath and stepped over him to get to Basil. He stood over the dead man. Luke knew as soon as he confessed, he'd chosen to die.

"You're bleeding," Tyler said, pulling at the materials of Luke's shirt and inspecting his arm. "Looks like a graze. You'll need it stitched up."

Luke didn't feel a thing. He glanced down at the floor. "Where's Brody? He was here curled up like a baby a moment ago."

Tyler cursed. "He must have taken off. He's not going to get far." He headed out of the room while Luke remained waiting for the crime scene team. Once they arrived and the medical examiner had been called, Luke took one last look at Basil's bloodied body and knew that he'd only stopped one of them. The reign of the Andino family was far from over. They might take a hit with Basil's death, but a criminal empire wasn't taken down that easily.

Luke released a breath he felt like he'd been holding since the start of the case and went to find Tyler. He got to the open doorway and saw the slew of cop cars, SWAT team, and more officers than he could count standing around.

In the middle of all of them stood Tyler with Brody in handcuffs.

Luke glanced to his right in time to see Captain Meadows and Terry Jordan walking toward the house. He left the porch and closed the distance meeting them at the edge of the lawn.

Terry extended his hand to Luke. "I had for a long time questioned whether we had a traitor. I had suspected Brody but couldn't be sure. I caught him in my office about two weeks ago. He said he was looking for a file. I believe that's how he found Mandy's name. Up until then, no one but the FBI knew about her. We appreciate your support on this case. The FBI isn't too happy with you stepping on their toes, but you were in your full right. The murders were your jurisdiction. Good police work, Det. Morgan."

Luke appreciated the compliment and he didn't much care what the FBI thought. "Will the federal case against the Andinos be able to go forward?"

Terry nodded. "I believe so. Your detectives got full statements from those who were working for them. It certainly helps to continue to build our case. Without Brody sharing the information, we will have some work to do. I believe it will ultimately be successful."

"That's good to know." Luke was glad that his police work helped in that way. "What do you think is going to happen with Brody? He admitted to luring one of the victims to their death. We know from a witness he was there at the early stages of the planning. There's also another witness who hasn't come forward yet who knows a good deal of information. That's how we got the intel on Brody. She'll need to know she's safe before she comes forward."

Terry looked to Captain Meadows and back to Luke. "We've been talking and, if it's okay by you, we'd like to turn Brody over to the FBI. The goal is to get him to flip. I'll make sure he receives a long prison sentence and is stripped of his ability to ever practice law. In exchange, his information should prove useful in our prosecution. He'll only be given one chance to redeem himself though. I'm not playing games. Your witness, whoever she is, will be fully protected."

Luke agreed with that. After Terry walked off and two FBI agents showed up and pulled Brody out of the back of the police cruiser, Captain Meadows, Tyler and Luke stood watching the scene.

"Good work from you both," Captain Meadows said. "This seems like the perfect time to tell you I'll be retiring next month and Tyler will be taking over. His promotion has been approved."

"That fast?" Luke asked not hiding his shock.

Captain Meadows slapped him on the back. "It's been a long time coming. I should have retired years ago. You're in good hands with Tyler."

"That was never in question." He turned to his long-standing partner. "I guess this was our last case."

"I guess so," Tyler said with a grin. "I'm not going anywhere and will need your help. Right now," he said, clocking Luke's arm, "you're dripping blood all over the place. You need stitches and that's an order."

The three of them laughed together before Luke headed back to his SUV. He waved to Cooper as he went and told him to meet him at the hospital. He had been neglecting their friendship because of work and it was about time they had some quality time, even if it was in the emergency room.

CHAPTER 40

It had taken me most of the day to decide where I should stage the confrontation I hoped would elicit a confession. I didn't want to do it at her work or home. I ended up deciding the best way was to ask her for drinks after work. I let it slip I found the evidence needed to go to the cops that would clear Tim and pointed to Alex's real killer. I figured that she'd be interested enough to show up.

At a quarter to seven that night, I sat in an upstairs booth at the Troy Pub far away from other patrons below. I had been coming to this pub since it opened and stopped in frequently even after moving to Little Rock. I guess that garnered me some good will when I asked for a quiet spot.

Right at seven, Michelle appeared at the top of the stairs. She smiled as she approached. "Sorry, I'm running late. Long day at work." She slid into the booth and undid her coat, shrugging her arms out of the sleeves. "Are you eating? I'm starving."

She proceeded to read over the menu items and debate back and forth what she wanted to eat. It was like I wasn't even at the table with her. I watched quietly, allowing her to settle in and feel comfortable.

Once our server took our order, I said, "I'm glad you could meet with me. I found out so much."

Her eyes lit up with interest. "It's been hard to focus all day. I can't wait to hear. Who killed Alex?"

"Jason Thatcher," I responded evenly. "He lied to me about several things and sent me on a wild goose chase to New York City. He blamed the artist Tate Butler. It was easy enough to clear him though."

Michelle shrank back and feigned shock. "Is that who was upstairs with Alex that night? I was sure it was Tim. What are you going to do? Did he confess?"

"He didn't confess but I handed over all the evidence to the state police investigator. It's up to them to make the case. I found out something else that might interest you."

"Oh, really?" she asked, almost excited. The server came and dropped off our drinks. Michelle had ordered a beer while I stuck with water. I needed my wits about me during this discussion.

I waited until she was taking a sip. "There were a lot of inconsistencies in your statement that didn't add up for me, Michelle." I said the words and watched her reaction carefully. Her shoulders stiffened and she blinked her false eyelashes a few too many times in a row to have been natural. "I wanted to clear up your statement, so the investigator doesn't come after you because what I found will point him in your direction."

Michelle pulled back. "How could it possibly point to me?"

"You were the one who testified under oath that it was Tim who was upstairs and that you saw him leave." I rested my arms on the table and leaned forward. "Michelle, there were at least three people in the apartment that night not including the person who helped Jason kill Alex. You saw Tim outside of your window but you never once saw him enter or leave that apartment. Isn't that right?"

"I told you the cops pressured me to say I saw him, Riley. What was I supposed to do?" Michelle rubbed her forehead. "I heard him. I know I did. Yes, I saw him outside and then I heard him go up the stairs and down later. You didn't have to hear that fight and what he did to her. It was horrific."

"But you knew it wasn't Tim," I said confidently and waited. When Michelle didn't respond, I waited some more. I let the silence hang in the air. She squirmed in the seat and shifted her eyes back and forth. "Just admit you knew it wasn't Tim. That's all it's going to take. Either you were completely oblivious to what was happening upstairs or you were lying."

"It's been so long, Riley. It's possible I don't remember."

"Stop lying to me!" I pulled the thick trial binder from my seat and dropped it down on the table with a thud. I jabbed my finger down on it. "At trial, you said you saw Tim go upstairs and later you saw him leave. You testified to that under oath. You didn't say anything about Jason being there or even Gail."

Michelle's eyes got wide. "I didn't…"

"Yes, you did," I said more loudly than I meant and she shrank back in response. "There is only one way this can go. Either you were home and aware enough to know Tim went upstairs, had a fight with Alex and then left, which would mean in that span of time you'd have heard others going up and down the stairs, or you weren't home or couldn't hear at all and are making up the whole thing. There is no gray area based on your own testimony. Which is it?"

Michelle sat stone-faced and didn't respond.

I reached down into my bag and grabbed another photo. I put it on the table and pointed. "This is your best friend, Taylor."

Fear came over her face and her shoulders shivered. "Why does this matter, Riley? I don't understand."

"Why was Taylor waiting outside of our apartment that night? Why did she follow Tim when he walked away from the house?" There was an accusation in my tone Michelle understood.

"I didn't know…"

I slammed my hand down on the table, wincing as the sting shot through my palm. "You do know because she was back at your apartment later that night. I have a witness who saw the car. You're lying to me, Michelle. I need the truth if I'm going to help you."

Michelle shook her head. "I don't know why you're bringing all of this up now."

"You sound like Gail." I paused and laid out my evidence. "Taylor was an education major with you and Jason. I remember that because I remember you both going to classes together. Was it her who was cheating or was it all three of you?" I watched her face carefully and it was then I noticed the twitch near her eye. I didn't know if it meant anything, but I was certain if she wasn't cheating she knew about it.

"It was such a competitive program, Riley," Michelle said by way of explanation. She rambled on telling me the same thing Gail had said about Alex and the scholarship for her master's program. "We were all trying to find an edge to win that scholarship. We had to get our grades higher than everyone else's. If Alex told anyone she had found out, it would have destroyed us."

"She had to be stopped, right?" I said, hating that I sounded like I was agreeing with their actions.

Michelle shook her head and sucked in a sob. "I tried to talk to her nicely. I begged her not to tell anyone she had caught us cheating. Taylor got access to test answers. She never told me how she got them. To this day, I still don't know. One afternoon at the apartment, Alex was on the stairs as we were coming in and overheard us talking about the answers for an upcoming test. She knew we were cheating and she was going to tell. Then she won the scholarship and she had us in a death grip. Not only had she won money she wasn't even going to use, she was going to destroy all of us."

"Where does Jason fit into this?"

"He doesn't," Michelle said with a sniff. "He and Taylor dated for a while but broke up. It was after that Jason started dating Alex. We went to him to try to convince Alex not to talk about the cheating.

Jason wasn't cheating and he didn't want any part of it, but he also didn't want us to get in trouble. He couldn't convince her. He had his own issues with Alex, including her ongoing relationship with Tim. When she started talking about dropping education and changing to art, he lost it."

"Are you saying Jason killed Alex?"

Michelle looked away and wouldn't meet my eyes. She shook her head slowly. "It was Taylor." She paused for a second to collect herself. "We all played a part."

This was the closest to the truth I had been and didn't want to blow it. "What happened that night?"

"After we eat," she said as the server delivered our food.

I didn't know if she was stalling for time or trying to come up with a good story. If I pushed her, there was a chance she'd walk out and never tell me. I did what she asked and ate the burger I had ordered. I had never wanted food less in my life. There was a growing knot in my stomach and my mouth was dry no matter how many sips of water I took.

We ate in silence.

Finally, Michelle pushed her plate to the side and downed the rest of her beer. She didn't look at me. Her eyes focused left of me over my shoulder. "Once I found out Alex was staying behind that weekend, Taylor and I made a plan to stick around too. We were going to convince Alex one way or the other. It was a mess that night. None of us were expecting Tim to come back or Tate and Gail to show up. Looking back now, those were all signs we should have let it be. They were exit ramps to our plan we were too stubborn to take."

I wasn't sure I was understanding. "You planned to kill Alex?"

Michelle rolled her eyes to the ceiling and shook her head. "There was no plan. All of that was an accident." She expelled a breath and focused on that spot over my shoulder. "When Jason showed up, I called Taylor and told her I thought we should call off the plan. She said no and that she'd come over and watch the house and warn me if anyone else was coming. She said it was fine Jason was there, good even. Maybe he'd help us. Tate came and went quickly, but as he was leaving, Gail showed up. I thought for sure we needed to call it off. There were too many variables at play. Taylor insisted this would be our only chance before you got back."

Michelle was right, they had so many chances to stop and think through their actions. They didn't. "After Gail left, what happened next?"

"Tim showed up as I was getting ready to go upstairs. I saw him through the window. Taylor was still outside in her car and later she said she followed him to make sure he didn't come back. He would have protected Alex at all cost and we needed to make her understand she couldn't destroy our careers." Michelle focused her eyes on me and I saw the determination in her expression. "I waited until Tim left before I went up. At that point, Alex and Jason had already started fighting. That wasn't planned either. Jason lost his temper after Tate was there. He could handle Tim but to think there was another guy he had to compete with and this one was taking her away from their plan, he couldn't stand that."

"Tate and Alex weren't involved like that," I corrected her.

"We didn't know that then." Michelle took another deep breath. "At some point, Jason and I were screaming and yelling at Alex that she couldn't tell about the cheating. I told her she owed us since she took the scholarship funding, but she held firm. Then it got physical. Jason completely lost his temper and hit her in the face twice and she fell to the ground. I stopped then, completely shaken by it. That's not what was supposed to happen. Riley, I swear to you. We weren't there to hurt Alex, just to stop her from ruining our lives."

I swallowed hard and wished I had more water in my glass. Alex had already had a tussle with Gail and now this. I couldn't imagine what she must have been feeling. "Was she still alive?"

"Yes," Michelle said slowly. "Jason was freaked out. He kept saying he hadn't meant to hit her. He carried Alex to her bed and lay her down. He paced around her room saying that we needed to help her, but he knew he'd get in trouble. That's when Taylor came up. She saw how freaked out we were. Alex had even more ammunition on us now. She saw Alex lying on the bed not quite conscious and she told us to let her handle it. We said no but she pushed us out of the room. She was yelling at that point that she had it covered. Jason and I went to the living room. He had the phone in his hand and was about to call 911 when Taylor came out of the bedroom. She said that it was over and for Jason to put the phone down."

"I don't understand," I said even though I understood perfectly. "You let Taylor kill Alex and then blamed it on Tim?"

Michelle locked her gaze on me. "There was no other way. We didn't know Taylor was going to kill Alex. We didn't know what was going to happen. When she came out and said it was handled, we still didn't understand. When she told us what she had done, we decided that the three of us would never tell anyone what had happened that night. No one could know. We trashed the kitchen to make it look like there had been a big fight. Maybe someone broke in and was looking for something and killed her. We weren't sure but none of us thought Tim would get blamed."

"You told the cops he was there!" I cursed loudly at her then, not even bothering to control my temper. "You let an innocent man take the fall for something you did!"

Michelle furiously shook her head. "I didn't kill her. I didn't kill her."

"You might as well have!" I was breathing hard, sucking in sharp breaths and breathing them out through my nose. I couldn't believe what they had done, the gall of it, all over cheating on a few tests. "You destroyed Tim's life." I also believed in that moment that while Michelle might not have planned to kill Alex that night, Taylor had. By Michelle's admission, Taylor calmly and methodically went to Alex who was injured and unconscious and smothered her. To be capable of that, she was capable of anything.

The weight of what Michelle admitted finally took hold. She reached for her wallet and threw cash on the table. She pulled her coat from behind her as she slid out of the booth. "You can't tell anyone, Riley. I'll deny the whole thing. We'll all deny the whole thing."

"It's too late, Michelle. You've done too much damage to walk away from this," I said and slowly pulled up the bottom hem of my shirt to reveal the wire. "Inv. Grogan with the New York State Police was listening in the whole time."

Michelle stared at the wire and backed up slowly. "We were friends, Riley. How could you do this?" She kept backing up right into the arms of the cops. When Inv. Grogan gripped her arms and told her that she was under arrest, Michelle's legs buckled under her and she slipped to the floor. She wasn't crying or fighting, she had a blank expression of defeat on her face.

Inv. Grogan looked over at me. "We have it from here. Good job, Riley."

I knew it took a lot for him to say that. It had taken time to convince him to wire me up and listen in when he had been so convinced of Tim's guilt. I grabbed my things off the table and walked past them. I stopped for only a moment and looked down at Michelle. I wasn't sure what I was feeling – happiness the truth had come out, regret for all that had happened, and betrayal from the people I once thought I knew so well.

All I wanted was to call Tim and see my mom and sister. After that, I needed some downtime at home with Luke to be reminded of the good things in life.

It was time to put this chapter behind me.

Epilogue

"I can't believe you had no idea that was going on back then, Riley," Adele said to me as we stood at my kitchen counter fixing margaritas. The four of us had gathered together for dinner at my house to celebrate Adele winning her case and the successful conclusion of Luke's case and mine.

I hit the blender one last time before responding. As I poured the concoction into four glasses, I explained, "I had so many different groups of friends back then. I wasn't necessarily spending all my time with Alex and Michelle even though I lived there. They were all in education classes and I was focused on psychology and sociology courses. Our paths didn't cross a lot."

Even though I had a reasonable explanation, I'd carry guilt for a while for not being more observant at the time. Alex was a lot to handle and sometimes she was overwhelming for me. She didn't make the decisions I would make and sometimes it was hard for me. No one deserved the end she had. It was also a reminder that people, even those closest to us, aren't always what they appear.

Adele and I carried the margaritas into the living room where Cooper was sitting on the couch with his legs propped up on the ottoman. He had a good visit with his doctor earlier that day who told him he was finally healing nicely and on his way to a full recovery. The doctor cleared Cooper to go back to work part-time, which couldn't have made him happier.

"Come on," Luke said with his laptop positioned on the coffee table.

Cooper told him to wait. "I want to hear the end to Riley's case."

I sat back in my favorite chair and curled my legs under me, careful not to spill anything from the glass. "The New York State Police tracked down Taylor out of state and arrested Jason at the ice rink. Michelle is looking to take a plea deal for three years in prison if she testifies against the other two. It sounds to me like Taylor and Jason might also plead guilty. The evidence against them is significant."

"What about Tim?" Adele asked, cuddling up next to Cooper on the couch.

"He started a civil suit for wrongful conviction. He has a good case and, if I'm called to testify, I'll be there. He thinks there will be a settlement."

"I hope he gets everything he deserves," Adele said and I couldn't agree more.

Luke had already told us the federal case against the Andinos was moving forward. There had been more arrests and it appeared the FBI was making dents in bringing down the whole empire. It would take time for a successful conclusion. The woman working for Brody Barrett had given a full statement to the FBI. She finally felt safe and he was looking at a long time in prison, even though he spilled his guts five minutes after being in handcuffs.

Cat O'Conner profiled the murders on her podcast Rock City Killers, which was what Luke was itching to hear. We had all gone from being wary of the podcast to loving it. I had listened to a few episodes on the drive back. Luke and Cooper had also been trying to catch up. Cat was smart, had a unique perspective, and scored good interviews. Luke was being featured in this current episode, which was why he was so eager to listen to how it had all come together.

He didn't wait for us to stop talking. He hit play. Cat's melodic voice came through the speakers of the laptop and quieted us. She did a great job at setting the stage for the first murder, then moving on to Mandy's, even highlighting Cooper's role in it all. Then she touched on the last.

"What happened to Jimmy?" Cooper asked to Luke's annoyance.

Luke rushed an answer. "He's back in rehab. His parents finally got all the messages after getting off the cruise. They stayed at Jimmy's uncle's for two days and, when it was safe, they came back. The grief hit them hard but their focus is on getting Jimmy clean."

Luke pointed to the laptop and we got quiet again.

Cat moved from interviews with the victim's families to a statement from the cops. When Luke heard his voice come through the podcast, he scrunched up his face. "Is that what I sound like? I sound terrible."

I laughed. "You waited so long to hear this and now you're complaining. No one likes the sound of their voice. You sound hot to me."

Luke rolled his eyes. "Cat did a good job."

She had a way of crafting a compelling and factual story. We listened to the rest of the hour-long episode. As she began to give her closing remarks, there was a knock at the door.

Luke grumbled, "Who is here at this hour?" He jumped up to answer it and was surprised by the visitor. "Cat, we were just listening to your latest episodes. You must be proud of how well it turned out." He let her into the house and closed the door behind her. She had visited once before when she was scripting the podcast and had dropped off information for Luke.

"I'm sorry for interrupting," Cat said as worry lines creased her forehead. "I'm sorry about bothering you at home." She stumbled over her words and couldn't seem to focus her eyes.

It was clear something was wrong. I hit the stop button on the laptop and stood. "Cat, is everything okay? You're shaking."

She held out an envelope and as Luke went to take it from her, she stopped him. "It's evidence. You might want to put on gloves. I got this in the mail yesterday but didn't read it until tonight."

I stepped toward her. "What do you mean evidence?"

"It was marked with yesterday's date, the day I received it. There's no postmark which means it was hand-delivered to my office." Cat opened the envelope, pulled out a type-written letter, and read. "The summer of 1977 in New York City has gone down in infamy. Record heat. A blackout. Murder. Tomorrow night, I will continue what he started. No one is safe. I own this city. Fear me."

"That's tonight!" Cooper said as he got to his feet.

Confused, Adele asked, "What happened in the summer of 1977?"

"The Son of Sam." I recounted what I knew about the case. "He targeted young women with dark hair or at least that was the theory. Women were terrified. They cut their hair and dyed it. Some wore wigs. The killer David Berkowitz claimed he had mental illness and there was something about a dog. I can't remember all the details or how many people he killed. It was a huge story at the time."

"We don't know that this is real," Luke said, trying to calm us all down. He checked his watch. "It's nearly eight and nothing has happened yet. This might be a prank."

Cat shook her head. "It's not a prank, Luke. There was a shooting about an hour ago not far from my studio. I couldn't see what happened because the road was all blocked off. I had to go five streets out of my way to get here. I thought you'd want to see this immediately."

She thrust the note toward him but Luke didn't touch it.

He glanced down at it and then went for his phone which was charging upstairs. Cooper, Adele, and I exchanged a worried look.

"Cat, sit down," I said, moving toward her. "Let me get you something to drink." I gave her the chair and went to the kitchen to get her some water. By the time I made it back into the living room, Luke stood at the bottom of the stairs.

His face drained of expression. "A woman was shot in downtown Little Rock. One shot to the head from a distance, a long distance according to witnesses. They believe the bullet came from a sniper perched above her. No suspect has been apprehended."

There was an audible gasp in the room. I rushed to him. "Go, Luke. Go to work and do whatever you have to do. We'll be here waiting for you," I said, knowing he'd want to be there on the scene. Luke went back up the stairs and came down a few minutes later dressed and ready to get out there.

"Cat, I'll need you to follow me to the station." He went to the kitchen and got a plastic bag and using tongs, slipped the letter and envelope into it. Luke kissed me goodbye. "I'll let you know as soon as I know."

When they were gone, I sat down on the couch stunned into silence. So were Cooper and Adele. It was one thing to be shot on the street during a robbery but being gunned down by a sniper on a city street was unheard of in Little Rock.

There'd be no rest tonight and possibly not for a long time.

About the Author

Stacy M. Jones was born and raised in Troy, New York, and currently lives in Little Rock, Arkansas. She is a full-time writer and holds masters' degrees in journalism and in forensic psychology. She currently has three series available for readers: paranormal cozy Harper & Hattie Magical Mystery Series, the hard-boiled PI Riley Sullivan Mystery Series and the FBI Agent Kate Walsh Thriller Series. To access Stacy's Mystery Readers Club with three free novellas, one for each series, visit StacyMJones.com.

You can connect with me on:

- http://www.stacymjones.com
- https://twitter.com/SMJonesWriter
- https://www.facebook.com/StacyMJonesWriter
- https://www.bookbub.com/profile/stacy-m-jones
- https://www.goodreads.com/StacyMJonesWriter

Also by Stacy M. Jones

Watch for PI Riley Sullivan Mystery Book #10 FEAR CITY in Fall 2023

Access the Free Mystery Readers' Club Starter Library
PI Riley Sullivan Mystery Series novella "The 1922 Club Murder"
FBI Agent Kate Walsh Thriller Series novella "The Curators"
Harper & Hattie Mystery Series novella "Harper's Folly"

Sign up for the starter library along with launch-day pricing and special behind-the-scenes access. Hit subscribe at
http://www.stacymjones.com/

Please leave a review for What He Saw. Reviews help more readers find my books. Thank you!

Other books by Stacy M. Jones by series and order to date

FBI Agent Kate Walsh Thriller Series
The Curators
The Founders
Miami Ripper
Mad Jack
The Fuse
Dead Senate

PI Riley Sullivan Mystery Series
The 1922 Club Murder
Deadly Sins

The Bone Harvest
Missing Time Murders
We Last Saw Jane
Boston Underground
The Night Game
Harbor Cove Murders
The Drowned Boys

Harper & Hattie Magical Mystery Series
Harper's Folly
Saints & Sinners Ball
Secrets to Tell
Rule of Three
The Forever Curse
The Witches Code
The Sinister Sisters
Scandal Knocks Twice

9 798218 182144